EDITH FAIR AS A SWAN

James M. Hockey

Wyrd Sisters Publishing, Bristol, UK

www.wyrdsisterspublishing.com

WYRD
SISTERS
PUBLISHING

Image Credits

Front Cover: Dirty Design / dirtydesign.co.uk
Copyright Charlotte Hockey-Berry 2014

Maps: Copyright James M. Hockey 2014
Maps produced by Luisa Stamp

ISBN 978-0-9566871-4-2

**Published by Wyrd Sisters Publishing
Bristol, UK**

WYRD
SISTERS
PUBLISHING

Acknowledgements

This series of books is dedicated to Pamela my wife with my thanks for her infinite patience as I deserted her, to go play in my imagination or with what she calls 'the mistress on my lap', my Laptop. Also to Charlotte my clever and patient daughter for all the time she took out from her busy life, to design the covers for my books and to help me in my battles with stubborn and perverse software.

With two such helpmates what can you do but give heartfelt thanks and love?

More wholehearted thanks go to Jo Field that patient and hardworking editor who has erased mistakes and ironed out wrinkles to help me produce something I can be proud of. Jo can be found at www.newwritersuk.co.uk/jofield.html

Contents

Maps in Britannia

The Heathen Calendar --- The Festivals and Months of the Year

Christmas .... Yule. Mothers Night

January .... After Yule

February... Mud Month

March.. Hreth Month

April .... Easter (Oestre) Month

May .... Three Milkings Month

June .... Before Mid-Summer, (Aerra Litha)

Mid-Summer.. Litha

July....................... After Mid-Summer, (Aefterra Litha)

August... Weed Month

September...................... Holy Month, (Harvest Festival)

October .... Winter Full Moon, (Start of winter)

November..............Blood Month, (Winter Cull and Offering)

December .... Before Yule

The Christianisation of Britain led to the replacement of this calendar by the Julian but here the country folk are still using the old calendar.

Some Roman terms are used:

Calends is the first day of the month.

Ides is the middle of the month

Nones falls nine days before the Ides.

Some days are identified also as Saints feast days. Here the feast of St. Peter Apostle by Roman Rites is 22nd February.

What is the power of a curse?
Know this.
That which is not in the weaving of the Wyrd has no power.
It is as the crying of a child in an empty house.
It is words of anger borne away on a rushing wind.
Know this. Even the Gods must bow before the three.
Even the end of all things is patterned in the weave.
What is woven is what will be, the sum of all that has been.
Gæð a Wyrd swa hio scel! *

Edda of Wodanaz

* Fate goes ever as she shall

Song of Hastings

In the time of the need of the king of the people
Axe wielding warrior choice of the Witan
The ring burnied brand wielders, hearthband of courage
Gave their lives for their lord as they fell all about him
Struck down by darts from the cowardly foemen:
All fearful to wield bitter blade in fierce battle.
All alone stood the king in defence of his people
Sharp honed strong broadaxe in shining arcs wielded
Death dealing scythe man doomed foes in great numbers.
Then the desperate Duke who desired the domain,
The Duke who was oathsworn to kill in lone combat,
Feared for his life before the king's death arc.
And called others to him that four against one
Might give him the strength his lust to fulfil
Called three to guard him whilst he spurred on his charger
Two warriors grim to lend their strong arms
One fat cheeked boy to bring shame to his home hall.
Our king stood alone, upright and fearless
Above waved his banners gold woven by Gytha,
The gold fighting man flag and dragons of England.
The Duke drove his mangaff shining and sharp honed
Drove it with strong arm straight through our king's life shield
All weakened with brand blows and splintered from strong
strife.

The bitter edged spear point by Iron arm wielded,
Burst through the life shield, which failed in its promise
Iron parted the burnie of our hard fighting slayer.
Pierced through the breast as our king staggered backwards,
Pressed by the fey metal, bitter edged mangaff.
Another foe leaning far down from his stirrup,
A hard man from warring for William the Norman.
Wielding a honed blade made famous in battle
With fatal stroke sundered the neck of our king.
Straightway down fell that far faming warrior
Ringed by those feymen his axe stroke had doomed
Piled all round him in death his loyal Huscarls
And thegns of the land who died for their lord.

Anonymous, from OE.

AD 1062 Rome

Prologue

AD 1062

Rome

He stood by the polished table, far finer than any I had seen anywhere, and picked at the signs of his wealth laid upon it: a golden writing set; a goblet; a small golden platter on which were sweetmeats for his refreshment while he worked.

And then, he came to the matter that was in his mind.

'I have been given to understand that you have a crucifix, my son, a particularly fine one in black flint; one that belongs to Holy Mother Church?'

'I have a holy cross, yes, it was found on the estate of my standard bearer by the village blacksmith. It hangs in Waltham Abbey and has worked a miracle for me. It could have come from anywhere, why from here?'

Ildebrando stood in thought, his fingers tapping rapidly on the table the only sign of his agitation. 'There are records showing that this cross was promised to Holy Church, that it in fact belonged to the cathedral in Sirmium. In time of trouble it was sent to Rome for safekeeping. It was stolen by the Vandals and lost for many years until discovered in what you wish to claim as your kingdom.'

He moved to look out of the window and then, as if idly talking of the weather, added, 'Duke William talks of a crusade to reform your Church when Edward dies. If His Holiness supports him he will have no lack of eager crusaders.'

His point was crudely clear; on top of all the other power he sought in my country – the reforms that would bring us on our knees to Rome – he also wanted my cross from Waltham. Suddenly I snapped; a feeling of revulsion, of bile, rose in my stomach and rage started to build. I wanted to smash him to the ground, this grasping priest. Like all of them he would not stop until he had squeezed the last drop of blood, greedy bloodsucker that he was.

He saw my rage and drew back in alarm, crossed to the other side of the table and called for his servant priest. The cleric entered quickly. 'The audience is at an end,' said the Archdeacon. 'Please see Earl Harold to his escort.'

He turned to me, 'Go in peace, my son, and think on what I have said. His Holiness cannot support your claim unless he is satisfied on all points.' And he laid stress on all.

I bowed curtly and followed the servant out of the chamber.

AD 1687 Somerset

Chapter 1

If you have followed my tales you will know of Bowdyn the gleeman, how he came to our farm and of the stories he told.

Every year for much of my young life he came back to us in the winter, for when the snow was on the ground and the hedgerows glistened with hoar frost, a pedlar's life was exceeding hard. It eased the ache in his bones, he said, to come to Browan Farm. To work for my father as handyman and to sit around the fire in the Cold Cot and tell tales to our eager villagers, this was comfort and joy to him.

I shall not tell you much of how we chopped wood and set the fires, nor of the talk between Bowdyn and the villagers, or the magical way he lost himself in fireside shadows and took on the voices and characters of his taletellers, for those of you who have followed these stories can imagine this for yourself. What I will do is tell you something of my own, for when he first came back to us something fearfully strange happened. I discovered there was more to my friend Bowdyn than was in plain sight and I became party to a great and dangerous secret.

It was the late autumn of the year of Our Lord 1687, when brown sere leaves with their ribs showing plain were laying thick on the ground in the wood beyond the duckweed pond. Dry and cold it was; shuffling weather, when the wush and shush of feet brushing through dead leaves was a pleasure to the ear. Through these woods on times I walked the path to Ham Hill and saw in my mind's eye the Gewissae of Bowdyn's tale on their way to their meeting with the Fates at Baddun.

The day before my fateful day, when I found out more than I wanted or was good for me, I was not idling in the woods. I had come back from the west field ploughing. Looking along the road towards Ivelbridge I saw a pony and cart coming along the road. My heart leapt in my chest. I strained my eyes and then felt the cheer rise in my throat for, early as it was and against all expectation, it was my friend Bowdyn returning to us.

I dropped the sacks I was carrying. The harvest being over and the weather being dry, we were scouring the field for loose grain, but there was precious little and my sacks were empty. I ran to greet him and he reined in, jumped down and clasping his arm around my shoulder, pulled me to him.

'Greetings friend Jo,' he said. 'How goes it with you?'

'Bowdyn, it's so good to see you, it seems so long.'

''Tis only since spring Jo, lad,' he grinned. 'Still, I'm with you on that, I've missed the fire and the talk on many a night.'

'Will you start the tale telling again?' I asked.

'If your father will have me, for now the cold draws in. At any event I need to talk to him, 'tis that which brings me here at this time.'

I was surprised to hear him say this, but supposed it concerned some goods my da had asked Bowdyn to get for him up Bristol way, and so I asked no more, but clambered up

8

beside him as he took his place on the cart once more and gathered up the reins.

When we passed through the gateposts to Browan farm it seemed that Beth had been watching from the pantry side-window, for the word had been passed and my da was already waiting in front of the big black door to the house. Handing the reins to me Bowdyn jumped down and shook my father's hand, leaning close and murmuring something I could not hear. I had an uneasy recall of the bad times after Sedgemoor when there seemed to be so many quiet words and meaningful looks passing between my ma and da and others, to which I was not privy.

Our da listened carefully and then a frown creased his forehead and he nodded slowly.

Straining my ears, eavesdropping, 'not now', I heard him say, 'nor tonight, I will enquire for tomorrow that all is '. He became aware that I was nearby listening and stopped speaking.

'Jo, put Bowdyn's cart away and see to the horse, there's a good man.' He had taken to calling me "man" rather than "boy" ever since the time I brought my mother and sisters, Margaret and Ann, home from Ivelbridge after its cruel occupation by the Tangiers.

I was not stupid; it was plain that my da wanted me out of the way so he and Bowdyn could talk. I knew that a gleeman carried news as well as stories and wondered what news could be so urgent and private that I must not hear it. But I did as I was told, and with a feeling of worry in my chest put the cart in the plough shed and saw to the pony's comfort.

Bowdyn was friend to all in our household and in no time had blended back in as if he had never left. And so, falling into our old routine and expecting he would start his storytelling as soon as the village could be gathered together, I asked him if he would come with me to gather timber in readiness, as in the past. He frowned and shook his head.

'There is no hurry Jo, I shall tell a story, that is certain, but there are things I must do first and people I must see.'

This was a puzzle to me for never before had he gone calling on folk in the village, although the reason for that was plain whilst the King's provosts had been scouring the land for rebels. He still showed the scars from his beating by soldiers of the Tangiers Regiment.

Being impatient for the storytelling to start and wanting to do whatever I could to speed the time, I resolved to rebuild our firewood stack myself. The next day I took the light barrow and a saw up to the woods and started my search for windfalls from the late March winds. My father did not tell me to go nor did I ask him. If I had, I think, knowing now what came to pass, he would have sent me to work anywhere than up the Hill that day, for it was from there that I saw what I saw and did what I did, which led to my da and Bowdyn telling me things they would rather have kept from me. They took me within their secret, I believe, because they thought that for me to know held less danger to all than for me to be making fantastic tales in my head and perhaps repeating them where enemies might hear them.

But I get much ahead of myself and am making a mystery where there should be clarity. What happened was simple: it was the coming together of the merely unusual, and me, puzzled, inquisitive, poking my nose into things that were not my concern

I was standing at the edge of the wood in the gathering dusk. I had found a fine windfall branch and was holding it on the low fieldstone wall with my knee and sawing the timber into lengths. Browan farm was slightly to the left of my view and from there the road stretched straight to the hall gates before curving to the right on its way to Bishopston village.

A movement by the farm caught my eye. Around the east side of the house came two figures, which my gaze revealed, even in the failing light, to be my father and Bowdyn. This in itself was so unusual I stopped work to watch. They turned left out of the gates and walked down the road towards the village. I had half made up my mind that they were bound for the tavern, perhaps to proclaim the winter opening of the story house, when to my great surprise they turned towards the great wrought-iron gates of the hall, opened the small postern gate at the side and started the long walk down the cedar-flanked avenue to the hall.

This concerned me for I did not trust his lordship. He had never come to listen to any of Bowdyn's tales and I was frightened. Perhaps, as our magistrate, hearing in some way of Bowdyn's return, he had summoned them to answer to some crime of sedition. With that thought in my head I abandoned the half-loaded barrow and ran downhill towards the hall gates. I don't know what I had in mind, what I hoped to do if my suspicions proved true. Perhaps I thought that if our folk were taken captive I could raise the alarm, and in those rebellious times the farm folk and Bowdyn's friends in the village would storm the hall and release them. At my age, at that time, my grip on reality was weak and coloured by the recent history of poor Monmouth and the savage aftermath of Sedgemoor.

Anyway, I slipped through the postern gate and melted into the shadows cast by the cedars, slinking from trunk to trunk until I crouched behind the wall not forty feet from the pillared portico and front door of the house itself. I had hardly crouched there in the deepening dusk when the door opened and my father, Bowdyn and his lordship came out. Lit by the doorway oil lamps, they stood for a moment under the stone canopy before walking together. Talking low, they passed but a few feet from me. My heart beat so loud I thought they would surely hear it. They stopped walking and I froze. Bowdyn was facing towards me away from the wind, his face shadowed in the brightening moonlight as he sucked noisily on the old clay pipe he sometimes smoked, making the ash glow cherry red.

I ducked behind the cedar trunk; I was certain they must hear me. I held my breath and waited, face screwed up, for one or other to challenge me, but no challenge came. Instead, they huddled in conversation. I did not hear all that passed between them, but what I did hear was enough to make me mess in my britches.

'Keep your voices low, the servants may not hear, but you know the king has ears in the trees.' I could swear my father looked straight at me as he said this, but I dared not move further back.

'Is it true she is with child?' This from milord.

'Aye,' said Bowdyn, 'true enough and if we do not act now, then for all our pains and blood, we will find ourselves one day with a Catholic king.'

'Then it is certain?' said my father.

'Indeed,' Bowdyn nodded. 'The ships are on their way to fetch the Staadtholder now, so at long last we shall have a Protestant king of Saxon blood.' I peeped round the trunk, for I could not believe my ears alone.

'Shush, keep your voice down man,' said his lordship glancing around. 'What does the Hunt want from us?'

'First, only that we stand ready to muster men, stout men who fought at Sedgemoor and dodged the noose,' said Bowdyn. 'It is not thought the king will have many to stand by him. Second, should all go for nought, that the Hunt stands ready to hide and shelter the Staadtholder and smuggle him out of the country at need, so that he may, at a better time, try again.'

'Understood and agreed,' said milord. 'We will meet again when all proceeds. You will keep me informed?'

'Of course,' said Bowdyn, 'that is my task. I will stay here for the winter so that all may find me with ease. The couriers from the coast know I am here.'

I listened to this, feeling as if my stomach had risen to my throat and shivering with fear at the danger of what I had heard. My father, Bowdyn and milord were talking treason – more than enough to get them hung, drawn and quartered. The screams from Ivelbridge after Sedgemoor still rang in my nightmares.

'Then we are agreed,' said my father to milord. 'We will bid God be with you and depart.'

But then something exceeding strange happened, for the three conspirators turned to each other and clasped arms to make a circle. And then, as we do sometimes in church, each chanted soft and low in turn, to my fear and amazement.

'May the unrighteous be driven in terror,' chanted my father.

'May the Hunt howl and feast on their horror,' sang Bowdyn.

'May their mad souls be driven to Hel,' droned milord.

'Hail, Hail to Wothan, Hail, Hail the Wild Hunt!' they chanted together and then, with a final clasping of hands, Bowdyn and my father slipped back down the avenue, through

13

the postern and turned right for Browan, whilst milord returned to the hall.

I sat with my back to the giant cedar, shivering with fright, for what I had seen was so strange and fearful it was as if men from the moon had ridden a moonbeam to Earth and performed some savage rite in front of me.

After fetching the barrow and the logs from the wood, I walked carefully home in the dark, my mind flying around and side-to-side in my head like some desperate wild bird in a cage.

There was worse to come. When I had stacked the wood in the Cold Cot, which serves as Bowdyn's story house, I went home, for now I was hungry and it was time for dinner. I entered by the side door into the dining room. There behind the table sat my father and Bowdyn and it seemed clear they were waiting for me.

'Come, stand here boy,' said my father.

With a sinking heart I noticed my drop in status from man to boy as I moved to stand where he pointed in front of the table. Both he and Bowdyn regarded me with grim looks.

'So when did you become a spy?' said my father.

I looked down at the floor where I traced patterns with my foot and made no answer, although I could feel my face reddening under his scorn.

'I saw you in the trees,' said Bowdyn in a more kindly voice. 'How came you there, Jo?'

Relieved that he at least was not angry, feeling I must explain myself or lose their regard forever, I told them how I had quite by chance seen them going to his lordship's house and how, fearing they were in some sort of trouble and about to be taken captive, I had planned to rescue them.

They watched me carefully as I explained and then looked at each other and I almost thought I saw a faint smile curve their lips, but if I did it disappeared quickly and when they turned back to me their expressions were grim. 'What did you hear, son? Tell me truly and tell me everything,' said my father.

And so I did, everything, including the weird chant at the end before the plotters went their separate ways.

The silence in the room seemed to last forever, broken only by the drumming of my father's fingers on the table. Both men looked up and regarded me right sharp, then looking at each other they seemed to reach a decision at the same time and both nodded.

My father gazed at me, his farmer's wind-burned, sun-tanned face, with the lines of care each side of his mouth, grim. 'You have put me in a difficult position by your conduct.'

'I am sorry sir.'

'That's as may be, but the secrets you now know are not mine alone and your knowledge endangers the lives of many. It could give rise to another Sedgemoor. If you were a stranger I would kill you without a thought. I cannot do that...' he paused then continued, 'but I cannot let you run free with what you do know, for fear it will reach the wrong ears. So I should imprison you until what you know is stale news, for good or ill. However, I do not think your mother would permit that. There is only one other possibility...' he paused again.

The silence stretched; a log cracked and spat on the fire. I glanced pleadingly at Bowdyn, but he dropped his gaze. I waited, listening fearfully to hear what my father's judgement might be. After a long while he spoke again.

'There would have come a time when you would have had to know some things that are secret. This is not that time, for you are but fifteen years and I would have wanted two years more. However, your rash actions are forcing me to bring that forward.'

He leaned across the table and took my hands in his. 'This knowledge may bring you danger my son, are you willing to swear your most solemn oath that you would rather have your throat slit, your belly opened and your guts pulled out than ever disclose what I am to tell you.'

To say that I was startled would be to fall short of the truth, but I could see no way out of it, also my curiosity was now raging. Thinking back on it now I think my father spoke in so dramatic a fashion to really impress on me the urgency of my silence.

'I will so swear.'

'Then swear.'

And he took me through it word by word until I had sworn to be gutted rather than reveal his secret.

'Now you know how seriously your vows must be held I will let Bowdyn tell you the story and you will understand. This is something that he and I were born into, with many others, and now you too are as bound as we are.'

Bowdyn sat staring at the table for a while and then looked up. 'I will not tell you the whole tale for there is much to it and it will take too long. Some of it you will hear when I start the tales to the village again, for your father has once more invited me to stay and follow the gleeman's calling whilst the frost and snow are on the ground. Often, in the tavern my stories are told and retold, but now I have new things to tell and part of them involves the secret, which we, your father and I, shall now disclose. And so they told me.

In the months to come, our gleeman was to tell the history of that secret, wrapped in a tale he told to our village. So for now

I will tell you only what they told me on that night. To Bowdyn will fall the task of telling the full yarn to all; straightforward as each storyteller tells it, for this is a tale of sorrows and I would not seek to divert with lightness, nor spoil with my lack of skill.

What they told me was of the fight against tyranny, one that had been waged for six hundred years and more. They told me of the brutal vengeance against those who stood up to injustice; how the Danes' law of Murdrum had but imposed fines on all for the death of an invader, and how the Normans took it up and worse, twisted and perverted it, using it to visit maiming and slaughter on the innocent poor. They told me of the tithings, where poor folk must belong to groups of ten and each must betray the other, so that none could fight for freedom for fear of betrayal. So freedom had gone into the deep woods, hills, dales and fens and lived in hiding. They told me of greed and larceny, of the Norman and French churchmen who saw it as their task to enrich themselves and their French foundations with English church treasure.

Then they told me of the legend of the Wild Hunt, by which Wothan pursued evildoers through the skies, and how the persecuted had formed a secret Brotherhood, a Wild Hunt to frighten the foreign churchmen and castle men, but which in time came to fight in secret against all evildoers. How it was the Hunt that had plotted the overthrow of King William, the bastard Duke of Normandy, and in failing had brought down terrible vengeance on the poor and helpless, man, woman and child. Even then the Hunt had continued in secret to harry and terrify the thieves who stripped our country of its treasures. It took vengeance on the king's son and in due time it took vengeance on the foreigners who murdered our land, paying them in the same coin one hundred times over. Many years later, the Brotherhood came out of darkness and conspired to overthrow and execute another king and planned the building of the Commonwealth. Thus the people took back some of their ancient freedoms, the power of Rome being destroyed in the land, the powers of the king curbed. These freedoms now were sadly in danger of being overthrown by the wilful and greedy. They told how the Hunt was the power that picked up the banner of freedom after Sedgemoor and now led in the plotting to supplant King James. Not this time with any bastard son or English lord like Monmouth, but with someone far from Norman blood, a Hollander with German blood, but with Tudor and Stuart blood too and as near to an Englishman as this poor country has had since poor, murdered King Harold.

My father then told me that he and milord were brothers in the Hunt, and Bowdyn the chain that linked groups of brothers together, carrying messages from only he knew who to only he knew where. Through him and others like him the Hunt was brought together.

When they were finished my head was spinning. My father placed his hand on my shoulder. 'You have much to think over Jo. Go, walk in the woods, sit under a tree and think on what you have been told. But remember, you must hold this secret of the Wild Hunt tight to your chest and never give even one hint to anyone. Not your mother, not your sweetheart, nor even, one day, your wife; not until she has earned your uttermost trust. Remember, the life of whoever holds this secret is in danger and he holds the lives of others in his hand. Do not share your danger around. Sharing will not lessen that danger. The danger of a secret grows the more it is shared. Share it with one and the danger is doubled. Do you understand?'

'Yes sir.'

'Then go, let all that is strange sink in, let it be forgotten from everyday thought. Put it in a special fortress in your mind with strong walls around it.'

I nodded and, head down, left the house. It was dark now, clouds had covered the moon so I could not walk in the woods, but I wanted to be somewhere I could think in peace without being questioned. I had by now quite forgotten any thought of eating. I went to the stables and sat in the trap whilst my mind churned. This morning I had been a contented idler. Then, happy with the coming of Bowdyn, I had worked to prepare for the opening of the story house. Now in the evening of the same day I was a plotter against the king and in danger of a death painful beyond imagining. I wished that I had been ill and never risen from my bed that morning.

The sound of my mother's worried voice calling my name roused me from my anxious thoughts.

'Josiah, where are you?'

She always called me Josiah when I was in trouble. The trap creaked as I rose and jumped down. I opened the stable door a crack and then slipped through. 'Here Mother,' I called.

'What are you up to my boy? It is way past dinner time, we are all waiting on you.'

'I'm sorry Mother. I was wool gathering, thinking about where Bowdyn's last story ended and wondering where they shall begin again.'

'You and those stories, I declare you live more in them than in the life around you.'

I knew she was not serious for it was plain she enjoyed them as much as I. 'I don't know why I sat so long Ma - my stomach thinks my throat's been cut!'

She laughed. 'That sounds more like the Jo I know. Go and wash your hands and sit up to table. Beth is waiting to serve, she needs to finish and get away to her rest also.'

The next day my father and Bowdyn again left the house together in the early evening. This time they did go to the tavern, to announce the opening of the story house after church on Sunday next. I know this news was greeted with pleasure and a round or two of drinks. I know this for when they returned to our candlelit drawing room I could smell the cold air on their clothes and the ale on their breath.

AD 878 Sumorsaete

Chapter 2

Brother Anfeald's Tale: The Riving of St. Michael's

On the Saturday before the stories were to start again I laid the fires in readiness, not wanting to have to hurry and perhaps delay the start after church.

On the Sunday I was the first in, but not by much, for I had no sooner lit the fires than the villagers started to arrive and pull down their benches and stools from the stack at the Cot's end. I think it was their breath rather than the fires that warmed the Cold Cot in the beginning. In any event the fires were burning brightly, the daylight had faded and the shadows were deepening by the time Bowdyn and my parents made their entrance.

My father and mother settled themselves and gathered their things around them. Bowdyn sat comfortably in the story chair, which I had placed in readiness for him, and turned to greet the villagers. The Cot was packed with people. All the old listeners were there, but there were some new ones swelling their numbers.

Bowdyn bade them all welcome. 'Eat, drink and be merry,' he said, 'for the story I would tell you starts sadly, how it will end we shall see.' And then he said, 'you will remember the first story was about Gewis and how he set about rescuing his

23

people from famine? You will remember the second in which the folk, now the Gewissae, settled near here and through their bravery and that of their staunch and true friends set about the mending of broken Britannia? In spite of tragedy, the death of Gewis and Elwine, the folk survived and in time prospered.

'I cannot promise you such with this story, for the history of folk is like to great waves at sea. The first two stories are like a rising wave. This story takes place after their great success; it follows after the building of a rich, well ordered and, for the most part, happy kingdom. It tells of its ruin, of slaughter, of the folk sliding down the watery slope, sinking into the depths, of starvation and misery at the hands of a cruel and vicious foe. Do not look for joy in this tale for there is little. But do not complain, for it is your story, your history and it is by no means finished yet. The Commonwealth put an end to tyrants for a while, for just a little while. Then they were with us once more, as many here have shed tears to attest. But cheer up, my friends, for the waves of time are with us and this poor country may be riding the wave upwards again at last.'

I quaked inside, I thought he steered too close to the truth for safety, but I now know that only my father and I understood him. The feeling grew on me that his words were meant to begin to prepare all here for what was to come and to receive it with joy, but his audience of farm and village folk looked only puzzled by this as Bowdyn continued.

'First we will follow the Rood, for its baneful presence has loomed over all of our stories so far and still does, up until the doom that befell us poor English, and then it vanished from sight and now perhaps is finally locked away from the sight of man in some dark cellar in the foreign land from whence it came.'

There was silence whilst the village folk thought about that; some remembering; some scratching their heads having forgotten where the stories had left them, some raising a murmur as they reminded the forgetful ones what Bowdyn was talking about. Only the tavern men sat quiet, for the stories had been much discussed in the tavern since the last story time and were still fresh in their minds.

'First we will hear Brother Anfeald's sad tale,' Bowdyn said, leaning back in his chair. And then, as always, he merged with the shadows and from them came the thin, high, reedy voice of an old man.

My slavery is my punishment and I will tell you nothing of it for it is also my penance. What I will do is tell you how it came about – of my shame, for perhaps it will save you from a sin such as mine and from the misery of such atonement. Would that they had taken my head also, but that was not God's judgement.

There was a pause as if Brother Anfeald was gathering his thoughts, which old men sometimes do for their memories go back many years and take time to be gathered together. Then the thin, high voice, like the scratching of a fingernail on slate, continued.

It was in the early morning of the twenty-second day after the calends of mud month, in the year of Our Lord eight hundred and seventy-eight. That date is written on my mind and is the only one, for now time means nothing to me except that through its passing I will escape this life and my sorrow.

I was young, a novice in the brotherhood of St. Michael and so I was first awake. I worked quietly by the fireside preparing for the feast of St. Peter Apostle. My brethren still lay sleeping, for it was not time for Prime. There came a knocking at our door and I crept quickly to it not wishing to waken the others, most of all not to wake Senior Brother Sigismund, for he thought little enough of me.

It was Wulfstan, the baker, at our door. He was greatly unstrung. He had removed his cap but his hands that clasped it moved endlessly, turning it round and round. He had been running up our hill for he gasped for breath and through these gasps he strove breathily to speak. 'Brother Anfeald, I must see Senior Brother.'

'He sleeps friend Wulfstan, I dare not wake him, what ails you?'

What he then said sent cold shivers down my back and cramped my guts.

'The Northmen are here, they are burning the land; you must run to the Burh!'

He meant the fortified area at the east end of Lutgaresburh. I grasped his hands. 'How near?'

'Not far, see,' he pointed, 'out Ilcaestir way.'

I looked to the northeast and sure enough in the dark I could make out dull pinpoints of red light. Burning houses. I thought what I should do, balancing Brother Sigismund's anger against the Northmen's rage: the Northmen were far off; Brother Sigismund was near. I decided.

'I will watch to see if it comes nearer and wake him at need. Blessings on you my friend. Go, look to yourself.'

I watched the baker as he ran off down the path that led towards the Burh. So steep was the path down he seemed to be swallowed by the ground, first his legs then his body. When his head left my sight I turned back to our house of song and prayer. As I crept quietly through the door and into the stink of sleeping bodies I took the stew I had been preparing and hung it over the fire to cook. I paused then and thought further on what I had decided to do. Jesu forgive me, for that was the point at which I started on the road to horror and lifetime of regret. I listened to the peaceful sound of snoring and looked behind me, the fires were far off. If I woke the brothers for no good reason Sigismund would scold and think even less of me than he now did.

I made my choice: I would not wake them; I would don my warm brown mantle and sit on the stone chair of contemplation, my back to the wall of our house, and watch and pray. If the flames came no nearer then I would allow the night to continue in peace, if the flames seemed to spread towards me I would wake Sigismund and he would lead us to the Burh. We could not carry arms to kill, but at the least we could pray for the success of the arms of the townsmen and the levy, we would be welcome for that.

I sat there saying my prayers for the defeat of the Danes and the safety of our people, until one by one the fires blinked out. When the last one did so I was left freezing my bottom on the stone seat, looking out on blackness, there being no gap in the clouds through which the moon and stars could light the countryside. After some time the cold started to strike through my habit and the mantle in which I had wrapped myself. I saw nothing, though I opened my eyes wide and stared until I started to shiver. My duty done I used my staff to thrust myself, groaning with stiffness, to my feet. Gratefully I entered the stinking and saw-rasping darkness, from my unwashed and snoring brothers in song. I lay down on my pallet and sighed as the warmth beneath my woollen cover soothed away the chill of my cold limbs.

I cannot say how much later it was that I woke with a start, knowing something amiss, not knowing what. I thought it might have been the chill, for the fire was out. I pulled my wool closer about me. My mind of a muddle, I could not link the cold fire with the red flickering on the window's edge and the wall behind. I got to my feet quietly. There was no dawn lightening of the sky for it was not yet Prime, but I could see the sky framed by the window and it was dyed a reddish hue. Fear gripped my gut. I plunged towards the door, not caring now about waking the sleepers.

I stood on the hilltop edge outside our house and felt my knees weaken and bend with shock. The fires were burning again, not far off by Ilcaestir as before, but nearby in the town and at the foot of our hill, the hill of St. Michael whose house of song we were. Even our fishpond house was burning. Faintly in the distance I could hear screams, but they were near enough to make out the pain and fear.

I watched for a while, hoping that our height and our silence would keep the secret of our place and being. Fool that I was, for even then speed might have saved some. And then I heard the sound of harsh voices nearby, loud enough to drown out the distant screams, near enough to know they were the voices of those who climbed our hill. Only then did I do what I should have done in duty long before. Stumbling in my hurry back to the chamber of sleep, I made to wake Sigismund and raise the alarm. The brothers, bleary eyed, came awake to horror. All too late, thanks to me, to make an escape to the Burh, for the lands between here and there were ablaze.

'Shhh! Wake up, wake up, shhh, quiet.' And as they woke, I beckoned hastily, 'Quickly, come see!'

Our song master, Senior Brother Sigismund, hissed sharply, but also quietly, 'What is it, why have you wakened us Brother Anf?'

They crowded to the door and to the window; they saw the flames; they heard their doom climbing towards them.

They did not know then that my petty fears had cursed them, some never knew. Those who came to that knowledge did so far too late to do more than cast a glance of reproach in my direction. It was this charity, this forgiveness that galled my conscience. It was this that made me step forward in defence of my brothers, and this that saved me from the terrible fate of one and the death of the rest. My foolhardiness in opposing them made our invaders suppose I might be worth something as a slave and so they enslaved me, made me, the unworthy one, live my life of regret whilst they slew the rest. For the soft hands of monks, whose lives were spent in prayer, had no value in the slave markets and, coming from poor families they had no value for ransom.

One thing alone Sigismund had us do. We lifted the glory of our house, the Halig Rood, down from its place above the alter, placed it in its silver case, glittering red with reflections of the fires surrounding us, and carried it to its prepared hiding place, outside beneath the rowan tree. We slid the stone over it and scuffed the earth on top and then stamped and shuffled until the area beneath our feet merged with that around and about.

We had barely finished our labour and huddled outside our house; a little group of six with Sigismund in front, when the Danes reached us.

As they crested the top of our hill and trod the flat space on which our house was built, I looked at them, in fear certainly but also with curiosity. There were ten of them, and they were not what I had thought: they were not monsters; they looked like our own fighting men. They wore helmets or leather caps as ours did, all grew the warrior's hair on their upper lip and many were bearded. Their helmets and bernies were clean and scoured, they were clad in furs to ward off the cold, their clothes were like ours, their hair, some blond, some dark, some red, was grown long and gathered back in braids. I felt some of the fear leave me, such civilised men could not mean us harm; we were men of peace, once they saw that surely they would leave us in peace?

One of them, the leader, stood forward. He waved an arm and as if we were men of smoke, four of his men pushed us aside and entered our house. We could hear them banging around inside and the sound of overturning furniture. And then the flicker in the doorway as the light from the torches they carried forewarned their return. They burst through the door, scowling.

'There is nothing, nothing,' shouted one.

'It is as bare as a bairn's arse,' shouted another.

Their leader, a thin, hollow-cheeked warrior with a golden boar atop his helmet turned to Brother Sigismund. 'You are the leader here, yes?'

Brother Sigismund nodded his head.

'All you Christian crows love gold more than you love your God. Where are your treasures?'

'We are a poor house of prayer Lord. Our only treasure is our love of God.'

'We have no time for this dung. I will ask you only one more time. Where is your hoard?'

Brother Sigismund looked at the ground and said nothing.

Golden Boar signed to his men. Two stepped forward and threw our Senior Brother, twisting, roaring and fighting, to the ground face down. They knelt on his arms, pinning him to the trodden earth. Another took his knife and cut Sigismund's mantle from throat to waist exposing his skinny backbone.

30

Then, reaching across to his weapon belt, he pulled out a small hand axe.

I watched with a sickness in my stomach and horror in my heart for I thought I understood what this portended. I threw myself at Golden Boar.

'No! No! You must not, he is a holy man; he is all goodness. We have nothing, take anything...'

Two men seized me. I struggled and lunged towards their leader. One turned slightly from where he gripped my arm and hit me just below where my ribs joined above my gut. The pain brought flashes before my eyes; I could not draw my breath and for a short time must have fallen into blackness.

I woke to the sound of hoarse, agonised screams. They came from Brother Sigismund. He was pinned to the ground by the men on his arms, but now two more had joined these and were sitting on his legs. The axe man was hacking into his back either side of his backbone as though butchering a carcase. It was this that caused the screams.

Sick with horror I threw myself again at Golden Boar. 'Stop this, stop this, you must stop!'

This time it was his hand, thin but strong as a giant's, that punished me. He caught me by the throat and skilfully choked off my protest, I say skilful because I know that he could easily have killed me, but I woke from blackness with nothing more than a sore throat and the pain in my gut from the first blow.

When I woke it was to a horrible noise, a harsh bubbling underlying a mewling of agony and grief from the brothers. When my gaze alighted on its source my stomach heaved and I, sick with horror spewed. Brother Sigismund lay face down in a pool of his blood. Where the axe man had severed his ribs from his backbone they had been pulled apart to reveal the inside of his chest and from there they had pulled his lungs. Exposed to the air these flattened sacks fluttered, but the screams had fallen silent. The bubbling came from his mouth and died away, the mewling of his flock was all that was left of his screaming, for he had not air to produce his own and from its lack, by God's mercy, he died.

'Now tell me. Where is your hoard?' said Golden Boar to us remaining five brothers.

Brother Acey fell to his knees, his voice trembling with fright. 'Lord, what little we have is beneath the altar and there is one other thing of great value,' he pointed to the rowan tree. 'It is buried beneath a slab there.'

Those who went first to the altar returned with glum faces. 'There is a box,' they said, 'in it are but five silver pennies.'

Those who went to the rowan scuffed the earth, found our hiding place and set my brethren to digging. They fetched up the slab to disclose the prize of our hoard: the Christian centre of our house of song. That which had stayed with us and purchased prayers for the dead Gewis and Elwine, heroes of old, so it was said, for three hundred years and more. Golden Boar had his men lift it out of its hiding place, the silver case glittering in the torchlight.

'Open it,' he said.

He glared at what lay inside. 'Is this it? Is this all, some filthy Godgield?'

He bent and looked hard to make sure there was nothing more beneath the earth and then lifting the Rood from its silver case he threw it back down into its grave and tipped the slab back over it. He waved the case in the air.

'If you can show me nothing more than this then you are all dead men.'

We all started saying our paternosters, for in truth there

was nothing more to give him. We had no hoard of offerings; few pilgrims came to see our Halig Rood now Danes strode the land.

Tetchy at such a poor outcome Golden Boar gestured to his men. 'Kill them, throw them in their house and burn it.'

One giant, clutching a mighty war axe, walked among the clamour of pleading and prayers and one by one smote the brothers' heads from their shoulders. When he came to me in the silence of the end, I was prepared to meet my God, for I had a heavy penance to pay and only God could properly judge. By my cowardice, my failure in duty through fear, I had caused the torture of Sigismund and the death of us all. My earthly executioner raised his axe.

'Wait,' said Golden Boar, 'bind him and bring him, he has spirit, he may have some value as a slave. He can toil at an oar to roughen his hands for the slave souk. We must have at least some gain from our work this night.'

As was their way, the Christian house an affront to their true Gods, but mindful of the afterlife of the dead, the Danes threw the remains of the brothers inside and fired the building. The beams, the floors, the roof, burned with greedy flames, lighting the hilltop; the flames rose as our house was consumed, a funeral pyre for our Order; the calm and sweet song, the prayers for our benefactors now cut off forever. The gravel outside our house, beneath the seat of contemplation, the meeting place for many for as far back as any could remember, was now tainted by agony and death and stained with the blood of the good and innocent.

My captors bound a leather cord about my throat, which made my breath rasp, then tied and trailed a length of rope from this collar. With me in tow by this rope like some bedraggled stray dog, we left. As I was dragged down the hill, fighting to keep my footing I heard a rumble and a crash. The walls of our house had collapsed as the wooden cross beams supporting them burned and fell. A great column of flames and sparks rose in the air. I liked to think it was on this column that the souls of my good brothers sped upwards to God and that his gentle mercy soothed their hurts and calmed their fears, forever and ever, amen.

And so I survived, to live through many years in which I cursed my life and nursed my guilt. I cannot fathom God's ways but if, as I think, this was the start of his punishment in life, I fear what may be waiting after death. My only comfort is that for all of time, since their deaths until our own, our Order had stayed faithful in prayer to our gift giver, Creoda, King of the Westseax, the son of Elwine and Gewis of the Gewissae….

Here the thin voice paused.

Bowdyn looked into the faces of his listeners, recognising many, and spoke to them. 'You know, of course, how Creoda in fear of the Halig Rood had gifted it to purchase prayers for all time for Elwine and Gewis. After the sack, the price for those prayers lay buried beneath stone and earth. Only one knew its hiding place and he far away, a slave in Muslim lands.

'But curses are not dismissed so easily, it was not the fate of many that the cross should languish in secret with the curse helpless to wreak its will on all who held it in awe.

'The bishop, cursing that he had not taken the Rood into his possession long ago, sent priests to search for it, in vain. It lay hidden for nigh two hundred years more, until the blacksmith of Lutgaresburh, digging for arrow and spearheads to add to his stock of iron, chanced upon the great honey-coloured stone slab and the Halig Rood lying beneath it. He gave the Rood to his king's thegn, Tovi the Proud, a Staller and a great lord. Tovi sent it to his church at Waltham and hung his sword by it as a gift. When that church was taken up by Harold, Earl of East Anglia, and became the seed of his gift of Waltham Abbey, the school for priests, the Halig Rood passed with it and Harold's mother gifted a jewelled diadem to hang at its head.

Harold kept it to show God's blessing when he became king, the legend of how it had cured him from a dread sickness attested its power. He hoped that this, in the eyes of his army, would overcome the Pope's banner and the rumour of the popish curse. In that way the cross of ill omen became the chant of a whole army of Englishmen defending their country and their freedom against a vicious, ambitious, foreign tyrant. As always with the cross, woe followed it, whether by accident or fate, who can tell? What happened then was either a bad choice, the carrying of the cursed cross to war, or two separate things meeting by chance: the death of Harold and the history of the cross. One thing is true, in the history of the cross all those who loved it and held it in awe died foully. Harold too, of course; murdered and mutilated beneath his standard by Sang Lac, the Lake of Blood.

The flower of English nobility that had called on the cross also died. Only those who had fled, to be hunted down by the gleeful Normans and their mercenary minions, survived. Some of them, at least, survived with pride: those who took their revenge in the dikes and ditches, where horsemen yielded advantage to foot and axe. These turned at bay and killed and killed again; paved the hollows with Norman dead then fled on and were lost in the darkness of nightfall. Many, including Asgar the Staller, oath sworn and true, took refuge in London, where waited another force denied to Harold at his time of greatest need, by treachery.

Would that the earth had sped on its axis and night had fallen one small hour early. What would that have cost the world compared to the misery visited on the English by that one hour; the hour that would have stopped the murder of a king, that would have saved the protectors of the English nation and by that have saved the English from all the hardship that was to befall them?

And here it was that Bowdyn stopped his tale for as he said, there was much to tell, but what had been told tonight set the stage for the real story that was to start at the next telling. He set that time for the hours after church the following Sunday and wished everybody a good and peaceful night. There was some doubt on the faces of the listeners as they shuffled and clattered, packed up and left, for the tale just gone, as the Goose Mother complained, was more the stuff of nightmares than restful sleep.

AD 1066 Sumorsaete

Chapter 3

AD 1066

Asgar the Staller

The next storytelling night Bowdyn ignored the complaints of the nightmares the tale of St. Michael's chantry had caused. He reminded the folk that his tales were true and little that happened where the cross was involved had joy in it. It would get worse, he told us, more harrowing and darker, before it grew lighter.

'This sad story,' he said, 'flows from the greatest disaster to be borne by the English people. Its beginning is told by a man of power, Asgar, grandson of Tovi the Proud, a Dane and Staller, or Constable, to King Harold. Asgar when we meet him carries a drear load of guilt. In his mind he has betrayed everything he loves. And yet he is sick with the wounds he bears in fighting for those things. He fought for poor Harold who, for all his Danish blood, is now accounted the last true English king.'

And with that Bowdyn performed his magical trick with the shadows and from the darkness spoke out the deep authoritative voice of a large man, confident in his station.

I am Asgar the Staller. I will tell you what I know, though grief chokes my voice. I loved our good Earl Harold who became king, although he held much land that should have been mine, lost to me by my foolish father. I was there at Harold's fall; I took these wounds in his defence. I was at London, the great town that had withheld its fyrd behind its walls when, if sent forth to Senlac, they could have turned the tide of defeat. I was there afterward when still we could have denied the Norman the land of England. I, God rot my over-proud soul, was deceived by the monster. He swore and thus forswore that my word should rule the land on behalf of all the English, that he as victor would take only the name of king. I told his lies to the fearful elders of London and they eagerly grasped them and the gold he gifted and yielded up the town and all its fighting men, and thus was lost our last good chance. In guilt for my weakness and foolishness and in love for my dead king, now all my love goes to his lady and my life is hers. The saving of her and her issue is all I can now give to my butchered lord.

The voice fell silent, the silence lengthened, the listeners started to shift, stools scraped, the noise of restive folk started to rise and then Bowdyn raised his hand, silence fell and the voice continued.

On the first day of Oestre, in the year of Our Lord one thousand and sixty-six, our good King Harold called together the fyrd for fear of the ruin that Duke William sought to bring upon our country. It was the fourth day before we received his call and by the time we had bade goodbye to tearful womenfolk, certain they would never see us again, by the time we had sought out and donned our war gear and gathered together in the Burh, the sun was rising on the fifth day.

As thegn and constable, commander of what few horse warriors we had, I rode, as did my men, but the others walked, until from pity they were given turns with the men on horseback, thus none were left behind and we went as fast as we could. But it was the evening of the ninth day of Oestre by the time we arrived at Steyning where the king had his foothold. There we were shown where we should go to await the call. Our orders would come to us, they said, at a place ten miles to the east, near a great signal fire. When we got there we waited.

Five full moons we saw and still we waited, eating our king's food until it failed, and by Holymonth we were hungry and going witless that the crops would rot in the ground and all the folk go hungry come winter. All the fyrd felt the same and there was some anger that our leaders had brought us to this place for no good purpose.

Our good King Harold, knowing our worries, sent the men of the fyrd home on the eighth day of Holymonth, but no sooner had we got here and started to bring in the crops than a horseback runner came through with the summons to re-gather. Had you been there perhaps you also would have said such things as our men said then, but like me, some you could not, for I have never heard them before or since. Only great anger can bring forth such new ways of cursing.

Anyway, this time we were told to bring a heavy load of food in our sacks and to fill our skins with water. We were not to return to the old place but were to walk as fast as we could on the ditch road from Escancaester to Lincylene and thence to Yorvik. The King would make sure we were met and joined with his army along the way. And so we set off, and because the sun shone and because we knew our Earl Harold would give us victory – for when had he not? – we sang at the start as we strode along.

Why we went north and what foe we were to meet and what do, I did not know and nobody told me then, if they even knew. The only thing that was told and was clear was that we were to hurry. And the singing stopped as hurry we did, until the blisters rose and burst and bled and still we forced our raw feet to trot.

Asgar ceased speaking and the listeners in the Cold Cot, still silent, looked to Bowdyn for the reason. The gleeman waited a space and then explained.

'For the moment we must leave Asgar, gone to the wars. First he goes to glorious victory and then to grim defeat. We shall not talk of that last disastrous battle; there are many who have. Suffice it to say that our feyman lord king fell, and the flower of the English well born were there slain with him. You have heard as much here as is needful. Later you will hear more from one whose tragedy starts and whose happiness ends with that accursed hill. It is of the aftermath that I speak now, seen through the eyes of a young man. A brave young man who, but for a badly knit leg, would be feeding carrion with the rest at Sang Lac Hill, the Hill of the Lake of Blood. The name of this young man is Edmund and it is he who will tell most of this tale as his eyes saw it.'

Bowdyn's voice changed again and so great was his art that now, in place of Asgar, we heard the young, crippled farmer's son, take up the story, and we listened enthralled.

Chapter 4

AD 1066

Edmund's Tale: Wirt

Every morning at sunrise I dragged my crippled leg up the slope to the wood's edge. The pain was grim but I suffered it for the pains of battle it had spared me. Every morning I looked to the East, into the rising sun when the skies were clear, and to the grey world's edge when they were not.

Six weeks had passed since our thegn had gathered the spearmen together and gone to answer the call of our Earl Harold, now our king. Six weeks since the on-again off-again summer had come to an end. Six weeks since the ceorls, my father and brother amongst them, all owing duty to the thegn and through him to our lord king, had donned their war clothes, picked up their spears and gone striding away up the ancient ditch road.

First they were gone and then, as the harvest was starting to spoil in the fields, they returned, doffed their war gear and became farmers again. The harvest was no sooner cut than off they went again leaving us to thrash and grind the grain.

And me they left behind. I begged, but they said they had far to go. There was fighting to do in the North, my leg would not carry me so fast or so far and they feared they would lose me on the road. So they went, and the outcome was the same, for they left me behind anyway and were forever lost to me, save one and he but for a time.

As the men rode and strode off into the distance down the old ditch road, taking turns on horseback, I cursed the axe that felled the tree that broke the leg, which never grew straight again. The womenfolk were kindly. They knew my heart and never mocked me. They gave me tasks to do, for my shoulders were broad and my arms strong. They valued me it seems and were glad I stayed behind. I, on the other hand, mocked myself and damned myself for a useless cripple who could not answer the call of our thegn and our king. The men-folk trotted away to save the kingdom whilst I, the useless one, stayed to work at kitchen tasks; a warrior bestrewn with girdle irons instead of a sword.

And so, each morning I mounted the slope to look for tidings of battle, my pain my penance for not being with kith and kin in the shield wall.

As each day passed, with my gaze on an empty road, I started to count the days. How long would it take to get to the North and, once the battle fought, how long to come home? In the eye of my mind I watched them go, riding and trotting together up the road and with that eye I saw them ride victorious and laughing back down the road to home.

But in truth that was the last I saw of them, until one came home broken. And then, because that was just the start of it, Asgar the Staller, our thegn, grandson of Tovi the Proud, who owned the Halig Rood and gave it to Waltham, came home and brought all of my troubles with him. As for those who laughed and sang and strode and rode away, we saw most of them no more. Ever.

And so I dragged myself up the hill every day, out of guilt and false pride, to look for our farmer-warriors. As time went by the days grew cold and I wrapped myself in wool and donned the wolf skin coat that my brother Wirt had given me.

Even so, by the time the sun had set, darkness, hunger and cold drove me down to our Hide.

After three weeks and a day of Winter Moon my watch was rewarded, for I saw movement along the road from the east: a lone figure. I thought him to be the first of many and I waited until the sun had fallen below the edge of the world before it grew on me that only the one was coming. My gaze followed him until he turned into the drove way that leads to our Hide. Overcome with my need to know, I descended as fast as my leg would allow, which in truth is slow and painful.

When I passed through the gateposts onto our Hide and stood before our hall I was one of many. Our farm folk were streaming in like ants on the march, all packing into the hall, all come to see the new arrival for his news, for since the men, the husbands, fathers and brothers with living families, had left, we had heard nothing.

The door to the hall was packed with standing men and women. As my folk were the farmers and this was my home, I felt angered that I was thus once again shut out. I let my anger show as I roughly pushed my way through. My growls and my jostling sounded loud to me, for the hall was silent but for a strange noise. No sound, not even that of protest came from the folk I thrust aside, all their heed was inward to the hall, eyes staring. As I pushed on I found myself at the front, part of a circle around an open space. Within the space crouched my mother and one other, and from him arose the strange noise, a whining, snuffling sound, like that of an anxious hound. It was the sound of a grown man crying and mourning. Shocked, I saw then that it was my warrior elder brother, Wirt.

My mother now knelt, her hand on his left shoulder. She bent, so that her eyes looked up into his. In them I could see the question.

He shielded his eyes with his hand as if he could not bear to see her look and then, taking his hand away, he looked about at the staring crowd and the horror on his face will stay with me forever.

'All dead,' his voice rose from a groan to an anguished shout. 'All dead, all the warriors of England, the king, the thegns, the huscarls, all dead, slaughtered,'

He paused and then his head lowered until it rested once more on the hand he held across his eyes and he shuddered. The silence held all in a grip of icy iron around the room, not a listener stirred as all strained to hear the slightest sound, as if by stirring they might miss the core of the dreadful news or perhaps find that it was not so and we could all go laughing on our way.

Then the silence was broken as he continued in a small voice, 'All dead; all but for those who broke their oaths and ran away. Me amongst them.'

Of course, we thought the battle had maddened him, that what he said was laid on with a shovel because he had run. To run was to lose one's honour forever, yet what he said in excuse, that the king and all were dead, could not be true. He would say no more and we could see that his strength was spent as he slumped to the floor.

The crowd, still silent, looked around as if only now seeing where they were and guilt-struck at forcing their way into our home. In ones and twos they turned and left our hall only to gather in huddles in the yard to murmur together as if trying to lay out in plain sight what had been said so that they might make sense of it. Slowly the groups broke up and the folk drifted away, silent, heads down, as if they could read the truth of the matter on the ground. All except Ulf, that is. He alone came back and sought out my mother.

Ulf was he who set all in order on the lands of our lord. Before Asgar, our thegn, had left he had gathered together all who held land from him and owed him service. At that meeting he told them that Ulf would stand in his place. If weighty things were to be decided, Ulf would do the deciding. If justice needed to be meted out, then Ulf would do the meting. In all things we were to hearken to Ulf as if he were Asgar himself. Ulf could not go with the spearmen. He was old and slow, his wind failing with the years, but he was wise in the ways of the land. Furthermore he liked his ale and was not mean with his pennies or his advice when called on in the tavern. Ulf was a good choice and everyone was relieved that our thegn had the wisdom to leave one such as Ulf in charge.

When all had gone from our hall, Ulf and our mother, our two ancients, sat in isolation by the fire. My sister and I sat in silence at the board in the kitchen listening to the murmuring that rose from their talking, although we could make nothing out from it. My mind churned with heavy thoughts and there was a sickness in my stomach at the news that Wirt had brought. Still I did not believe it and wondered what the truth was, although if even one finger-part of a handful were true then the news was all bad.

Wirt, who had cried until he could cry no more, now lay silent on his side, on bedding we had spread in the corner of the kitchen. There he stared at the wall and gave great shuddering sighs from time to time. After a while, in love and pity I sat on the floor beside him and held his hand. It seemed strange to be holding the hand of my warrior brother, who I held so high in my thoughts, as if he were some grieving child. Perhaps he felt the same for after a time his sobs died away and in a little while more he drew his hand away, opened his eyes and looked at me; at me, not at some sight of horror far away. He spoke low as if ashamed that folk should hear him, as if telling some dirty secret, but I heard him.

'We ran twice, you know. The first time we did not know why. Afterwards I found out that Eadnoth the Marshal and Harding his son owed more loyalty to Rome than to Wessex. They led us away because the Pope had sworn that all who fought for Harold were damned to hell eternal. They cared more for their souls, they said, than for England. And so our part of the Western fyrd did not join in the battle. Later a horseback runner came and called us to the fight. Harding tried to stop him from speaking, but he came direct to us and begged us honour our oaths. It was then we found what Eadnoth had done. Some, whose word was stronger than their fear of hell turned back. I was amongst them, but all was too little and too late. The battle line was thin and ragged when I joined it, so many dead from lance and barb, although I rejoiced to see the Norman dead piled high before us. Still our shield wall shouted "Out! Out!" and "Halig Rood! Halig Rood!" But always the barbs flew and again and again the Norman horsemen charged at us in groups of three or four, knee to knee. I saw King Harold off to my left, a tireless death dealer, and while he cleaved the Normans so did we. And then…'

Wirt paused and again his eyes lost sight of us and looked in pain at something far away in place and perhaps in time. Then, on a racking sob, he said, 'I saw him die. Those who stood around him were driven back and for just a moment he stood alone and at that time four horsemen drove at him. One I am sure was the Bastard. He drove his lance clear through our king's shield and pierced his chest, another's sword swung into his neck and with a mighty blow cut off his head. While I watched in horror another lance pierced his gut and came out hung with tripes. The fourth Norman jumped from his horse, hacked off our dead king's leg and shamefully his manhood; his pintel and apples, and carrying all over his shoulder, remounted and galloped away to the mass of horsemen, carolling his poor triumph...'

My brother's voice died away and he spoke no more that night.

I was falling asleep with my head resting on my arms on the kitchen board when a hand shook my shoulder. It was my mother. She beckoned to me to follow her back into the hall. My eyes were gummed and I blinked to moisten them and got to my feet. My leg ached from its stay on the bench and I limped my way behind her.

Ulf was sat at the high board and my mother gestured I should sit facing them as she took her place beside him.

Once we were seated facing each other my mother looked closely at me and spoke.

'You heard what Wirt said?'

'Yes.'

'You are the man of the house, Edmund. What do you think will happen now?'

'I don't know. Is it true, how can it be true?'

'Say it is true. What next?'

I thought about this. 'There will be a new king. He will send our thegn back to tell us what to do.'

'For all we know Asgar is dead with the rest. We must bear the thought that your father has fallen as well. The slaughter was complete if what Wirt says is true.'

This thought had not struck me. The cold stone in my stomach grew heavier and colder still, it pained me like a blow just below my breastbone.

They were still looking at me, expecting an answer. I marvelled at the icy grimness of my mother. The grief, the tears, I knew would come later. First there was a threat to deal with. I thought about it. What would I do if I were part of a conquering army? The answer was plain.

'A strange thegn will come. He will bring troops to enforce his word. They will take what they wish from us to show their power and his.'

'Yes, that is what must happen,' my mother agreed. 'And we, we must arm but submit. Not to wage war, for the war is lost for a time. But to show that to rape and pillage will be at too great a price.'

Ulf nodded his head, 'To submit, to show the new thegn that we are a people in arms but that we will not oppose his rule,' he said.

I waited. What they said was grim enough. That a foreign thegn would come, that we must accept him without bloodshed. But then, what was new about that, Tovi after all was a Dane? Now we poor Saxons and Danes would need to bow the knee before a Norse turned Frank.

'When they come,' said my ma, 'we will need to be awake and armed. That way, when the new thegn comes forward to explain himself and talk peace, then we can agree there will be no rape or burning of hall or home.'

'We need to keep a good look out on the road for their coming,' said Ulf.

'They won't come by dark,' said my ma.

'They'll likely come at daybreak, hoping to catch us at our sleep and with the whole day ahead to do their will,' said Ulf. 'So we want you to carry on watching from the hill, Edmund, from before daybreak until after sunset every day.'

They waited for my reply, eyes watching carefully, and

although their thoughts on what faced us hurt my stomach, nevertheless I was pleased that they had asked me, had given me this duty. At last I could do something useful, unhindered by my god-rotted leg. And so I was pleased to agree and see the satisfaction in their eyes. It being now nearly sundown, we resolved I would start my watch the following day.

Chapter 5

AD 1066

Edmund's Tale: Asgar and Frida

There was silence as Edmund ceased speaking and then Bowdyn spread his hands in question to my father and mother and the villagers.

'Why do they send Edmund to watch for the Normans? I will tell you, because their whole history betrays them. Conquered only by the Danes and ruled then by a Danish king, Knut the Wise, they cannot imagine what the Normans will do. They think they can talk with them, reason with them and that they will rule but otherwise leave alone the freedoms and the property of honest men. They do not understand that the Normans do not reason, they only enslave and rule by force. They are powerful reavers, no different in their minds to the Vikings of old who came to kill and steal. They have won the country and would kill all in it but that they need slaves to grow and harvest the crops and to build the castles by which they will be oppressed.

So the next morning Edmund wakes to darkness. He lies under the covers awaiting the first light of dawn to signal the start of his day.' Bowdyn's voice faded into silence and then out of the hush the young voice of Edmund took its place.

I awoke the next morning before the sun had risen. As the dawn light lit the overcast of the clouds a pale grey I splashed cold water on my face from the bedside bowl and rubbed my teeth with a wet finger. Shivering, I hastily pulled on my clothes and wrapped my wolf skin about me.

I picked up my thumb stick, fine for walking but also iron shod and balanced as a fighting man's quarter staff, and set off in my limping, crippled way to the top of the slope beneath the hazel hedge, yellowing already, the leaves beginning to fall. The nuts also were falling and were scattered amongst the leafy layer on which I lay. I cracked the shells in my teeth and feasted, it was partly because of these that I stayed where I was behind the hazel hedge. I would have been able to see further from the top by the ruined chapel of St. Michael, near where our blacksmith's father had found our Halig Rood, but I was not easy with that thought, for it is a holy place. Also, the trees on the slope had overtopped the flat area at the summit and were now so tall that the view along the road could not be clearly seen without moving about, even though the leaves had fallen. So I stayed behind the hazel trees at the base, seeing but unseen, eating the harvest of nuts.

On the first day I saw nothing.

On the second day all my troubles and heartache began. I still saw nothing in the gloom before dawn, but just before the sun began to lighten the sky, I felt a cold ridge across my throat. Without thinking I snatched for it and feeling pain I cursed and drew my hand back. I was fearful to see blood on my fingers.

'Keep silent,' hissed a whisper in my ear. I gasped and made to turn, but stopped still as the cold pressure against my windpipe grew greater. From the blood on my hand my sense told me that a sharp blade was held at my throat. Gently, gently I turned my head around. Asgar's grim, grey-bearded face loomed close to mine. The whisper came again.

'What are you doing here, who do you watch for? Who are you?'

'Lord,' I spoke over my shoulder, 'do you not know me? I am Edmund.' He looked blank. 'The cripple... from Browan farm?' I added.

From the corner of my eye I saw him looking closely at me. 'Why are you here?'

I explained that it was my duty to watch for the coming of the Normans. The hard, cold ridge at my throat went away.

'A good thought, but they will not come yet. They have much to do, wounds to lick, a new king to crown and more battles still to fight. They will not come here until the king gives out his gifts to all who fought for him.' He fell silent and then I felt him move back. 'We need to talk,' he murmured. 'I've put my blade away; you can turn and face me now, Edmund.'

I did so and bowed towards my thegn, my hand going unbidden to rub at my throat. Asgar's face was grey and deep lines of pain scarred his mouth, he stank of ill flesh and I could see yellow and black stained cloth wrapped around his body and limbs beneath his cloak.

'My lord, you are wounded, how can I help?'

'Enough of that, boy, let us talk of that which must be done. Where is your father?'

The cold lump in my gut returned.

'Only my brother Wirt has come home lord; of our father there is no sign and we fear from Wirt's news that he may have fallen.'

'Where is Ulf?'

'He is at our Hide. Mother is in charge there, between them they seek to plan for the wellbeing of the folk of our Hide and of Lutgaresburh.

'Then I must see Ulf and your mother. But I must not be seen. There is much for me to do. Can you bring your mother and Ulf here? Do not mention my name aloud; none are to know I am alive.'

'My mother does not climb this hill, lord, for her to do so in company with Ulf will draw many an eye and start many a whisper.'

'You are right, it will not do.' He paused, his forehead furrowed, thinking.

'Tell your mother and Ulf in secret that I will come to them after dark, but they must do what they must to keep my visit and our meeting hidden. I will be in the byre at midnight when honest men and wives are abed.'

Bowdyn fell silent. And then, looking at his audience, he smiled. 'So, we come to a mystery. Why must Asgar talk to the leaders of Lutgaresburh in secret? Perhaps the reason will reveal itself as the story progresses, perhaps not, for once revealed it is no longer a secret.' Bowdyn smiled at our folk, I think he did so, so that all would not be gloom, for when he spoke it was not of happy things.

'To know what happened next in our country after the lost battle you must know something of William's army. Some owed him service, for they held land from him; some he paid in gold. Most he paid in promises; promises of land, baronies and halls in England. No other conqueror had done this. Under Knut the defeated English mostly kept their land and served him. But William dispossessed the English of their land, all but the great earls. And then he also replaced the great earls with Normans, until all the land of England was in Norman hands and all the English under the Norman yoke. When you understand that then all becomes plain, how nobles became outlaws.'

'What about my land then?' said my father

'Aye, and mine?' said other farmers in the room.

'Are you owners or tenants?' said Bowdyn.

'Why, tenants of course,' said another, 'the hall do own all the land 'round yere.'

'Then go back six hundred years and you will find a Norman moving his household into the hall. But let us go back, to Edmund's tale, for we could talk all night about the wrongs forced on the English by William.'

There was silence and no argument, so Bowdyn returned straight away to Edmund's story and the young man's voice continued from where it had left off, as if our homecoming and sleep and work and talk itself were the dream and the story real.

When I awoke at daylight there was no sign of Asgar. What was spoken of at that midnight meeting I was never told although in time it became plain. The servants moved silently about and life went on under the pall of dread that was now cast over us. I climbed the hill and spent my chill damp watch seeing nothing, the best of my day being to eat the cold meat and cheese packed for my food by my mother.

The next day from my perch beneath the hazel hedge I saw that which was to bring about a change in my life beyond anything I could have thought of. There, walking towards me along the road from Lutgaresburh, I saw a small forlorn pair, a woman and a young girl.

I ran in great leaping bounds, down the hill to the hall. There I gasped out my news to my mother. Strangely, she showed no surprise but called for Ulf, sending him to meet the travellers almost as if she awaited them.

I stood quietly in a corner, hoping no one would notice me and send me back to my lookout on the hill. I did not want to go until I had found out all there was to know about the strangers.

It was not long before Ulf and his wards turned off the road and walked the path leading to the gate, built of wooden palings eight foot high in our outer wall. My mother, watched by our servants, all wondering at the meaning of this unusual event, met them at the gate. Ma threw her arms wide and clasped the woman – tall, brown-haired, not old but with an air of weariness about her – in her arms. Both the woman and the child were dressed in ancient, worn, road-stained clothes, in sore need of washing.

'Oh Frida, it's been so long, are you well? Come you must be tired, and hungry and thirsty. Come, come, sit by the fire and when you are rested you must tell me news of Scaepterburh.'

'Come everybody,' my mother called, 'come meet my cousin Frida from Scaepterburh.'

My sister and I came forward to greet the newcomers. I was puzzled. I knew my mother was born in that town and had left there to come with my father to our Hide, but I had never heard before of a cousin Frida. I wondered whether she was child of my mother's brother or sister, for in truth, with her red-shaded brown hair and slim build she looked nothing like my mother, fair-haired and now thickset in middle age.

We embraced her and sat with her at the board. The girl, perhaps twelve years old, perhaps thirteen, but quiet, withdrawn and thus seeming still a child, sat silently. For one so young she was strangely subdued, almost as if frightened of us. Later I learned that she had been taught to stay silent, to be afraid of all strangers, for there were many who would bring her to harm in a country grown lawless. She sat across from us, her eyes downcast.

'Come,' said my mother, 'how are things in the old town?'

'So far the worst is yet to come,' said Frida. 'The Normans have not yet reached there, but the tale of their deeds runs in advance.' She started to cry silently, fat tears running down her cheeks, she wiped them as though ashamed and then the dammed up sorrow flooded out. 'My man is dead,' she wailed. 'I thought only of here for safety. I was alone but for servants, you know my family is far away. We would not be safe there, not even children, so I have heard.'

'We have heard nothing of any Normans,' said my mother, 'perhaps they will not come here.'

'They will come, they will come everywhere; there is not a blade of grass they will not possess in their greed. There is a cloud of tears and pain and loss drifting over the land from the east. The cloud will bring with it the rumour of their coming and when they draw near that cloud will feed on your sorrow and move on in warning to the west. We fled in fear of its coming. Cousin may we stay with you?'

My mother sighed, 'I fear also that my man and many from this place are lost, but you are welcome to stay.' She moved round the table, gathering them to her, a sisterhood of shared grief. 'I cannot promise you safety but you will be as safe here as anywhere.'

Weeks went by. Still the Normans did not come. Frida and her child merged with our folk until there was nothing to tell them from us. And so she stayed for two years, throughout which time the Normans came and trampled on us, doing their worst to us, until we boiled over, and from that came about the great turning of my life leading it down pathways I could not have imagined in my wildest beer-sodden dreams.

The voice of Edmund faded away and Bowdyn spoke. 'But those are other stories for another day.'

Knowing from this that we were at the end of the tale for this day the folk rose to their feet with much clatter, cleared everything away and with their usual chorus of thanks, they left, their hubbub of chatter fading away in the night air leaving nought but the crackling of the dying fire and silence.

AD 1067 Sumorsaete

Chapter 6

Edmund's Tale: The Castellan

The next storytelling night, when the fire was glowing, the story house filled and warm, Bowdyn lit up his old clay pipe and looked with approval at our folk, all packed in. Those who had come without waiting for their evening meal bit into the contents of their satchels and swigged on the apple beer they had brought, it being the season and the cost being cheaper than well water.

When his pipe was drawing well he spoke.

'And now the lost battle at Blood Lake comes home to roost right here. You may not know this, but the Lutgaresburh of the tale is here, where you live. It has another name from Norman times, named after the castle. What castle you might ask, for few know the story of this place or of the history of England that has played out here?

When you leave here tonight, pause and look up at the hill, St. Michael's Hill. Battles have been fought there in ancient times. The Holy Rood was found there. The Normans built a castle there, Montagud Castle. When you look up, see in your mind the castle on the top and the local folk storming up the hill to pull it down, at terrible cost to themselves and their kith and kin; so great a cost that many of you sitting here tonight are incomers. Folk brought here to work an empty land. It is in that direction the story goes now. And Edmund, who was there and saw it all, will tell you the sad tale.'

Bowdyn settled back in his chair and the voice of Edmund spoke out from the shadows.

For a year and a bit after Frida had come into our lives, I watched from the hill every day. Wrapped in my wolfskin against the cold through that first miserable, dread-blighted Yule, then on through the pleasures of spring and summer and the growing gloom of another autumn. Wrapped once again in my wolf skin through the bitter onset of winter I kept on watching until I and everyone else wondered what it was I watched for. News we had in plenty of other places where the Normans came and took everything and where no English were left with any land to call their own, but still they had not come to us.

Frida and the child, Gytha were still with us. They were so much part of our kin that no one noticed them any more as strangers. I was glad they stayed with us for I took great joy to be in the same room as my cousin Frida. I found that my gaze followed her everywhere. It was foolish I know; she was much older than I, a woman of wide knowledge and a sharp mind, I but a cripple who knew nothing and had been nowhere. But that apart, I knew secretly in my heart that I would die happily if by so doing I bought the safety of Frida and her child. I daydreamed the dangers that might face us when the Normans came and always in those dreams I and my trusty staff saved both from the Norman soldiers.

Of Asgar we knew not. Since his visit and secret talk with my mother and Ulf he had gone into the West, so they said.

We knew not where, nor did we see him for a long time. By the next time we saw him we were in deadly trouble. He told me then that while he had been away he had stayed with the old king's mother at Escancaester. They, brave souls, had refused to submit to William the Bastard, but as always in this land of greed without honour, the country thegns thought more of the possession of their carucates and halls than their freedom and that of England. Perhaps if a Harold or an Alfred had been here to lead them, it would have been different. But they were not, and so the citizens of Escancaester were alone. Thus, when the Bastard gave them promises that he would not empty their purses, they submitted to him.

It seemed to me that Asgar was a War Raven, that wherever he went he caused trouble for William of Normandy. This was his plan to make good on his reckless urge to rise to greatness. It must be hard to have been at a tipping point. If the Bastard's lies had not deceived him perhaps he could have rallied the London fyrd. Certainly huscarls surviving the battle and the fight in the dykes and ditches had made their way to the walls of London, they were many and the fyrd was swollen by them. Perhaps they could have saved England, for the Normans had suffered many dead and had none standing by to draw on. Although, as Asgar once said to me, if the Normans had been forced to take what ships they could to escape, they knew the English fleet, still offshore, would have destroyed them and so fought all the harder for knowing that. But defeat at the gates of London could never have happened because Asgar, tempted by the Norman devil, had sold his soul and England too, as he knew to his cost when his devil's bargain unravelled and he saw he was betrayed and that he had betrayed us all. And so the foray that our greatest city put forth was but a token, numbered in hundreds not thousands, too little to do more than sally and then run.

The sun was rising and causing the dew on the grass to sparkle when that, for which I had watched so long, to the hurt of my crippled leg, came to pass. Many times in these many long days I had cast my gaze over the ground between the hill bottom and the far world's edge, starting to the west and sweeping through north, ending in the east. After each sweep, if I saw nothing I would walk around the hazelnut girdle until I came to the south of the hill and repeat my task. And so it went, day after endless day, sweeping my gaze to the north then to the south, until the sun set and I went to my food and rest, only to start again before sunrise the next day. Many times I asked to be let off, my mind told me that the Normans had passed us by, and many times I was denied.

It was the tenth day after the feast of All Hallows in the year of Our Lord one thousand and sixty-seven, one year and two months after we lost our country and our freedom, and I sat as always keeping my useless lookout.

At first I saw nothing but a shadow on the ground to the east of Lutgaresburh. But as I strained my eyes, I saw that it moved. As if by moving it came into clearer air, the edges sharpened and I saw the shadow was a column of mounted men. As they neared and the sun rose higher, so scoured helmets and spear points started to shine and I saw this was a column of mounted warriors.

I set off to run down the hill, but in my haste I over ran myself, sprawled full length, rolling down the steep slope and through cowpats, adding stink to the disorder of my clothing. I stretched my arms asunder and stopped my progress, got back on my feet and, more carefully this time, again started to run down the hill. By the time I entered the door of Browan I was unkempt, breathless and stinking of cow shit. I did not need to say anything while I was recovering my breath; my state was enough to draw everyone around me and to have my mother sent for. She knew instantly what my condition portended.

'Where?' she said.

I pointed to the east with my right arm, drawing great whooping, heaving, breaths.

'Oh sit down,' said my mother, 'what use is it running so quickly that when you get here you stink but cannot tell what you have seen?'

I plonked my arse on a bench and gasped out, 'Armoured horsemen, coming towards the Burh.'

'How many,' this was Ulf, arriving in the hall.

'Not many, maybe ten or twenty.'

'Good.' He turned to the watching men folk. 'Stand to the fyrd, tell them full war clothes. Muster at the Burh.'

The men hurried off about their tasks, I could hear them shouting to others as they went.

Ulf faced my mother. 'Well my lady, I think it best you wait here. These may be rough men. Who we are will mean nothing to them. They may not take orders from a woman, no matter how great hereabouts, it may move them to do things they will not otherwise do. I beg you stay here and let me deal with this.'

My mother stared at him, considering his words, I thought she drew herself up and would snap back at him. Then, as if something had drained out of her, she sagged and waved her hand in assent.

'Very well, friend Ulf, until we know what kind of men these are, you are right, it is best you deal with them; you it was our thegn charged to rule here.'

He bowed to my mother and then gestured to me. 'Stay here and guard your mother, let no one enter the door.'

I nodded and rapped the metal-shod end of my thumb-stick

quarterstaff on the flagstones and Ulf turned and left, walking quickly to set all in order at the Burh before the Norman horsemen arrived.

My mother grasped my arm. 'Listen to me. I am in no danger here. If it is women they want there are many younger ones, they will have no interest in me. You go; go to the Burh, listen to what is said and then come back and tell it to me. But first, go to Cousin Frida and young Gytha and make sure they are hidden safely in the stable loft. They will not search for women there when there are many others in plain sight.'

I did not need to search; Frida and Gytha were by the door to our hall, standing with the servants staring down the road to the east, from where the Norman column would come. Tongue-tied and stumbling I told her my mother's wishes, that I should hide her in the stable loft. As she turned her head I noticed that her red-brown hair now showed ice-white at the roots, giving lie to her youthful appearance.

She looked calmly at me and with a little smile said, 'that will not do. Consider this: standing here I am but one of the servants to the hall. Why would they bother with me?'

Besotted by her beauty I could think of many reasons why. I could not say what was on my mind and started to protest, but she held up her delicate, graceful, long-fingered hand and stopped me.

'However, if they find me hiding in the loft with my child will they not wonder why I hide there when everyone else clusters here to look at them? Will they not perhaps ask questions I would sooner not answer?'

She looked at me, I could swear fondly. 'To please you, I will put on my oldest travel clothes, Gytha also. I will rub soot in her hands and smudge grease on our faces, and I will wear a snood to cover my hair. Does that please you young Edmund?'

'It does, Cousin Frida, but please do it now for soon they will be here.'

She smiled and smoothed my cheek with her hand making a shiver go through me. 'I have found, young Edmund, that bold is best. If you are bold none think you have anything to hide.' And with that she put an arm around Gytha and moved away to go and change her clothes. She left me wondering what it was she had to hide. I had only thought of Frida as our cousin before, but now, as I hurried towards the Burh, I wondered if there was something else I should know.

I ran through West Street and entered the Burh to find it in uproar. The trained fyrd of the town had marched to battle and none returned except my brother Wirt, but he was not here. To my shame he said he was broken, done with fighting, if they wanted to kill him then let them, he deserved it for not dying with our king. The remaining fyrd of the town were those too young or too old to go to war and those of an age like me, but too crippled or weak to go.

None of us had armour of any use; the best pieces had gone to battle and were worn either by the dead, the stealers from the dead, or the few survivors who had fled. What we wore was what was left and a forlorn and patchy bunch we were. I wore nothing but my day clothes: my wolf skin coat and my leather cap, my only weapon my quarterstaff. We were not such as would frighten trained soldiers but that we numbered a half hundred, many with huntsmen's bows, perhaps enough to overwhelm the small number approaching.

We stood behind the palings on the fighting step of the Burh, too few to meet the rule of one man for every four feet length of wall. And so, hoping we looked more than we were, we clustered on the side towards the approaching horsemen and stood there shivering with fear for the most part while Ulf went up and down our line to encourage us.

'So small a number will not try to storm a manned wall,' he said. We looked at him in some doubt, for these were the destroyers of our huscarls, the best warriors in the West.

'This fort stood against the Vikings,' he said, 'and what are these but Frenchyfied Vikings?'

After a while of this we started to feel less frightened. We were only here to talk, after all, to agree that we would not resist them if they promised not to harm us.

They approached from East Street and stopped, bunched together, overlooking us. In their polished steel armour with their lances and with swords hanging from their waists they were a forbidding sight. Then a small party of one man and two companions rode towards the centre of the palings and faced them. The leader looked to be a noble of some sort. He carried a shield shaped like an upside down teardrop, not at all like our round shields. It was the most beautiful deep sky-blue and on it in shining gold was some strange dragon beast with opened wings. It was the finest shield I could ever have dreamed of; its owner I knew must be a rich noble to have such a shield.

He drew up below our walls, but it was the companion on his right who, in heavily accented English, called up to us.

'My master says why do you wait behind walls and clad for war? Your false king is dead, your army slain, our king is your king; he will be crowned on Christ Mass day. To stand against his servants now is treason.'

Ulf leaned over the wall and spoke, 'we seek not to stand against the king, nor to hinder his servants. Tell your lord we wish only that he will not allow his soldiers to abuse our womenfolk and children and that he will not burn house and hall. If he agrees on his honour, we will submit to his authority.'

The one who spoke English turned to the shield-bearer,

clearly his lord, and waving his hands towards Ulf and then towards the whole town, translated what Ulf had said – or so I imagined, for I had not heard Norman French spoken before. Looking up at Ulf, the shield-bearer said something to his companion, who nodded and turned again to Ulf.

'My lord would know who you are that you speak for all?'

'I am Ulf, overseer to our thegn. He left me in charge of his lands and hall when he rode to war.'

There was another rapid, low conversation between the two Normans and then the companion spoke again. 'If your thegn has not returned then he is dead.'

I knew better, I had a fluttering in my gut, for I now knew that my knowledge was dangerous to me. I said nothing and looked off to one side as if bored with the exchange.

'Whether or not your thegn is dead, he has been replaced. The king has given this land to my lord.'

'And would your lord be so good as to tell me his name?' said Ulf.

Again the muttering and then the companion, smiling, said, 'my lord's name is Drew. He is Drew de Montagu, a great lord in his lands and a friend of the mighty. He wishes to know the name of that hill.' He pointed to the hill around half of which our town spread.

'You are welcome, Lord Drew,' Ulf said, 'if you come in peace and not to hurt and burn, we will be your men in all things. The name of that hill is Saint Michael's Hill. It is a holy place hereabouts.'

I did not understand what happened then. When the companion translated what Ulf had said in their foreign tongue, the Lord Drew of wherever looked quickly up at the hill, his mouth dropping open as if amazed, and then he laughed and clapping his companion on the shoulder he spoke at some length.

The man at his side listened, thought a while as if setting his thoughts in order, then said, 'my lord says we come in peace; we will do you no harm. We will not despoil your women; Lord Drew will not permit, on his honour. We will not burn your town or your hall. Rather, you will work for us and we shall pay you for good work. Today will be a happy day for this place. What is its name?'

Ulf, looking more cheerful than he had for a while, said, 'Why, Lord, 'tis Lutgaresburh.'

There was another long exchange of words and then the companion spoke. 'That is an outlandish name. My lord receives this land from his lord, the Duc de Mortaine, who is the king's brother you know, and what he says must be so. He has told Lord Drew, who is his friend, that he must name this place after his own possessions at home. Henceforward this place will be known as Montagud.'

There was a low rumble of protest at this but Ulf hushed it before Lord Drew heard it. 'Let them call it what they like,' he said to us, low-voiced, 'and between ourselves we will call it what we like.'

Poor Ulf. Thinking back now, I know he hadn't understood that no argument was permitted. When he found out, it was too late for him. Later, it was too late for everyone, except me, Cousin Frida, little Gytha and Asgar our thegn. But I am getting ahead of myself.

'Come down, thegn's overseer,' said the companion looking up, as did his lord, the sky-blue shield now hanging at arm's length; he seemed no longer to fear our darts. His other companion, clearly bored and not understanding what was said, was looking all around. His horse, perhaps catching his mood, stamped and shifted restlessly. The group of soldiers, seeing no risk, still sat astride their horses, but were talking and joking together and there was laughter and occasional loud exchanges in their foreign tongue.

'Come down, my master wishes to talk with you,' the English speaking Norman said again.

Ulf, now happy that all was going well, climbed down from the fighting step, unbolted the postern gate in the main gate and walked through.

Everything seemed so calm, no one could have foreseen that this was the point at which fate doomed nearly all those I knew. All, down to the smallest and most helpless, became feymen or feywomen; all doomed to die except those with dark hair. Isn't that strange? To the Normans, folk with fair hair were English; those with dark hair deemed Welsh and akin to the Bretons, of which there were many in the Bastard's army. But anyway, once again I get ahead of myself.

As Ulf came through the gate so Lord Drew dismounted from his horse. He put his hand on Ulf's shoulder and turned him so that he looked up at our hill, Saint Michael's Hill, named thus for the holy house, which 'twas said had been there for five hundred years or so, even before the Northmen burned it and slew all of its brethren nearly two hundred years ago.

Just thirty years ago our blacksmith found there a religious relic of great power, a Halig Rood. Our thegn in those days was Asgar's grandfather, Tovi the Proud. He had it sent to Waltham where it passed to our Earl Harold, turned king. It had cured him of a crippling disease, so it was said. Had I known Asgar then as I know him now I would have asked that I might go to Waltham to plead the blessings of the Halig Rood. Perhaps it would have cured my leg, although it did not save our king in the end.

Anyway, my point is that Saint Michael's Hill was a religious place, a holy hill and a place of great power to us.

73

As I watched, Lord Drew, speaking through his companion, pointed and then traced a pattern on the air with his fingers. Ulf looked aghast then shook his head and spoke forcefully. At the same time he made motion of bending his knee. Lord Drew again said something and Ulf gestured behind him to where we stood lined along the fence standing on the fighting step.

Lord Drew paused and turned away as if thinking and then turned back and spoke long and calmly, even placing his hand on Ulf's shoulder as his companion translated his words.

Ulf moved away from the hand on his shoulder and again shook his head and then turned back towards the Burh, re-entered the gate and climbed up to his position on the fighting step.

Lord Drew stared after him a moment and then shrugged his shoulder – a gesture I was to see again and again from Normans, usually before they struck someone down. Here though, the Lord mounted his horse, waved to his companions and the three of them re-joined the main group. With little more said amongst them, they all trotted away back up East Street the way they had come.

There was silence in the Burh as we watched them go, then we all gathered as near as we could to Ulf.

'Well?' we said, all together.

'He wanted us to build him a castle,' said Ulf.

'Where, here?' said someone.

'No,' said Ulf, 'that would have been easy. No, he wanted it on top of Saint Michael's Hill, over the ruins of the old holy house. It seems that his lord, the Duc de Mortaine, sailed to battle under the flag of Saint Michael and so it bodes well to build his chief castle, Drew called it his Caput, on top of our hill.'

There were sounds of anger from all gathered there.

'Did you tell him it was a holy place to us, did you tell him about the Halig Rood?'

Ulf was silent for a while as if thinking to himself what best to say, if anything. Frowning, we looked at him.

'Come on man, out with it,' one said.

'Yes, I told him. He said he didn't think his lord would care about an English holy place, that everyone knew the English were heathen and that our false king took his woman in a heathen ceremony and forswore an oath taken on saint's bones. And in any case, he said, the Pope himself has said that any English who oppose King William of England, Duke of Normandy, are excommunicate.'

'Is that true?' the boldest of us asked.

'How should I know, do I know the Pope? I'm just telling you what he said.'

'And what did you say to that?'

'I said that we believe it to be holy and we are more than five to one against him. That no, we will not build his castle.'

'And what did he then say?'

'He said that it wasn't his castle although he would probably be castellan. The castle would belong to the Lord of Mortaine, brother to King William, whose power could not be denied. He said he would take everything he had learned back to his lord and that we should expect to see Bishop Geoffrey's Vavassour next. He would make us wish we had agreed to work for Lord Drew when we had the chance.'

There was much I did not understand in this. Who was Bishop Geoffrey, a bishop must be godly surely, even a Norman bishop? And what was a Vavassour – if a servant of a bishop then surely also a servant of the Church? But the last words of Lord Drew denied that and filled me with foreboding.

And so ended our first meeting with our new masters and apart from the threat in his last words, which chilled Ulf and me and, I think, my mother, everyone else seemed to think we had sent them away defeated. The idea that they might build a castle on Saint Michael's Hill went around the town and the countryside like wildfire. Everybody was outraged, partly because it was a holy place and a castle would defile it; partly because it was our holy place and therefore the Normans' act would be like rubbing our noses in shit, showing that even with God's help we could protect nothing and the Normans could do with us as they wished.

Winter was dying and spring giving birth in the year of Our Lord one thousand and sixty-eight when they returned. For, with a new season upon them, the Normans decided it was time to revisit their possessions at Lutgaresburh and enforce their will. We knew nothing of these possessions. Asgar was nearby, for he came to me on the hill from time to time and he asked after Frida and Gytha. Once he gave me small packages, which he said were for Frida. Why he should take such interest in my mother's cousin and her child I did not know, dared not ask and he did not tell me. I gave her the packages, which she hurriedly put away, her finger over her mouth spelling 'Please keep this secret'. The next time I saw her, her old woman's white hair roots were gone. That she dyed it surprised me and I thought it strange that Asgar should run errands to soothe her womanly vanity. I did not care about her white hair; to me she was both beautiful and young.

Ulf continued to order everything as if Asgar was still away about his tasks of mystery and he did not, I believe, know that Asgar was in fact nearby. In truth I think I was the only one from our place and amongst our folk who did know, except now Frida. And I was sworn to silence.

The first thing amongst the many and grim things that happened, the first thing that, had I been able to read it, I would have known forewarned the destruction of our folk and everything that had meaning and warmth and love in my life – until I turned it to serve my new and secret love – happened on just another grey day that spring.

Although there was no sun shining on their burnished helms and spears, I had no trouble spotting the approaching Normans. There were now ten times the ten at the first visit. As I ran to raise the alarm they started to run also, the horses stretching over the ground. Again Ulf sent for the muster to gather at the Burh, but by the time we got there it was filled with Normans. They had a plan. They set ropes to the tops of pilings and with these tethered to chain traces they set teams of horses to pulling. The Burh and its timbers were old, rotten with wet at the ground and under it. Section by section they destroyed our fortress whilst half their strength held us at bay.

My Lord Drew was there with his companion. He approached where we stood; we were confused at the destruction of our fort and with no orders what we should do. Now Drew spoke to us all through his companion.

'I thought, perhaps we could speak more clearly without your fortress.' He turned to Ulf, 'we are going to build a castle; quite a simple castle, of wood. Bring together all your men of working age and begin to clear all the trees from the hill. Before we start to build, the slopes must be bare. Small wood you can have for your fires, although my men will have first choice. Large, straight wood you will stack for building. I want all clearing of the slopes done before the early summer rains; we will need the earth soft to sink the post-holes. Do you understand?'

'No,' said Ulf, 'we will not do it. It is a holy place and you shall not despoil it.'

Again I saw that shrug and a slow, lazy smile.

'I will return when the slopes are cleared. Another man will come to plan and oversee the building of the castle. His name is Bigo and he is the best of all at building castles. Your overseer for the clearance and the building work will be the Vavassour. You will work for him I promise you. As the site is so holy you will be pleased to know that your overseer, Hugh Vavassour, is vassal to Lord Geoffrey, Bishop of Coutances. What land in this place is not owned by my Lord Robert is owned by Geoffrey. I am sure the bishop will give pardon for defilement of the hill by those who work at the building of the castle. On the other hand, Robert, Count of Mortaine, is the brother of your king. The castle is to be built at the king's orders and so resistance is treason. You know that such traitors are excommunicate by orders of our beloved Pope Alexander II. So do not speak to me of a holy site, the site will be holy when the castle is built, we will rebuild the chapel to Saint Michael inside the bailey for the soul of Lord Robert. The builder of the king's castle at Hastings will come to build this. Be joyful, your castle will be special.'

And with that he turned and mounted his horse and followed by his men he rode away east, leaving us standing in the wreckage of our Burh.

Five days later they returned. Drew was not with them but many more mounted soldiers were; at least twenty more. The lord in charge was the castle-maker, Bigo. He, unlike Lord Drew, carried neither shield nor any other trappings of nobility, although as we had heard, he was castellan of the castle at the site of Harold's grim and fatal battle. He built that one, so they say, in Normandy, and put it together on the shore, near to Senlac. He cared only to build this castle now and needed men to do it, other than that he troubled us not. He had no need; all our trouble came from the true leader of the horsemen. His name? Hugh the Vavassour; he was the fount of all our grief, a demon and a vicious foe. At the time if I could have ripped out his guts and hung for it, I would have swung happily. Now of course he is just a memory and all things change. For me now that memory is a happy one, but I get ahead of myself again.

Hugh wasted no time. Ulf and I and our sad little fyrd were waiting at the site of our old Burh for want of anywhere better to wait. He rose in his stirrups and looked down on us, speaking in English, a sneer on his lips. Strange to say for such an evil man you could not tell the blackness of his heart by his looks. In truth he looked like us with fair to brown hair and blue eyes with the sort of looks that would draw a maiden to him, strong yet kindly and smiling. This as we found out was the mask he wore to hide the heart of a monster.

'I am Hugh, servant to the holy Bishop of Coutances. I am your overseer; you will all work for me. Tonight my men will rest. Tomorrow you will come here and I will make you into two work groups. First one group will cut wood; the second group will carry and lay. Bigo the builder will sort the wood so that you will put it in two heaps, one for burning and one for building. I see there is a mere and by it an oak. This tree you will leave, I have a use for it. You may go now. Be here tomorrow.'

Once we were out of his hearing we gathered round Ulf, a mass of angry men.

'What shall we do?'

'Will we let the Normans befoul the hill?'

'Will we let the Normans befoul us?'

I have often thought of that angry gathering on the road west from the Burh. If only Ulf had thought more carefully. If only the women had been there to calm us down. But they were not. We made plans in anger and destroyed everything. For the anger did not go away, if anything the Normans blew on the fire of our rage and made it burn more fiercely. What happened to poor Ulf helped build up that fire until it consumed us all, or at least nearly all. Asgar saw most clearly, and so he and I, and my heart's burden and her child, survived, but only we few.

What happened was this.

At our angry meeting in the road it was agreed that we would resist. That we would not come to the Burh to be made into work gangs to please the Normans and to befoul our holy hill. And having thus made up our minds we went to our homes.

I told my mother what had passed at the Burh. To my amazement she flew into a rage. 'Oh men, oh men! Stiff-necked fools, what have you done? You have destroyed us all. Go; tell them they must do as the Normans want. What good holy ground if it is befouled anyway and no one alive to know it was once holy. Go tell Ulf to re-muster the men, tell him to build their castle for they will have it anyway.'

I swear I tried. When I found him he was already asleep and not pleased to be awakened. When I repeated what my mother had said he was even less pleased.

'Tell your mother I respect her, I bow before her but this is men's business. It was I, not she, Lord Asgar left in charge and I am with the men. The Normans must be made to know they cannot drive us wherever they think to, like cattle. We will do what we said we will do, tell your mother that.'

I knew this would not satisfy her and for want of any other plan I went up the hill to seek Asgar, for I had long thought that he concealed himself above the town and came out as he wished. I called and called for him, but I found him not. And so I went home and gave Ulf's message to my mother. I was right. It did not satisfy her and she wept for fear of what his foolishness might bring about. Really I think she was weeping that my father was not there, for if he were he would have ruled and she would have ruled his wisdom at need.

Bowdyn ceased speaking. This time he looked seriously at his listeners. 'So my friends, we have had a long story tonight. It is a workday tomorrow so you will need your rest. Go, sleep well and be warned. There is rebellion in the air in Lutgaresburh. The Normans will have their castle nevertheless. There are cruel acts, which may also give you nightmares as Edmund continues his story. If this alarms you, do not come to the next storytelling.'

The folk thanked Bowdyn and my parents and quietly, perhaps thinking over his words, stacked their benches and went thoughtfully on their way.

And so we were warned. Especially, he had given fair warning to those who claimed nightmares from the tale of the sack of St. Michael's. But I had to ask myself, were these real nightmares or just a chance to speak, to seem higher than they were, in front of the other folk? In truth I do not know, but this I do know: I did not see anyone stay away.

Chapter 7

AD 1067

Edmund's Tale: The Vavassour

The following Saturday we came to the Cold Cot mindful of Bowdyn's warning. As soon as we were settled, after looking around to see who was missing and finding none, we fell silent. Bowdyn greeted us and smiled on us, glad I think that all had returned, even the Goose Mother. He did his trick of voice and shadow and Edmund started his story once more.

The next morning we stayed in our homes in defiance of the Vavassour; it was not for long. By midday there was a din of cries and screams and then our own door banged open and armed men burst in. The servants ran through from the kitchen carrying what weapons they could lay hand to, but my mother bade them stand back.

'By what authority do you come unbidden here? What do you want?' she asked, holding herself high, for she was used to being second only to the thegn in authority when my father was not there and sometimes also when he was.

The Vavassour strolled through his men, looking around at our feast hall.

'Why Madame, by my authority; which I draw from Lord Robert of Mortaine and he draws from the king, his brother, so I suppose you could say by authority of the king.

I have come as a courtesy to you Madame. I wish personally to take you and your household to the mere. There is something that I wish the whole town to see, from the lowest,' and here he bowed, 'to the highest.'

And with that he waved to the soldiers crowding the hall doorway and they came around us and with their spears aslant across their chests as barriers started pushing us ahead of them.

'You do not need to push us there, we will walk,' said my mother. Her voice sounded strong and yet I could see her face was white and her hands trembled.

The Vavassour smiled slyly at her and waved again at the soldiers and they fell back and ceased pushing. As we climbed the slope to the mere so it started to rain; cold autumn rain to increase our misery.

When we walked around the lower slopes of the hill, dragging cold feet through the wet grass to the mere where the oak tree stood, we could see the people of the town were already gathered there. Huddled together, clothes pulled over their heads against the cold, wet drops soaking their hair and trickling down their necks, they did not look happy; many looked frightened.

We, it seemed, were the last to get there. Whatever this was about had not yet begun, as though awaiting our coming. We joined the throng and waited. And then, when the Vavassour felt we had waited long enough, were cold and wet enough, had soaked up the feeling of his power enough, he started to speak.

'I am here on the king's orders to build a castle for Milord Robert, Count of Mortaine. Robert is a lord of great power; to defy him is treason. Your thegn's man is a traitor; he has brought this town to the point of rebellion, which would lead me to destroy it. But Lord Drew promised there would be no burning and so that weight of punishment must all fall on the man Ulf. Let there be no more defiance, and there will be no more punishment. Defy me more and every day you will see this repeated.

'Your thegn's man saw us Normans as blind and thought we could not see his treason. For this he forfeits his eyes.

'Your thegn's man spoke as a traitor against us. He spread the lie that you, the people of a perjured, heathen king, could hold your holy place to be greater than my lord's castle. For that he shall forfeit his tongue.

'Your thegn's man wished to contest whose might ruled here. To show that our might prevails, that he is no man compared to us, he will forfeit his manhood.

'In mercy, when these symbolic punishments have been carried out he shall hang.'

All the while he was talking we kept silent, trying to understand what he said; not that he didn't speak English clearly for he spoke it like an Englishman. No, it was not the words, but the sense of them we struggled to understand, so mad did they sound. There was a roar of anger at this last, for hang we did understand. At that we found ourselves facing a forest of levelled spears.

With an evil smile he waved a hand and the centre of the spear-carrying soldiers parted to reveal Ulf staked out indecently on the ground, with his leather hose awry.

We, held at bay, facing a tight wall of spears, could only watch as Hugh the Vavassour, drawing the knife sheathed at his belt, walked slowly across to Ulf and knelt down beside him.

Ulf, who was already bleeding about the face from rough handling, his arms and legs drawn out and secured to pegs, stared up at him. Eyes stretched wide with horror he whined, 'No, no, please, no.'

Without holding back one instant, Hugh thrust his blade into first one and then the other of Ulf's eyes. Mouth wide, our overseer let out the most terrible scream and whilst his mouth was yet open, Hugh plunged his fingers into it, grasped Ulf's tongue and with a flash of his dagger sliced off the end.

At the screams and the sight of blood flowing from Ulf's eyes and mouth there was a roar of rage and the crowd surged forward, only for those at the front to be painfully impaled, skin deep, on the firmly held spears of the soldiers. Shouting and struggling they tried to pull back to get away from the punishing spear points, but the unharmed back line carried on pushing forward. In the end, spurred by pain, the front line won. The crowd quietened, those impaled trying to staunch their bleeding. Those behind them no longer engaged in the game of push and shove turned their horrified gaze once more on Ulf and the Vavassour.

Hugh, who had been watching the struggles of the crowd, the smile never leaving his lips, turned back to his screaming victim. He reached down and with a quick sawing motion removed Ulf's pintel throwing it to the ground. The screams redoubled and then died away to a hoarse, bubbling moan of agony as the blood spurted strongly, splattering the wet grass.

At a wave from Hugh, a soldier who had been standing beneath the oak approached carrying a length of noosed rope, which I could see led over a strong branch of the tree. Hugh placed the noose around Ulf's neck and at a signal, six of his soldiers heaved on the other end of the rope. As it tightened, the pegs holding Ulf down resisted and then were dragged out of the ground. Legs kicking, he was hauled through the air, coming to rest swinging back and forth under the branch, the animal sounds issuing from his throat choked off. The stakes still attached by their ropes swayed wildly to a different beat. He was then hauled into the air, his legs kicking as he came to rest, swaying back and forth under the branch. Swinging gently from side to side, his face turning blue, he hung above the ground, tremors running through his body, feet jerking. The blood streaming down his face and chest mingled with that from his crotch. It mixed with the rain to make a thin, steady stream, falling to the grass beneath, foretelling his early release from pain, if lack of breath did not kill him first.

When he was silent, and was thus thought to have passed into the care of our Lord Jesus Christ, we were released, but not before Hugh had had his say one more time.

'If Ulf had done his duty to our king there would have been no punishment. Think on this, the beaten must yield. Be at the muster place tomorrow at sunrise and we will start to build this castle. Any who are not here I will take to be traitors and will choose one of you each day for punishment such as this.'

As we went home from Ulf's martyrdom, the womenfolk weeping, we men stricken to silence by what we had been forced to witness, I saw that Frida and young Gytha were walking ahead of me. Gytha was being guided by her mother and wore a mantle of wool over her head so that she could not see. I drew up beside them. Under Gytha's hood I suspected there were pads over her ears to dull the hearing. She should not have been there but for her mother's fears to leave her behind unguarded with the Normans in the town. Hard choices were becoming part of our daily lives since our warriors went away.

'I am sorry that you had to see that, Cousin Frida. If in any way I could have spared you I would have done so.'

She turned and her face was stern and hard, like a mask of stone. 'Thank you Edmund, but I have seen worse, much worse. That was but a drizzle compared to the storms of blood I have witnessed.' And with that she looked to the ground and said no more.

Not for the first time I wondered about her. The more I knew of Frida, saw her, heard her, the harder it was for me to think of her as my mother's cousin. She seemed to have seen and been used to more than I would have thought Scaefterburh could have shown her. But these were idle thoughts and I had no time to chew on them, for under the hardship of building Lord Robert's castle all such idleness was lost to me.

There was silence in the Cold Cot, almost relief when Edmund's voice ceased. As the folk shifted on their benches and mulled over what they had heard, Bowdyn looked around him and must have seen our distress, for he spoke to us in a gentle, soothing voice.

'It is sad, I know, but we needed to hear this for it tells us something about Hugh's nature. He speaks good English and why should he not for he is half English by blood. His father was an Englishman, an exile, an inconstant mercenary in the wars between Poitou and Normandy, who had fathered him on a tragic, fallen woman of the court. Hugh learned his English from him, before his sire, false as always, deserted them to stalk some other fey wish. His feelings for his father were visited upon us I fear, or his mind was steeped in evil, for otherwise who could understand his foul spite?

'It is needful for you to know that, for Hugh appears again and again and inspires fear at each meeting. He has something of madness about him. Certainly he is cruel, but it is cruelty from which he draws pleasure. It is strange that there are people of this sort. Not demons, although they act as if they served Satan himself. And yet, think to yourself, were those who tortured the condemned of Monmouth's army any different? Were they demons or men like us? When the judge gives out the sentence for treason, "Hang, draw and quarter," who carries out his order? Is it a demon or a man like us? And Hugh was of this sort. The brave lady, of whom I will tell you later, for much of this story is hers, shudders at the thought of falling into his hands. He it is who is ordered to pursue her. Edmund's stomach rises to his heart at the sight of him. We will see that Hugh is the monster of more than one woman's nightmares, one in particular whom we have yet to meet. But, for the time being, the story moves away from such cruelty, for the castle is indeed built and from it stems the tragedy of the murder of the shire from which Edmund, with his cousin and her daughter, must escape. And now I will bid you a good night and urge you not to dwell on what you have heard until we meet again for the next telling.'

Some, notwithstanding Bowdyn's warning, had come to the telling and went away disturbed; perhaps to more nightmares and wishing they had not. Anyway, the matter was not forgotten and was raised in protest again at the next telling.

AD 1068 Sumorsaete

Chapter 8

AD 1068

Edmund's Tale: The Castle

When next we met with Bowdyn there was a difference about the audience. My father said nothing, for he had tried before to contain the stronger parts of Bowdyn's tales. It was not he so much as the womenfolk who set up an outcry before the next part of the story began. Alice, the Goose Mother led in this.

When Bowdyn was in his chair, but before he had a chance to speak, she piped up. 'Friend Bowdyn,' she said.

He turned his head slowly as if scanning to see who had spoken and when his gaze came to Alice he looked surprised for she rarely spoke, had not done so since the beginning, the earliest days of the stories.

'We know you must tell the stories as handed down to you. We know that you tell true tales, but can we not find some more cheerful road to walk down? Since we have started this story we have had the slaughter of the English and now we have tales of torture. We know these things go on and even, since Sedgemoor, that they have gone on here, and in public. But surely, stories should help us to forget, not remind us of the cruelty of those in power over us?'

Bowdyn sat silently thinking. Then, I believe to take more time to dwell on his answer, he fetched a spill from the fire and set light to whatever fragrant mix he had in his old clay pipe. When he had puffed it into burning steadily so that he could stoke it with nothing more than his breath, he answered.

'For those who have suffered loss there is nothing I can say to make that dreary sorrow less. Reminding folk that others are as badly dealt with is no cure. For those who have not suffered the cruel loss of their loved ones, and most here are of that sort then, so that we may get on with life, it is worth remembering that what has happened here has happened before and far worse than I have yet told. The story I tell you now has something of love and tenderness and honour in it, but for the most part it is sorrow. If you would not have me tell you these things, which are true things and your own history, then we do not have to have stories at all. But we have started the long tale of the happenings to your folk of long ago and you must choose whether we go on or not. For these things we speak of here are happening to the blood of the Gewissae and from that blood came most here.'

He paused and looked around the room. There were shocked looks to faces about the Cot. Was he saying, really saying, that they should stop the stories?

'Go on, go on,' this from nigh everyone in the room. I looked around and saw some not joining in, one of them the Goose Mother. But when we did indeed go on I never saw any stay by the fire in their home hearth when the gleeman was telling a tale, not even she.

Waiting until the clamour had died down, Bowdyn gave a nod and we, relieved, settled down to listen as once again Edmund's voice spoke from the shadows.

After the grim ordeal and murder of Ulf my mother called me to her. 'I have a hard task for you my son.'

She looked at me through eyes red-rimmed with sorrow. 'Without Ulf I must govern as best I can, but our thegn must know what has come about. He will need to name another to rule in his place. And so, my son, you must still go to your watch every morning, for it is only through you that he can make his wishes known. Now Ulf is dead only you and I know that Asgar lives. No other must know until he names him.'

I stared at her in surprise, for I had thought that only Frida and I knew that Asgar was still hereabouts and that he sometimes sought me out. I should have known better.

She looked sorrowfully at me. 'It is hard for you my son, because you must work with the folk to build the Norman castle, but you must also keep watch so that Asgar may rule through you and me.'

'I can do it, Mother, for Asgar knows where I watch; he will find me if he wishes. Trust me, Mother, we shall satisfy the Normans and also work to try to destroy them.'

Suddenly, my mother looked worried. It sounded in her voice when she spoke. 'Do not be brave and foolish like Ulf. Brave I know you to be, but bravery now is to tolerate the Norman shackle. You must not, not at any price, bring Norman trouble to this house. There is more reason than I can tell you.'

'Trust me, Mother,' I said again. 'I do not understand, but I will do as you say.'

And so the next morning whilst still dark I limped up the hill to start my watch. As the light started to show in the east I ran leaping and limping downhill to be at the remains of the Burh as the sun rose.

Hugh the Vavassour was a hard overseer. He worked us from sunrise to sunset as if driven by some demon. Our work was never enough. In the beginning out of wrath and bitterness we did work slowly, but after whippings and near deadly beatings on some of our number, and under the goad of Norman spears, we gave the work our best efforts, thinking that if our masters could not be denied then it were best done quickly.

First there was the whole hill to be cleared of growth. This would have gone poorly but for Bigo, who brought forth many axes, saws and iron bars, many more than could have come out of Lutgaresburh.

The hazel hedge that girdled the whole of the bottom made it harder to move the cut wood down from the hill. The work would have gone more easily could we clear ways through this in each of four directions, but Bigo would not have it. He said the hedge was a natural barrier that would direct attackers only through the gap at the end of the road leading down from the bailey. And so he forbade us to cut any more gaps, which meant that some wood had to be carried halfway around the hill to be sorted.

As we cleared and stacked and the piles of small wood grew greater, we consoled ourselves that at least we should have warmth in the coming winter season. Alas, what Drew had promised us was not to be. Hugh laughed when we asked to carry away the small wood for our fires.

'You shall have it,' he said, 'when you pay me for it. Norman wood is not given free to English dogs come sniffing for scraps.'

We vowed we would freeze in our homes before we put our coin, if we had any, into thieving Norman pockets. I tell you this so you may see how a bad time was made worse; how the Vavassour inflamed things and helped dam up our rage until it spilt over and the dam broke in an outpouring of violence that killed us all, or nearly all, for of course, had it killed me I would not be here to tell the tale.

And so we chopped and sawed and cleared the slope. Bigo chose the wood that he could use and laid it in a third mound. He stood on the hilltop with line and rod, once it was cleared of growth and the stones from the ruined holy house had been removed. He hammered in stakes, and then we were set to dig outside the stakes and pile the dug earth and stones inside.

Bigo said we would work better if we knew what we did, and so he taught us, step by step, how to build a Norman castle. Where we piled earth would make a high mound, he said. On top of this he would build a tower. Where we dug the earth we should keep the ground flat, digging evenly across the whole length and breadth of the hilltop. When this was done we would close the whole within a strong wooden wall. The tower, he said, was the motte, the flat ground within the wall, the bailey. Within the bailey and up against the wall, with roofs to make a fighting step, he would build guardhouses, stables and store rooms. The tower was for the lord, the castellan and the hearthmen. It was also a last refuge for all should the outer wall be taken. And so he made clear what it was we slaved over and I was betrayed by my inner nature to want to build it right.

We started to clear the woody cover in Blood Month, one year and two months after the death of our King Harold and the loss of all our warriors. We finished building the following Aefterra Litha, in the warmth of midsummer. It had taken us seven months from start to finish, ceasing only for calving and lambing time. We had worried that perhaps the Normans would ignore our farming needs and not stop the work, but we should not have worried. As the Vavassour pointed out, all the flocks and herds now belonged to Lord Robert or Bishop Geoffrey and so it was their wish that everything should be done to save their livestock from loss.

At the end of it, when we had built the Norman's castle, there was a road from the west side of the hill winding round until it reached the gate of the bailey. Once inside the gate there was an area of flat ground leading to the buildings backing onto the wall, but there was no straight path to the motte. To find that path a man on foot would need to walk half way round the mound we had raised and there he would find narrow steps, suitable for single file, leading up to the door into the tower. This tower had windows and slits for defence, but was roofed over with a sloping roof.

Standing at the foot of the hill looking up at Montagud Castle, as it was called, I felt quite proud, wrong-headedly. I wondered why we English had not built such fortresses, for had we done so, the Normans' task would have been much more trouble and with much greater loss, so much so that they might have given up and gone home. It was clear to me now that they never would. I think this was plain to all who laboured as their slaves to build this castle; just another thorn, the constant pricking of which swelled our rage.

Later, when I had seen more of their works, I understood why they built castles here and we did not, for if they came against our castle they would simply ravage the land around about, as they did before Hastings and later in the North. We, on the other hand, if we came against one of their castles in our countryside, would not ravage the land, for it and the people were ours – although we did burn their towns sometimes.

When the building work was finished, well enough to make Bigo light hearted for the first time since we started, our work was still not done. For now we English had to fetch the stores; bring water in many, many buckets to the top and empty them into the tanks. This while the soldiers lounged around fires and grumbled that their lord had forbidden them use of the womenfolk of the town. Hugh did not care how much they abused the English, but Lord Drew had given his word, which was golden, and the Normans feared his wrath when he returned.

The nearest water was the mere, but this was not fit for drinking. The tree had been used for hangings for as long as any could remember and if no family came to claim the body to bury it then sometimes it just rotted and fell into the water. So it was said anyway, and the mere did stink, that I know. It was covered in a smooth, treacherous coat of duckweed, as fresh and green as any spring leaf, but underneath this pure inviting ground was black stinking water. At the bottom of the hill there was a fresh clean stream, which led away east towards the Ivel. It was about five hundred paces away and every pail had to be carried that far and up the hill to fill the tanks. That was done once we had made them, and plastered them, and dried them, and prepared them with resin to make ready for water. I tell you this so that you may know there is much more to building a castle than throwing up a few walls.

All this knowledge was to become useful to me in times to come, although I could not then have guessed at it, or under what lay of the land that would be. Even so, I took some interest in the building of Castle Montagud, but I was, I think, the only one. Perhaps because of my leg, the work I was given was easier. As I have said, Hugh made sure that the task was a running sore to all.

There was a time when we came upon the stone slab beneath which the Halig Rood had been found. This brought home to us how much the Normans had forced us, under fear of grim punishment, to foul that which was holy to us. The anger, which had hardly started to die down, now sprang up anew, like red fire on which a basket of kindling has been thrown.

When the castle was built, when the stables had fodder, when the tanks were full of water, and when the cookhouse store rooms were groaning with food, some of which had been sent by Lord Robert with escorted Waggoner's; some of which was gathered by thieving soldiers foraging in the surrounding countryside; then the soldiers, the overseer and the builder moved into the castle with flags flying. It was stuffed with soldiers and brooded over us, a wen on the hilltop, always in our vision. Where before had been a holy house, and then nothing, there now crouched the means of our slavery. When Lord Drew did not return, the insolence of the soldiers, who now could sally forth and then retreat, no longer surrounded by Englishmen, grew beyond bearing. There was bullying and theft, but worst of all there were tales of young women who had disappeared, to the grief and horror of their families. All this rightly blamed on the castle. And so the countryside was now in terror: no woman younger than a grandmother dared leave the home without an escort of family men folk. Metal was hung so that alarms could be sounded, so that neighbours could help neighbours defend against thieves and women hunters. Farmers from outlying farms abandoned their homes and moved into the village, for as they said, better a long walk to tend the land than risk attack and murder. And all of these things lay on top of the outrage, still a weeping sore, over the befouling of the holy site and the memory of what had been done to Ulf.

I still spent from sunset to sunrise waiting under the shadow of the castle for Asgar, until one night in Holy Month, like a moon-shadow fleeting noiselessly over the land, he appeared beside me. I was alone, and then I turned my head and he was there. He told me later that moving like a shadow was a trick he had learned on the Welsh campaigns with Harold, in happier times.

Here Bowdyn stopped and with a grim expression looked over those assembled. 'Now things in our story go from bad to worse. Once the castle was built and provided shelter, so the insolence of the Normans was boundless. What they could conceive, they did. The rage of the people increased daily at this. You must remember, until Hastings this was a free people; they were strangers to the unfettered lawlessness of the Normans. Before then, the thegn had given out justice and if the folk thought him unjust they could discuss this at moot and send to the lord for judgement.

'There was foolishness on both sides. If the Normans had been constrained to good government of Lord Robert's holding then perhaps the people would have accepted it as being better than what might happen if they did not. Perhaps if Lord Robert had been there all would have been well, for he was a stern soldier and a good one, but was not a bad man and would perhaps have controlled the milites, the soldiers, of the castle. Perhaps if Drew had been there he would have honoured his word and there would have been no carrying off of young girls and women, but he had gone travelling around the lands of his friend Lord Robert de Mortaine to impose his lord's authority and to set all in order. For the time being the castle builder Bigo was castellan of Montagud. He hated the land of England and the whole conquest. He just wanted to go home to Tilleul, to peace and quiet and his family. He took little interest in anything but waiting for the day he would be free to leave, and by this made his state worse.

'Much of the land to be seen from the castle belonged to Geoffrey, Bishop of Coutances, more familiar, so they said, with drilling troops than with teaching monks to pray. He left the guarding of his interests to his Vavassour. Hugh, bursting to visit his evil on the land, was pleased to stoke the fires of resentment and rebellion, for through this he would be able to shout treason and punish the land of his father, perhaps as he would have punished the man himself did he but know where he was.' Bowdyn paused and his face kept its grim look.

'The Normans, goaded by Hugh, raised the bitterness of the English to a white heat. The English had no leader they would heed; none who seeing their danger could have bade them be calm. Perhaps an arrow in Hugh's back would have led to revenge killing, but this would have been a small thing measured against what came out of storming the castle of the king's brother.

'Next time we meet we will start the story of how a group of lightly armed, unskilled, simple men worked to storm the castle of one of the greatest in the king's court, to then free the captives and to kill their Norman tormentors, and what then befell them.'

He fell silent and his audience, now so well drilled in the way of the story telling, got up to go.

The castle on the hill was just tumbled stones and everyone knew of them, but that the folk had stormed it was news that would be discussed over many a pint of scrumpy. There was even betting of small amounts on the outcome to be revealed at the next story telling.

'Oi bet we threw em out,' said old Bill.

'If that be so 'ow come it t'be such a mishap?'

'Wait and see,' said Alf.

And they did.

AD 1069 Sumorsaete, Edith

Chapter 9

AD 1069

Edmund's Tale: Asgar's Secret

Since Bowdyn had returned I had spent some time, with my father's permission, in building the firewood stack, needful as the year crept deeper into winter. So it was that on the next Saturday evening I had two good blazes going, warming the Cold Cot as the village started to crowd in. It was now a month since Bowdyn had resumed his tales and other than a lesson in the history of our hill we still didn't know where this story was going or who it was about, aside from Edmund, and in truth we knew but little about him other than that he was lame and was passed over for many things because of it. We knew that he bitterly resented his place helping the women about the house when his heart would have had him stride away to war with the others. Whether he be hero or whiner we had yet to find out. I think Bowdyn knew this and would not be hurried, but he also knew that unless he gave us someone to follow, someone we would care about, then there was not a proper story, to his loss and the tavern's gain.

When he next took his place in his story chair he waited until all was a hushed, expectant silence and even the coughing had died down before he spoke.

'And so my friends, through Edmund you have had a

history lesson about your village; you know something about the loss of our country to the Normans and you know something of the building of Montacute castle, although now the hill is bare but for some tumbled stones.

'Today I want to bring someone else to you. It is a lady, a tragic queen fallen low by the working of malice and fate. Have pity on her for it should not have been so.

'The tale I tell is of her courage, her love and her strength of purpose. Many of her station in life, beaten down by the hammer blows of fate, would perhaps have taken the Roman way and let out their blood. But the lady of our story had more boldness than that, she had a secret, which she kept close, to reveal when the time was right, and a child to nurture until full grown. And so she endured whatever grief and hardship she must, until her journey's end.

'Let me start at the beginning. The Gewissae, as you know from our other tales, helped in the founding of Wessex. This kingdom over time brought all the other kingdoms together to make our country of England. There were four earldoms, over each of which was an earl and over them the king. Those earldoms were Northumbria, Mercia, Anglia and Wessex.

'The greatest earl of all was Earl Harold of Wessex. He had two wives. One, Ealdgyth, sister to the Earl of Mercia and widow of Gruffudd ap Llywelyn, King of Wales, Harold married through Christian ceremony for purposes of policy and Ealdgyth became queen. The other wife was a love match, and her he married outside of Christian ceremony in the Danish handfast fashion. This wife bore him seven children of whom six survived and was a true wife to him. It is her story that I now tell you.

'She was a great beauty; her name was Edith, called 'Fair as a Swan' for her regal grace and loveliness. But under the comeliness beat a strong and courageous heart. When Harold was killed it was Edith who protected his honour; Edith who withheld that which William would give anything to possess. And to preserve that honour and withhold that possession she fled. It is this flight we talk of here, for this land of England was not easily possessed after the fatal battle at Senlac. In her passage through the land we will meet some of the brave souls who helped her and carried on the fight long afterward. To hear her story we will listen to the voice of Edmund, for he was with her until her voyage end and it is through his voice that the story has come down to me.'

As Bowdyn paused, Gert, who was Watt the herdsman's wife, called out.

'What did she look like? I mean to say, you tell us she was a great beauty but that don't tell me nothing. She could be from Cathay or a handsome Blackamore for all that tells me.' There were murmurs of agreement from the other womenfolk.

I won't say that Bowdyn sighed for he didn't, it was me. Gleemen, I think, love to talk around their stories and so he answered Gert and painted a picture that we all could see, and the story was all the better for it. As usual with Bowdyn, it was probably his intention to go up this lane and if Gert hadn't asked the question he would have poked someone else into doing so.

'Edith's family,' he said, 'were Angles of East Anglia, some of the original settlers who had been there for hundreds of years, which they had used to their advantage for they were rich in land and rich in gold. Edith was tall and slim, but with a wiry strength; grey of eye, but with long, silver hair the colour of birch tree bark. She was mild and courteous, always calm, always moving with the grace of a swan on the water. But underneath she was a warrior at heart. She could hit the gold with a light, hunting bow and carried a bodkin dagger concealed about her clothing. She was the womanliest of her time and place, yet she sailed and rowed a boat, spoke four languages and had a keen and questioning mind. She could do many things that some would think manly. Although enraptured by her, Harold knew it was bad policy for his ambitions to marry her. By taking her as his handfast wife he created a marriage that was not recognised by the Pope, thus leaving him free to marry as policy dictated, in a Christian ritual.'

'I don't think that's fair,' said Gert. 'He did 'er wrong; he married 'er boi a lie. He told 'er they were married but they weren't. Why did she put up with it if she were so clever? There were a girl down Martock way got taken in like that, though he ran off when 'er family made it hot for 'im.'

'Ar, oi rember that,' said someone else, 'pretty girl with red hair, baby were pretty too.' There were murmurs of agreement from many of the women, one or two crying out, 'shame on 'im.'

Bowdyn sat quietly with a smile on his face and then gave a loud 'Hrmph,' which shut the womenfolk up and made everyone who had turned around to look at Gert turn back towards him.

'If you remember,' he said, 'at the last telling, Edmund was keeping a look out for Asgar. Let us listen as he continues with his tale.'

At first I jumped with fright because Asgar had startled me, suddenly appearing alongside me so silently. He took no notice, except perhaps with a sly smile then asked me for news. He had passed through the land before and saw the castle rising and then again when it was built, but having nothing to tell us had not stopped. As he said, the more he stopped the more likely that the Normans would learn of his visits and the greater the danger. Not to him, he said, but to others.

I told him all that had happened from the coming of Drew to the present day; of Ulf's murder and of the spiriting away of young women. Lastly, I told him of the anger.

His face was grim and he looked into the distance, thinking.

'There is something I must tell you,' he said.

I listened with all attention for I could tell from his manner that what he had to tell was weighty. He paused and then spoke, his voice hushed, dead and lifeless.

'When our king was killed, Duke William bade that his remains should be gathered together and buried, without Christian rites and in mockery, under a cairn on the seashore. The man he ordered to bury the king was a miles, a soldier of his court by the name of William Malet.

'Here he made a mistake, for William Malet was half English on his mother's side and also, perhaps because of this, had befriended Harold during his forced stay in Normandy. He sorrowed for the death of Harold and felt his own honour besmirched by such a task. He feigned that he could not find Harold amongst the carnage and so Duke William sent to Waltham for Harold's beloved, Edith Swanneschals, and ordered her to seek her lover's remains on the battlefield. Again he made a mistake, for William Malet and Edith plotted how they could have Harold buried by an English priest who would care not for the Pope's curse, and in a place where he could lie in peace and secrecy until England needed a martyr to rally the kingdom to drive the Normans out. I know this was Edith's wish. For William Malet, I think it was enough that his friend could have an honourable burial. And so when Edith found her husband's mutilated body, she took him in secrecy to be buried in a place known only to herself, while William Malet buried another in a cairn on the seashore. By chance he found the ring of Wessex stolen from dead Harold's arm. Perhaps Malet did not know how much Duke William wanted it, or perhaps he did. Either way, he gave it to Edith and so she now carries it about her, this ring that Duke William covets for himself, it being the ancient jewel of the kings of Wessex and England.'

Asgar paused and a smile flicked for just a fleeting instant across his face. 'Duke William opened the cairn and knows that it is not Harold buried there, but Will Malet has escaped with no worse punishment than banishment to the North, for he claimed that Edith deceived him. The Bastard now believes that Edith can tell the true resting place of our king and thinks, rightly, that she has the arm ring, and so he seeks her with all his power.'

I listened to this long tale of high deeds, of kings and queens and wished he had not told me, for enthralling as it was, it was nothing to me and yet put me in danger, for now I knew things that a king wished to know.

Asgar must have read this in my face for he said, almost in a whisper, 'Queen Edith is with us here.' He looked at me. 'Do you not know?'

I shook my head, mouth agape.

'Look boy, I can foresee what is to happen here. Hotheads will stoke this fire; swains of missing girls will want to tear down the castle walls to find them. Glastonbury's monks will curse the Normans for befouling the hill; Ulf's family will stir the ashes. There will be a blaze, boy; they will try to burn the castle down and then the might of the Normans will fall on this plain and many will die. They will kill all the English they can catch – man, woman and child. We must get Lady Edith and the child away.'

And then the blindness fell from my eyes and everything came together. Then I could see, where before I was befogged.

'Frida and Gytha?' I asked wide-eyed.

'Of course Frida and Gytha, you share a house with them, did you never sense that all was not as it seemed?'

I had to confess that I had and now all of these feelings made sense. Not Frida and Gytha, but Edith and Gytha.

'We must get them away before the storm breaks,' Asgar said. 'There is another child, the youngest, Gunhild; she is safe with the nuns at Wilton, too young for the hardships of exile. So, you have your choice, boy. You can stay home to guard your household and die, or you can come with me and guard the queen and her knowledge of where our king lies buried. I want you with me. A wife, a crippled husband, a child and an old father moving north away from trouble will not draw too much attention, especially if we look poor and hungry.'

'But what of my mother?' I said, aware of my duty. 'Does she know?'

'Of course she knows. Life is full of hard choices, Edmund,' he placed his hand on my shoulder. 'Your mother has a household to protect her, if they cannot, adding in a cripple with a quarterstaff will make little difference.'

I thought about this, what he said did little for my pride, but should armed and armoured soldiers pour through our door facing me with my quarterstaff, for all its iron-shod foot I did not see that I would hold them back for long. Better by far that my mother went on a visit to her real cousin in Scaeftersburh.

I saw myself the defender of Frida and her child, better I thought, to let the name Edith stay in the back of my mind. My heart swelled within me for I had thought before and now thought again that I would die for her if I must.

'I am with you Lord Asgar. What must I do?'

'The first thing you must master is not to call me "Lord". From henceforth you must practice calling me "Father", for on the road that is what I must be. Frida, for never must you call her otherwise, must be your wife and Gytha your child. It's as well your beard adds ten more years and that Edith belies her age.'

'Where do we go, old Father?'

'That I cannot tell you until we start, for none must know our road. William's bloodhounds will follow soon enough once we are missed. The castle is our doom. Frida could have stayed here forever, as one of the folk if not for that, but once the folk rise up all will be fey.

'Can we not warn them not to oppose the castle?'

'Who would do that, a crippled boy, a dead man, your mother?'

I could see that he was right; it was hopeless. 'What would you have me do now?'

'You must carry my word to your mother and to Frida. They must prepare. Pack water and food, get as well shod as can be, dress in old, not too clean but strong clothes. Bring money, but conceal it well. Send your mother on her way; leave behind only those folk needed to care for any livestock that cannot be turned out to thrive running free. Tell her she must take the household with her. If any ask she is to say she is going on pilgrimage through Ilcaestir to the Abbey at Edwardstowe, for her health and to pray for the peace of the kingdom. Frida and the child must go with her; we will wait for them in Ilcaestir and take them on from there.'

'All is not now as it was. Tell her to avoid the bishops' sees and any folk of a bishop's household. If she must seek refuge along the way tell her to seek the abbots, monks or friars, or nuns.'

I must have looked my puzzlement at this, for he explained. 'Since the battle and the death of the king much has changed, many on high have shown themselves traitors and not least some holy men.'

I thought this over and then asked, 'Why is it we can trust the abbots but not the bishops?'

He paused, thinking on his answer. 'Well, young Edmund, I think this is the way of it. An abbot or abbess has that which he or she most desired in life when first they entered the abbey. He or she has the rule of it and possesses it. If to keep their place either must then lick the sole of another's shoe, by doing so they admit that person's mastery over them. And so they then must accept that the abbey is theirs only until someone else comes seeking their place and to gain it licks the piles of that master. So, abbot or abbess, they wish only to stay still and are prepared to fight to the death to defend their abbey and the rights of the brothers or sisters in Christ to elect their own ruler.

'A bishop, on the other hand, is a dog seeking a bone. He fights and schemes to get his see, but then he is not content. He seeks his pallium, his vestment of power, and will serve any and betray any, and play the rogue to the utmost to get it. He must have the king's approval and so he bends the knee and submits. He must have the Pope's approval, and he knows the power of the Pope lurks behind the Norman king and so he strains his sinews to show that he serves only him. Many a bishop would have us killed and then serve up Edith and Gytha spitted and roasted, if by that he could prove himself to be the chiefest of the lickspittle road lickers.'

I was silent considering this. Asgar was talking of men so high in my regard I had never before uttered their names or place without respect. He was crumbling my world with the hammer blow of his words, although Wirt's tale of Eadnoth's and Harding's betrayal had already rocked my belief in those above me.

'Oh Asgar... Father,' I said, 'nothing is as I thought it was, we are beset, as was our king, by treachery and ambition at every turn.'

'Welcome to the world, young Edmund,' said Asgar, 'nothing is new, and it was ever so.' And he fell silent, grim-faced and deep in thought.

After a while he spoke again. 'You must pack and join me here at sunset tomorrow. Rest during the day for we have far to go in the dark. Let's hope the clouds let the moonshine light our way.'

I had already thought this all through whilst he spoke and I knew what I must do. 'I cannot. You speak truly that I cannot defend my home and that my mother must go, but I cannot let her go alone. I will give her your message but, for my honour, I must stay with her and cousin Frida until Ilcaestir to lend weight to her command of the household on the road. We will join you then, whilst my mother goes on to Edwardstowe.'

Asgar thought about this for the time it took to say it then nodded. 'Perhaps it is best. You at least know what can happen. Make sure you leave in good time. If the castle falls do not think the danger over, it is then it will be at its greatest. I will see you all at Ilcaestir. You will not see me when you arrive for I do not wish any to know I live. Especially, do not look for me for I will come to you. As the household passes through have Gytha seem sick. Have Frida and Gytha stay at the inn, you wait behind to guard them. Your mother must say that

Frida will hire guards from the town watch; that you will catch up along the road when Gytha is well. Counsel her to lead the folk to Edwardstowe, not to wait, but to pass on as if none had tarried.'

'And when we three do not reach Edwardstowe, what then?'

'Then it will be a mystery,' said Asgar and was silent.

I waited, but he said no more. I looked down the slope, to see that the dawn was shedding its grey light on my way home and when I turned back to bid Asgar farewell he was gone; drifted away like smoke while I had looked away.

Early as it was, my mother was waiting for me in the hall, as if she knew that the purpose of my watch had been served and much had now to be furthered.

I sat while she put a platter of food in front of me and I must confess I found I was starving. My mother, one of the calmest and most patient of women, waited in silence for my news while I set about stuffing my face and filling my belly. I managed to spit out the message that Asgar had given me. That I now knew who Frida really was told my mother the importance of the message and its urgency. She was not happy.

'If we abandon the beasts and the home Hide, how will I live in Edwardstowe?' she said.

I told her what Asgar had told me to tell her, for as always he had foreseen this problem. 'You will take refuge in the abbey, mother. Asgar knows the abbess; unlike many of our sees the abbeys are loyal. The abbess is a good Englishwoman who has no love of the Normans; they will unseat her one day, if they can. Until that day you and the household are safe there. You will be in retreat and the servants will be found work to do in exchange for their bed and board. Leave someone you trust to sell the beasts and bring the money to you. The Hide, if we are allowed to keep it, will be brought back to use when times get better. Asgar says that all who fought for Harold are having their lands taken and given to Normans. Do not expect that we will be able to keep our Hide. Best sell what can be sold and go. Maybe one day they will let us buy it back.'

This speech, perhaps the longest of my young life, and also probably the most important, had an extraordinary effect on my mother. She stared at me, mouth open, and suddenly tears came into her eyes. She reached out her hand and cupped my chin. 'Your father would be so proud of you now, my son. Praise be to God that your leg kept you here when all others went away.'

Chapter 10

AD 1068-1069

Edmund's Tale: The Storming of the Castle

'All of our party knew what we must do. My mother, Frida and I met together in secret. I told Frida that I knew her to be the Lady Edith, our dead king's wife, and that the Bastard sought her for the secret locked in her head about her husband's place of burial and for the ring of Wessex that she carried. I told her of the plan, such as it was, to make her part of a pilgrimage to the abbey at Edwardstowe and that we would go by way of Ilcaestir where Asgar waited to take her to safety, God knew where.

She had sent Gytha to help in the kitchen before we sat to talk and all the while I was speaking her clear grey eyes watched me gravely, as if seeking to divine the entire truth from what I said. When I gave her Asgar's reasoning that soon the castle would be attacked she nodded.'

'Yes, it will come; all of the women say so. The fyrd know your mother will be against it so they do not bring their plotting to the hall, but they say there is news from the North. There is to be a rising; they say that the taking of the castle will be part of that rising. There are not enough Normans to be everywhere; they will need to go north for the greatest test to them is there. The fyrd say that my countryman, King

Sweyn, will help the great northern lords drive the Normans into the sea.'

'If this is true why does Asgar not know of it?' I asked. 'He is everywhere; he was at the rising of Exencaestir. That failed for lack of help from the thegns. What news is there that the lords of the North will be different?'

'Oh, they will fight when their hoards are at risk,' said Edith. 'They know William will seize the gold they left with the monasteries for safety. He knows that their gold is a greater danger to him than the anger of the church. He needs gold to pay those who fought for him to whom no land was promised.

'As for Asgar, he does not tell all that he knows. He tells that which is needful to make good his designs. But there are others passing through who in happier times told their news to your father. They now tell your mother as the price for bed and board.'

I knew she meant the pedlars who passed from time to time.

I needed to think this over and also to make sure that Asgar knew and had made his plans with this news in mind. And so I set off up the hill to seek him, but he was nowhere to be found. He had, I thought, already set off for Ilcaestir, or perhaps he went further afield to prepare the way by secret paths. I could not fathom this for he had not told me his plans for Edith and where he hoped she would find safety. My guess had always been a nunnery, but that would be no hurdle at all to a king who would raid the monasteries and steal that which they held in church trust for others. If he knew where she was then he would take her.

Thinking back now, it was as well perhaps that I could not find our Thegn. For perhaps with the news of the uprising in the North he would have held back whilst the castle on Saint Michael's Hill was stormed, thinking as Edith did, and I also did, that the Normans would be too busy elsewhere to bother with us. And in that I misread the greed of a churchman, his fear of losing what his brutality had gained and the ferocity that fear would set loose.

As it was, foolishly, and without Asgar to guide us, we did not follow his orders. When great change is threatening it is in the nature of folk to hope it will go away and to cling on to straws to stay afloat instead of striking out for the river bank. That is what we did. Not wanting to leave our Hide to lurk in an abbey, my mother saw the rebellion in the North as giving us an escape so that we need not go. For, as she said, if we took the castle, we could hold it against any feeble force the Normans could send since they would be against the whole shire in arms, for that was how far the anger now reached. And so we foolish folk fooled only ourselves, looking for grounds for not doing what we did not want to do. And that is how, by staying to protect my mother as well as Edith, I saw the first part of the horror and tragedy that unfolded. I had enough sense of the importance of the duties Asgar had given me, to take action in time to get Edith and little Gytha to safety, but my mother would not leave and I never found out what happened to that proud, stubborn woman. It breaks my heart that she perhaps suffered the plight of the rest: hunted down, mutilated and bled to death in an unknown grave, tossed in with the rest under the game fold.

First there came the stoking of the anger. I think the ale that flowed at Yule at the year's end was part of this. For folk came together for the feast and as we all know, as the ale flows in so sense is pissed out and down the privy. Vows were made at this time, alliances forged that could not be avoided in the light of day. After Yule this was inflamed in meetings in many places, but always with small number so that the Normans knew nothing. And then there was a gathering together of all. For the Normans were known to sally forth on their foraging sweeps with half the castle numbers at a time. And so it was judged that if we could catch them in the open and destroy them, the garrison could be much reduced.

Where the fyrdmen gathered for this they did not tell me. Why this was I don't know, nor did I ever find out. Perhaps because of my lameness they thought me of no use and therefore it was not needful for me to know. If so then my lameness saved my life once again, just as it had spared me a death at Blood Lake. Perhaps also they thought that as my mother believed it all to be folly, to tell me ran the risk of my betrayal of their plan.

This is all I know: that the plan failed. Worse, that it was a grim mishap. Our men watched for the foragers and attempted to destroy them. But as I have already said, all our trained warriors were feared dead, our fyrd was a poor, left over thing and we had never fought expert mounted troops before. Instead of waiting in hiding in wooded country, our brave but foolish men formed a shield wall. They should have sent a herald to ask, 'please destroy us'.

When the word came back we learned that a poorly armed and unwarlike two hundred fyrdmen were put to flight by twenty battle-hardened horseback warriors; that sword, axe, mace and lance wielded from on high by the milites of the Lord of Mortaine cut a swathe through our shield wall and cut down those behind it. We took many losses for little gain. All that saved our men was that the Normans, for fear that the whole land had risen, ran for their castle and the command of their castellan, Lord Drew.

And so went our first affray against the Normans; it does not deserve the term 'battle'. It was like a flea attacking a dog. Like a dog they scratched us out and leapt away. Of our folk, many took wounds that day and some, feymen, took death. Like bad children running home to their mother, those who survived fled the fight and came, beaten, to our hall, to patch up their wounds and to settle their fright and their shame.

Of the two hundred that beset the Norman horsemen perhaps three out of four were fit to try again. Of these, many who had not lost womenfolk to the castle were minded to go home. I think if they had, hard as that would have been on the fathers, husbands and swains bereft of their womenfolk, that would have been the end of it and all would have given up. Would that was how it turned out, but fate spun the wheel and another more tragic end fell to us. For, just as all our plots were about to crumble, there came from the north of our shire a party of fifty or so who had heard of our plight. These were the same hardy stock, swollen by a sprinkling of Aeglenoth's monks from the abbey at Glastonbury, who had fought off Harold's pups and who had been in the field when Eadnoth died. I said nothing, for I had heard Asgar name him traitor. That he had perished at the hands of the sons of the man he had helped to kill while serving his Norman masters seemed to me no more than he had earned.

But then, as they said, the athelings, if you could call them that now, had come pillaging the land with Irish pirates and could not expect a welcome from Englishmen. Neither, they felt, could the Normans and so hearing of our sorrows they had come to join us. The fyrdmen, angered by the tale of the womenfolk and Ulf, came seeking their pride and English dignity; the monks outraged by the despoiling of our holy site came shouting of Norman unbelief and preaching holy war.

Thus encouraged, while the Normans hid inside their castle we held a moot to decide what to do next. Those who feared their womenfolk were captive would not have it other than that we stormed the castle and rescued them. It was in our hall they gathered together to make their plans, so they could hardly deny me a part in this. My mother was much in wrath at the foolishness of it. She feared, quite rightly as it turned out, that we planned for our doom.

But let me say this, for it is something I have learned since. Castles can be overthrown and taken, but it is an art and every castle must be studied and the plan to destroy it must be for that castle and that alone, for each is different. None of our folk had ever stormed a castle. Indeed, most had never seen a castle before they built this one. This was entirely true for the men who had joined us from the North for they had never seen more than the type of stronghold we call a Burh.

The pattern was set. We had choices we could make. We could have chosen one where we would all have gone home to bewail the injuries done to us – and lived. Or we could have chosen another, where the first would have seemed good fortune indeed compared to what then befell. For we chose the second; we decided to storm Castle Montagud.

At Oestre time in the year of Our Lord one thousand and sixty-nine, we set about storming the castle. We took ropes to pull down the bailey walls without thought to the soldiers defending those walls. There were some bowmen in our company, but not enough to clear the defenders from the wall top. We took cooking grease to help build fires at the foot of the bailey walls, and spades to dig out the uprights.

To our cost, all our thoughts and eyes were downward to what was at the end of our noses and not up to where our enemies stood, which was wrong and foolish for they were there to rain death on us. Later, when our eyes should have been looking downwards to the roads approaching the town and the hill, so by then all our thoughts and eyes were turned upwards. Thus whatever we did was wrong and things went from bad to worse, for our enemies above had seen all this before and were well prepared.

When we climbed the road to the bailey wall we found that from the ditch that fronted it we could not throw our heavy ropes to the top, for it was over three man-heights high, and so we abandoned the idea of pulling down the wall. We decided instead to burn it down.

We gathered kindling and branches and built a great fire against the bailey fence. All the while we were piling this so the crossbow bolts, arrows and sharpened stakes came hurtling down at us and we took many wounded, for we suffered a lack of shields and had not thought to build even rough wooden ones that we could move up to the wall and shelter under. The wood being damp we larded it with the buckets of cooking fat we had brought for the purpose. When the runner who guarded the flame was summoned he ran up the hill and thrust his torch into the fire and flames spread quickly through the greased logs and started to catch in the kindling. But now the soldiers on the wall tipped pails of water and, from the smell of it, man and horse piss onto our small fires and put them out before they could properly take hold. And so our plan to burn the bailey wall did no better than our plan to pull it down, and with each failure the list of the fallen, whether from death or wounds, grew greater.

We then planned to dig out the wall's strong posts, those uprights in the centre of the longest stretch of wall. We took the spades and set to starting to dig, but the posts were sunk deep and the work was slow. Again this was not easy. Try one thing, try another; and all the while we worked at each attempt we were pelted with those arrows, bolts, spears and sharpened stakes, of which the defenders seemed to have many. I at least had a shield that I had brought from the hall, which I used to protect myself and as many others as I could from the deadly rain, but still men dropped all around me. When the water they poured on the fires became scalding hot, so we withdrew, dragging our dead and wounded with us. All the while we clambered down the hill away from the bailey wall we were pelted with stones and slingers' pebbles, relics from the ruined holy house.

All those who were left gathered together and crouched at the foot of the hill behind the hazel hedge while the dead and wounded were taken to the hall. Sober counsel now came to the fore. Partly this was because many of the hottest for the fight, the fathers and husbands and swains of the missing womenfolk, had been carried off on stretchers made of branches – an unlooked for use of the timber we had cleared from the hill. Those left, now much less inflamed than before, saw the storming of the castle as unwise as had been the ambush of the milites. There was much talk backwards and forwards but all were clear that throwing ourselves under the walls of the bailey once more would win nothing but our deaths. Even ladders, which we could make, could not be used they said, for the slope of the hill was too great. I did not see why we could not use sheep hurdle shields and under cover of these dig pits to make footings for ladders, but no one asked me, so I just listened.

They understood now, they said, why the Normans had chosen this hill on which to build their castle. Wiser heads said the only way we could take the castle without great loss was to starve the Normans until they came out. Some put forward the idea that we should shoot fire arrows over the wall to burn the stables and the storerooms. Even for this the steepness was against us, for our bowmen must creep close to be near enough to reach the fence and would be easy targets for the bowmen on the walls firing downhill. All the wood having been cleared there were no sheltering trees.

In the end we made up our minds to lock the Normans in their castle, to make a circle of iron around about it until they starved or agreed to come out and give the castle up to us.

We blocked the road to the bailey so that the only way down the hill for the milites was on foot. Thus we thought to take away the horseback soldiers, which were the main strength of the Norman forces. If they should try to ride straight down from the castle they would come up against the hazel hedge that girdled the bottom of the hill. This was old and so thick and strong that no horse would try to force through it. Once the road out was blocked it only remained to set watch, lest the Norman foot soldiers, the pedites, should try to force our road block or cut a way through the hazel hedge to make an escape way for the horsemen.

It was plain to us that to encircle the castle was the best plan to win the day without more great cost. We — I say 'we', but of course I was not part of this and speak only of that which I heard. By 'we' I mean our folk, for I was with them in my heart even if they had no need of my shoulders and strength or the subtlety of my thought — we now set about planning that.

Having blocked the road we made more barriers to stop all movement out; dug ditches around the hill and hid them with branches to bring down any that thought to avoid our barriers by taking to the hill. And then we made camp, as comfortable as we could be and waited for hunger and thirst to do our work for us.

At first we kept good watch, but when no attacks came out we rested, sure that we should win, given time.

There was silence throughout the Cold Cot as Bowdyn, and through him Edmund, ceased speaking. When the puzzled silence had lengthened he said, 'Now we have an advantage over Edmund for we are permitted to know what happened with the Bishop of Coutances, Lord Geoffrey, the master of "meat hewer" Hugh, as they had dubbed the Vavassour. What the English encircling the castle knew not was that at this time Lord Geoffrey had expected to meet with Bigo to talk about building his own castle to the west. When Bigo did not come at the appointed time the bishop sent a messenger to summon him. The messenger drawing near espied the truth of the matter and sped back to tell his master.

'We who tell the story know this because, like all churchmen, the mace-wielding bishop, slayer of men, liked to talk and boasted of what he had done so that all about him knew the story and the Normans gossiped amongst themselves until it became well known, even to the English servants.

'Now, as expected, there was rebellion in the North. Most Normans went north under William, but all the new castles were left with their garrisons. So the Bishop of Coutances sent out scouts to find the way of things.

The scout sent to WinCaester came first.

"What is with WinCaester?" asked Lord Geoffrey.

"My Lord Bishop, WinCaester has its garrison and can spare you forty milites and fifty pedites."

"Return, tell them to send every man they can but keep enough to hold the castle."

'Then the scout from Salisbury brought word of fifty horse and sixty foot, and the scout from London brought word of seventy horse and one hundred foot already on their way.

'The story goes that Geoffrey and Hugh raised their glasses to each other thinking there would soon be sport aplenty.

126

With the forty mounted miles and the thirty pedites already in Montagud castle he would soon unleash over four hundred trained and blooded warriors, more than half of them mounted. These would fall on the heedless men of Sumorsaete in the midst of Holymonth, almost three years to the day from the Duke his Lord's victory at Hastings and the death of the English king.'

Bowdyn fell silent, staring into the fire. Then he said, 'So you see, there they were, Edmund among them, encircling Montagud castle thinking all the Normans fighting English and Danes in the North, and hopefully losing. They knew nothing of the Bishop of Coutances and his mustering of troops from the South, from London, Salisbury and Winchester. They had no idea of the doom that approached. Even had they been well led, the Norman troops would have spelled their doom. Edmund's sad fyrd of poorly armed, poorly trained farmers had chosen to go to war against the best warriors of Europe. For these were certainly the best now the English huscarls were destroyed. Our fyrd thought they had freedom to do as they wished. In that they were sadly misled, to their great sorrow and misfortune.'

Bowdyn ceased speaking and started to charge his pipe with tobacco. Then smiling a contrast to the drear words he had just spoken, he added, 'There we must leave the story for today and continue tomorrow.'

With a feeling of gloom upon them that what they would hear at the next telling would not be cheerful news, the folk went home.

AD 1069 Flight to the North

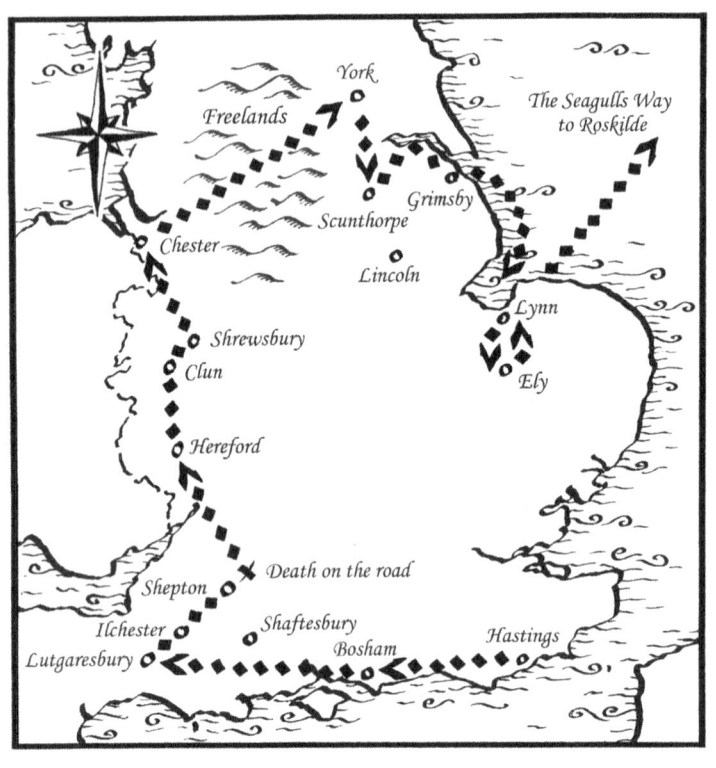

Edith's route into exile

Chapter 11

Edmund's Tale: Flight from the Murder of the Shire

On Sunday, when the fires were burning brightly, when my mother and father were sitting comfortably, Bowdyn smiled at and greeted the folk. Without any ado he reminded them of the Norman troops advancing on the siege of Montagud castle. He faded into the shadows and from them Edmunds voice spoke out continuing his sad story.

As I said before, when we should have been looking up at what the defenders on the castle walls might do, so we were looking down and when we should have been looking down from the hill to see what was coming, so all our thinking and gaze was now up at the bailey walls. All it would have taken to save many lives was to have stationed look outs to the east and the west, but so taken were we with thinking how we might bring the castle down that we did not see the strung out mass of mounted soldiers coming towards us from the east, until they were close by. When we did see them we were seized by dread, for it could be seen they were many. Those of us thinking of the undoing of our fyrd of two hundred by only

131

twenty mounted milites saw at once that the numbers coming were too great for us; that to oppose them would lead nowhere but to our utter destruction. And so the word was passed to run, to hide, to disarm and take up the look of farmer once more.

Our fyrd ran. For a brief time the hill looked like a disturbed ants' nest as every man ran towards his home. Within the space of ten paternosters the hill was empty.

I ran too, limping as fast as my leg would carry me. Not to save my life, but in guilt that I had perhaps left it too late to do that which I had sworn to do: to get my mother, our household and most of all Frida and Gytha away from here before they were caught up in the doom sweeping towards us. I cursed as I ran for not having the foresight that the Normans would strike at us so quickly for challenging them.

As I burst through the door I raised a shout.

'The Normans, the Normans are coming we must leave now.'

'Calm yourself,' said my mother, catching hold of my arm. 'Tell me what Normans, from where, how many?'

'A great host, from the east, they will be here within the time it would take me to walk to the mere.'

'All is ready, take the food sacks and lead Frida and Gytha north; you will soon cross the ditch road that leads to Ilcaestir. I shall not come with you nor will my household.'

'What? What; why?' I gasped, thinking I had misheard, not understanding what she said, sure I had it wrong.

'Don't stand there asking stupid questions. Go!' she said, picking up the food sacks and thrusting them into my hands. Frida and Gytha had entered the room and stood, dressed for the road, listening.

'But why?' I repeated.

My mother sighed. 'Oh, God save me from the son who is the town halfwit. If we follow the first plan then when the

Normans come they will find an empty hall, they will think we have left and carried our hoard with us. They will certainly pursue and because we have newly left and are so many they will catch us. If I and my household are here to greet them they will not learn until later that one son and a cousin with her child have returned home to Scaepterbyrg, by which time they will not bother to pursue, they will have no reason to. So go, your safety depends on me staying here. I will be safe, they may take the Hide, but they have no reason to harm me. I will ask their permission to join you in Scaepterbyrg. I will be there within the month and will be surprised and in fright that you have not arrived. I shall blame the Normans; they will blame bandits and do nothing. You will get further away by the day, and Asgar will fulfil his plan.'

What she said made sense, but I felt she was not telling all, that she used our flight as the excuse but truly did not want to leave our Hide to the Normans. I think she wished to be here to claim authority within the town, not trusting any to sell the flocks and bring the money to her. Perhaps she hoped the Normans would leave her to rule and would not possess her land. My mother was a proud and stubborn woman and would not give up my father's land easily.

All my life since I heard what happened when the Normans came, I have carried the sorrow that I obeyed her. But I was young, I had always listened to the authority of my mother and always obeyed her wishes, and so I did now. What followed, followed and what happened to her I never knew, for I only ever found one left to tell the tale and she did not know my mother's fate. I live in hope that she escaped and one day will return. I fear that she was mutilated like the rest, her body and lopped off limbs thrown into a shared grave somewhere beneath the old hill.

On that fateful day I heeded her word, kissed her farewell,

begged her be careful and was lost to her and she to me. I picked up our bundles and bowing to my mother for the last time until journey's end, bade Frida and Gytha to follow me.

So that we might not be trapped with the Normans between us and where we must go, we set out right away to the north, heading across the fields until we met up with the raised droveway that led to the old chief city of Somerton and its market place. I knew that if we followed it we would cross the ancient ditch road that led northeast to Ilcaestir – and from there God knows where. I knew from Wirt it was the road that our men had followed to victory in the North at Stamford Bridge by York. What roads led them to our downfall at Hastings I knew not.

For the first two miles we crouched in ditches and crawled through the bottom of hedges until we were sure that the Normans would not see us. We were made firmer in our resolve to move in this way by the noise of shouts and screams of anger, pain and fear that arose in the distance behind us, marking the Normans' arrival in our town.

I was restless to get to Ilcaestir, in part because I feared the Normans; in part because I wished Asgar to take my precious burden from me. I feared I might fail and betray Lady Edith and her child into danger through my own foolishness. If I had known the fate that the Norman planned for her and Gytha I would have been frozen with fright.

It was with relief that I shepherded them across the ancient ditch road. We turned to our right and followed the Ilcaestir road, walking not on its raised surface but down in the dry ditch beside it, still hoping that we would not be seen by any pursuers,

I should not have feared that my foolishness would betray us. In truth, my dread, which had sped us away, had saved our lives. For although the Norman Duke sought Edith for what she knew and thus wished her taken alive, her pose as my mother's cousin Frida would have been her death. This I found out later from one who hid and from that hiding place witnessed the brutal rage of the Normans. For in revenge for our resistance and as a warning to others like us, they murdered the shire. As the lady who hid told me, weeping, they sought not the innocent or the guilty. They had made up their minds that, like the wild woodsmen elsewhere who laid their steel against Norman flesh, the English were to blame. They could not blame all, for if they killed them as they wished, who would work their land? And so they decided to punish the English and spare the Welsh, of whom there were many around about the castle.

Hugh the Vavassour was in command at the bishop's behest. He it was that decided in his bloodthirsty and mad way that every man, woman and child with fair hair should be slain if they resisted, or maimed if they submitted. He collected the right hands of these in sacks and threw them in the grave he had caused to be dug by the grateful Welsh for the dead English. There was but one great pit, west of the town, close by the slopes of Hamdon.

Did my mother submit? I am sure she would have for thus she counselled all. But would she have told of Edith and where we had gone? I cannot imagine that she did, stubborn loving woman that she was. But at that time, fleeing with my lady and her child along the road to Ilcaestir, I knew nothing of what happened behind us. I did not hear of it for many days, not until lurking in the forests with one of the Silvatici that had caused the Norman's rage. There I met the sad wife who had survived her man and all her children. She had shorn her black hair off in shame that she lived and those she loved, all fair, had died.... But I wander from my story. I will come back to her tale at the proper time and you shall hear of the fiendish fury of our Norman masters.

After a while our pace slowed. Not only were we tired but also it was coming on dark and cloudy and I knew we could not walk further without something to light our way. We were in a place where there were mud holes churned up by the cattle that passed this way and I was in fear that one or other of us might fall and take a sprain or perhaps, God forbid, break a leg. I had been looking around for a place to rest and the best I could see was a dense copse off to the right of our pathway. We were near the hall of Cilterne at that time. I did not know whether the hall would be a safe place or not, after Asgar's warnings about traitor bishops. Perhaps, I thought, if there were traitor bishops and traitor stallers there might also be traitor thegns. Certainly there had been many at Escancaester willing, for their own interests, to betray the old king's mother.

Aware of the need to keep silent lest there be Normans on our trail, I pointed at the trees and laid my head sideways on my hand miming rest.

Edith looked to where I pointed, raised her eyebrows and mouthed, 'There?'

I nodded and we headed for the clump, across a muddy field where cattle grazed. They stared at us judging our threat then sheered away leaving us passage through them. The small stand of trees was dense enough to hide us from the road, but not so dense that we could light a fire and not be seen by travellers. Yet without a fire the chill of the evening quickly soaked through our clothes making our teeth chatter. It was Gytha who first whispered her wretchedness at this.

'Mother, I'm cold, can't we have a fire?'

'No child, they will see the flames.' She did not make plain what creatures 'they' might be and neither did the child ask, clearly she knew.

I gathered arms full of dried twigs and spread them on the ground. There were not enough for two pallets so I made the one as large and roomy as I could and spread my wolf skin cloak over it to further ward off the damp. When I was finished I waved my lady and young Gytha to rest. Edith sank down, smiling; her arms around the child, and waved me down beside her. I shook my head for I did not feel it was fitting.

At that moment Gytha whined her complaint again. 'Mother, I'm really cold.'

I, who knew nothing of the wiles of women, saw nothing but truth in this complaint, but Edith, her arm about the child's shoulders, drew her close and murmured, 'Is that better?'

'Half better.'

'Perhaps Edmund will sit by your other side and so between us you will be so warm you will melt away.'

Gytha chuckled. 'That would be nice.'

Smiling, Edith looked up at me, eyebrows raised – Jesu, she could say so much with just a twitch of those eyebrows! Obediently, I moved to place myself alongside the child. Gytha pressed close to me and put her hands about my arm, laying her face against it. I know little of children, but this was so innocent that if she had placed her thumb in her mouth I would not have been surprised. Of course, Gytha had just entered her sixteenth year at this time and so my thoughts were more a sign of my innocence than hers. I did not know then that my part in getting them to a place of safety had cast a shield of gold over my crippled leg and uncouth ways and had made me into a warrior saviour to Gytha. Nor did I see that in her young and tender heart she had found a place of girlish favour for me. I for my part had a heart full to bursting for her mother. A strange group we were, but much of these different threads of feeling could be laid at the door of our flight and fear of being hunted and pursued. My Lady Edith – although in the depths of my mind I still thought of her as Frida – had no such entwinement. Her feelings were constant, as was the strength with which she hid her grief so that it did not take our eyes and ears from the task before us. However, this night, sitting pressed together for warmth, after Gytha fell asleep between us with her head on my arm, us both feeling cold and though tired, not sleepy, I plucked up the courage to ask her what was on my mind.

Keeping my voice to a whisper so that none could overhear me even if there were someone crept up nearby, which I believed there wasn't, I said, 'My Lady, I know what you did, for Asgar has told me. Can you tell me the story? For when you have gone over the sea and are far away there is reason why the story should stay behind. I do not wish ever to hear where our king is laid. There will be others to say that, when the time is right and the people need a martyr, so says Asgar. What I would wish to spread is the story of how you defied the Norman duke and laid our king with Christian rites in a secret grave so that he may rescue our poor England, gathering all behind his banner like Saint Edmund. Let the people hear that, for perhaps it will give them hope of light to come, when the days are dark.'

Chapter 12

Edith's Tale: Of Hastings and Harold's Remains

Frida, who is Edith, sat staring into the darkness, her breath forming little clouds of steam in the cold night air. She sat for a long moment, thinking, and then spoke. Her voice was present, but from the cast of her head her eyes were looking far away and she spoke in a sad, soft voice, so softly I had to strain to make sense of her words. This is what she told me.

'Already they make legends. I have heard it said that I awaited the outcome of battle sat under a nearby apple tree. It is not true. I knelt the whole time at the school and abbey of Waltham. I prayed for our success and the life of my man throughout the time of daylight and, when no news came, curled on my side to save my knees and still I prayed. I prayed to God the Father of Jesus Christ, I prayed to Jesus, I prayed to Wothan that he should save my man; I prayed to Freya that she send my love to protect him, and I prayed to Tiw that our arms would be successful. Perhaps my trust in the old gods is unwise. Perhaps only the Christian God now has power over these things. I did not know it at that time but my prayers were not granted. I heard nothing until William Malet came to the abbey seeking me. The battle was lost, he told me. The Norman duke wanted to dishonour my man, place him under a cairn on the cliff tops in mockery, without rites like some heathen Moor, but Harold's head had been struck off and they were unable to find the body. So the duke sent William to fetch me in belief that of anybody in the world, I should know my lord husband by his headless remains.

I should tell you about William Malet, Edmund, for if ever a man was cursed with loss of kin place it is he. His mother is English and for love of her he loves the English; his father is Norman and for love of him and duty to his land, he serves Duke William. He was a friend of Harold in Normandy and for love of him he bows to me. His honour suffered from the task he had been set, to mock his dead friend and deprive him of wake, rites or absolution, and so he defied his master to help me.

We took horse from Waltham and rode three days to Senlac sleeping by the wayside under our cloaks and mantles. I in dread, but certain that I must do all I could to show my love for my dead lord. William Malet rode at my side and we had with us an escort of six Breton serjeants-at-arms. He ordered them to fall back so that we could talk in private and when they were out of earshot he told me a great secret. My task, he said, was a false one for he had already found my husband's body. Knowing Harold by sight from the time of their friendship, he had first searched for the head, but found it not. Then quite by chance he found my lord's body in an unlooked for way. Spying a scavenger picking through the bodies near to where he was searching, William, sickened with disgust, grabbed the man, held a knife to his throat and looked in his sack. In it he found that for which beyond all hope he sought above all else, for in the sack was the dragon-marked arm-ring of Wessex, the emblem of royalty that none but a king should wear.

'Where did you get this, scabby dog?' William demanded, his knife still held to the scavenger's throat.

'From a dead man, lord.'

'And where lies this dead man?'

'Why yonder, lord,' the man pointed to a spot perhaps forty paces to the south.

When William reached there, clasping the looter by his mantle and towing him behind, he found the banners of England and Wessex, along with that of the Fighting Man – Harold's own banner stitched in gold thread on red by Gytha, his mother – lying in the mud surrounded by dead huscarls. There also lay the remains of my poor lord. He alone of that mound of dead Saxons lacked a head, and thus did William know him.

William held the royal arm-ring of Wessex towards the wretch in his grasp, he who stripped and defiled the dead, and as the man came nearer and reached out a blood-caked hand to take it, William, with a slash of his dagger, slit the scavenger's throat and he dropped to the ground, the look of greed on his face turned to one of surprise and horror. Still holding the ring, William reached for the dead man's sack of loot and tossed it to the watching serjeants-at-arms.

'This Saxon dog had no honour,' he said, 'he steals even from his own dead countrymen. Here, take his pickings, take what you wish, you at least fought and conquered. You won what is here. This man will no more steal from the fallen nor dishonour them.' But even as he spoke, in his head he was saying, 'nor will you, despoiler of the dead, tell the duke my master what you found here or who, for I cannot obey him in this.'

For a time William Malet and I rode in silence, each lost in grim thought, and then he said, 'And that, my lady, is why I told him I could not find your lord, who was my friend, but why I have come for you goes beyond that. Between us we may be able to get his remains away. You must take them, get him absolution for the good of his soul and given Christian burial in some secret place that only you will know.'

I looked at him in doubt. What trickery was this? Did the Norman think he could so easily deceive me? That I would pick out my beloved so that the bastard duke could piss on his body to further crush us poor English?

'Why would you help me?' I asked him.

'Why would I help you?' He paused, his eyes looking into the distance as if gathering his thoughts. 'You will not know it, but in the battle my horse was felled from under me. I fought but I was surrounded by foes and knew I must die. I made my peace with God while I scythed with my sword, but God did not want me at that time, for along came de Montfort, swept my enemies before him, gave me a horse and sent me off to kill more Englishmen.'

William turned to look at me, pausing for a long moment. 'I think God saved me for a purpose,' he said at last. 'I think He gave me mercy so that I might in turn show mercy. Perhaps it was to make sure that my friend was buried honourably and that his beloved, of whom he spoke to me so fondly, should find what little comfort is left for her. No?'

I believed him and knew then that I would accept his help and be guided by him.

In silence we rode on up the ridge on the other side of which lay the battlefield. Reining in his horse William turned in the saddle and spoke to the serjeants-at-arms riding behind us.

'Wait here, guard our backs, let none approach for I fear that Gytha's Saxon dogs may come in force seeking the dead king. Warn us of any that come near. I will call for you when my task is complete.'

As he and I rode to the top of the ridge there was a strange noise, which increased the nearer we got to the crest. Like the drones of some great sac-pipe the air itself seemed to shudder with it. As we crested the ridge I cried out in horror for the flies and crows we disturbed rose up in great clouds, all the while making the noise. Their massed flight disturbed the calm air, for the wind had dropped to nothing. It stirred up the stink of blood, death and shit from the gore-strewn mass of bodies that carpeted the ground and lay in heaped up lines. At first I thought that only the great blue flies and black rooks and crows were moving and all else was still, and then I picked out womenfolk moving about within the field of the dead, seeking the bodies of their fallen to carry off for burial. Pulled up behind the lines of corpses there were carts, horse- or donkey-drawn, and onto these those lucky enough to find their dead were loading the bodies of those loved ones.

There is nothing fine about a battlefield, young Edmund, thank the stars that your leg saved you from it. All I carried away in memory from Hastings is the noise of the flies, the stench, which brought my stomach to my mouth, and the stillness of the shrunken dead. Oh, and of course the crows and the seagulls feeding on the corpses. And amongst this stinking, humming field of death I came upon the remains of my beloved where William Malet had put them. And I knew him at once by the mark of love low upon his neck, which was still faintly showing from our passion the night before he left for battle. He had chided me gently, for his men he said would mock him, but he did not mean it; it was but in jest.

William stood in silence beside me. We had dismounted and left our horses a short distance away. 'How did my lord die?' I asked him, for he had been there, or so he had said. At first he did not wish to speak of it, but I pressed him for I had to know. Looking down at the butchered remains of my husband, my lover, my lord, I tightened my stomach, straightened my back, held my mouth tight and asked calmly, as if I were asking the fate of a favourite slaughtered calf, 'Tell me, Sieur William, how did he suffer? Tell me true.'

His face bleak, William was silent for a long while, gazing blankly over the bodies to the far sky as if in his head he was looking back to that which he would rather forget, and then his mouth twisted in a grimace and he spoke.

'There is little to tell, it was quick as a lighting strike. Our duke had boasted that he would meet your man in single combat, but King Harold, his guard laid low around him, was cutting down our men like a scythe-man at harvest. Seeing how death surrounded him and his flashing sword and axe, Duke William's spirit quailed and he called three others to help him. I saw this, but for my honour's sake I did not join him. Your man stood still, head high, facing four men on horseback falling upon him at speed. He raised his sword to bat aside Hugh of Pontieu's lance and used his shield to fend off the duke's point, but he knew not the strength of our duke and the speed of his horse. William's lance, held solid as rock, pierced Harold's shield, already pitted and thinned with sword and axe blows, and then it pierced his breast-mail from which his blood started to flow. Stunned, he staggered or was pressed swiftly back and lowered his shield and sword. Eustace of Boulogne, himself a mighty man, leaned from his saddle and with all his weight, which was considerable, and his force, which was fierce, swung his bright sword and cutting by chance between Harold's helmet and his mail, removed your lord's head from his neck with that one blow. The head fell and rolled to one side, the crown fell off into the mud and the body dropped straight down. He was well dead but, wanting to join in and earn Duke William's gratitude, Geoffrey, Lord of Pontieu, lowered his lance, skewered your dead lord's belly, split it end to end and pulled out his tripes with his lance tip.

'Harold and I grew close in Normandy and it grieves me to say this of Norman nobility, but it was fat-faced Gifart who hewed off my friend's leg and shamefully his pintel and apples. He rode through our army brandishing his pitiful trophy, won so bravely from a dead man. He, but a youth, so puffed up with childish glee he did not see how it shamed him to so demean one, the soles of whose cattle-herding boots he was not fit to lick.

'When the duke saw what he was doing his rage and shame were without limit. I judge he already feared what they had done, for killing God's anointed king is no small thing. Should God not strike him down for it, it would prove that such a thing was tolerable to Him. Already the duke felt and feared the risk this brought on him, who sought to be king. He wanted to distance himself from the deed, for to have killed a king and then to have abused his dead body in so vile a way was more than William's fears could bear. As always, his fear turned to violence. He had the chubby-cheeked abuser brought before him. Red-faced, William stood facing him, feet apart; sword in hand.

'"Kneel you dog," he shouted, and when Gifart knelt, kicked him powerfully in the belly stretching him on the ground. White foam flecking his lips and spittle cascading in the torchlight, the duke shouted his rage, and, perhaps, fear.

'"You filth, you dung without honour, you wretch, not fit to be milites nobiles. You disgrace yourself; you disgrace me; you disgrace your family. You are dismissed this army, you are unfit to say you served with the heroes who today won a kingdom. If your family still has honour they will hold you dead for this day's work. It is only from love of them that I spare your wretched life. If you have courage you will fall on your sword to requite its shame for that which you have had it do. Go! Get you gone out of my sight, back to the ships."

'Having risen to his knees, Gifart stayed, white-faced, head down, only his eyes lifted, peering under his brows in fear at the duke's face. At this last he jumped to his feet and hurried almost running to his horse and there hauled himself creaking into the saddle and head still down, looking neither to left nor right, spurred his mount back towards the ships at Pevensey.

'I tell you this, my lady, because I have heard it said that Walter Giffard did the deed. Him I know to be a brave man and the duke, now king, has honoured him for his part in the battle. The family name of the chubby-cheeked one I know not.'

William Malet ceased speaking and then, 'Time passes we will lose the light, we must get on.' He paused again for a long moment, thinking, his hand, still encrusted with blood, stroking his shaven chin. Then as if having made up his mind, he became suddenly brisk. 'Let us find two bodies that could pass in size for Harold.'

Surrounded as my beloved was by the bodies of the big men of the Godwin household this was not difficult. When we had found two, I turned to William and asked, 'What do you mean to do?'

'Why, I shall cleave them in parts as our good Harold is,' he said, lifting a fallen battle axe from the ground and wiping blood from its handle with a handful of grass.

I put my hands in horror to my mouth. These were honourable men. I said as much. He looked sternly at me. 'Being honourable men, fallen in defending their king, their shades will be honoured to be buried and named as their lord. And we must hurry before their people come for them.'

146

There was truth in what he said, for already the weeping women moving through the dead, searching for husbands, brothers and fathers to take away for burial drew nearer. So I protested no more. Averting my eyes I moved away while he went to his grizzly work, although I had trouble keeping my stomach out of my throat as the stink of his labours rose up with the flies.

When he had finished he called forward three of our escort of serjeants, who stood guard beyond the ridgeline hidden from our sight as we were from theirs. When they approached he pointed at the fruits of his bloody work.

'Here is the body and parts of the pretender Harold, load them on a cart, take them to the shore and build a cairn over them. Leave me a spare horse.'

When his orders had been carried out he called forward the remaining serjeants and pointed at the other body. 'Here are the parts of a man who looks like the usurper, take these on your horses to Waltham Abbey, tell the monks it is Harold Godwinson and have them bury him, that the Saxons, thinking someone has defied our good duke and carried their false king to a Christian resting place, will not seek him in the cairn and steal away his remains.'

When this party had departed he turned to me. Dark was falling and although I again found the body of my love where William had left him and where I had marked him to be, we searched but could not find his head or his missing leg and privies, or his half leg and foot. William picked up my beloved's tripes and tenderly put them back where his guts should be then pulled down his Bernie.

Though I struggled to control the urge to void the contents of my stomach, beneath my horror and grief I was content that we at least had the part wherein my love's great heart was contained. William bound him with a bloodstained banner to keep all in, lifted him up and onto the spare horse's back and tied him, covered with a cloak like some bundle of old clothes. Then he hoisted me onto my beast and handing me the reins of the serjeant's horse looked up at me. I wept tears of gratitude for this generous, honourable and brave man. Brave because I knew enough of his master that William Malet was doomed to torture and death if the truth came out.

'Go now Edith, take him where you will, do not tell me where. If aught of this comes out I must say that you misled me. Duke William may kill me, but for foolishness not treachery. One thing is sure: in that event, he will seek you, so you must flee; pass into darkness beyond the view of man. For both our sakes you must never come back into the light. Here, take this.' He held out his hand in which something glittered dully. 'I told you of this. The scavenger took it off your lord's body. It was on his arm, concealed beneath the mail. Take it, keep it hidden, none must see it now. My master the duke wants it above all other things. It is for this and the crown to come that all these gallant fellows on both sides lie dead.'

I looked down at what he pressed into my hand. It was the Godwin arm-ring, the white Saxon dragon and the red dragon of Wessex carved and enamelled into the gold.

William raised his arm to wave, 'Farewell my lady, may your task be fruitful and may you be safe. God be with you.'

With these words in my ears I rode away, leading the horse with its hateful burden. Through the night I followed the coast until I came to the place where lay the stone coffin that Harold had shown me when once we had spoken of his death. There the priest of the church and the town helped me lay him in his final peace, there he spoke the funeral rites over him and covered him in a shroud of secrecy in the ground. Not that that would worry his heathen soul....

Lady Edith ceased speaking, and looked at me. A weary, wry smile lit up her face and belied her red-rimmed, weep-swollen eyes. 'And so, young Edmund, you find me here, bereft. You are the first to whom I have told all of this tale, and you will be the last.'

As first Edith's and then Edmund's voice faded into silence, Bowdyn looked solemnly around at his audience, all of us sat quiet and still.

'And so we see the death of the last English king,' he said, 'for all that followed him to England's throne were incomers, foreigners, most from Normandy or France, one briefly from Spain and of course the Welsh and then the Scottish ones, the Stewarts, who have caused great troubles for this land and do so still.'

'You will have heard, perhaps, of how Harold was killed as if by God's will by an arrow in his eye. The tale you have just heard is the truth, I think. It suited William's purpose, great liar that he was, to have folk believe that God and not Duke William killed Harold. But it is not the purpose of this story to fight again or to mull over the battle that led this country to such misery. From the tale you can see that Edith had two possessions that William coveted. She carried locked in her head the knowledge of King Harold's burial place. Perhaps she thought that one day the right time may come to let the English know where that was, to become a place of pilgrimage and perhaps the start of resistance to the Norman kings'.

'As I told you at the outset, Duke William opened the cairn and found that the remains were not those of Edith's husband, though how I do not know, but William Malet had been clever: rumour that Harold had been buried in Waltham quickly spread. Duke William did not want the English to have a martyr. Perhaps he knew it for a lie — certainly he put the monks of Waltham to the question in the most brutal manner — perhaps not, but he was sure that having found the body, Edith must also have found the arm-ring of Wessex, and he dearly wanted to wear this jewel of the English kings. So for these reasons and because she knew that if he caught her he would rack the truth of Harold's resting place from her and then not let her or hers live, it was needful to the utmost for Edith to go into exile. It was Asgar that warned her that once the King had taken what she knew and what she carried from her he would act to kill the tale of Harold. My lady he purposed to burn at the stake, her children to be openly strangled. Thus he hoped to destroy all that remained of Harold so there was nothing left for the English people to follow. How she escaped him is what I shall next reveal. But not now, tonight we will go home and sleep. That story will start at our next meeting.'

And so we all went off to our beds thinking of our lost king and our lost freedom, still waiting after all these six hundred years to be won back. Even removing the head of one wanton king had not prevented another from oppressing the people of this land. Perhaps the one to come will take note.

Chapter 13

Edmund's Tale: Ilcaestir

You may notice that when relating future meetings in the story house, I no longer begin by describing how my parents and Bowdyn entered the Cot; how the Gleeman sank into the shadows and his voice became that of the teller of that part of the story. Let me tell you why this is so.

On one story telling day I was collecting wood from the pile I had built up over time since Bowdyn's return and as I went through the usual routine of setting the fires, it came to me that I was making too much of my part in things. Each week I built the fires and warmed the Cot before the villagers arrived. Each week they came, mist on their breaths, rubbing hands against the cold, stamping their frozen feet as they took down their stools and benches from the stack at the Cot end.

In the summer the Gleeman went about his business and we made our living from the land. It was in the winter when nothing useful would grow and we had only the beasts to tend; in the winter when Bowdyn found it too harsh to travel around buying and selling those small things that folk wanted but would not travel to the city to buy; in the winter when folk were idle and it was down to the tavern or early to bed, that our story telling took place. To me, there were only two good things about the winter: the first that it was when Bowdyn returned and we opened up the story house; the second that it was the time of year when the tavern could make good strong ale, for the moon on icy nights gave it strength.

You might think that folk would stay home in the warm, but for some time now, this being the third of the great tales that Bowdyn told, the story telling had become part of the fabric of life in our village and all around about. Without the stories I believe the tavern would fall silent, for the Gleeman's tales were the subject of much beer-wetted talk. But my part in it was always the same: I fetched the wood, laid and lit the fires and set out Bowdyn's chair for him, placing it according to where he felt the shadows would best fall.

So on that day when I was collecting firewood, I thought about this, how it was always the same, and it came to me that it was not needful to keep repeating what I did week after week, and that being so, I refreshed my resolve to mention my part in it and Bowdyn's greeting only if there was something different to say. And so, unless something new is said I will begin each story telling at the point when Bowdyn, in the voice of Edmund or any other, continues with the tale – as Edmund does here when he, Edith and Gytha are fleeing to Ilcaester.

Fearful of moving in my sleep and waking Gytha, sleeping at my side, I slept but little and when the first light of morning crept dimly through the trees I was already awake, worrying. I strained my ears for any sound other than the usual woodland chirping of birds and rustling leaves, but heard nothing. My courage bolstered by the silence, for either the Normans had not come here or were sleeping off their grim deeds in the town, I gently whispered my lady awake. Her eyes snapped open, looked all around taking in the view and then turned to me, and I swear they softened.

'Good-morning to you, good Edmund, are we safe?' This also whispered.

'Yes Frida,' I said. 'All is at peace; I believe we are safe, but we must hurry towards Ilcaestir and Asgar whilst the sun is up and all stays quiet. I thought we should ready ourselves, eat, drink and be on our way.'

Which just went to show that I could not be more wrong for as I said it I heard the sound of hoof beats, just a rumour at first and then stronger until they were a mild thunder. We crouched down and as they came to their loudest so they stopped and silence fell, bar shouting and the jingling of harnesses.

Gytha slept peacefully as the galloping horses approached but as they milled outside our copse her mother set about gently and quietly waking her. She still lay against my arm and when she stirred and sat up I missed the warmth. She stared about her in fright but Edith had trained her well and she did as she was bid, silently and quickly.

I waved Edith and Gytha down and they lay flat, faces pressed to the forest leaves and needles. Moving as quickly as I could and still be silent I picked up the pallet I had made from dead branches and swept the branches over the women. What was left I tossed over myself to break up my outline. There was the noise of feet treading through the undergrowth and snapping dead twigs. The crackling and rustling stopped some distance from us, but one of the seekers came nearer and nearer. I feared he would walk into me and even the dim light and the woodland shadows would not save me. Then there was talk in whatever tongue they spoke, which meant nothing to me. The footsteps stopped and then retreated.

We held back our shivers as we lay on the cold damp ground. The footfalls went away and then the hoof beats started and the Normans rode away, back towards Lutgaresburh seeking God knows who. When all had been quiet for a while, birdsong broke the silence and the copse returned to normal. We got up, brushed ourselves down and let the shivers die away. I could not say whether they were from cold or fright, a little of both perhaps.

When they had gone, Edith, who had understood their words, whispered that they were looking for traces of a fire. That we had taken such care in not lighting one and instead had huddled together to keep in our warmth had saved our lives, for not seeing one they agreed that no one had been hiding in the copse. As far as Edith could tell from their muttered conversation, it seemed they were not looking for us, but for anyone at all who had fled the murder in and about Lutgaresburh. They were there to make sure no one escaped, she said.

I feared for my family and from that and feeling the chill I shivered. Deep in gloom, I missed sitting around a cheerful fire while we took our first food of the day. Cold water was poor fare in place of ale, but thinking to the day ahead while I ate the cheese and crunched dry bread, I hardly tasted the food my mother had packed for us. Water we drank for wayfaring, we did not know what we would find along the way and ale makes thirst and dulls the senses.

When we had finished eating and were in all things ready for the road we once more set out, but now, as we seemed beyond the limits of the murderous searchers, we trod the road instead of the ditch, although I kept a careful watch, always looking around about and listening for sight or sounds of Normans.

I had no idea how far we had to go; only that the Ditch Road led there and so it was a surprise and a relief when we came upon the houses of Ilcaestir after only three miles or so of walking.

The town was not large nor, with the sun just risen, thronged. We knew we had to look for the inn, for it was there that Asgar would meet us. Once there had been a mint in the town so I had been told. The inn had been built to give bed and board to the noble visitors to this. Now the mint had been gone some years, moved to be safe against Viking attack and the inn, named 'The Ivy Bush', had fallen into disuse other than as the local tavern, but still gave some space to travellers at need.

There being only one street and that the one we were on, it did not take long to find the inn, falling down heap that it was. At first I thought it was burning down, for smoke rose in thin clouds from the thatched roof, but there was no shouting and rushing about so I knew that either all was well or all inside were dead.

When we knocked upon the door and it opened to us I felt a feeling of freedom wash over me. For the door was answered by Asgar and a different Asgar from when I last had seen him. Gone were the stained and stinking cloths he had worn on his wounds. Cloths there were in plenty, but all now clean and sweet smelling. A look that was alert and hale had replaced the thin and spent look about his face when I saw him last. Nevertheless, he looked upon us as if we were roast meat and he a starving man let into a feast.

'Thanks be to God,' he said. 'God and Jesu bless you young Edmund. I feared you all lost.'

He pulled us into the dark and gloomy common room lit only by a glowing central hearth and a single candle, all the windows being shut to keep in the warmth. The inn was older than any could remember, it may have been the second built after the mint, and had no hearth chimney or vent hole. The smoke from the hearth drifted upwards and gathered in clouds beneath the thatch of the roof where it seeped through until it leaked into the outside air, giving the roof the on-fire look I had first seen.

Asgar called for the innkeeper and ordered him to bring food and to prepare the best room – there were but two – for the womenfolk.

'Now,' he said, 'tell me about your journey.'

'We left before a mass of Normans fell upon the town, although the fyrd had run from the castle as they rode up. We fled over the fields, but still we heard the screaming and shouting. Do you know what happened in the town?'

Asgar had a sour look to his face; he was silent for a long moment and then spoke. 'The fools did not listen to a wiser head than theirs. I know little, but what I heard is that for miles around Lutgaresburh most are dead or maimed, slaughtered or torn through Norman rage. Only one came to tell the tale, she a small woman who, fearing rape and death, had hidden in an old badger sett. As far as I know only she and any who outran the Normans escaped.' His eyes looked his pain and sympathy.

Asgar's words hit me like a hammer blow to the stomach, worse than when I heard Wirt's tale of the slaughter of our warriors; worse than when I feared and accepted the death of our father. He and the rest had been warriors. They had gone to war and some were fey men and doomed to die. No one who values them wants it, but everyone knows that if the fates will it then death or laming must be abided. But my mother was a spinner and weaver of cloth; Wirt was sick and spent; my sister the soul of kindness. I did not expect harm to come to them and would never have left them, notwithstanding my feelings for and my duty to my lady, the queen of this land. The Mercian widow of the Welsh king might wear the crown, but to me, handfast or not, Edith was King Harold's widow and my queen. But in honour I would never have left had I thought any risk to my family. Why would I? They could not take up arms, two women and a broken man.

'Where is she, this woman? I must find out about my mother, my family.' My fear was so plain in my voice that both Edith and Gytha stretched out their arms to lay comforting hands on my shoulders.

'She is gone,' said Asgar. 'I have sent her ahead to the place to which we go. She will be safe there as will we be. You may question her when we reach there, if she lives.'

'Should we not move on now, may the Normans not come here?'

'We keep watch but I think we are beyond their net.'

I felt my shoulders slump and only then knew how tight they had been in fear of the horse soldiers. There was another question that I must ask. 'Tell me now where we go. If you fall down a ditch and break your neck we will search forlornly for safety on the road if we know not.'

He smiled. 'Then I must tell you. It was a secret kept only for safety, for if it became known where you went foes might seek to forestall you.' He smiled again. 'Do not believe it was secret to protect him to whom we flee, he is so nose deep in the Normans' cess pit he is past saving and would not have it any other way, but to bury him in it they first must catch him.' He paused, thinking, his brow wrinkled.

'If I cannot guide you, follow the Fosseway road. Five days from here there is a crossroads. No walker could miss it for pedlars and merchants throng it to live off travellers. Turn left and you are on Watling Street. Follow this northwest for many days, ten perhaps, more or less, until you come to a bend where the road now turns southwest. From here you must ask other travellers the way to the hall at Clun. The man you seek is Eadric, by some called "the Wild", by the Normans called "Silvaticus". He has not submitted as yet to Duke William and he is in constant warfare with the castle the Normans built at Hereford. He is an ally with the Welsh king and they fight side-by-side and together against the Normans. He will protect you while he can and will send you safely on your way when he cannot.'

At that time the innkeeper entered carrying a wooden platter loaded high with roast sheep. Now it was my turn to be the starving man at a feast. As the smell wafted over me I suddenly felt the depth of my hunger and joined with Edith and Gytha in eating from the platter. So hungry was I, I forgot myself. In my eagerness to fill my belly I picked slabs out with my fingers and filled my mouth to overflowing. Edith and Gytha drew their food knives from their girdles and cut small mouth-sized portions to chew on. Seeing this I felt so uncouth. I felt the heat of my blood running to my face and belatedly drew my knife. Edith smiled at me and picked up a fat-edged slab of sheep and filled her mouth with noises of glee. I knew she was easing my mind out of kindness. At that moment I loved her beyond all bearing.

The innkeeper entered with a pail of ale and beakers. I poured for all and took a big swallow covering my shame.

'We must not linger too long,' said Asgar, 'for there is far to go and the Normans spread out like fog upon the land. We must get to Clun without meeting them on the road. Tomorrow at daylight we will make a start. We will walk at a brisk pace and every five miles or thereabouts we will rest for the count of two hundred.'

He turned to Edith and Gytha. 'The rooms here are poor; there are tiny crawling things and those things that prey on them. You may find it more peaceful to sleep here by the fire, if you do so I will rest here at the board and guard you.'

I was angered at myself for not making such an offer first.

Edith smiled at Asgar. 'Your offer is courteous and kind, Father,' she said, 'but I think not. Poor folk on the road will carry many little riders on their way. We have none, so for safety and for show we must invite some to ride with us. What are a few fleabites against what could arise on the road?'

Old Father Asgar bowed slightly and said, 'Daughter you are wise beyond your years.'

Thus Asgar and I shared a flea-infested room the size of a dog stall. Edith and Gytha retired to the best that the inn could offer. It was also flea-infested, but at least had, so they said, a comfortable pad to sleep on and a room of fair size.

Chapter 14

Edmund's Tale: Death on the Ditch Road

The following morning the fleas that had chosen to ride the road with us, impatient to get out of the filth of the inn into the clean fresh air no doubt, renewed their attack on us until they drove Asgar and me early from our beds.

We splashed water from a bucket on our faces; rubbed fingers across our teeth; scratched our heads and chests and underarms and – standing privately in corners – other hairy places. Whilst waiting for our womenfolk we supped ale and stuffed our sacks with the food the innkeeper sold us. The Norman foragers from the castle had not reached this far and food was still plentiful. We bought smoked meat, both bull and pig, good yellow local cheese and slabs of flat bread. As soon as Edith and Gytha had joined us and we had broken our fast on cold meat left over from the evening before, we passed from the smoky haze of the inn into the sweet, cool fresh air of the early morning, which was ringing with the tuneful song of birds.

We walked for half a day. It was easy. We were rested and we were fed. Asgar's rest times were as much as we needed and so we travelled quickly, always on the lookout for marauding

Normans. At the end of the day we passed through a group of houses that Asgar said was a gathering place for the sheep market. Thus it was called Scepetun. We had not gone far past this place when we came to a long, steep hill. Being tired and the sun now setting we agreed to stop for the night. We turned aside from the road into a group of trees. There we had some of our food and water then wrapped ourselves in our mantles and laid our tired bones down to sleep. I blessed the weather, for although it was cold it was dry and so much easier for us to keep warm, even without fire.

The weather next morning failed us. When we woke, our mantles were beaded with water droplets and our faces wet. It was not raining, but there was a steady fog-like drizzle. We ate hurriedly, readied ourselves for the journey and then moved out of the trees.

The hill stretched away to the east ahead of us. As we neared the top of the long, steady climb we stopped to catch our breath and rest our legs, for the walk uphill had tired us. It was a bad place to linger and we were foolish, but Asgar, the wisest of us was also the oldest and still weakened by his newly healed wounds. He was thus the most drained by the long climb and needed to rest.

I say foolish because as we topped the hill the road became flat, but also curved around a copse of trees standing out from the thick woods to our left. We were unsighted and could not see down the road ahead. If we could have seen what was around the curve we would have hidden off the road. But we could not see and thus did not hide, and what then happened happened and from that our journey was entirely changed.

As we moved on at a snail's pace, still gathering our breath, so around the curve came a trio of Norman horsemen. From

162

their arms and the shield of one I took them to be a miles and two serjeants-at-arms. They reined in when they saw us and stood watching us as we limped and shuffled along the road. Then at a word from the leader they spurred towards us.

They halted two horse lengths away. I grasped my quarterstaff, ready to fight, but a growl from Asgar told me to hold.

The horsemen leaned forward on their mounts' necks to get a better look at us. There was a speedy passing of speech between them in their outlandish tongue. I did not need to understand their meaning. It was all too plain as they gazed steadily at Edith and Gytha.

Edith also understood only too well. To my horror she walked up to the leader and smiled at him, laying her hand on his thigh.

He exchanged a look with his serjeants and laughed then swinging his leg over his horse's back dropped to the ground, walked around the beast's head and stood grinning at Edith. The two serjeants, their harness and saddles creaking, also dismounted and stood holding the horses whilst their master sauntered towards the woman and her child. He stopped by Gytha and placed his hand under her chin, lifting her face and smiling down at her. As he put his arm around her shoulder and drew her to him he turned, spoke to the two serjeants and waved towards Asgar and me. They laughed and drew their swords.

Asgar was shuffling forward towards the serjeants, whining, 'Please sirs, they are my son's wife and daughter, have pity I beg you,' edging closer to them all the while.

Edith was the entire mistress of the occasion. She placed her hand on the shoulder of the miles, drawing his attention away from the child. Sinking to her knees in front of him, causing his serjeants to pause, watching and smirking, she lifted the hem of his mail coat with her left hand. He thrust his hips at her and leered a look of pride and scorn.

Everything that followed happened so quickly I barely remember it. As Edith bent forward to perform her shameful task so her mantle caught beneath her knees. With an apologetic smile she reached behind her to free it and tugged at the mantle. Then, faster than I had ever seen a hand move, her right hand shot up under the mail coat with the speed and spite of a striking viper. The miles gave a shriek of pain as the bodkin dagger she had concealed in the waist of her mantle bit deep into his groin. His legs folded and he fell, to lie screaming, legs twitching and trembling, blood pooling under him. She leapt to her feet the dagger poised to strike at the serjeants.

They stood frozen, their minds struggling to grasp what had happened. Whether they ever understood I could not say, for Asgar, now close to one of the serjeants, took three quick steps forward, reached into his hood and from a sheath concealed beneath it, drew a seax and plunged it into the man's throat. I was busy by then, but from the corner of my eye I saw the serjeant drop his sword and claw at his throat as he tried to draw breath and draw out the knife. Asgar held him onto it, his hand round the back of the man's head. As his breath ran out the serjeant hammered weakly at Asgar's chest, but Asgar held fast until the blows weakened and then stopped altogether and he slumped to the ground. I saw that happen clearly, for my part in this was over much more quickly.

As I said, I was busy. For you to understand that I must tell you something of my staff. It is iron shod at the end for a purpose. It is to do with the value to me of the quarterstaff as against the half-staff. The half-staff is for closer work where a swipe from a strong pair of shoulders can easily crack an unhelmeted head. But I, with my crippled leg, am not lively enough for that. To be that close and slow moving is to ask for a sword or spear point in the gut. The quarterstaff, on the other hand, has nearly a sword's length of extra reach. With my quarterstaff I do not side swipe; I strike along its length as an adder strikes and, with the iron shod end and all the power of my arms and shoulders behind it, it will easily shatter a man's skull if it strikes where I wish it.

The Normans all wore stout helms of steel covering their heads and with a guard to the nose, but there was no guard to the eye. An armed and armoured man will laugh at a staff of wood if he knows no better. That is until my iron heel, thrust hard and fast with all my strength, blinds his eye and cracks his socket and skull. This was my hope at least, but my practice since first I took the staff as my weapon, had been aimed at that small mark on the skulls of sheep. Never before had I thrust it at a living, fast moving warrior, but the risk and insult to my lady brought down the red mist. As the miles shrieked and crumpled from my lady's subtle strike, his soldiers looked to him and not to me and so I struck.

My foe did not, I think, see the end of my staff. I do not believe he felt it either, for it hit his brow just above his left eye. As his legs crumpled beneath him he dropped straight down, his helm tumbling from his head. My rage was still upon me and I struck down and heard the noise of breaking bone as my staff drove into his temple.

And so it was over as quick as a thunderclap. One second a miles and his two serjeants faced us: a wife; her crippled husband; his aged father and a new grown woman-child, and ten breaths later the Normans were lying dead on the road. Gytha had not moved but stood, her hands over her mouth, her eyes wide with shock.

Asgar held up his hand for silence and listened for anything beyond the wind in the branches and birdsong. There was nothing; no sound or sign of movement on the road. It seemed so strange to me that the flight of three souls, evil as they were, should be followed by such silence. I felt there should be more for an event of such importance, important at least to the dead men. Asgar bent to lift one of the bodies and signed to me to help him. Between us we rolled them all into the ditch from which the road takes its name.

Edith stood to one side and plucking a great handful of grass coolly cleaned the bodkin blade and returned it to the pocket sheath in the back of her mantle.

As soon as we were ready, the bodies well covered and road dirt brushed over the blood, both on the road and on Edith's skirts, I turned to catch the horses, which had wandered away to crop at the grass beside the road.

'Hold,' said Asgar, 'we dare not make use of the horses nor take the Norman's weapons. Poor folk do not ride, nor do they carry arms, we would only attract attention. Drive the horses back down the hill, we must leave the Ditch Road.'

I must have looked at a loss, for he said, 'Wake up boy! We can no longer go this way. The Normans will come looking for the miles if not for the serjeants. They will search until they find the bodies and then they will search for us. There is only this road, we cannot hide in the woods until they give up and our food will not last, even if we can find water. If we stay close by the road to follow it, we will be seen.'

'Then what…?'

'We must go north through the woods to the river.' He paused, thinking, and then spoke again. 'There are two ways to get to where we are going. One is by Watling Street and that is now barred to us. The other is by river, but that is hard for we must cross the wide Severn and all bridges will be guarded. Then we must boat the Gwy to Hay, but we have no boat. Then we must cross the land to Eadric at Clun. Have you money?' he asked. 'I have but little.'

Edith sat listening, 'I have some beneath my skirts, a little at least,' she said. She went behind the bushes by the side of the road and a moment later returned with a pouch well weighted.

When Asgar spied the gold and the silver pennies his eyes widened. 'Little for a Godwin is much for most, my lady,' he said with a wry smile. 'I will use mine for I can replace it where we go. But I will ask for a little of yours at need. We cannot ask a boat from a loyal Englishman for I know of none closer than Glastonburh I would swear to. Where we go is amongst the Welsh. They will help us if our coin is enough. Until then hide your coin again, my lady.'

She smiled and went swiftly into the trees to do so.

'After you, Father,' I said.

We drove the three riderless horses away, startling them into bolting back the way we had come, then we left the road, taking care to scuff away our footsteps and leave no sign of our passing. We headed northeast while we could see the sun and the moss on the trees. We relied on Asgar, for direction; he had spent much time now living in the woods and could find his way with the greatest of ease. Even so, it was hard going, as the way underfoot was thick with ferns and brambles.

As the sun sank beneath the world's edge, gloom grew under the trees and we made camp before darkness overtook us. Asgar forbade a fire for he said we were still too near the road. So we sat as the nighttime chill set in and we washed morsels of meat and cheese down with cold water.

We started to shiver as darkness fell and we huddled together for warmth. Edith and Gytha sat together in the middle of a cushion of soft branches that I broke from the trees about us. Asgar put his arms about young Gytha whilst her mother warmed her from the other side and I leaned against Edith. I worried lest she hear the beating of my heart as her sweet warmth seeped through the wool of my tunic, but I could not move away if it meant my life. And then, as if to put my fears to rest, she put her arm about my shoulder and pulled me closer. I know this was only to better trap our warmth, but my heart rose in my throat such that I could hardly breathe.

And so we spent our first night, one of many, hiding from our Norman foes with me wishing the night would never end.

The following day we broke our night fast from our now thin supplies and again moved northeast through the trees, heading towards the river. We saw not a soul; it was as if we were alone in the world. This stumbling but otherwise silent progress continued until at nightfall we struck the edge of the woods. Now Asgar had hard judgements to make. To move out of the trees during daylight was to risk being seen, but we could not tell in the dark how near we were to the river. He decided we would stay where we were inside the woods until we knew more and so we huddled together once more and slept as best we could, although with Edith's arm around me I didn't care if I ever slept again. Yet I did; I do not remember falling asleep, but know I slept dreamlessly until morning.

It was with some gladness that through the trees we saw the shine of bright grey water lit by morning light. Looking about us we came carefully out of the cover of the woods and onto the soggy grass of the water meadows running alongside the wide River Severn.

Asgar stood silently, deep in thought, staring at the rippled water, muddy now we were close enough to see the moving river and not just the daylight shining off its surface. He looked at Edith and gave the slightest bow, so slight that a watcher ten paces away would not have seen it. He spoke to her softly so that a listener five paces away would not have heard it.

'My lady, please, you must wait back inside the woods. You need to wait here for me, for we must cross the river, ebb or flood and as yet I do not know how. I must go and seek a way.' He turned to me.

'You, young Edmund, must wait with our lady and Gytha.'

Nothing could have pleased me more, although I nodded my understanding without giving away my pleasure at this sweet duty.

We moved back into the woods. Once Asgar was sure we were deep under the trees so that none on the river would see us, he waved farewell and soon was lost in the woods that stretched to the east of us. The river ran, I knew, from east to west and so he set out in the way of the narrowing of the river. I was thinking on this when Edith spoke.

'Tell me Edmund, where does Asgar go?'

'I know not my lady, for he said no more to me.'

Edith smiled, 'It is mannerly of my husband to address me as "my lady", but do you not think you should call me Frida as Frida's husband would?'

I blushed at my foolish and perhaps even dangerous mistake. 'I am sorry, forgive me my la… Frida, I shall practice as I do with our old father.'

'It would be best,' and she smiled a smile of such sweetness that my heart and stomach lurched within me.

'Tell me, husband, if you were Asgar where would you be going now?'

169

'Well Frida, the river narrows to the east. Now I know we were to go east on the Fosseway and then north on Watling Street. And so we were to walk north. Now we have left the road, yet still we are moving north, so we must cross the river. Asgar follows the narrowing of the river. Perhaps he seeks a ferry, a ford or a bridge not guarded by Normans. The river is deep and wide so I think not a ford. A bridge will be guarded for certain and I think there will be no bridge before Gloucaestir and such a city will have many Norman soldiers. For these reasons I think a ferry most likely to be that which he seeks. If there is such it will be guarded, for the Normans will be those making most use of it.'

Edith, whose smile had for some cause been growing wider as I spoke, broke into a peal of laughter; it was the first time I heard her laugh. It sounded like a merry peal of little bells, it cheered me to hear it.

'Well young Edmund, you argue clearly that Asgar is gone for nothing for there are no possibilities.' She smiled kindly and I felt stupid.

'I have faith in my old father, Frida. If none of these things will do then there is something he knows that I do not, and so we must await his return.'

Gytha, who sat in glum silence while we spoke, suddenly complained. 'I'm cold mother, can we have a fire?'

I looked to the north but could see nothing of the river and so judged that from that direction and certainly from the road, a small fire could not be seen. I set about building a hearth with stones from the riverbank and collecting kindling and dry branches from low on the fir trees that grew all about us. I looked with care, choosing those with beads of resin on them that would catch alight the easiest and produce less smoke. When I had a small fire laid I set to lighting it with flint and iron.

As I waited for the wood to catch I used yew tree branches to make screens to hide the firelight from the river and the road, whilst by the heat of the small flames Frida and Gytha warmed their cold hands and feet, wet from the water meadow grasses. Once the fire was burning brightly and gaining a red heart we spread our over-mantles on the needles of the forest floor and rested our aching bones from the long day's labours. Gytha lay down, closed her eyes and at once fell asleep. Frida wakened her with a dig to her side. Gytha gave a muffled whine.

'I know you are tired little one,' said her mother, 'but before you can sleep you must eat, for who knows when we must rise and how hurried we must be.' Gytha looked at her, wide-eyed and frightened, but Edith said nothing to comfort her, almost, I sensed, as if she prepared the girl for a lifetime of flight.

Chapter 15

AD 1069

Edmund's Tale: Pursuit

For four days after Asgar left we lurked shivering in the woods, deep enough that we could see neither the road nor the river. Fire we had, but small and smokeless from what small dry branches I could find.

At the end of the first two days I had started to worry, sure that if all went well Asgar would have returned by now. When four days had passed since our killing of the miles and his serjeants I was frightened; I felt it foolish to be waiting so close to the ditch where we left the bodies. We had crossed a field to the woods and kept under their cover, but we were headed in the same direction as the road and were not so far from it as the crow flies. I wanted to be far away, but was afraid to move from where Asgar had left us in case my fears were groundless and he could not find us when he returned to the place where we now huddled around our sad fire.

I could not rest. If I could not move us far away from this place I must at the least watch for our enemies and make sure that we fled well away if they came seeking the killers of their men. I spoke my fears to Edith. As always she considered my words calmly, nothing seemed to frighten her. I think that all her greatest fears had come to pass and nothing left to come stirred her. She agreed that I should stand guard closer to the road and she would be prepared to move quickly east along the river should I whistle the warning note we practised. And so, leaving Edith and Gytha nestled together beside the fire, I limped along the way we had come that led back to the road.

For most of that day I moved with care, stopping to listen for the sound of men on foot, but heard nothing. When I neared the wood's edge and the road itself I stopped still as a deer scenting the hunter. I could hear voices. Slowly, one step at a time, watching the ground for trips and crackling branches, I moved nearer to the edge of the trees until I could see out to the road and the place from which the voices came.

There were armoured men and horses, perhaps ten, clustered on the road. Some were standing on the crest, others down in the ditch. They appeared to be searching the ground and had plainly found the bodies where we had pitched them. The ones on the road were standing facing towards me, shields in a line as if fearing an attack, perhaps from bowmen in the woods. I thanked Odin and Lord Jesus that I had come upon them in silence and with great care, for if they had heard me I would now be fleeing for my life.

As it was, I lay low peering beneath bushes, the brown of my cap like the brown of the carpet of wet leaves that covered much of the woodland floor. The soldiers clustered about their leader as he started to give orders. Then in ones and two's they spread out and started to walk to north and south casting about the ground on either side of the road.

I started to back away slowly, making ready to return through the woods to warn Edith and Gytha and to put some easterly distance between the searching soldiers and us. It was then, as they moved away and left their commander looking about him, that I felt as if I had taken a heavy blow to the gut.

Fear washed over me; not fear for myself, although in that moment I knew that my fate if we were caught would be violent and painful. It was fear more for my lady and the young one. For the face I saw was that of evil; the Devil and cruelty in human form. The leader of these soldiers was Hugh, the Vavassour to the Bishop of Coutances, the torturer and murderer of Ulf. I shuddered to think of our ends should we fall into his hands.

I did not know it then but it was to his brother Robert and the bishop that William the Bastard had given the task of finding Harold's grave and it was to Hugh that Bishop Geoffrey had given the task of pursuing Edith. As I later heard, it was from the ravaging of Sumorsaete and the raising of the siege of Montagud Castle that Hugh had learned of the arrival in our village after Hastings of a noblewoman and her child in the guise of ordinary folk. He learned, I shudder to think how, that that woman was Edith. Only Asgar, my mother and I had known that. The sorrows of Hastings spread out like ripples over a pond and even those who did not die there are washed over by it.

But as I peered through the bushes at the hated Vavassour, I had no knowledge of this. My fear, which had struck me to stone when I saw Hugh, ebbed and left me enough movement to creep, oh so carefully, oh so softly, back towards the river. I slept for a while wrapped in my cloak, but was sure I was well clear of the soldiers when in the dawn kissed early hours of the following morning I arrived back at the clearing, which had been our home now for five days.

Both Edith and Gytha still huddled by the small fire pit, arms wrapped about each other for warmth. It seemed to me that they had not moved since I left and my heart jumped for fear they were frozen to death. But it wasn't so cold, only the autumnal chill. I whistled softly and entered the clearing, heart starting to beat again as Edith turned her drowsy face to look at me.

Though the fire was burned low, for safety I scooped earth and pebbles onto the embers from the heap I had laid ready to douse it and kill any smoke or smell of smoke. Edith stared at me, eyebrows raised, suddenly wide-awake.

Not wanting to wake Gytha nor re-awaken her fears, I whispered, 'They are here, they have found the bodies and Hugh the Vavassour leads them.'

Even my always so calm lady looked shocked at that. Drawing Gytha close she kissed her on the head and woke her with tender words. 'Come my love, wake up. Wake up sweet child. It's time to go; time to walk along the river. Come on Gytha my love, Edmund's come back, wake up now, there's a good girl.'

Gytha knuckled her face and looked around her as if to discover where she was. And then the fear came back into her eyes and she came fully awake. She gazed up at me and then looked to her mother for orders.

Edith got to her feet and held out her hand to her daughter, the young woman so slight and biddable I still thought of her as a child. I lifted our much-lightened bags of food and we walked towards the river.

As if to show us that not all things go from bad to worse, at this point our luck changed much for the better, for we had not crouched our way over two water meadows in the growing light of day, pushing through the thin hedges that kept them apart, a distance of perhaps four furlongs, when Asgar rose out of a dry ditch in front of us and pulled us back down into it.

'Where are you going, what is happening? Why did you not wait for me?' he asked.

Edith waved a hand towards me, as if to say, you tell him. I think she was angry that he had been gone for so long that we had been left in danger. A worse danger I think than she had ever imagined there would be. In the eyes of our minds both of us could still clearly see Ulf's tortured body hanging from the old oak.

I told Asgar about Hugh and he listened gravely then nodded. 'You did well, Edmund. Follow me; we will soon be where they cannot come. I fear I have been longer than I wished, but I think all will now be well, at least for a time.'

He turned and continued in the easterly direction we had travelled to meet him. Over water meadows and through thin hedges we walked for much of the day, until even my lady begged, for the sake of the youngster, that we must rest.

'Not long now,' Asgar said. 'We must catch the tide right,' and he kept on walking. My leg was a throbbing fiery hurt now and Gytha, who'd had little sleep these past nights, was dozing and wandering as she walked and would have fallen into the river had Edith not taken her arm and steered her straight.

As the sun was sinking to the horizon we came at last to where Asgar wished us to be. In front of us was a small pill from which a stream wended its way south over the land. By the light of the setting sun I could see it flowed over flat land that rose suddenly in the distance to a long, level-topped hill mirroring those rising on the other side of the river.

In the inlet, swaying on its anchor in the water was an object which, because it floated I took to be a boat, but like no boat I had ever seen. To begin with it was egg-shaped or rather, like a hollowed out half egg. The framing of the boat was hazel or willow, I could not say which, and the shell of this egg boat was made up of what looked like stitched together animal skins that had been daubed with something black on the outside. This was to seal the stitching, Asgar explained, and to my amazement it worked, for the inside of the boat was quite dry. 'Come,' he said, 'this is what we need. It is called a cooroogle in the Welsh and it means that our walking days are over. Now we shall ride to where we go.'

Edith and I looked at this egg-shaped hole bobbing in the water with some foreboding. She it was who asked the questions on both our tongues.

'Is it safe, it looks weak? Will it take all of us for we can leave none behind?'

'Yes and yes,' said Asgar. 'Its worth is twofold for it has both great strength and yet is light enough for two men to carry easily, one man at need. And yes, this will carry five shoulder to shoulder. We four with ease.'

'But why do we need such a thing?' said Edith.

'Because the road is now beyond dangerous, we must avoid roads. But where we must go we can reach by water. I cannot tell you yet how, for there is much we must learn upon the way, but I can tell you it is close by Hay, which is near to Hereford, on the river Gwy, the place where armies cross into Wales. And therein lies our safety, for the man to whom we go is an ally of the Welsh. Hugh Vavassour and all the servants of Duke William, who calls himself king, cannot enter the lands of the Welsh in safety. The river though is shallow in places and we shall have to walk in water to our calves, and there Edmund and I shall have to carry the cooroogle, but as I said, it is light enough that we can do it.

'Come, I will drag it alongside the shore and we must all

climb in. The tide is strong here and we cannot row against it. Let me warn you, it will be cold, we will be in the craft for a long time for we must let the ebb take us towards the sea whilst we row towards the middle; across the tide we can do it. Then we must let the flood carry us back again, but also across to the far shore. With a little paddling we can let the flood carry us into the mouth of the Gwy. There we will anchor through the ebb and then go up the river on the flood, but only in darkness for the Normans are already building a castle on the west bank at the market place of Chepestow.

I listened to this with fright, which I hid from the womenfolk. I knew nothing of boats made from wicker and skins, nothing of rivers that flowed where they had a mind to, could swim but weakly. So I listened with great care to Asgar, afraid if I missed something it would be the death of me.

'We will be fishermen in the mouth of the river. From two miles off they will not see much, and then after dark we will pass the castle, sliding up the east bank, and they shall not see us at all.'

I was thankful we were once more under the arm of Asgar, for although he had been gone for longer than we had liked he had learned much that was needful to us and also got this strange looking boat which, as I found out later, was the only sort that could do what we wished of it.

We waded ankle deep through river mud to the cooroogle and Asgar held it steady for us to climb in. I now saw two wooden paddles and a bundle of fishing net lying in the bottom. Gytha was light enough for me to lift and carry. I offered the same service to my lady, but with a wave of her hand she dismissed it and pulling up her skirts vaulted lightly into the boat. Using my quarterstaff I followed. Lastly, Asgar climbed in, pulled the anchor – a hole-bored stone attached to a rope – up into the bottom of the boat and rested it on wood bearers, to which he lashed the end of the rope. He then picked up a paddle and pushed off.

And so began our crossing of the Severn River as we pushed and paddled out into the ebb tide.

Chapter 16

Edmund's Tale: Sneaking up the Gwy

I will not bore you with the tale of how we crossed the Severn and entered the Gwy. I am no seaman myself and things happened that were a mystery to me. Much of the time it was black night and we could see nothing. The womenfolk slept under the cover of our mantles and when Asgar handed me the paddle, I paddled and that kept me warm. Enough to say that it all turned out as Asgar had said: first we passed downriver towards the sea whilst paddling slowly towards the other shore and then, after seeming to stop and make no headway at all, so we started to move back the way we had come, the cooroogle moving faster and faster towards the northern shore until, as a new dawn lit the sky, we were being swept towards a gap between cliffs. The tide was fierce here and we paddled hard to keep off the land but still hit in places. The cooroogle was built, I believe with this in mind for each time we struck it bent and then just sprang back into shape without breaking or tearing the tough hide.

So, striking and bouncing off the shore, we entered the mouth of the Gwy. Here Asgar, who seemed to know what he was doing, threw the anchor stone into the water and paid out the rope until we lay barely moving, our craft attached to the end of the stretched out rope, the anchor dragged only slightly by the current.

'Now we are anchored,' said Asgar, 'and we must sit facing the water and make as if fishing.'

Although now full morning it was still cold and again we yielded up our mantles to keep the women warm. I thought that Edith's long hair might cause a problem if we were seen, but she still wore the dark snood as she had promised me at the farm when first the Normans came. Asgar said it did not matter because often the Welsh women worked alongside their men whether farming or fishing so those at the castle would think nothing of it that there were two women and two men in the boat. The snood was a double blessing though, for whatever dye Edith had used to make her hair red-brown was now starting to fade, leaving it lighter by the day. Also, at the roots it grew ice white showing what colour would be revealed when the dye grew out. Not the sign of ageing as I had first thought, but her natural colour; silver, as some said, as birch tree bark.

Of the castle there was not much to see. Unlike the castle at Montagud, which I had worked on and been amazed at how quickly it took shape, this castle was different. Mostly this is because from the beginning it was built of stone. The first part to be built was a tower and the rising of this was all we could see, for there were thus far no bailey walls. Stone may be stronger and will not burn, but it is much slower to build. Aside from the beginning of the tower, we could make out the piles of stone and the hordes of workers driven under the lash to fetch and carry, to the directions of the castle builder. What we could see of them, which wasn't much, was all they could see of us and so I was not fearful as we sat there drowsing, nibbling on the cheese and oaten biscuit Asgar had brought back with him, slaking our thirst on river water and drowsing whilst we pretended to fish, from time to time casting the net into the river and hauling it back. We took it in turns to watch, even my lady took her turn at this, but Gytha was beyond tired and we let her sleep.

Once the sun set below the western edge of the river and darkness fell then Asgar fetched up the anchor and we started to paddle using the fires lit around the castle building works as marks to steer by. After a while, as the flood took hold we stopped paddling so that we made no splashing and we all crouched in the bottom of our low-slung cooroogle so as to make as small a mark as we could. We slid past the castle building, close enough to feel the warmth of the fires that were burning on the shore for cooking the workers' day-end meal, but I think those looking at the blazing fire would have seen nothing in the dark of the river. There were no calls or challenges and we drifted past and were gone.

Once clear of the castle builders Asgar again threw out the anchor stone. There were shallows and rapids to pass, he said, and it would be foolhardy and needless to attempt them in the dark. In any case, until it rained, the bottom of our craft was dry and so we should take our advantage and what sleep we could. And so my lady and Gytha nestled beneath our mantles while Asgar and I wrapped our arms around our chests, and shivering, but at least out of the wind in the dry bottom of the cooroogle, fell asleep.

When we woke the following morning the light was just creeping up the sky over a ridge of wooded high ground to the east. We were in a deep narrow valley and the land to the west was also high and wooded, but there the sky was still dark and we could make out nothing. The narrow river on which we floated stretched but a small way ahead of us before vanishing around a bend to the left. This we discovered was the wont and way of this river and it needed careful watching because neither hazards nor foes could be seen far ahead and every curve, of which there were many, could have hidden one or the other waiting to leap on us as we came around the bend. I soon began to wish for the road and to curse our meeting with the miles and his serjeants, for the river was difficult and dangerous. Aside from this, there were bodily needs to which we must attend. Because of the quality and modesty of my queen and our princess we had to put into the bank from time to time, easy enough to do, but a constant cause of delay to our passage.

The danger was brought home to us quickly and it was probably better so for it meant that we were never at ease and harbouring false hopes of safety. We had hardly rounded the bend in the river to the left when we found ourselves being pushed back by the tide the way we had come, landing on mud on the left bank. Had we known of this swirl of the tide, said Asgar, we would have paddled to the right at the bend. The depth of tidal water fell so quickly that we could not float off the mud in time and had to climb out of our craft. Sinking to our knees in soft mud Asgar and I carried the cooroogle to the deeper water and once the womenfolk were on board we pushed off and threw out the anchor stone. To our fright the tide dragged the stone and once more pulled us back downriver towards the castle builders.

'Paddle!' said Asgar.

Fighting the tide we paddled upriver, making no headway but slowing our drift almost to nothing. By the time the tide went on the flood and we could lift the anchor-stone we were bone tired, but because of the fright the river had given us we could not just let the boat drift, and so we took it in turns to watch and sleep. This watchfulness had to be kept all the way up the Gwy, for this was the usual way of this hateful river the whole length we travelled.

Let me tell you another of its tricks; one amongst many. At one place two days from the castle at the Chepestow there was an island. To the left we could see the white water of a race and so we decided on the right side for our passage. The water was low, for the ebb tide, which ran at all times now, had started to run faster. We had been anchored in a pleasant haven out of the tide and were now riding the calm of low ebb. Imagine our horror to find that the right-hand passage was filled with flat-top rocks through which we now must paddle. We bounced from rock to rock as we passed for they were less than a hands breadth below the surface. Once again, only the bendy build of our craft saved us from disaster.

At another place the water rushed in a weir over rocks that had fallen into the river making a dam. Unable to hold the cooroogle against the press of water we saw we must carry it around. The climb out was so steep at that point that Asgar and I would have struggled to lift and carry our craft without the help of Lady Edith. God bless her. How many queens would fetch and carry in that way?

At yet another place, what we at first thought was a race was a stretch of the river so shallow that we needed to carry the cooroogle one hundred paces to pass into deeper water. The bottom was gravel on which our feet slipped and once again, it was only with the help of our strong-hearted lady that we were able to carry our boat to where it would again float. Looking back I know now that between my crippled leg and Asgar's still healing strength, there was not one good man between the two of us. Without Edith's strength we could not have won through.

Not a mile from the gravel bed where we went aground was a Burh. Asgar said he thought it was Burh St. Leonards, held by a Saxon thegn, but tempted as we were to stop there for food and rest, Asgar knew not whether this thegn had made his submission to Duke William and in any case, as he said, 'If we stop, he will want to know our story, which I am not prepared to tell. He will then be in wrath and the story of the distrustful strangers will spread from here to Normandy.'

And so we passed by the Burh. It seems that besides death the Normans have brought distrust with them and it seeps everywhere. We cannot trust bishops, we cannot trust thegns, and we cannot even trust stallers and marshals. The Normans are like the plague: if they do not kill our land in one way they do it in another, for if the plague does not kill us directly with pustules of poison we do it to each other, whether through starvation or betrayal, either way we die.

Although still daylight, Asgar led us to pull into the left bank under the shadow of low hanging trees and there made our craft fast.

'We will rest now,' he said, 'for we shall be at Hereford in but a few hours and must pass by the castle in darkness. It will be hard for us because here there are shallows and a ford by which the armies cross the river. We too must cross the ford and I do not know where it is knee deep and where ankle deep, and thus we must feel our way and may need to carry our craft in darkness. Gytha must stay inside it, for we cannot take the risk of losing her to the water in the dark of night.

'There is one other thing. Before Hereford we must pass Monmouth and that will be a test for us. There is a wooden castle there. Here fate is with us for it is four hundred paces or so from the river, but I am told there are two channels, the right hand one shallow and with many rocks. To try to carry our craft over them at night will surely lead to broken legs. The left-hand channel is clear, but close to the bank. Any watch set by the castle on the bank itself would be sure to see us.

'There is yet one other thing to tell you. There is another river, the Monnow, which joins from the left. The flow from this will sweep us towards the right bank and when this happens we will know the castle is nearby.'

We sat for some time thinking about this. 'The threats cannot be made less,' I said at length, 'we must choose which we would meet. The shallows are too great a threat, the channel along the bank also, for if the castle espies us then either we must halt and answer for ourselves or they will pursue and fire darts at us until we are dead. I do not wish to be a target for the crossbows of Monmouth Castle.'

'There is perhaps another way,' said Asgar, 'but whether it lies within our strength I do not know, for your leg is weak, Edmund, and I must tell you I still do not have the strength I had before Hastings.'

'Tell us what we must do, old father,' said Edith with a smile, 'and we, Gytha and I, will help.'

Asgar seemed as if about to say nay to this, but then paused and thought some more. 'Then listen well; it is this. We have a rope. If we land in darkness on the far bank from the castle, the right bank, then perhaps if we walk the bank or pull ourselves along by branches in the water we can tow the boat until we are clear of the castle. It has its dangers but is less than the rapids, for we will have handholds. With three, perhaps four, on the rope, no matter what the tide we should win.'

I was not hopeful but all the ways were grim. As Asgar said, at least with hands as well as feet to keep us upright, the threat to our legs was less.

187

And so that is what we did, and our luck was made by our bold deed for it proved easier than we thought. When we passed the mouth of the Monnow River, as Asgar had been told the flow swept us onto the right bank. Grasping tree branches and bushes we pulled our craft into the bank and clambered out. The water was cold and the flow clutched at us, pulling at our feet, which had sunk into the mud of the soft bottom. But the riverbed here was flat and shallow, for over time the bank had collapsed and the river widened. It was easy to walk close to the bank as long as the walker took care not to trip or become ensnared in the tree roots that twined just below the mud.

My lady tailed on the rope and pulled heartily with Asgar and me. The help of Gytha was not such a good idea. She soon caught her feet in a root and fell beneath the water with a shriek. As she thrashed by me, caught in the ebb. I gripped the girl by the mantle and held onto her until Asgar growled she should be put back in the boat. When this was done we stayed silent as deer, listening for voices from the castle or the far bank. There was silence. If the watch had heard Gytha's shriek they must have thought it the cry of prey caught by a fox, or perhaps a vixen's shrill bark. There were no calls from the bank and so after a while we went on our way. There were unwelcome outcomes from this mishap. Gytha now saw me as her saviour twice over and her warmth towards me grew ever greater. This took me aback for I did not wish to hurt her feelings; I kept her safe as I would any child, but also for her mother's sake.

Once back in our craft we paddled towards Hereford. I was not looking forward with any glee to yet again seeking to avoid a castle and carrying our boat, this time across the ford of the armies, with its risk of broken legs or ankles. I said as much to Asgar but he chuckled.

'There may be no need for I have a plan. I had forgot to tell you that soon we will see a stream off to our right on a great bend of the river. This is the River Lugg, which will carry us near to where we go. It does not pass in sight of Hereford castle and is thus away from Norman eyes. That is good, but it is narrow and twists and turns and is shallow enough that we must needs carry our craft in many places. What say you all?'

Edith and I were clear in our voicing that anywhere away from the Normans was good no matter the trials it put on us. We feared that if we were taken we could fall into the hands of meat-hewer Hugh. Young Gytha said nothing; her fall now had her balancing death by dagger or death by drowning. I think she wished with all her heart she could be somewhere else.

Thus it was that we passed Hereford and its great wooden castle without seeing it, nor did it see us. The Lugg, as Asgar had been told, was twisting and shallow but it was also largely still. With my lady to help us we carried the boat with ease; Gytha managed not to fall in the river and all went well. There were uprooted trees floating by the banks in places and many overhanging branches. I thought when rains were heavy it would be a threatening place, but now the Holy Month sun was shining, lighting up the autumn colours of the leaves and the wind had fallen to almost nothing, it seemed a peaceful place. For the first time since we had met the miles and his serjeants I started to feel the happiness of hope.

When we reached a stretch where we were able to paddle I asked Asgar, 'Old father, how much further do you think we have to go?'

'Truly I don't know, son,' he said. 'My plan is that we go as far as we can and when there is no more water to float us then we hide the Cooroogle and set off north overland. As soon as we find people we will ask for Eadric. He will be well known for he is the protector of the folk hereabouts. Already he and Prince Bleddyn have shown the castle that Normans are not the only law around here.'

That was the plan but like many it ended in a different way, from causes we could not foresee.

As I said, I was happy as we made our way down our peaceful and twisty river. We approached a great bend and paddled around it. Here the trees came down to the edge of the bank, their roots in the water and their branches hanging their heads, hiding the bank in gloomy shadow. As we paddled peacefully along, my nose started to twitch for I could smell burning. One by one my senses came to life. I saw smoke in the sky and then I heard the distant sound of shouting. Last of all I saw movement in the trees and as I turned my eyes to look more closely, I saw that beside the movement there was much that was still. The still shapes were not trees and bushes; they were men. No sooner had I spotted them so too did they start to move. From standing silently watching us, now there arose shouting and yipping like the sound of a pack of hunting dogs.

AD 1069 Silvaticus

Chapter 17

AD 1069

Edmund's Tale: Eadric's Hall and the Wild Hunt

To the front and the back of us men jumped less than waist deep into the water. I dropped my paddle and bent to my staff. Asgar waved me to drop it.

'What would you do, go to war with Wales?'

He was right, there were far too many to fight so I waited quietly to see what would happen next.

The men in the water looked a rough lot. Bearded, clad in cloth wrapped and strapped about the legs, with thick leather jerkins to serve as war coats, some sewn with metal strips, others not. Some of the men wore helms, others thick leather caps. It seemed we had fallen amongst outlaws and looking at their fierce faces I began to wonder whether we would have fared better with the Normans.

Our craft was towed to the left bank and we were told to get out. If they were indeed Welsh, thankfully there were some who spoke English, more than could be said for most Normans. They held out their hands and helped the womenfolk out without roughness and in a mannerly way; I started to hope their rough looks belied them.

We were brought before one, no different to my eyes from the rest but who must be their leader. 'Who are you?' And where are you going?' he said.

'We are going to see Eadric the Wild. Who we are, is between him and us. All I can say is that he should be expecting us,' said Asgar.

'Maybe so, maybe so; perhaps you will see him sooner than you think, but you must give me your names.'

'That I cannot do, but I will give you my name, when you tell it to Eadric then he will see me; I am Asgar the Staller, please tell him that.'

'He does expect you. I am Gruffydd. If you will follow me we shall go to see Eadric.' He strode off to the top of the bank watched by a tall, thin man astride a short horse waiting there.

When we stood looking up at the horseman, Gruffydd grinned. 'Ladies, sirs, I present you with Eadric Silvaticus, the jolliest rogue north of Hereford.'

I looked up in surprise, as did Asgar, Edith and Gytha. It seemed we had reached the end of our journey.

'In good health, Asgar,' said Eadric.

'And to you, Thegn Eadric.'

'And this is she of whom your messenger told me?'

'Indeed,' said Asgar.

Eadric slid from his saddle jumping nimbly to the ground. He went on one knee before Edith and she placed her hand on his head as if in blessing.

'My Queen,' he said, 'you are most welcome here; I am your servant in all things as I was to your husband. If you will come with me to my hall at Clun there will be food and drink and all that is there for your comfort and that of your lovely daughter. It is far to go and we came upon you all unlooked for. Please take my horse, my lady. Princess Gytha can ride up behind you.'

'You are kind and courteous sir, but until now we have kept close the secret of who we are. Would it not be wise to continue doing so? I have not claimed to be myself since the battle.'

'You will always be my queen,' said Eadric, 'and if I cannot keep you safe from the Normans with all of Wales to the west to hide in, then there is no safety anywhere in this land.'

'I thank you sir. Your words make us feel safer than we have for many a month.' So saying my lady mounted Eadric's horse and reaching down pulled Gytha up behind her. Our queen is stronger than any would think looking at her willowy slimness.

'Where away?' she asked.

Eadric smiled up at her, 'Follow me,' he said, and taking the horse's bridle in his right hand started to walk away from the river, Asgar and I limping along at his side, followed by his men.

In truth it was far to go. After we had covered two miles or so, Asgar asked Eadric how he had come to be so close to the river and so far from home, as if he had come to greet us, although he surely could not have known we had yet arrived in his lands.

'It was just fate that we met you,' he answered with a smile. 'Why we are so far from home is simple. The Normans of Hereford Castle have taken these lands. They raid my lands and I raid theirs. Perhaps one day they will learn, before I burn their castle about their ears. Do you smell and see the smoke? It's a hall burning; a Norman settler on lands that once were mine. Well he has today suffered such loss that perhaps he will give up and go home.'

'You left him his life then?' said Asgar.

'A Norman life is forty-five marks under the Norman laws of murdurum. No Norman life is worth that. I will burn their halls and their crops, but I let them keep their lives and I my money. One day, when we burn the castle down, there will be no murdurum, I will kill them all and they can try and collect the fine then. That is the law in the Freelands where there are freemen who work their vengeance on Normans that fall into their hands. Those folk hold no land but what they camp on by the night, and to take the murdurum fine the Norman earls must first catch them. They will never do that, for the earls fear to go into the mountains. The Normans call me wild, but the true Silvatici are the freemen of the dales.' He stood, deep in thought then looked up and spoke on.

'Here on the plains we are not yet strong enough to go to battle with William the Bastard, but one day, perhaps. Ah, my lady,' he said, turning and looking up at Edith. 'I deem there will not be a day when you do not wish your husband alive. You are not alone in that. If before the battle the land had risen up when Harold the warrior led us, then William would have been thrown into the sea. Now the land weeps that it did not do so and wishes to rise, but does so in fits and starts. It has no one to lead and bring all together in a mighty force that would destroy the Normans and wipe them from the land. Alas, Edgar the Aetheling is no warrior.'

'Now,' he said. 'Asgar has told me as much as I need to know. We must see, my lady, about getting you to a place of safety. You are safe from Hugh the Vavassour here. Even if he comes with an army we do but fall back to Welsh lands. Our friends there have armies to buffet his ears.'

He halted and turned again towards Edith, 'Here is my plan,' he tapped his nose with a finger. 'You will only be safe over the sea with your Danish kinfolk. We must get you across the country to take ship. Best to go from York where many Danish ships come, some for war and some for trade. There is a man I would trust with my life: Prince Bleddyn. He will take you safely up the Welsh lands to Caester. From there you must cross the Freelands of the mountains. All the way to Mancaester and from there to York the land is hills and valleys and forest. This is deadly dangerous for there is no law there and it is peopled since the rebellion and William's destruction of the North with starving folk and outlaws.'

We looked our puzzlement for we knew nothing of this having come up from the South. He read our faces and said, 'I see you have not heard the dire news. I will not tell you now; soon you will meet someone who can tell you much better than I. He is Swein, son of Sicga. He will take you safely through the bandit country for he is one of the greatest of them and a bitter enemy of the Normans. He will bring you to York and from there you must take ship. I think King Sweyn Estrithson will greet the widow of Harold Godwinson with warmth.'

'But for now, I must bring you to Prince Bleddyn. You will like him. He is the best among rulers. He is merciful, well bred, loved by those who know him, generous to the poor and a defender of the weak. That you seek refuge, are a widow and that your men support you in all things will commend you all to him. He was a friend of Harold and bound in alliance to him. In him you can trust.'

We walked for half a day and at length came to Clun and Eadric's hall. It was the usual fenced wooden building, simply a great dining hall about a hearth, with rooms off for the household servants. There were stairs and a gallery with doors to private family rooms. It was large and open, like the man himself who owned it and called it home. There was no wife to run it. His life was spent in harassing Normans and I think he had no wife or children for fear of giving hostages to his foes, although, according to legend, Eadric had a fairy wife who had left him due to some fatal sin on his part and his life was spent in search of her.

We waited in his hall for the arrival of Prince Bleddyn and while we were there I wandered about the estate and came across an exceeding strange thing. As I said, it was Eadric's delight and his life's work to harass Normans. I found something out about this whilst I was in the stables where I had gone to admire the horses, for these were a fine, warhorse breed. I noticed they were all blacks, but when I looked more closely I saw that not all were so by nature. Some showed signs of being dyed so that, whether pied or bald-faced, all were black all over. The exception was their eyes, for about their eyes were white rings, which I could see were painted on.

Then, in the corner of the stables I found the most peculiar things piled up. They were great curved goat horns, in pairs joined together by straps, which made it clear these were false horns to be strapped on a horse's head. As I looked closely at these and puzzled what they might be for, I heard a cough and jumping with lurching heart, turned to see Eadric watching me.

'So, you have found our little joke against the Normans,' he said. 'Sit down,' he waved his hand towards a bench against the wall then picked up one of the sets of horns and sat alongside me, turning it over in his right hand.

'How well do you know the legends of our people, Edmund?'

'Not well, lord, only those things local to our Hide that my mother told me: King Alfred and the burning of the cakes at Somerton, things of that sort.'

'Hmm. Well this is something older; much older. How well do you love the Normans, Edmund? Would you fight them, kill them at any chance?'

'That I would. A Norman killed our town elder most vilely; he may also have killed my mother. I think he may at least have hurt her sore, for I believe he now knows something which only she, of all those left behind, knew. I do not think it chance that he pursues us. I believe he has found out who Edith is and guesses the direction she heads in. If he learned this from my mother he must have hurt her more than I want to imagine, for she would not give it lightly. Given my chance I would kill him and all Normans, or do anything towards it.'

'Then let me tell you this. There are men, some of them great, who can render great service against the Norman Duke, and there are others who are small and yet whose small service is important.' He paused, looking into my face to make sure I listened closely.

'An old legend of our people is of the Wild Hunt, known by some as "Wothan's Army". This ghostly army pursues wrongdoers across the sky to their torment in Hel. To see the Wild Hunt is to know your death is near. These folk of whom I speak, great men and small, are banded together in a Wild Hunt. We hunt down and harass Normans, tell them their death is nigh and, when we can, we kill them. Those who get away from us carry back tales of ghosts, thus spreading fear and dread amongst our enemies.' He turned the horns in his hands. 'You are a good man, Edmund. When you return home you might serve the hunt from there. Would you join with us?'

'It would do me great honour to join your fight against the Normans in whatever way I can,' I said.

'Then let us shake hands on it and be in oath and honour-bound to silence before all others.'

'Gladly.' And we shook hands and I saw then that he brought his left hand from behind his back and slipped his dagger back in its sheath.

I pointed at the horns he had put down on the bench while we sealed our oath. 'And what are these?'

He smiled. 'Legend has it that Wothan's armies are mounted on great horned goats with eyes the size of plates that glow in the dark. The huntsmen are swart and blow horns to drive the pursued. They have with them great dogs that bay to the note of the horn. He waved at the horses and the goat horns. 'These are our goats and we paint circles about their eyes. The paint is made from a powder. We make it from green crystals dug out of the ground in West Wales. When treated it will glow in the dark. We paint it on before we ride and wash it off when we come home, for it changes the colour of the hair. By bad luck not all will wash off, as you have seen. We use it not only on the horses. Some of our huntsmen own big wolfhounds. We gather them together, paint around their eyes and let them run loose.' He laughed,

'We do not have to teach them to bay for they think we chase wolves and they bay to split the moon. So there; you know our secret, young Edmund, and because you are who you are and we are oath sworn, I trust you never to speak of it.'

'What of Asgar, is he…?' I started to say.

'Yes, Asgar is a huntsman,' he smiled. 'When you return to your home perhaps you and he can find a way to punish those who have murdered your kin.'

'I am told you are safeguarding a kinswomen of mine who bears witness to the slaughter, for so Asgar has told me.'

'It is true. She suffers great ill from her sorrows but I will show you where you may go to see her and then I too must go. Tonight the Wild Hunt rides to Scrosburh and tomorrow, with the help of Wales, the castle will fall.'

I followed Eadric as he left the stables. He pointed to a small dwelling place against the fence. 'That is the living place of our Wise Woman,' he said. 'There you will find the woman you seek, but take care. Before you speak with her, ask the wise woman, for she will know best.'

Chapter 18

AD 1069

Wilda's Tale: The Murder of the Shire

I did not wait the time it takes a leaf to fall to the ground. Ill or not, if the woman had any news of my mother I must hear it. I knocked at the door and straightway it was opened by a crone, hale but old in years, that I took to be the Wise Woman.

I had been practising in my head what I would say for I wished to see a sick person under her care, but I need not have done so; as soon as she opened the door she took me by the arm and drew me inside. 'Welcome,' she said, and then surprised me with her next words. 'I have been expecting you.'

The woman I sought, who they said came from my home ground, was unknown to me. Her black hair had been shorn from her head and grew only in the spikes left by blunt blades. Where it had been hacked too close, scabbed-over cuts showed dark and ugly. She sat, staring straight ahead, her eyes were red and tears ran down her thin, hollow-cheeked face.

'She has been like this since she came here,' the Wise Woman told me. 'I don't know where all the tears come from. I give her a potion to make her sleep, but as soon as she wakes she weeps again. Is she of your blood?'

I shook my head, 'I do not know her, but there are many I

have never seen. If they come not to the gathering places, where would I see them?'

'But you must know places she knows. Her name is Wilda. Talk to her of your village. Perhaps it will bring her back to us, for without doubt she is in a dark and strange place.'

I sat on the ground facing Wilda. She stared through me as if I was not there, so I took her hands in mine. She looked down at them as if surprised; as if they acted with a will of their own, but she did not glance at me.

I started to talk. 'Do you remember the hall at Saint Michael's at harvest time? Do you remember the ale at Harvest Home and the singing and dancing?' She stared ahead, but did not by any glance show that she heard or knew what I said. Silent tears ran unceasing down her cheeks as I talked and talked. I spoke of happy times and those not so happy. I spoke of the winter floods when the meadows sank beneath the water and all turned out to drive the flocks to the high ground. I spoke of the Yule feasts when all those who worked the thegn's land, and all others from round about, gathered at the hall for the music, the dance and the glee. I spoke of Holy Month when the flocks were culled and meat was plentiful.

Nothing drew her glance to me until I spoke of summer, of the smell of sweet primroses in the meadows, of violets under the trees, and then her face crumpled and from her throat there came a groan as if torn from the depths of her body; as if a place inside her was part of Hel and from that came up the protest of those sad souls held captive there. And then she spoke.

'All dead, all dead, my little ones, my sweet love, all dead,' and great racking sobs replaced the silent trickle of tears. I took her in my arms and held her close and she clung to me as if drowning and only I could save her.

After a long while the sobs died away and she pulled away and looked at me and I could see that for the first time she truly saw me.

'You are from the hall,' she said, 'you are Edmund, Edmund the cripple.'

'That is true,' I said, 'but excuse me, who are you?'

'No tavern drinker you,' she said, 'for I am Wilda the pot girl from the tavern in Lutgaresburh.' Her face crumpled, 'Oh sweet Jesu, Lutgaresburh is no more, all burned, all killed or dying.' Again she started to weep.

Once more I held her close, pulling her tight to me, trying to comfort. After a while she ceased her crying and lay her head against my shoulder, sniffling.

'Don't speak of it more,' I said, 'for it pains you so.' I waited and then, 'It's just that I left before they came to our hall. I saw nothing and I was hoping for news of my mother.'

'I will speak,' she said, 'for the more that know, the more that hate the Norman devils, the better I will be.'

And she started to tell her tale and did not stop until everything was revealed, except the one thing I, poor wretch, greatly wanted to know: the fate of my mother and my family. This is what she told me.

'When the horsemen came, the fyrd scattered to their homes, took off their war clothes and put on their farming clothes until there was not a fighting man to be seen in the whole shire, except for a lucky few who kept their spears and hid in the woods and copses and fled by night.

As the Norman horsemen encircled the hill, so the men from the castle came out to greet them. They'd had a fright and so were in great wrath. The tavern is at the foot of the hill and we could hear the angry shouting voices from there, although it was drivel to us being in their foreign tongue, and then the castle men and the horsemen came on foot, a great force of armed men. They drove all the folk from the town and round about into the open space of the old Burh. When we were all there and guarded by spearmen, the horsemen mounted up and spurred away. The following day they returned, driving parties of folk from the out villages until many of the folk of that part of the shire were crammed into the space of the old Burh. We were hungry, but most of all thirsty by then. We complained but our guards gave us nothing.

'When it seemed that no more were being driven in, so Hugh, the Norman overseer from the building of the castle stood before us. He spoke to our guards and they came amongst us and dragged two men shaking with fright before them. These men had seen Ulf's fate and I think feared the same.

Hugh pointed at one man and said, "This man has dark hair; all those with dark hair stand at that end," and he pointed towards the high end of the Burh. Then he said, "All others stand there," and he pointed to the low end.

My hair is dark, the colour of charcoal my husband used to say, as dark as his was light. His and that of our children was the colour of wheat….'

Wilda started to sob again. I reached out my hand to comfort her, and soon she stopped for she had much she wished to say.

'And so there we were, the dark-haired at one end the light at the other, and I was set apart from my family. Then Hugh stood in front of the dark ones, and said, "You must go with these men now," pointing to some soldiers standing to one side. "Obey our laws and you will be safe." And bewildered the dark-haired ones left that place as quickly as their legs would carry them; except me, for my husband and children were there and I would not leave them. Instead I ducked away towards the great oak tree.'

I nodded. I knew the one she meant. Great of girth, it had stood within the Burh time out of mind.

'I knew that beneath it was a badger sett. The mouth had collapsed and then been cleared such that the way in was great, or at least large enough for me. No one was watching me and so I dropped to the ground and wriggled through the loose dirt until my legs were deep underground and only my eyes were clear, so I could see what the Normans did. And all the while they brought about the mad evil of Hugh I stayed where I was. For what could I do? And I feared what they would do to me. And so I watched, my eyes, popping with horror and sorrow at what I saw.

'He gave an order and all the Normans in ranks lined up before those left behind, all the fair-haired of Lutgaresburh. First they threw their spears at them and then the archers fired their darts and amidst screaming and shouting the folk fell in heaps and still the Normans shot at them. Some, although not bearing arms seized the Norman spears from the bodies of the fallen, charged the spearmen and archers, but armoured soldiers, standing ready, cut them down with sword and axe. Those who were but wounded, men, women and children, Hugh had them gathered together and then he personally wielded a cleaver and cut off their right hands. There were many children, for some bowmen had not wished to fire their darts at young girls and boys and so had fired into the ground. Hugh had these little ones carried screaming to where he wielded his blade so that he might inflict his evil on them and then they might bleed to death. With a great scream, silent in

205

my breast, I saw him cleave the hand from my little girl, I heard her high thin cries and then in mercy, she fell, I hoped the shock had stopped her tiny heart. Of my boy and my husband I saw nothing and thought them dead.

'When all was done, heaving for breath from his brave work Hugh spoke. "To the dark-haired Welsh I have shown mercy. It is the English who will not understand they are beaten. And so I shall show the other shires what happens to those who shed Norman blood. The English we killed, as fate would have it, but those who lived after our spears and darts, I took their hands that they may never take up arms again. If after that they still live I will take that to be God's judgement and spare them as long as they are loyal to King William."'

Wilda tried to say more, but had started to cry again, her voice shuddering and breaking, 'I let them murder my baby… I let them put to death my husband and my boy, and I did nothing…'

I rocked her in my arms. 'What could you have done,' I murmured, my lips against her stubbled head, 'you could not have stopped it?'

'No, but I could have died with them. If I had we would have been at peace together and now for my cowardice I will never have peace for the whole of my life. Always the picture of their deaths will burn me sore like a brand in my gut. I watched as they threw the bodies onto carts as though they were logs of wood, my girl child with them, for through God's mercy she had bled and died, poor little mite. They collected the hands onto a cloth and threw it on a wagon. With whips they drove the living handless ones away to die from wounds or bleeding or starvation.'

Still holding her, I asked the question though I feared to hear it answered. 'You knew me, so you must know my family.

206

Did you see aught of them?'

'No, I did not see them, neither in the Burh nor among the dead.'

'You went amongst the dead?'

'No, but I followed the carts from a distance. None noticed me. I could see them on the road and by the clouds of carrion that flapped about the place I saw where the Normans took them. They went to a meadow under the afternoon shadow of Ham Hill. I hid in the bushes and watched. There the dark-haired that Hugh called "Welsh" were made to dig a great pit, shoulder deep, fifty paces by thirty paces. When they were done, they were made at sword point to unload the carts, toss the bodies in and then cover them over with the earth piled up there.

'Some who lived I know were dark-haired English and some who died, red-haired Welsh. I say Welsh, but you know these were not like the Welsh, these were not foreigners, they were our neighbours; they had lived in the shire since before my family came from overseas. They have lived beside us since then and I could not say whether any were Gewissae or not. I do not know if dark hair and light hair makes us different. It is, I think, another part of Hugh's madness, of his hatred of the English.

'My husband and my children lie there in that great pit with all our kin. When all had gone I knelt and cried and prayed and cried again all that night. And then I set out north to be as far from mad Hugh as I could be and to tell my tale to all who would listen. But the more I told the more I cried, until I could not stop, and so you found me.'

'How did you get to here? It is a long hard road.'

'That was easy. I set out and every day I asked where I could find men who killed Normans. None would admit they knew much, but all said they had heard rumours, and all rumours came from the North. One I met who knew me, he took me to his cot of branches and saved me from abuse in the Freelands, he said that those who fled north live there as reavers now. Those who stayed he knew naught of, but I do, for I saw it all, the murder of our shire.

'Sometimes I walked and sometimes I rode. Men would give me help and food, some from kindness, some if I gave them what they wanted. Few cheated me and for myself I did not care what they did with me for it was my penance for not dying with those I loved. And so I ended here, under the care of Eadric, but is it not strange that once I was safe again the tears came and until you found me nothing would stop them? And what of you; how came you here, Edmund?'

Looking into her thin face I could see she had been pretty once, but was now worn with sorrow and hard living. 'I left Lutgaresburh before the Normans came seeking vengeance,' I said. 'My mother told me they would not harm the women and children, and I in my foolishness believed her. I would not have left her but that we had a highborn lady and her daughter in our care and I was tasked to get them away.'

Wilda did not ask who and I was glad, for even though Eadric had thought it safe to name Edith as his queen, I felt the fewer who knew the better, at least until my lady was safe across the sea.

'We are seeking safety with the Danes,' I said. 'The Danes kill Normans too. We cannot stay here, for the Normans will not brook Eadric forever. They will make peace with the Welsh and leave him hanging in the wind, or he will see his danger and will submit to Duke William. The duke turned king is cunning I am told, he may see Eadric as more useful as a friend than an enemy.'

I paused as a thought came to me. 'Perhaps you should come with us? My lady might welcome you as maid and companion. It is hard for her with only men to talk to; her daughter is yet young and not strong.'

Wilda looked up at me, 'Do you think she might? I know nothing of ladies. I am only a farmer's wife. I can milk cows but not dress hair.'

'I am sure she would welcome your company, I will speak to her.'

'And I will consider it,' she said. Not for the last time I admired her pride and her courage.

We lived with Eadric for two weeks. We had shelter, we ate well; we recovered from our journey and soon were ready to move on. We did not fear Hugh while we were there, for we trusted Eadric and the Welsh to defend us against any odds.

One day Eadric came before us as Edith and I, with Gytha sitting staring into nowhere, were wrapped in talk about where we should go next.

'There is a Norman,' Eadric said, he meets the description you have given me of Hugh the Vavassour. He is at the castle of Hereford and I am told he asks after a crippled man travelling with his father, wife and child. I think it is time for you to go; we must move you on before your presence here is betrayed. I fear not for my hall for it will take a great Norman army to take it as long as I have the Welsh to stand at my back, but I fear that they will lurk near all paths out and take you when you leave. Best to leave now. I will bring you to Prince Bleddyn tomorrow and he will start you north to Caester.

The following morning as we ate our first meal of the day Eadric joined us at the board. With him was a man of middle years, his beard and hair of russet. His clothes were fine but threadbare and worn in places. This was a man of worth leading a hard life.

Before sitting he bowed the knee to Edith. 'My lady, I am Bleddyn ap Cynfyn at your service. I was an ally of your husband, I grieve his loss; he was a great man, a fine warrior and a trusty friend.'

'I have heard much good of you Prince Bleddyn, but I ask you not to talk of Harold to me now or we cannot plan what must be. When I talk of him I grieve and we must keep clear heads I think.'

'You come at a time when great things befall, my lady. Tomorrow Thegn Eadric and I will go to Scrosburh. The Normans build a wooden castle there, we go to tear it down or burn the town to teach them their castle protects nothing. I think you will be safest from he who pursues you if you and your company travel with the army. Then, whilst we set about our business, you, with an escort of stout armed men, will ride on to Caestir. It will be easy for there is an ancient road from Scrosburh to Caestir. There is also one from Caestir to Yorvik, but you cannot travel it in safety even with many guards, my lady. The road passes through the Freelands of woods and dales. They are infested with those who have fled the Normans or been starved into outlawry.'

'So Eadric has told me, but I fear the Normans will seek them out and destroy them? They must live somewhere, even in forests. Once the Normans have hunted them down they will kill them will they not?'

'It is not so easy in the Freelands, my lady. There are forests, yes, but the whole land there is like a cheese riven though with caves and every cave has many ways out, many places to lay a trap. The Normans know the reavers are there, but fear to enter. When bold ones do so, either they see the light no more or they do not find those they seek for their quarry have left by another door.

'What I say now is to all of you; pay heed. Caestir has not yet submitted to William the Bastard, he will come there to force it to his will and so you must not linger. You will meet a man there. His name is Swein Sicgson. Do not ask for him, he will seek you out. If you are delayed he will not wait for you, for every bit of time he spends there is a danger to him. He is an outlaw with a small hoard offered for his death by the Sheriff of York, patron of Benedict of Selby. Since the harrying of the land by William many villages and towns are laid to waste. The land, salted and unploughed, is without crops or stock. The people starve and many have taken to the hills and forests, for to prey on the Normans or other travellers is the only way they can keep their lives. Hunger knows no country. To cross the Freelands is to lose your life. You must not stay in Caestir and you must not leave except with Swein Sicgson. If aught goes wrong, come back to here.' Prince Bleddyn paused and gazed frowning at Edith. 'You see now that your journey has within it more threat not less? You must go with great care.' Then he smiled, 'But after Scrosburh and until Caestir you will pass with me across my kingdom of Powys and for that time at least you will be wholly safe.' His smile grew into laughter, 'Please forgive me, my lady, for now I must go and bring together our harsh awakening for the Normans. I will send men to guard you when it is time to go.'

The following morning a soldier came to the hall. He had with him three horses for us to ride, with Gytha up behind her mother, and Wilda – for she had agreed to come with us and my lady welcomed her company – behind Asgar. When Eadric and his guard joined us we set off at a merry pace following our guide. We had not been on our way more than the time it takes to eat a good meal when we came upon the army.

Unlike the English who, to their undoing, relied on foot soldiers and the shield wall, much of the Welsh army was made up of light horse soldiers. Which is good for land battles in the open, for the heavily armed and heavily horsed Normans found the swift moving, nimble Welsh hard to deal with. Much of what remained of the army was made up of archers using a bow of great length, which required much strength. As I have said before, my leg is weak but my shoulders are strong, and yet when I tried a Welsh longbow I could not fully draw it.

Asgar looked sad. 'If only Harold had married Wales as he married Gruffyd's widow. If we'd had five hundred bows like these at Hastings then William would have died in battle and our good King Harold would rule us yet,' he said.

It was as if his words had set light to Edith's mantle, for she came upright in the saddle. Quivering, eyes flashing, she spoke with such venom I would not have believed it had I not heard it for myself.

'Gruffyd's widow! Gruffyd's widow! That whore? She would have married the devil himself if he made her Queen of Hel! She married my husband with her own murdered husband still warm in his grave. The Mercian bitch had married Gruffyd for the crown of Wales and as soon as she saw her chance she married Harold for the crown of England. And for why did he? To creep and lick the ground before Pope Alexander, that's why. And to what end? It gained us nothing from the treacherous dog but a curse and a banner for the Bastard. You speak true Asgar, five hundred Welsh bows and an arrow in that bitch's heart would have saved us.'

We said nothing. I'm sure my mouth dropped open. I had never heard my lady anything but calm and her angry bitterness had struck us all dumb.

And yet, for all the Welsh archers and their longbows and the swift light horsemen, the Normans were still better at the making of war than were we, whether English or Welsh.

Prince Bleddyn was joined by his co-ruler, his brother Rhiwallon, who brought with him more foot soldiers but no wood or carpenters for the fashioning of the battering ram and wall storming machines, without which, so Saint Michael's Hill had taught me, the castle could not be entered and overthrown. It seemed that our friends had no more idea how to overcome a castle than the men of our shire of Sumorsaete. I could not advise them for although what I had seen told me what was wrong, I did not know then how to tell what was needful. I had a bad feeling in my gut. I looked at Edith; she also showed no good cheer. Gytha, staring about her at all the horsemen and archers and listening to the flow of their musical foreign tongue, was spellbound and for once did not seem frightened.

I learned two more things that day. The first was that light horsemen may win a fight with heavy horsemen, but they are of little use against castles and must be taken back behind lines and their riders come forward on foot. The second thing I learned is that archers can keep a bailey wall clear and that leads to fewer dead men at the foot of the wall, but by themselves they cannot cause a castle to fall. And so I saw all over again the failure I saw at Lutgaresburh. We did not take the castle.

Again we gathered about the wall and the ditch. This time while they shot arrows at us we also shot arrows at them. We killed some, which was better than our attack at Montagud Castle. Also, Scrosburh Castle was not built on so steep a hill so we were able to swing ladders against the bailey wall. We swarmed up these but could not overcome the defenders. Perhaps in time we might have done, but it was decided to encircle and besiege. This was much quieter and much safer and I think everyone agreed with it because climbing the ladders and trying to clear the wall had proved to be hot work and the numbers of wounded and dead were rising.

The next thing I cannot say I learned, as I already knew it. Encircling with a view to starving a castle may be a peaceful way to win, but only as long as the whereabouts of the enemy's main army is known. We did not know that at Lutgaresburh and it killed us. We did know it here, however, for word came in that Duke William was not far away to the north. And so encirclement of the castle was quickly abandoned, but in order that the Normans should not feel they had beaten us and driven us off with little loss to themselves, some of our horsemen carried flaming brands into the houses and set light to the town. We watched it burn merrily for a while and then we left.

That night we slept in a shelter that Prince Bleddyn had put up for Edith and Gytha, Asgar, Wilda and me. His plan was to draw in more men and build an army of Welshmen and Englishmen that could defeat William in open battle, but we never saw this army for we left for Caestir long before it formed. I did hear of it later. It was cursed by the same madness that has struck down our country ever since William came. I heard that, as William's army drew near, Eadric had a falling out with the Welsh and fled with his men to the hills. The Welsh and the few Englishmen who had stayed true fought William at Stafford and were defeated. And so another chance to restore our country's freedom passed us by. I do not know why this happened. I do know from Asgar that William

214

is greatly cunning. Had he not tempted Asgar into betrayal of the English cause? Did he do the same with Eadric? I do not know. All I heard later was that after the battle Eadric submitted, his lands were restored and within the space of two years he was fighting alongside William against the Scots. It seemed that Eadric, for all I thought much of him and for all that he had told me of the Wild Hunt that day in the stables, valued holding land more highly than he valued his honour.

This could not be said of Bleddyn for he remained true to his word. He and his men took Edith, Gytha and we her servants to Caestir as he promised, even though there was need for him to be elsewhere. He left Rhiwallon to bring the army together knowing he would be back before the gathering was complete. It seemed to me then that what had started out, as a way of punishing the castlemen of Hereford and Scrosburh was now becoming a revolt against the Normans. I began to hope. For with the Danes in the East and the Welsh in the West and all the angry English in between, how could we fail?

The Story House fell silent as Edmund's voice faded. Bowdyn emerged from the shadows, sitting forward in his chair to smile at his audience. 'That is all for today,' he said.

He sounded tired and I, who had been lost in the story, only now realised how long he had been talking, but the devil was in me at mention of the Wild Hunt and for once I asked a question, which I will relate to you.

As folk began with much clattering to gather their things together, I said, 'what can you tell us of the Wild Hunt, Bowdyn? Is it still with us to fight for our freedom? Bowdyn looked keenly at me, daring me to say more. I knew I had already said too much and kept silent, waiting for his reply.

Lowering his voice, he said, 'Well Jo, the Wild Hunt is a long and great story and will perhaps be told one day. It was and is, I believe, the best way in which we can fight for our freedom when it is threatened. Think of the accomplishments of some of our great men. Take Oliver Cromwell, he it was who freed us from the power of a wilful king. We had a wilful king again, but not for long. Our new king may rule, but he himself will do so under the rule of law. Perhaps the Wild Hunt toppled the last one? Certainly, Oliver Cromwell showed us what could be done. His great uncle Thomas Cromwell freed us from the tyranny of the church. I tell you these things to show you what great men can do. I do not say that either of those men were brothers in the Wild Hunt, although they fought to free us as the Hunt does. Who knows what great men are in that brotherhood? One day, if it is not dangerous to you and me or anyone else here, I will tell you what little I know of its story.' He paused, raised his voice and called over my head to the departing villagers, 'We will meet again next Saturday.'

With a chorus of thanks they went home, except those whose fondness for discussion and concern for the wellbeing of the tavern keeper sent them scurrying to the tavern to examine, over a thirst quenching beaker of ale, what had been said about Edith's flight and the secret brotherhood of the Wild Hunt.

AD 1070 The Freelands

Chapter 19

Edmund's Tale: Swein the Outlaw

When we had gathered once more in the Cold Cot the following Saturday, Bowdyn looked across at me, the firelight casting flickering shadows on his face.

'You asked me to tell you more about the Wild Hunt, young Jo,' he smiled, 'but that is for another time.' He leaned forward as if to gather in his listeners.

'You will remember last week that Edith and her escort were about to set off for Caester, guarded by Prince Bleddyn and his men at arms. There they would meet with another who would safeguard them and conduct them through the dangerous, outlaw-infested Freelands. Prince Bleddyn could only stay with them to the gates of Caester for he was needed to join his brother Rhiwallon, both of them, along with Eadric, raising an army to oppose William in the West while the Danes face him in the East and the Scots in the North. Edmund has already told us the sad outcome of that battle and Eadric's betrayal. For now we will continue with Edmund's tale of Edith's escape, for from it we can learn much of the curse that the Normans put upon the land.'

Sinking back into his chair, Bowdyn waited until the audience had settled and the only sound was the crackling of the fire, then Edmund's voice filled the Story House once more.

The following day, with Prince Bleddyn and twenty of his hearth companions we rode inside the boundaries of Wales and at every hall there was a noble and his sworn men to swell our numbers. It would have taken a bold and well provided for Norman lord to attack us. The Bastard himself with all his army could easily have overwhelmed us, but before that happened, as Prince Bleddyn said, we would have faded into the lands of Powys and Gwyneth and the further we retreated, the bigger our army, until we swallowed up the invaders in trap and snare.

This being so we were at peace as we travelled north, the burning town behind us with only our failure at the castle to take away our good cheer. Bleddyn said that as they had failed to take Hereford castle before, much needed to be done in planning how to take a Norman castle, for if we could not take a wooden motte-and-bailey, which would burn, what chance did we stand against a stone-built castle?

He said it would take us two days to reach Caestir. The road we were on stretched from the southeast of Scrosburh all the way there, but it was so old that few could guess at its builders. Sometimes it was a dyke above the land but sometimes it merged with the land and was hard to find. Here again, Asgar, the old soldier, seemed worth his weight in gold for he could find the road when it was lost to me. But the ride was pleasing. We felt safe with Prince Bleddyn and his men. We had food and each night we gathered around a warming fire. The two days passed easily and then we were riding into Caestir. Bleddyn came with us, our guard stayed outside.

The first thing that took my eye was the way the river wrapped halfway round the town, which was enclosed by a strong wall. I could see why the elders of the town felt they need not submit to William. To take Caester would not be easy if stouthearted men manned these walls.

By whichever gate was entered all roads came together at a crossroads in the centre of the town. The inn we sought, where Swein would meet us, was the War Horse on Foregate Street. It had been chosen for us by Prince Bleddyn and was both clean and comfortable, but not too great for the folk we claimed to be, and at least it did not have the little riders we collected from the last inn. It had taken days and many soaks in cold, river water, to float them away.

Once we were shown to our rooms, one for Edith, Gytha and Wilda; one for Asgar and me, Bleddyn embraced us, wished us the greatest of good fortune and strode away. I know he had much to do, the time he had spent bringing us safely to Caestir was a princely gift indeed. As he started down the stairs he paused and turned back.

'Your lives depend on waiting for Swein Icgson do not think to go on without him.'

We each in turn, even Gytha, told him that whatever happened we would not. It was a timely reminder, for the next day, without his warning in the forefront of our minds it is believable that one or other of us might have been panicked into running through the town gates to be forever lost.

When I awoke the following morning, leaving Asgar still sleeping I met with Edith, Wilda and Gytha, all of us intent on breaking our night's fast, for having had no good meal the day before we were hungry. The taproom not being yet open, the four of us decided to take a walk in the town to seek food at the market, for whilst clean, the inn had an old, stale smell and we yearned for fresh air.

Turning right out of the inn door we walked towards the cross and wended our way down Bridge Street looking for the market, thinking to find hot food to eat but also to refill our food sacks. Suddenly, Edith stopped walking, Wilda gasped and Gytha, breathing quickly, grasped my arm.

I looked up to see that our way was blocked by a small group of men. At first I did not understand why, and then I looked more closely and my stomach came into my mouth, my legs weakened and I almost fell over.

In the centre of the group was Hugh Vavassour; he was staring at us with a grim smile. 'My Lady Edith,' he said, 'how nice to meet you here. What a surprise. There are so many questions I wish to ask you. Indeed, there are so many questions the king says I must ask you.' He shifted his gaze, 'and this is Gytha, I believe. I'm sure she will help you to remember the answers I need and...'

He did not finish; the risk and insult to my lady brought down the red mist and I hefted my staff, hitting him in the middle of his forehead.

Taken by surprise he dropped without a sound. My rage was such that I wasn't worried about swords or spears. I swung my staff like a half-shaft and felled one of the other men. The three facing me stepped back and drew knives from their belts. To the one in the centre I gave my steel-shod snake strike and he flew backwards onto his rump. The other two crouched, heeding me now with greater care.

'Run,' I said. 'Frida; Gytha, Wilda, run!' I stood my ground facing the two men, now in a fighting stance and wary, each with a stabbing knife in his hand, the two points circling as they waited their chance. I knew that with all surprise gone I would be lucky to get out with my skin in place.

And then an odd but welcome thing happened.

People had gathered, as they do, and were watching eager for blood, when out of the crowd stepped a giant of a man with braided hair and beard. He moved so fast that my eyes and mind could not at first make out what he did. He grasped the skull of each of my foes in hands so big that their heads looked like apples in his grasp and then he banged them together with such force that they fell like stones down a well.

I held my staff at the ready still struggling to take in what was happening. He at least seemed to understand, for he stepped over the fallen bodies, all four of them, and grinned at me. 'Well done young man, that's a handy bit of stick you have there. I think you may be waiting for me, I am Swein Sicgson.'

'Waiting for you I am, and very pleased to see you, for I think you have just saved my life.'

'Perhaps, but you are fast with your staff. You may well have done for them without me.'

The crowd that had gathered, seeing no blood or any likely to come, started to drift away. I became aware that the two people in the world I most cared for and was responsible for had obeyed me and run for their lives. I now grew frightened for them. In the shock of seeing Hugh standing before me, I had wanted to run through the gate, swim the river and never be seen again. Even now my stomach was in my mouth as I looked down at his still body, a bruise like a pigeon's egg swelling rapidly on his brow. Seeing my foe lying helpless did nothing to lessen my hatred and I raised my staff to crack his skull. Swein held it fast and then lowered it. His strength was such I could not resist.

'Let me kill him, let go,' I protested, struggling to free my quarterstaff.

'Bad thought, for if you do the town watch may take us and there will be questions of blood money. Better to leave it for now. If we ever see them outside these walls then we will kill them. Now, take me to the War Horse and let us hope the womenfolk have gone there and not taken to the hills. That would be a very bad thing. Even I might not be able to get them back from there. While we walk you can tell me who we have just laid on the ground.'

Feeling like a dwarf at his side I led Swein to the inn and told him of the evil Vavassour. The more I spoke the grimmer grew his face and the more I regretted not killing Hugh while I'd had the chance.

'If we see him again leave him with me, for of all Normans his is the type I punish the most. Some say the gods will punish; some that perhaps Hel will. I like to be sure. If he comes into my grasp he will meet Hel on Earth and will bless death for his release.'

I believed him. Seeing the look on his face I shivered.

My fright rose higher as we entered the inn, fearing that the womenfolk had fled and were lost, or worse. I should have known better, for when had I ever seen Edith anything but calm and brave?

They were in the taproom, beakers of beer before them and Edith's bodkin dagger on the board by her right hand. Asgar was with them and looked angry. His seax was drawn from behind his hood and was also resting on the board. The women's faces lit up like sunlight as I stood in front of them, but if they were pleased to see me it was nothing to the thankfulness that flooded my chest. Not so my thegn.

'Why did you go out without me?' he scowled at me. 'You must never do that again; not ever!'

'I won't. I'm sorry, I thought there was no harm in us going to the market,' I said. 'It is thanks to this good man that we are safe.' I turned to Edith, 'Allow me to give his name. This is

Swein Sicgson, he that we await.'

Swein bent the knee, just slightly, not enough to be noticed from afar. 'I am at your service my lady,' he said quietly.

Edith smiled a welcome. 'So what happened?' she asked.

'This young man felled three Normans with his wooden shaft,' Swein answered.

'And this giant cracked two heads with his bare hands,' I added.

Edith laughed. 'With two such heroes, how could we not feel safe?' But her face did not carry the laugh and soon took on a thoughtful look.

'So Master Swein,' said Asgar. 'We are at your orders. What would you have us do?' I could see he was still angry, but Swein smiled.

'Tonight we shall drink beer and when we have had enough, we will sleep. Do not fear. Now I am with you and until we are in Yorvik there will always be watchmen standing guard. You will not see them; indeed, you should not see them, but they are here somewhere. They watch and will protect you.

'When you awake you must be fresh, for tomorrow we start the ride to Yorvik, over the fells down the dales and through the forests and at every step we will be in the company of outlaws and reavers. But they are loyal to you my lady, and also to me. You will be safe from Normans there for few dare enter the Freelands and of those that do, far fewer ever leave.

There will be fresh horses, one for each of us. Thus we shall ride in comfort. We may find that we have need of them for our safety.

Trusting Swein's word, that night we drank beer until warm, tired and at peace, then we went to our beds and slept soundly in the knowledge that unseen watchers stood guard.

Chapter 20

AD 1070

Edmund's Tale: Outlaws

Swein, whose mighty fists knocked like thunder on our walls, woke us early. 'Come sleepy heads; arise for we have far to go. Come, eat, ready yourselves.'

A short while later over our meal of oats and fowl he told us what we must do. 'Today we set out for Mancaester. The way is not hard, but perhaps half a day from here there is high ground and forest where there is a burned out farmhouse. It was Winflaed's farm and the ground still bears the name. That land is thick with outlaws for there are meres with fresh water and the means to slip away if stronger foes come. There are woods around the meres and the old road from Caester to Yorvik passes by there so there are travellers to be preyed upon. But do not fear, I shall be with you and thus you will be safe, for no outlaw who values his skin would dare to cross Swein Sicgson.

'From there we ride to Mancaester where we will stay one night to rest. After that we enter the fells and dales where our danger is greatest. There the Freelands start, but our danger will not be from Normans. It will be from those rendered desperate by hunger: men whose wives and children are starving. They will kill us for any food we carry. I have heard that some are so desperate they will kill us for our flesh. Thus has Duke William set about his vows to protect and love the people of England as a right true lord!

'When we come into the plains you will see empty fields of blackened earth all the way until we come to Ledes, which is Norman country. There you will find fields of wheat, sheep and cattle and you will see how differently the Normans deal with English and Norman land. But it will gain the Norman lord nothing for we shall burn his hall, reap his crop and feed it to the starving before their ravagers can fall on us.

'I must leave you for a while after we cross the River Wharfe. There is a priest at Selby, a saintly fellow, a Frenchman. He will give you shelter and help you on your way to Yorvik. Like all priests he hoards what people give him whilst the poor die from lack. I took it on myself to take from him and give to them. He and I are old foes; if he even sniffs me on the air he will bring the sheriff down upon us. But do not fear; unseen, my men will be watching not far away.'

I hoped that Swein's trust in himself proved true, he was, after all but one man, if a mighty one. I did not understand then that in his company nothing less than an army could take us. I learned that on the road.

We had little to pack and what we had went into saddlebags or sacks slung on either side of our mounts and on the one packhorse we took with us. Only Edith's bags held anything worth stealing, for I knew she carried the ring of Wessex for which Duke William so urgently sought.

The November day was crisp and clear when we gathered in the road outside the War Horse Inn. Swein waited until our mounts had ceased to move restlessly then judging us ready turned east up Foregate Street and led us to the stone tower of the East Gate and out onto the ancient road to Yorvik.

This was not the first ancient road we had followed. It seemed these roads, old before time began, stretched to wherever we wished to go. Before, we had relied on Asgar's sharp eyes to keep us on the road when it sank beneath the ground and thus became hard to see. Now, however, Asgar could take his ease. Swein knew the way so well he kept to the road without looking, even when it disappeared from sight, as if he could feel it through his horse's hooves.

We walked our horses at an easy pace until the sun had dipped halfway down the sky, by which time we had started to climb as the land sloped up ahead of us. On either side it was lightly wooded, but as we rode further from Caester the trees thickened into forest. Swein now came alert, looking from side to side of the road. Wilda and I talked as we walked our horses side by side, her crying had ceased and I made sure I spoke only of happier days in Lutgaresburh. Swein waved his hand for silence and cocked his head to one side, listening.

Then he waved for us to stop and called towards the trees. 'You can come out now.'

There was silence and then from the woods south of the road there was movement and men started to drift out of the trees.

One of them stepped towards us and shouted, 'Lay your bundles down and we will carry them for you. Dismount and rest your weary limbs. Tether your stewbag steeds and we will take and tend them.'

'We stood for a bit looking at the gang facing us. They were a wild looking bearded pack, clad for the most part in furs: badger, fox, wolf or deer hide. What woven cloth they wore they had worn to ruin. They both looked and smelled untamed, like wild animals of the woods.

'You are mistaken,' called Swein, 'us you will let pass.'

The womenfolk nudged their horses close, huddled knee-to-knee and clung together, Edith in the middle. Calm as always she had her arms about Gytha and Wilda.

'Your womenfolk need not fear,' said the mountain of fur that seemed to be leader. 'Women we have, but ours are starving. It is your food we want and anything we can eat. Think upon your good deed as you walk upon your way. Think of our bellies and those of our women and children filled with your mouth-watering horses. Why, they will last us a full turn of the moon. Be thankful we do not break our fast upon you. We are not that far gone, yet. Your beasts will help keep us from that evil.'

'You speak fair,' said Swein, 'but we have far to go. You shall not have our horses. Could we but buy food on the road ahead you would be welcome to what little we carry. But I know along our road as we pass through the Freelands there is none to buy. Folk there will not give up food, not for fear or money.'

The leader of the outlaws laughed. 'Did you think I was asking?' The laugh became a growl, 'Now! Tether your mounts and lay down your bundles.' He gave a wave of his hand and those of his gang with bows notched arrows and raised them.

Swein in his turn raised his hand and to my great surprise I learned something. For, as his hand went up, so with a swish and a thunk an arrow struck the ground at the feet of the wolf leader. This was followed by a flight of arrows, each one striking at the feet of the archers facing us. I turned and looked behind, yet could see nothing but the trees and hear nothing but the wind sighing through them.

'I am Swein Icgson,' said Swein. 'Perhaps you have heard of me?'

The fur clad leader bowed slightly, kicking gently, idly at the arrow a hand span from his feet, setting it aquiver. 'Indeed

I have Lord Swein,' he said. 'I am sorry for the uncouth greeting. The hunger of one's children is a sharp spur d'you see?'

'And so it is in the fells, and for that we cannot help I fear.' Swein lowered his voice and approached a few feet closer to the outlaw as if about to give up a great secret.

'However,' he said, 'we have but lately been in Caester. As always, while there I have talked, but in greatest part listened, in the taverns. Let me tell you what I have learned. The Abbey of Werburgh and Oswald is full to bursting with the coin left there by grateful pilgrims. Knowing that King William will soon come to take the submission of Caester and fearing the rape of the city if this is resisted, the coin is to be transferred to York for safety. They have begged guardians from York, and with milites and serjeants, perhaps twenty in number, will cross the land north of the meres and ford the Wharfe at Tadcaster. Both of these places might serve a hungry man seeking to relieve them of that coin to buy food in the markets of Caester, which are groaning with food from Powys and Gwynneth, for the Normans have not salted Welsh land, nor have they broken Welsh ploughs.'

'Why do you tell me of this, Lord Swein?'

'Because I know if you do this you will kill Normans and steal Norman gold. I will help to make your warriors and the arms of your bowmen strong. I will leave you our packhorse. He is old and windblown but will make a tasty stew.'

'Swein, you are a prince among outlaws. If there is aught I can do for you, you need but ask it.'

'There is one thing I ask: one man, old and slow but known in the Freelands. Give me such a man to ride with us, for some of us are very light and their beasts will carry two. Tell that man to tell the tale at need that you and I are allied and that you will be wroth if harm should come to us. We are safe. We are many you do not see, arrows do not fire themselves, for we have long lived in the woods and slide from tree to tree unseen like the wind, but I do not wish to kill Englishmen that do not see their danger. Give me one man to save the lives of hungry Englishmen.'

'I shall, and he will tell your foes that to your strength is added the arms of Wyman of the Meres. May he serve you well.'

And that is how Arian the bleater – for that is what he did – came to join our company. Nothing was right for him and nothing made him happy. By the end of the day I wished to end his life horribly and I understood that Wyman had given us a toothless horse he was glad to be rid of.

We dismounted and stretched our legs while we took the packs from our poor packhorse, whose reward for carrying our burdens was that we traded his life away. I did not think it a bargain. Made to choose between our windblown old horse and Arian, I would have taken the horse any day. These packs were spread around the other horses, but not mine, for my burden, in more ways than one, was Arian the complainer.

I helped him up behind me as we bade farewell to Wyman the outlaw. I have strong arms but even for me it was heavy work for he hung like a dead weight and did nothing to help, other than to swing his leg over once I had lifted him almost over my head.

'I shall not forgive Wyman for this,' he said. 'Why me? There are many here who have passed through the Freelands.'

I had not learned to ignore him by then and so answered, 'Perhaps Wyman thought they would remember you better than most.' I did not know how close to the truth I was.

'Slow down, slow down, I have no saddle,' he grumbled, I have no stirrups; you will pitch me off. I shall be no use to you dead.'

I slowed to an amble, but because the others trotted I soon fell behind. 'Hold onto my waist,' I said, 'I must catch up.'

He held my waist in an iron grip so I breathed in only shallow breaths. 'Loose off, loose off,' I cried, 'you are cutting me in two, I cannot draw breath.'

He loosed his grip a little bit and I kicked my mount into a canter.

Straightway Arian tightened his grip again and started to shout. 'Ease up, ease up, you'll have me off you young fool.'

I reined in and slowed to a walk. 'I'm sorry, but I have to keep up.'

'I'm no horseman, you know, I don't ride,' he moaned. 'If God wanted me to travel on a horse I would have been born with one between my legs.'

'How do you get around then, if you cannot ride?'

'Why, I do what any man of sense does, I walk.'

'Then walk now!' I turned in the saddle, grasped his upper arm, swung him off the horse's rump and lowered him none too gently to the ground.

He looked up at me as if to say, 'What have you done that for, you young fool?'

'We have fallen behind and I must catch up with the others,' I said. Starting my horse to trotting I looked back and saw that Arian was still standing behind, watching me go. Cursing under my breath, I turned the horse and walked back to him. 'Why are you waiting? You must walk and keep up with me.'

'You set off too fast for me.'

'Look, when I start now, hang on to my stirrup and do jumping strides. That way we will be able to catch up.'

He grasped my stirrup and I walked then started to trot. Hearing a cry I looked down. Arian was hanging on the stirrup but had lost his footing and was being dragged along. I slowed to a walk and then stopped.

'I'm an old man,' he cried. 'I can't do what you ask of me.'

'You can't ride; you can't hang on and walk, what use are you?' I asked, losing all patience.

'Don't talk to me like that, young pup, I'm an old man, old enough to be your grandfather.'

'So you keep saying, and my grandfather would ride and suffer in silence were he still alive.'

At this point Swein came riding back. 'Why are you hanging back?' he asked. 'We must all stay together.'

'You are going too fast,' said Arian.

'He will not ride for fear of falling off and he will not run at the stirrup because he is too old. Nothing is right and all he does is complain,' I said.

'That is easy,' said Swein. 'I have rope. I will tie him to a horse so he cannot fall off and I will lead it so he keeps up. You, old man, can have a mount all to yourself and can complain to the horse endlessly. Gytha can ride behind you, Edmund, and hold tight around your waist. From what I have heard she will like that,' he grinned at me.

I said nothing; not at all sure I cared for what he had heard. Had he sent Edith to ride with me I would have been in Heaven.

The others seeing we had left them had turned and come back to find us. Swein made clear what the problem was and within minutes we were cantering to make up lost time. Arian, his legs tied firmly round Gytha's horse was bumping in the saddle like a sack of rocks and complaining bitterly, perhaps to the horse but all our company could hear him.

Gytha lay against my back, her head turned and her cheek pressed against me whilst her arms were tight about my waist as if she would never let go. It was not unpleasant, not my choice, but I unwound and found I liked the warmth of her body on my back.

Chapter 21

Edmund's Tale: Freeland Fells and Dales

That night we made camp, for the following day we would start the climb over the fells and down into the dales of the Freelands.

Swein gathered us to him. 'There is much danger all about us here. We are well guarded but no one is to go out of sight. When the womenfolk go behind the bushes to be private there must be more than one man to stand nearby on guard. Our other guards will not come so close. Let us guard by pairs, Asgar with Edmund and I with Arian.'

'I am an old man,' said Arian, a fact of which he reminded us constantly. 'If we are attacked I cannot fight to defend.'

'Do not fear,' said Swein, 'for I can fight well enough for three, but I only have eyes to the front so your task will be to watch my back.'

'I am too old for danger, I will not forgive Wyman, I should not be here.'

The womenfolk looked at him with worry in their eyes.

I leaned close to him and spoke in a whisper. 'Shut up, shut up or I will close my hands around your throat and squeeze until your breath stops and shuts off your bleating, aged, fool voice. If you are afraid, keep it secret or I will give you something to be afraid of!'

He looked at me, his expression part fear; part smirk. Because of my age he loathed me; that much was plain. I cared nothing for his hatred, though I was glad he was not now sat behind me. Not that I thought he would have had the courage to try to harm me, but I felt my own dislike become hatred. So great was this that I feared it, for I felt there was risk enough in our journey without danger within our gang. Even so, it would have given me great pleasure to strike him down with my staff and still his bleating voice forever.

The ground beneath our feet became steeper and ahead we could see it rising through the trees. This was the first of the fells. Free because the Norman's tyranny did not rule there. We were now in the Freelands of the outlaws. This became clear within the space of a morning's walk. As the sun was overhead the path ahead was blocked by a single man clad in the furs and ripped cloth of the outlaw.

'Have you food?' he asked.

'We have not,' said Swein.

'Then you must walk,' said the outlaw, 'for we must eat your horses.'

'That we will not,' said Swein, 'for we have a long way to go and the women cannot walk that far.'

'Where do you walk to?'

'To Yorvik.'

'That indeed is far, and there are Normans on the way.'

'How so for these are the Freelands?'

'They are many, we many less, it is better to hide unless victory is certain.'

'What makes them risk the fells?' said Swein.

'They are led by some servant of the new king. They are seeking a father, a husband, his wife and their child. They come well provided for to risk these lands. It is the king's wish.'

My heart sank. It could only be Hugh the Vavassour. He had guessed where we were headed and was ahead of us, blocking our way. More than ever I wished Swein had allowed me to kill the devil while I'd had the chance.

'You will find that we are many, although unseen,' said Swein. 'Also we have with us Arian, a follower of Wyman of the Mere, to pass the tale that we are his friends and offense to us would be offense to him.'

'I know how many you are my friend. Do you think we have not counted your folk amongst the trees? We do not wish to lose our lives or earn the ire of Wyman for a mangy horse or two, but we are truly hungry. Give us one horse and you may pass.'

'Let us have an understanding. We know this servant of the king if his name be Hugh.'

'That it is.'

'Join with us. All our men are bowmen and skilled in the woods. Let us together destroy these Normans. Their horses will become yours. Then when we are near the walls of Yorvik all our horses shall be yours also.'

We stood listening to this when Wilda thrust forward and screamed the one word. 'No!'

We stopped and looked at her.

'Please,' she begged, 'do not kill Hugh, give him to me.'

I understood her and my fears for my mother punched me in my gut. 'Heed her,' I said, 'please, do not kill Hugh.' I turned and took her by the shoulders and looked into her eyes. She looked back at me, her eyes slitted in a face of stone. 'I will help you kill him,' I said.

She nodded slowly and then, in a long, drawn out hiss, spoke just the one word: 'Yes.' And I knew that for Hugh

Vavassour, death would come as a mercy.

'I also must help you,' said Swein, 'for it is my task in life to bring all Normans to know Hel in this life before they pass to Hel in the afterlife.'

'You are most welcome,' said Wilda, 'for you know what is in my mind. I find comfort in your task.'

'If it is God's will, we will deliver him to you,' said the outlaw and he turned and spoke into the woods, just speaking, not shouting. 'We join to destroy the Normans, pass the word to take the leader alive.'

I heard nothing, but for whatever he listened or looked he must have heard or seen, for he turned from the woods and spoke no more.

Swein walked back up the path and passed from sight into the trees. He returned in a short time and nodded that all was in order.

'We will wait here,' he said, 'they will call when all is fulfilled.'

I spoke to the man I had thought of so far as "the stranger" or "the outlaw". 'Sir, may we know your name?'

'You may indeed, if I may know yours and those with you.'

'I am Edmund of Lutgaresburh,' I said.

'And I am Swein Icgson,' said Swein.

'I am Frida and this is Gytha,' said Edith.

'I am Asgar, and this is Wilda, we are also of Lutgaresburh.'

From your speech you men are Wessex folk. Was King Harold your earl?'

'He was indeed,' said Asgar.

'Thank you, I am Aldan Hamal. I have been a captive of your earl's brother, Tostig Godwinson. My family wished to ransom me, but in vain. Cold and wet and hungry was the deep hole they kept me in, until the fall of Tostig found me freed. I will not weep for the fall of the house of Godwin. As

Tostig fell so I rose up. But the sins of Tostig were God's grace against those of the Normans. They will never take me alive and I will never submit to the Bastard. My hall is burned and all destroyed, all I loved are dead. I live only to kill Normans.'

'In that our hearts are joined,' said Swein.

As our guards had gone ahunting Normans we ourselves kept a watch so that we might not be taken by surprise. From the other side of the clearing where we slept, Aldan Hamal also kept watch, but we did not trust him enough, so while the womenfolk slept, Asgar and I took turns to hide beneath a bush and watch over them. Aldan seemed to understand this and not feel dishonoured by it.

I was off watch and falling asleep when I was brought awake by faint shouts, screams and the sound of clashing steel, dying away to silence again.

We all sat wondering at the outcome. Our leaders had shown no doubt that our attack would end with the destruction of the Normans and so it turned out. For within the time it took to get up, gather together and settle our fear, so our men returned. I looked at them with some interest, for the rumour of their presence within the trees and a handful of arrows were all I knew of them. They were true Silvatici for their clothes were the colour of tree trunks and leaves, and about their hats were sprigs of twig and leaf. By their sides hung half-filled arrow quivers and across their belts from right to left they carried the full seax, longer, heavier than the ordinary seax. Although not with the reach of the langseax, these were nonetheless long enough to engage with Norman cavalry swords.

Across their backs the Silvatici carried Welsh longbows. That not all the Normans had fallen to their arrows was told by the fierce clashing of metal that had woken me from my nap.

Chapter 22

Edmund's Tale: Hugh Vavassour

Within the mass of these men there was a toing and froing and the sound of angry voices. From out of this din was thrust a figure, arms bound behind his back. My guts churned in fear. It was our pursuer, the evil Hugh, killer of children; murderer of women; hacker of men. But I need not have feared, for driving him was Swein Icgson.

'I am the servant of the king, about the king's business, free me or you will feel his wrath, which is terrible.'

'I think all here have felt his terrible wrath already,' said Swein. 'That is what brings us here. We cannot punish him for he is not yet in our hands. Should he ever be, he would shiver.'

Swein looked directly at me, 'The Normans are all dead,' he said. 'We have kept only this one as friend Wilda asked. We will truss him and then each he has injured can speak their will. The choices are these. We give him mercy and a quick death or we give him the death he deserves: Hel on Earth and a slow death. Each of you that have felt the evil of this man should have your say.

Wilda stepped forward.

'He killed my husband and boy child. He cut the hands off my girl child, she had but five years, she died of the horror of it. He has not earned a quick death.'

'He knows that which he could only have gained from my mother,' I said. 'Only great evil could have wrung it from her. Tell me, Vavassour, what of the hall at Lutgaresburh? What can you tell me of the woman who holds it?'

He looked at me and laughed and in his hatred knew no caution. 'What should I know for I killed so many: men, women, children — some quick, some slow. If she knew aught that I wanted to know she would have told me,' and he spat at me, a great wad of snot. 'If you hope for good put it from your mind, for I burned the hall and all in it, that much I remember. It made a fine sight on All Souls Eve.'

'I damn him to Hel,' said I to Swein. Later I thought that perhaps Hugh's hatred had fathered cruel invention, for by All Souls the family and the household should have been in Scaeptersburh.

Swein nodded. 'I damn all Normans to Hel, but servants of the king must go through Hel to get there. I would not have them gain God's mercy. What of you my lady?'

'I will not speak,' said Edith, 'nor will Gytha. It is not seemly.'

'The man is evil, as was his treatment of Ulf, he does not deserve mercy,' said Asgar.

'I know him not,' said Aldan Hamal, 'I stand aside for those who do.'

Facing his accusers Hugh cried out, 'Let me free! Let me go, I serve the king, any harm to me will be punished more than you can ever imagine.'

But now, to my delight and I think the delight of all he had wounded, we could hear the fear in his voice. Gone the scorn, gone the insolence and gone the sneer of power over the powerless. Now he felt the fear his victims had felt as he bestowed his kindness on them.

Swein drew his heavy seax. He seized Hugh by the back of the neck and forced him to his knees and then with the flat of the blade and the strength of his mighty arms he broke both Hugh's left and right arms at the upper bone. Hugh howled with the shock, and I hope foreboding, at what he now knew awaited him.

While the king's servant lay howling on the ground Swein hoisted his backpack, delving inside and drawing out a length of light chain. He drew Hugh's wrists together, bringing forth screams of pain. He knotted the end of the chain about both wrists threw it over a low branch on the tree, wrapping the end around a lower branch and then, with a mighty heave, dragged Hugh up to hang by his broken arms, his feet a foot length from the ground. He secured the chain with a simple hitch.

Swein hadn't finished. Again he drew his heavy seax and hit the upper bones of Hugh's legs, breaking them and sending him swinging and screaming. I lost my taste for vengeance at that and started to feel I might spew.

Casting about the forest floor Swein brought together a small pile of dry wood and kindling which he piled beneath the Vavassour's dangling feet. I began to understand what he had in mind to do next and I would have walked away but saw that Edith stood firm. I could not bring myself to prove less unshrinking than she and so, my stomach heaving, I stood firm also.

Swein brought out flint and steel and set light to the kindling. Hugh, his face beaded with sweat from the pain of his broken limbs looked down and saw the grisly end that Swein planned for him. He began to beg and scream.

'I am the king's man! The king's man! You will all suffer; all you and yours. He will be terrible in his vengeance, let me down. Now!' This last a hoarse and drawn out bellow laden with fear as the first smoke from the kindling drifted up past his face.

For all the effect his bellowing had he might as well have sung a cradlesong. The wild woodsmen stood watchful, wolf-like, the only look on some faces, a grin.

The wood caught fire and being dry flared up with little smoke. I had heard that the only mercy of the fire was the smoke; that those who breathed deeply of it might die from it before the pain overwhelmed their will and they lost all dignity. Even that small mercy was to be denied Hugh. And so he lost all dignity and he screamed. He screamed as Ulf had screamed. He screamed as the axe-hacked children and men and women had screamed in Lutgaresburh. He screamed in satisfaction of horrors he had dealt in countless untold tales. He writhed in vain to avoid the flames and as he did so he heightened the pain of his broken limbs and screamed louder still.

Wilda smiled and hugged herself with glee. The fire was slow burning and Swein fed it to keep it licking higher until eventually the screams stopped and Hugh was no more.

'That,' said Swein, 'is how I deal with Normans.' And he laughed. 'Now he may have God's mercy, if it pleases Him to show it.'

Edith, calm as always had watched the screaming man twist and turn above the flames. I could see that even she, hardened to death as she was, felt disturbed by the sight and sounds. Gytha crouched down, eyes tight shut, her fingers in her ears.

When the sounds fell silent and Hugh hung quiet from his chains, a blackened corpse stinking of burnt meat, Swein spoke.

'Ah me, it is a shame that there is no way we can send this thing to the Bastard. If we leave it on the road as a warning he will punish the nearest town, even though outside the Freelands and innocent. It is not fitting that any more deaths should arise from such shit.'

The Vavassour's remains were lowered and left for the carrion crows. The chain, cool now, was coiled and stowed in its bag, perhaps ready for the next time.

Swein stood out of earshot and spoke with the woodsmen and they turned and entered the treeline then melted from sight.

He returned to us and said, 'we will keep watch, but it seems that all the Normans sent to pursue us have perished. The man, Arian, has spread the words of Wyman; we are welcome here as are our own woodsmen. A guide will go with us to ease our way.

He turned to Arian and untied his ropes. 'Thank you and thank your leader for your good service. You may return to your home in the woods.'

True to himself, bleating right up to the end, Arian slipped from his horse, 'Horseback when I'm useful but walk home when you've wrung me dry. Have you any idea how long it will take me to walk home and the risk I must take?'

Edith nudged her horse alongside him as he stood casting black looks all about. She reached down and passed a coin into his hand.

'You have rendered me good service freeman Arian. Here is money that you may buy food if there is any.'

He looked down at the silver in his hand and then up at Edith. 'Thank you my lady. These are rough men you are with for I see you are highborn; take care lest they deal you badly. And keep your silver hidden.'

With a last look of scorn at our company, he turned and plunged into the woods and was never seen by us again, I am happy to say.

AD 1070-72 York and Ely

Chapter 23

Edmund's Tale: The Harrowing

In the fells amongst outlaws with no priest to remind us of our saints' days it came as a shock to me to find that we had passed Christmas by without notice, and that it was after Yule and the year was now that of Our Lord, one thousand and seventy.

As we rode, Edith urged her mount forwards until she rode next to Swein. I followed, moving up to ride on her other side, Gytha trailing behind us.

'Why do you kill all Normans so painfully,' asked Edith, 'for I know they are not all bad? I have met with kindness and help from some. Although they are soldiers some milites are noble.'

Swein looked into her face, his eyes bitter, like chips of tree-hung frost. He turned, tugged at her sleeve and said, 'Follow me; it is not far, for this hereabouts is my country.'

When we had ridden off to the right for an hour we came to the burned ruins of a hall. 'Do you see that? That was my hall.' Waving his arm to take in all before us, Swein turned to Edith. 'I had a Hide from my father, which he had from his, from father to son back to the days it came to a kinsman who served Cnut as huscarl. I was a farmer, I had submitted to the king through his thegn, I caused trouble for no one, I did not care who ruled, only to make the land prosper and feed me and mine.

'I was at market when the Norman castlemen came spreading over the land. It was a good market day and with a fat purse I rode home with my herdsmen, my heart full of joy.

'The milites had been told to clear the mountain lands of farmers who could give support to the outlaws. These were the men of Robert de Comines, further south than they should have been. We saw the smoke from far off. We hurried, risking our steeds in our haste.' He paused, a faraway look in his eyes.

'The women and children were dead, the blood on the legs of all but the youngest told of rape before the merciful knife. Everything of wood was burned. All the beasts slaughtered and burned beyond use on great fires the milites had built for the purpose. On these also went all the stored crops and seed. Even the scythes and ploughs put beyond use, the wood frames burned and the metal blades smashed. Then, as if even this was not enough, they had salted the land and destroyed its fruitfulness The Normans killed everyone they could find and those they could not they saved for starvation.

This they now do throughout the whole of the North, all the lands about York and all the lands to Durham are at risk. The king's army advances towards York and as it passes it leaves behind wasteland and the dead. They are destroying the land so the people will starve.

'You wonder why I kill them without mercy? Killing is my mercy for I do not have the time to do as I would wish.' He paused again, a bitter smile twisting his lips. 'Except for those I bring to the Freelands in the mountains where all we farmers-turned-reavers live. There I can take my time.'

His mouth set in a grim face curved upwards in a mirthless smile. 'As for starvation, there are nests of Normans everywhere and so we steal their food, their gold and their lives and what we do not eat we give to those with nothing. Many have died from the Normans' evil, I cannot count how many have starved or will starve this winter, whole settlements, whole towns, many, many thousands; so many that the North will be empty of folk and the land gone back to wasteland. In towns, I have heard, those they kill lie rotting in the streets for there is no one living to bury them. Many flee to Malcolm Canmore of Scotland, others south into Mercia. We do what we can now. One day we will cross the sea and we will pay them back, if it takes one hundred years.'

Gazing about her, Edith said nothing, but I could see from her expression that Swein's words had affected her deeply. I shuddered, I was glad he was our protector for I should not like to cross the lawless mountains were Swein our adversary. Small wonder the Norman bishops moved overland with a small army about them. Small wonder the Norman ruled abbeys were armed camps with their own troops of soldiers.

Much as I had hated Hugh, over the next few nights as we rode towards Yorvik my rest was disturbed by nightmares, full of screams and dark things I could not see. Yet as my nights were disturbed so my days were peaceful for I knew we were well guarded and there were no Normans in pursuit. Only the villages we passed through raised up the horrors by day. All life was gone, all were dead and the bodies lay stinking on the ground; sometimes half eaten by wolves and wild dogs that loped away as we approached.

Within days we came down from the high ground and started our ride through grassy dales. There were no beasts grazing and where oats had been growing the fields were black where crops burned and salt had been strewn on the ground. It was as if the Devil had passed by, as if the end of the world had come.

'Why?' I asked Swein, too choked to utter more than that one word.

'The folk rose up against the Bastard Norman duke who

calls himself king and demands that we bow to him. Here in the North where many are Danes we did not even bow to a Danish king. Cnut ruled because he changed little except the crown. Men held their land and paid customary taxes and got on with their lives. The Bastard wants to take our good land from us and give it to his lickspittles. The great English lords who keep their hoards within the abbeys for safekeeping, fear their riches will be stolen, for the king has put his Frenchmen in the abbeys and his greed knows no law, either of man or God. Also, he knows that if we have no coin then we cannot buy aid from the Welsh or the Scots, the Cumbrians or the Danes.

'And so, from fear, the great lords rise up. I had made my submission. I honoured my word and did nothing, for all the good it did me. Now I live to kill them. William is sore afraid I think, for the Danes have landed here to aid the rebellion. They have taken Yorvik castle; they made great killing of the French. Earl Waltheof Siwardson of Northumbria hewed off many heads I have heard. Therein lies our danger, for the king's army now spreads across the land. He thinks if the land is destroyed then none can live here to defy him. What we must do is avoid the army and get to Yorvik before it falls to the Normans, for the Danish fleet is there and will carry you all hence for coin. Tonight we cross the Wharfe. There is a ford, but all eyes are on Yorvik, the king will spare no soldiers to guard a ford where none will be passing but Normans. All order comes unravelled, for the Danes hold king's sheriff, William Malet, and his family captive in the castle of Yorvik. Without him to shape all things, much slips by. This is good for us for the king cannot be everywhere.'

Edith touched his arm, 'Did you say the sheriff was William Malet?'

'I did my Lady. Do you know of him?'

'I know him to be a good man and more than half an Englishman, although in service to the Bastard.'

'Not for much longer my lady, for when the king approaches, the Danes will surely kill his sheriff.'

'That would be a great pity for I owe him much.'

Swein looked upon her with a steady gaze, then spoke, 'If we enter the castle before William arrives and you get to take ship with the Danes, perhaps you can speak in defence of the Norman sheriff, and being a lady of great quality it may be they will grant you his life.'

'Perhaps,' said Edith. 'And that would be true justice and a great thoughtfulness to me. We shall see.'

Chapter 24

**Edmund's Tale: The Castle, Earl Waltheof
and William Malet**

Bowdyn looked about him. There was silence in the Cold Cott some perhaps enthralled by the unfolding of the story, some still silenced by the Vavasour Hugh's cruel end.

'Let me be clear what is happening here. The great Lords, fearful for their treasure have joined with the Danes who have come in their numbers to retake the land from William the Norman. You must know that your land had been ruled by a Danish king, Knut the Great, and had been part of a great northern empire. There were many of Danish blood living in England who William dispossessed as he did the English who had settled for hundreds of years. Thus the Danes of England had sought help from their native land and king Sweyn Estrithson had sent aid to sweep the Normans into the sea. These Danes had joined the English in storming the great city of York and the Norman castle had fallen, but not before the Normans had set light to the town. William Malet, he who, out of honour, had given aid to Edith, who was the sheriff of York, had been locked in a dungeon and all his men and the castlemen slain. I will let Edmund continue with the story for a while, if you are willing and then we will take to our beds. We will meet again after the next church service.'

There were some cries of protest from those who found the story preferable to sleep. This died away to a waiting silence and then the voice of young Edmund spoke out.

Now, our speed becoming the key to life or death, the race began. Edith needed to get to the castle whilst the Danish shipmen were there so that she could flee by ship to Denmark, and perhaps also save William Malet's life. She needed to fulfil these tasks before the king and his army arrived. The risk she ran in this was great. I could not bear to think on her fate if she fell into the king's hands, the thought of it made me shiver.

Thus with half the day remaining, where before we had walked, now we trotted; trot became canter and canter became a gallop. We slowed our blowing horses to a fast walk to ford the Wharfe and to rest them and as Swein had foreseen, there was no guard. The milestone at the ford, ancient and worn as it was and carved in foreign words told us, so said Swein, that we were thirty miles from Yorvik. The sun was not one part in four from its peak and so we knew we would be at the gates of the town before sunset.

As we expected, the sun was still above the world's edge when we arrived at our journey's end: Yorvik. Our guide held up his hand to halt us at the bridge, looking for Norman guards before we went across.

'It seems to be clear, my lord,' he said to Swein. I will leave you here.' Before Swein could utter a word of gratitude, the guide had turned his horse and set off back the way we had come.

The bridge was still standing, but Yorvik was not, the

smoke still rose from its burning. Before fleeing in panic the Normans had burned the city. Only the castles now stood, garrisoned by Englishmen and Danes.

We made for the biggest of these to find the gate was guarded. We could not announce who Edith was as we judged it best to keep that secret up to the end. It did not matter, for Swein rode up to the guard and said, 'I am Swein, son of Icg, and we want to speak with the castellan.'

His name was enough. The guard bowed, spoke to his commander, who looked up startled and then with a word to his men turned and ran through the gate and into the castle. Asgar explained to me later that if William came and the rebels ran, they had only two choices: they could escape by sea or to the fells. If there were no ships, then to become outlaws in the fells they would need Swein Sicgson's good will. He was known here to be a king of the Freelands.

We dismounted and stood waiting. In a short time the commander of the gate returned with the castellan who waved us through the gate. 'Lord Swein,' he said, as we led our horses inside the bailey, 'how can I be of service?'

'I have with me a great lady; she wishes two things. The first is rather strange. She will ask you to release the sheriff, William Malet. He has been of great service to her and to King Harold. I can tell you no more than that. Although he is oath bound to serve William the Bastard, Malet is a good Englishman.'

'Who is this lady that asks the impossible?'

'That is secret and must remain so, but...' Swein glanced back at Edith, who nodded. '...but as we will not be here long, I will reveal it to you if you give me your sworn oath that you will tell it to no other.'

'You have my word, I so swear it.'

Swein leaned over and whispered into the castellan's ear.

The man gaped, looked quickly at Edith then glancing around at the castle guards, gave the slightest of bows and murmured, 'At your service my lady.' He turned back to Swein.

'And what is the second thing, Lord Swein?'

'My lady, her daughter and her escort,' Swein waved a hand at Asgar, Wilda and me, 'must go into exile. She needs to talk to King Sweyn Estrithson of Denmark to take passage on his ship.'

The castellan looked stricken. 'I regret that I cannot bring that about. The Danes, seeing the city burned and having nowhere to shelter for the winter, have left to build a Burh at Axholme. There are no ships bound for Denmark from Yorvik. Those folk still here may flee or stay, but the Bastard will not be kind when he takes the castle back, as he surely will. For myself I am going to Ely. There is a man, Hereward, who stands against the Normans and shelters behind mud and swamp. There lies the last place of safety in all of England.'

'Ah me, ah me; life is but risk and sorrow. I must be advised for I fear all my choices may be bad,' said Edith.

It grieved me to see my lady so cast down. All through our travels she had been strong and full of hope, but now it seemed her hopes were crushed, distress and exhaustion showed plain on her face.

The castellan spoke up. 'I would be honoured to guide you and your companions my lady. There is much coming and going of Danes I am told, with God's help you will find a ship somewhere to carry you to sanctuary.'

This news about the Danes almost struck me down. Everything during our whole journey so far had been working towards boarding a Danish ship bound for the court of King

Sweyn of Denmark. I moved back to where the castle guards stood waiting out of earshot and said to the nearest, 'Tell me, what is the name of the castellan who speaks so kindly towards the lady?'

'Why sir, that kindly man, as you call him, is Earl Waltheof Siwardson also known as "Armstrong" said the guard. 'Kindly he may seem but he is a dangerous man. Why, they say that singlehandedly he beheaded one hundred Normans with his sharp axe as they passed through the castle gate!'

'Is that true?' I asked for it seemed far-fetched to me.

'Well his skald sings it so,' he shrugged.

'Then we will be very safe with such a man as our guide.'

The sentry shrugged again. 'Like all dangerous men he makes many enemies. But he still lives and many of them do not.'

Waltheof set off and we followed him as he led us from the bailey, up the steps and through the great studded door into the feasting hall of the motte, its walls still bedecked with the woven arms of the now dead Norman milites. I approached this wolf-fierce axeman, for dangerous or not I wanted to know about the place where he said he wished to take us.

'It seems, my lord, that wherever we go the king or his minions are hard at our heels. Where is this Ely and will it truly be safe for my lady? Please forgive me for addressing you so, but I would not have those I must protect put at risk in any way.'

Earl Waltheof stared at me as if he had found me sticking to the bottom of his shoe.

Edith saw, as she saw everything. 'Lord Waltheof, I also ask your pardon. I should have introduced my escort to you. This is Edmund who, although young, is one of the truest of my friends. He has killed in my defence and I know he cares greatly for the safety of my daughter and me, as does Thegn Asgar, who was constable to my husband.'

Waltheof's expression changed. He nodded at Asgar, who with Wilda had moved to stand by the fire. He turned back to me and said, 'Then if you are indeed a blooded warrior in this lady's service I will be happy to talk about where I think it best she should go, but it will save my breath if I talk with the others of your party all together at one time. If you will just wait here a moment...' With no more explanation he turned and hurried away.

While he was gone, Swein Sicgson took his leave of us, for he was anxious to get back to the Freelands and now that my lady was in safe hands felt his task was done. He went down on one knee before her and I saw her lay her hands upon his head, though she was speaking too softly for me to overhear her words of gratitude.

'By the time Earl Waltheof returned, Asgar and Wilda had fallen asleep on a fireside bench. I envied them; even for what little sleep they'd had and wished I had the same. Nevertheless, I woke them and waited while they came back to this world from whatever realm of peace they had enjoyed.

'Frida needs your counsel, Father,' I said to Asgar, aware of listening ears. 'Did you hear Earl Waltheof's offer to help us?'

Not yet fully awake, Asgar nodded, said gruffly, 'I did.'

'Earl Waltheof is evidently a very violent, murderous man – he killed a hundred Normans in one day, so his sentry said – if true we could not prevail against him, but if we go with him we will be delivering ourselves into his hands. And yet... and yet he offers to guide us to a place of safety where there may be a ship to take our lady away. She waits with him now. We must go to her then he will tell us his plan and we will advise our lady what we think is safe for her and Gytha to do.'

When we were all gathered together sat at board, Waltheof sat facing us and began his tale.

'There is a place in Anglian country, in Harold's old earldom of East Anglia, where a thegn, practiced in the ways of Norman warfare from fighting in Flanders and other places, now resists and will not submit to the Norman Bastard. This man is Hereward. He is the protector of Peterburh Abbey, son of a brother to the dead Abbot Brand.

'The land is filled with lakes, riven with streams surrounded with treacherous swamps and this man is master of them all. William cannot come at him except by water, and only in flat-bottomed boats that draw little water at that, and we know he has none; he has no knowledge of the fens and no sailors to sail them. And so we will be safe there. But there is more.

'In the safety of the fens true Englishmen and our Danish allies will come together. If enough gather there William may leave us in peace, a small part of the old England of peace and liberty where men might live as Englishmen.'

Waltheof paused then spoke directly to Edith, 'should that happen, my lady, perhaps you might not leave for foreign lands but stay as queen in your own lands. I have heard that your family and their holdings are not far from where we go.'

'That is true, Lord Waltheof, but unless the Bastard is dead I shall never feel safe in these islands.'

'Then let us plan how we may get you oversea,' said Waltheof. 'There is a road that leads from Yorvik to Cambridge; it is an ancient road, Ermine Street by name. We will follow that road until we come to the river and then we will change direction to Peterburh. If the Normans are not already there then Abbot Brand's people, true Englishmen, will give us shelter and pass us into the care of his nephew.

Once Hereward has us we will be as safe as anyone can be these days.

There was the sound of movement in the room next to ours. Earl Waltheof smiled. 'And now my lady,' he said, 'I have a surprise for you.'

He got up from his chair and held out his hand to Edith. She took it, a smile already on her face for she guessed what he had in mind. Waltheof called out, 'Ready'. The door to the next room opened and a man was thrust through. He bore signs of battle or rough treatment for his face was bruised and blood streaked and there was blood on the sleeves of his filthy shirt.

He stopped, looked around the room as if wondering at the purpose of the crowd standing watching him, perhaps his death their aim. And then he saw Edith and his lips curved in a shining smile like the sun coming out from behind a cloud.

'My lady!' he said, falling to his knees. 'You are safe, God's blessing on you and all who have preserved you.'

'God's blessing on you too, William Malet, my brave miles nobiles,' said Edith. 'I have come to release you and your family.'

The sunshine faded. 'My wife and my family are already gone. My wife told my foes that she could not stand the shame of being married to a sheriff who had lost the county the king had given into his charge. "It were better that Waltheof had taken off his head with the rest," she said, and begged them to let her go. As they needed someone to carry the news to William that Northumbria, Yorkshire and the Danes awaited him, they let her go and kept me as hostage. They hoped that he would retreat to London and give them time to rebuild defences here. But their cunning was in vain for still he comes on and the Danes will leave, for they dread a full battle with William. Raiding the coast suits them better.'

He paused and then looked up at Edith quickly, as if a thought had come to him. 'But my lady, you should not be here, William comes and he seeks you. You must leave. Now!'

'And so I shall my friend, for Earl Waltheof takes me to safety in the marshes about Peterburh Abbey.'

'My lady, I beg you, take me with you. I can fight; I can defend you. The king has forgiven me once over the loss of Harold's remains. He will not forgive me thrice.'

'Thrice?'

'He believes I let myself be duped by you, my lady. To that I have added the crime of losing all the shire of Yorvik, and once again I am letting you slip through my hands.'

A small frown creased Edith's brow. She nodded then glanced at Earl Waltheof before returning her gaze to the man who knelt at her feet. 'It is not for me to say. What would you do once we get there? Will you join those who would fight against the Bastard?'

'I cannot, for I am oath sworn to William. To abandon him is one thing; to do harm to him or his is another. Leave word here that I have pursued your party wherever you flee and I shall still be accounted loyal. Let me go oversea with you, lady, let me guard you on your way.'

Watching Malet's bruised face, I was torn two ways by his plea. I hurt inside that he should also be Edith's protector, for that was my duty. On the other hand he was a warrior and trained as a Norman miles is trained, he would be more useful than I with my iron-shod stick. Leaving my heart pangs to one side I knew that having him as guard would mean greater safety for my lady. Also, he could entertain her with his talk, something I could never hope to do. In the balance then, I thought it better he should come, no matter that I should then be only the servant and he the friend.

Asgar now spoke, seeing clearly the need for speed, for not only must we be clear of the castle but also well away from the army heading towards us.

'Earl Waltheof.'

'Marshal Asgar?'

'The time is at hand when we must leave here if we are to escape the king. I think we should go now. Will you accept William Malet as one of our party?'

'Indeed, all swords in our lady's defence are welcome.'

Edith made a small movement of her hand and William Malet got up from his knees and bowed to her. Earl Waltheof then pointed at the board. 'Imagine this is the ground we must cover.' He touched a knot mark on the wood, 'we are here. The king's army is moving from the south, from London. We must go to here, to Peterburh Abbey.' He moved his finger to touch on a stain on the rough wooden board. 'As you can see, there is little between our line and the king's right flank. We must go with great caution, moving by night and sleeping in cold ditches by day. Pray that it does not snow for our comfort's sake. We do not know when he will be here, but be sure that he will come with all speed. God help us all if he finds us.'

I wanted to ask about a matter I did not understand. If the Danes were not to fight, what had been the point in overthrowing the castles and earning the king's wrath? I said as much.

Waltheof laid it out for me. 'When the English of Northumbria and Mercia joined with the Danes we sent to the Marches and to the West Country to rise at the same time. But when the Normans burned the town, they destroyed our plans. The Danes will not fight the Norman horse troops, they don't know how, no more do we. The plan was to take Yorvik and be warm and secure while outside William and his men

264

starved and froze their apples off through the winter. We would rest and grow stronger, he and his would grow weaker, many horses would die and in the spring we would strike. But, we cannot shelter in a burned down town. The Danes now wish to leave; they will not meet the Normans in the open in battle. Without them we do not have the strength to meet with and defeat William. You see many small outbreaks, but there is no one to bind them together, no leader that folk believe in who can raise the whole country in arms and throw the Normans into the sea.

'Our fighting men outnumber them one hundred to one, but there is no one they will follow. Look at Harold's sons: in olden days they would be the Athelings, the rulers in waiting, with greater rights than the Bastard. Yet when they raised troops and landed in Sumersaete they were driven off by an English lickspittle leading English warriors. We hate the Bastard; grieve for our lost land and freedoms, but without a Harold or an Alfred to unite us we waste our life and strength in little revolts that William's army brushes aside as a horse tail brushes at flies. We are doomed and until things change we must run. After my deeds here William will surely have my head. And so we go to the last man who holds land securely against him. That man is Hereward.'

Waltheof turned to William Malet, 'you must decide for your English mother or your Norman father. If you come with us will you be with us against William, to defy your oath and know it is your death if taken? Or will you decide for your father? In which case, we must lock you back in your cell until your master unlocks you. You may earn favour by telling him where we go. It will not matter to us for he knows there is now but one place that we can go.'

'I have said that I am with you,' said Malet. 'I will not fight

William, but I am with the Lady Edith and will stand with brave Edmund and Asgar to protect her against anyone who seeks to do her harm. It is in my mind to pass oversea with her and be quit of William forever.'

'How so Lord Malet?' said Asgar, 'The Bastard has held you high in his favour as Sheriff of Yorkshire and may do so again.'

Malet shook his head, 'I am minded of something the castellan of Castle Montagud said when I was sent there in search of Queen Edith, before I was sent to Yorvik and Hugh Vavassour took over the pursuit ' he started and frowned as if a sudden bad thought had come unbidden into his mind.

'I had forgotten Hugh, my lady, he it is that seeks you, have you heard aught of him?'

Edith looked coolly at him, calm as always. 'I believe sir that he got his due reward on Earth and that we need not worry about him ever more.'

William Malet stared at her, struggling to find her meaning. Finally he said, 'Then he is no more?'

'That is so Lord William.'

'Then I am gladdened to hear it. He was a devil without chains in Lutgaresburh and all around about. It was after that when I spoke with the castellan and the castle builder, Humphrey de Tilleul, known as Bigo, and he told me he was leaving. Bigo was castellan of Hastings, had made the castle in Normandy then brought it over in pieces and put it together near the battle site. He could look forward to great rewards, but he was giving it all up and going back to Tilleul. I asked him why and he said that his wife missed him and wanted him home. I did not believe him and said so.

'He said, "I am a builder of castles not a hewer of meat. This adventure of England is too rich for me. I am for my home where I can sleep without screams ringing in my ears." Then he grasped me by my arm and held me in his gaze. "Let me tell you something I have learned," he said. "Always when power lies on the ground for any who can stoop to pick it up, you will find it in the hands of the wicked and cruel. You know we Normans are not all like Hugh or Geoffrey of Coutances. I am a Norman and am sickened by these times. I am leaving, I cannot stay, my wife needs me at Tilleul, so I say, and so I shall go."

'Letting go of my arm, Bigo shrugged and looked down at his feet. "I have built for Robert before, I know him well. Do not blame him for the shadow fallen on this fair land. A good warrior he is but not cruel. Look no further than Geoffrey, for through him the Devil works in Holy Mother Church and Hugh is his Lucifer, his demon." And with this the castellan fell silent. After a while, looking up and seeing me still standing there he waved me away. "Excuse me my lord, but I have much to do for Robert before I go."'

William Malet looked about him at us listeners and then at Edith before continuing.

'He was fair spoken in all he said, this matter of England is not what many of us looked forward to. We came to England for two things, the priests for a crusade and the miles for land and then there were some, not Normans, who came for coin. In our minds there would be a battle, we would win, and the riches of the country would be ours. That battle was three years ago and still we struggle to subdue. And if the screams of Lutgaresburh disturbed Bigo's dreams he is lucky he misses what is already started or he would never sleep again. The screams that are coming will reach to Heaven and if God does not answer then there is no God. Either way, I do not want to be here for the answer to that question.'

We all looked at him as if thunderstruck.

'Please tell us what you mean,' said Edith.

'William is coming to destroy this land. For if no one can live here then none can take up spears against him. I have heard him plan it. He will sweep through this land and he will kill everyone he can find, men, women and children. He will kill and burn all the livestock; he will burn all the stored crops and all the seed for the year to come. He will burn all of wood, he will smash all of steel or iron, there will be no ploughs, no oxen to pull them, no forks, no mattocks, no spades. There will be nothing to delve the land even if there is hidden seed to plant. Then he will salt the land so that even nettles will not grow.'

'This is madness,' said Edith in despair. 'All the people will die they will starve and die. No child of God would visit such horror on even guilty people, but these are innocent.'

'Your mighty English lords do not know what they let in by not riding to Harold's rescue, my lady,' said Malet. 'William is a devil; there is no crime he will not visit upon those who oppose him. Those who do not do his bidding bring out this devil as if from the mouth of hell itself.'

'What can we do, what must we do?' said Edith, her voice no longer calm but filled with the pain she felt for the people.

'Do? Why nothing, we can do nothing. It is already too late for that. If you could have held the Danes steady, if you had bowmen, if Yorvik had not burned then you might have done something... if, if. You might even have thrown William into the sea, as you would have done had your husband had the Northumbrians and Welsh bowmen at Hastings. Now there is nothing to do except escape and shut our ears to the screams of a dying country.'

Edith turned to the rest of us. 'What do you think?'

'He is right,' said Asgar, 'there is nothing we can do against William, what he wants he will take. We must keep you from him my lady. We have no choice but to flee.'

Gytha clung to her mother's mantle and said nothing. Wilda sat looking at the ground and taking no part. I felt that I did not know enough to say anything and turned away, looking out of the window into the darkness.

'Then that is what we must do,' said Edith. 'Flee down Ermine Street, you said Earl Waltheof?'

'No,' said William Malet before Waltheof could answer. 'That you must not do, for William will send gallopers up the road to spread out and cut off those who run north. He will not order them to talk or take prisoners. There will be only one order and that will be to kill. We must avoid these gallopers like the plague.'

'Then what do you suggest?' Edith was now clearly taking charge, yet seeking advice as a wise king or queen must.

'Gather round,' said William Malet. We ringed the table and as Waltheof had done, he used its grained surface to draw a map with his finger.

'We are on the River Ouse, the Ouse runs down to the sea. On the north bank we have Myton Wyke, on the south bank Grimsby. Past Myton it will be too dangerous for anything smaller than a ship if the wind blows from the east, so we cannot go past there. A rough sea can easily overturn a boat and if I dropped my lady in the water I should have to fall on my sword. We could perhaps get fishermen to ferry us to Grimsby but perhaps not, it would be in the hands of fate.

There is another way. If we take to the water on the river here and pass downriver to the estuary we can then, in calm water, enter the River Trent. The Normans have a tower at Lyncilene so we must pass by there at night, but we can go by water as far as Escumatorp. From there we are but a short distance from Axholme where we can take passage with the Danes when William approaches and they run away.

'I have a boat standing ready for my own escape. It will take all here but not, of course, your horses, nor will there be room for the oarsmen. We must leave them behind, which means we have to ply the oars ourselves. I can, without trouble, can anyone else?'

'I can,' I said.

'I can,' said Asgar, 'my wounds are healed now.'

'And so can I,' said Edith 'I am stronger than you think and I can row. I played in boats all my unmarried life.'

'I never have,' said Wilda, 'but I can learn.'

'I will teach you,' said Waltheof, 'for I can row for two.'

'Then the sooner we start the better,' said Malet, picking up Edith's bundle and water skin and swinging them over his back. Plucking a flaming torch from a sconce on the wall he started for the door. 'Follow me, my lady, if you please.'

We followed him out of the door, down the riverside steps of the mound and through the water gate in the bailey wall. It did not appear to be guarded by Waltheof's men and we saw no one. There at the foot of the steps to the river was a boat, not a cooroogle but a proper boat of overlapping wood planks. It had side benches to sit on and cross benches to row from. On the top bar at each side of the rowing benches were thole pins to hold the oars; it seemed simple enough. There was plenty of room for all on the cross benches and so we threw our bundles on board, climbed in and sitting where we pleased, took up an oar from those laid along the side.

We waited thus until William had let go our tethers, climbed aboard and pushed our boat into the stream. Then he looked at us and laughed. Following his gaze I saw why, for not knowing where we went and the boat being double-ended, we were all sat facing in different directions looking at each other. If we had started rowing we would have gone nowhere.

William pointed towards one end, 'that is the direction in which we must go. All who can see that must turn around on their bench so that you all face where we have been, not where we go.'

Once we had sorted that out we again put our oars over the side, resting against their pins. William doused the torch and, as the only one amongst us who knew aught of the river, took the rudder then called the time to get us started.

And so, our plan to make for the fens and Hereward abandoned, by the light of the stars we rowed our boat away from the castle and through the choking smoke of the smouldering town.

Even with the time I had spent paddling and carrying our cooroogle I was not water wise. One stretch of water looks much like another to me. We rowed by moonlight through the night to the mouth of the river, mostly I think to the south, although it is hard to be certain for there were many changes of direction to east or west. When the river was wide William put the rudder over and we went to the right where the Ouse seemed to divide. I guessed this was the entrance to the River Trent.

By the new morning light we saw all the banks were mud; there was little growth of bushes or trees near the river and no dwellings at all. We rowed on through this dreary landscape, weary but eager for the safety of the Danish fleet.

At about midday when we were all hungry and aching with weariness we reached our destination. It was clear that many of the Danes had already gone. I heard they came in two hundred ships, I could not count more than twenty and my heart sank. Nevertheless William steered towards the largest and on 'up oars' we drew our looms smartly from the water and drifted alongside with scarcely a bump.

As we stopped rowing we could barely find strength to stow our oars. My muscles trembled and I slumped forward my head over my knees.

Chapter 25

Edmund's Tale: Betrayal

The small bump we had made coming alongside or maybe it was the jerking of the boat mooring rope alerted the deck watch.

We had hardly tied on when a line of Danish heads peered over the rail at us. Without asking permission, Waltheof stood, leapt up, grasped the ship's rail and swinging himself over onto the deck went beyond our sight.

After the time it would take to say ten paternosters he returned grinning and dropped down into our boat, which rocked wildly, nearly throwing him over the side and would have done so had he not sat down quickly.

'It is done, my lady,' he said. 'I had to fill their greedy little hands with gold but they agreed passage for us to Esbjerg, from where we must cross the country to the court of King Estridthson at Roskilde, but at least we will be safe from, the Bastard.'

Edith smiled, 'Thank you my lord, I will always be grateful to you.' She then leaned over and clasped the hands of William Malet. 'And thank you my Lord Sheriff, you are a true friend. If I can ever do aught honourable in return for you, then you have but to ask.'

Malet bowed his head, 'It is enough that you have allowed me to accompany you, my lady,' he said.

It was plain to me that the man felt the same for Edith as I felt and I found myself wishing him still held in a cell at Yorvik.

Waltheof pointed inland, 'There is a settlement where we can get lodgings just off to the east, it is called Escumatorp. From there we can await the gathering in of the straggling Danes. Our shipman thinks they will sail tomorrow night and will send for us, so it is a good chance for us to rest,' he said.

Gladdened by the thought of rest and sustenance, we let go and pulled the short distance to the shore and secured William Malet's boat to the small wooden hythe.

In truth there was not much in Escumatorp, no inn, but there was a hall, perhaps the one that gave its name to the place. There, having been looked at, at great length, through the door peephole and been seen to be not poor but perhaps highborn, the door was opened by the lady of the house to let us in. It was agreed that for payment we might make use of her privy and sleep around her fire until called to the ship. Coins were passed to her from Waltheof. She counted them then took herself away and had nothing more to do with us, neither to offer us food nor water.

Edith passed around her water skin, for we were thirsty, though we had all gone beyond hunger. By now we were more than tired, we were bone weary, and so we settled down in the warmth and slept. We did not think to post a watchman for we knew the Danes would wake us when they were about to sail. Or so we thought.

The light was greyly edging through the window when the householder came knocking on the hall door. I opened it and she stood wringing her hands, whether for us or from fear that we would kill the messenger I know not.

'I thought you were to go with the ships,' she said.

'That is so, Mistress.'

'But they are gone and the hill below is alive with soldiers. You must go, if you are their enemy they will burn my hall if they find you here. Go, go!'

My stomach lurched within me and I felt sick. Disturbed by the noise at the door my companions were coming awake. I quickly repeated what our householder had said.

Once the shipman had been paid, we thought we had a safe understanding, but either the Danes had no honour and intended to cheat us, or their fear of the king was so great that there was room for nothing more in their minds but to flee. That is what we thought – until the hammer blow of the truth fell on us.

As I was speaking I knew that something was wrong, but it took me a moment to understand what it was: someone was missing. Earl Waltheof was not with us.

I turned back to the anxious woman in the doorway, 'Have you seen the big man with the mighty shoulders. He slept by the fire.'

'He is gone.' said the householder, 'He said to tell you he has gone to see the king and that you should wait here, for to run would be useless. But you cannot wait here, I want you gone right now!'

Asgar and William rushed to the window and carefully lifting the covering, looked out. 'She is right,' said Asgar. 'The Bastard is here, the Danes have sailed. Waltheof has sold us. He thinks that you, my lady, will be worth more to the king than those one hundred Norman heads he took.'

'What can we do?' said Edith. Her voice was shrill with panic, her usual calm having slipped away. She stood with her arms around Gytha, who was quietly weeping.

275

'We must flee and hide,' said Asgar. 'And pray,' he added, so quietly that only I heard him.

'I cannot go with you,' said Malet. 'If William finds me with you, my lady, he will have my head. I will be more use to you alive than dead. Go, I will, in time, catch up with you. Before then I will seek out the king and tell him I followed you here in his service thinking Waltheof one of you. I will tell him I know you are going overland to Peterburh, so came to give him the tale and get a horse and some milites to help me. This will give me some chance of his forgiveness sufficient to keep my head, and you some chance of escape.

'Waltheof will have told William of our plan,' continued Malet. 'You must have the king think you mean to walk overland, that you believe if he is here then the further you walk the further you will be away. I will spin him the tale that you have on the garb of poor servants and that you are with Asgar. In truth, if you are stopped by anyone at all, only Asgar should speak. He must say you go to Peterburh Abbey to meet with the king there. I will tell William you think that because Asgar is a staller no one will question his word.' He smiled, 'I can make the king and even Waltheof believe that.'

'But will Earl Waltheof not gainsay you?' gasped Edith.

'Mayhap, but the king knows me for a friend. He will trust my word more than that of Waltheof, who joined with the Danes and is thus oath broken, both to you and to him.'

'But if he sends soldiers with you to catch us he must surely take us,' said Edith.

I shivered in my shoes. It is one thing to run away and think you are far ahead of your hunter. It is another to be almost within his grasp. We had not been so nearly lost since the escape from Lutgaresburh and I still had nightmares about that.

Again William Malet smiled. 'Well my lady, that is the

thing. Neither he nor I can catch you if you are not there. For you will not go overland. You will return to my boat and go back the way that we came. Leave it to Asgar, once on the river, he will find his way to a place of safety.'

I knew that what William proposed was fraught with danger. How could we get back to his boat and not be stopped? It would take only one Norman soldier to raise the alarm. But I blessed him in my heart for his bravery, for there was a slim chance that it might just work and of all the things the king might expect us to do, that was most likely the last. All would hang on whether Waltheof was still with the king to give the lie to William's story such that the king believed his word against William's and knew his former friend to be oath broken and false.

'Enough talk,' William picked up his leather sack and threw it over his shoulder. 'We must all go now, before the king's men come here. 'We will meet again my lady, be sure I will find you and that my sword will be yours to protect you oversea.' He took her hand and pressed it to his lips. She stood looking at him gravely.

'Indeed, my brave William, may the fates be with you.'

He waved to all there and then turned and walked out of the door. As we also started to shoulder our burdens, Edith said, 'Wait.' She beckoned to me, 'Edmund come with me.'

I followed her as she trotted to the kitchen and started stuffing hung meat and part loaves into our sacks.

The woman of the house protested shrilly, but when she tried to stop us Edith reached behind, pulled out her bodkin dagger and waved it in the face of the shrieking woman, who blanched, but still spoke boldly. 'You would not do this if my man was here. What land are we now where a poor widow is robbed and put at risk by outlaws pretending to be noble?'

'We have paid you well,' Edith hissed. 'The silver we gave you will buy this six times over. Now go, before I hurt you.'

Wringing her hands the woman backed away and stood by the door.

And so the five of us left the hall whilst William Malet strode off towards his dangerous tryst with the king.

Chapter 26

AD 1071

Edmund's Tale: Grimsby

Once again it was to Asgar that we now looked to lead us and with the owner's bitter bemoaning still falling on our ears, we walked away. Having agreed with William that our only chance was to row back the way we had come, we started to walk overland to the river. It seemed to me that having lost two of our crew, we were now too few to row, but Asgar said we could scull if needed, using only one oar at the stern. Again it was Edith who said that she also had rowed in this way many times and could help. 'My home in East Anglia was set among lakes, and water was easier to move on than the waterlogged bogs,' she said.

We could see Norman soldiers drawn up on the road ahead. It seemed they had not yet spread out to search and were a goodly distance away from us. We were not the only folk scurrying to be out of their way and after several days of travelling, tired, torn and dirty, my lady did not look to be highborn any more than did the rest of us. I suppose the Normans thought to find us, as Waltheof would have told them, still at the hall. He played as always a double game, all betrayal and submission to the Normans, and yet through the woman at the hall he had contrived a warning in time for us to get away.

The boat was still where we had left it, tied up to the small wooden hythe, but two of the Normans had already found it and were looking it over, perhaps wondering how its capture could be turned into coin. My hand tightened on my staff and Asgar drew his seax. I was sure now that all was lost, but again thanks be for my lady.

"Wait," she said to us then strode calmly out in front of us along the hythe, every inch the noblewoman used to obedience. The pedites, more interested in loot and perhaps being where they should not be, watched her approach, expressionless; waiting.

I could not follow what she said to them, for she spoke in Norman French, enough to change the tale around. She told me later that she had said we were her escort taking her to see King William and that the boat they could not take their eyes off was ours. Given the way we looked it was an unlikely tale, but either they were stupid or so afraid at the mention of the king's name that they did not know what to do. Whatever the reason they hesitated, letting Asgar and me get too close.

My staff and Asgar's seax flashed out together and tumbled the two unsuspecting Normans into the water, the weight of their mail dragging them out of sight below the surface.

'Quick, quick as lightning,' said Asgar, jumping down into the boat as the ripples and bubbles from the drowning men spread on the water. Edith lithely followed, then, turning, helped Gytha and Wilda down while I set about letting go the lines.

As I dropped on board, my crippled leg making me stumble, Asgar already had the oar in the stern notch and was sculling us away from the shore and turning upriver, back the way we had come.

When Asgar began to tire, we all took turns with the oar, but Gytha and Wilda showed no skill at it and for the sake of speed were set in the bow to watch for shallows. I also had little skill and our craft moved only slowly with much thrashing and white water when I tried. Only Edith was adept, for as she explained, she had often sculled like this in the past. My task was to keep us heading in the right direction and give Asgar and Edith small rest in the middle of their stints.

I kept scanning the water behind us, fearing our killing of the two pedites had been discovered and someone had managed to raise the alarm, but perhaps their mail had kept their drowned bodies down and they had not been missed, for no boats put out to chase us. The sun was behind a grey overcast of cloud, but the disc shone whitely through. I guessed it to be about midday. The wide waters where the two rivers met I remembered to be half a day's rowing. By this reckoning we should reach open water at dark-fall, and so it turned out. By the dim light of dusk we saw the banks stretch out to east and west and found ourselves in the River Humber.

Once clear of the Trent, Asgar heaved over the anchor stone. Edith, who had been taking her turn with the sculling, sat down and breathed relief.

'Now,' said Asgar, 'we must wait for daylight, for I do not know these waters. You and I, my lady, will rest and you idlers,' he grinned at me, Wilda and Gytha, 'can set watch. Edmund is in charge and must make sure the three of you keep a sharp lookout. Rouse all at first light, for we must move on lest the Bastard learns he has been deceived and finds a craft to follow us.'

I shivered. An open boat is cool in summer weather. In late year, in early Winterfylleth as we were, it is bitter cold. All thoughts of royalty and decency must give way to survival. In the bottom of the boat Asgar took Edith in his arms like a father would his daughter and kept the warmth of their bodies from escaping, their cloaks thrown over them both. On the side benches I placed Princess Gytha between Wilda and me and we held tight to each other, our cloaks arranged around us hiding all but our eyes beneath them. We agreed between us who should watch first and that as there was no sun or moon to judge time by, we would change over when the watcher could no longer stay awake. I told them I should be woken at every change of watch, but in fact I stayed awake for the first three changes for I was afraid the watch keepers might fall asleep without waking their relief. But they did not and all night we kept watch thus and no Normans came hunting us.

At dawn we roused Asgar and Edith. We ate the fare we had taken from the hall, thinking the silver and the householder's whining a price well paid. When we had eaten and having emptied Edith's water-skin, washed our food down with river water, which tasted faintly of salt, we gathered around Asgar.

'We are on the south side of the Humber now,' he said. 'If we follow the bank to the east we will come in time to Grimsby. There are many fishermen in this place. They live from the sea and have no thought of who rules and who not as long as they can conceal their catch and not pay taxes. They are nevertheless Englishmen and Danes with no love of Normans. For payment of silver they will carry wanderers one way and seek fish on the way back. With them we can pass along the coast, whatever the weather, until we get to Lynn. From there we can seek a boat to take us to Peterburh, it is not far, but the ground is treacherous to those who do not know it and the causeway may be watched.'

And so we sculled along the shore until, with the sun halfway down the sky, we saw the masts of the big fishers of Grimm's Haven. We turned towards them and soon were through the breakwater and tied up alongside a fishing craft, I swear as big as fifteen paces long.

Asgar climbed over the side, watched by the crew of six peering over the rail at us. He passed out of my sight and I could not but think of Waltheof doing the same thing yesterday, but I knew Asgar would never betray us and felt at ease that he would make everything come right.

It was sometime later that he returned. So long was he gone I started to worry that ill had befallen him. I said nothing to Edith and she seemed unaware, perhaps knowing that Asgar could deal with anything, such was her trust in my thegn. At just that time when my guts were starting to churn, so there was the sound of voices, a clatter and Asgar sat on the rail and jumped down into our boat.

He was smiling. 'At last fate smiles on us my lady,' he said. We sat looking at him, waiting to hear the tale.

'There is a boat, a small flat-bottomed ship not one hundred paces from here, captained by Eadric, the steersman, and crewed by thirty butsecarls. He it is who was charged with the defence of the East coast under Abbot Aelfwold of St. Benets at Holme. He awaits great lords who are coming to join Abbot Brand's folk at Peterburh. Morcar and Edwin are coming, Maerlsewein the Sheriff of Lincolnshire also. He and Abbot Aelfwold are going together to Denmark, for King William has sent word they are exiled.'

Here Asgar clenched his fist in glee, his face flushed with excitement. 'But first Maerlsewein goes to Hereward, for the Danes are coming again. Perhaps we can fight Duke William and win. If not, if the fens are hard enough fighting, perhaps he will leave us to have a little England of liberty in East Anglia. Here we can make our stand. Hereward knows well the Norman way of war for he has fought for years in Flanders.'

Asgar waved his hand, palm upward, taking in the surrounding land. 'Was it not land like this where great Alfred came to the end of loss against the Danes? Is not Athelney lake and fen, like Ely? Did he not come forth with his army regrown and win?'

'Yes but...' I had been going to say that the Danes sought only loot. They were not led by a madman who wanted to be a king and did not care if he was king of an empty land even if he had to kill all to be so. But looking at the hope that stood so clear in Asgar's eyes, I said nothing.

Edith also was not won over. 'Fight him if it pleases you and you think you can win, but do so when Gytha and I are safely away. William frightens me more than any man I know, more than Hugh Vavassour even. Please help me flee, and then war against William if you can.'

'My lady, it will be as you wish.' Asgar got to his feet. 'Safe as we are here we will be safer yet under the care of Eadric and thirty butsecarls. Let us go there, for he awaits us. There is no one he would sooner serve than his queen and her daughter. No one he would sooner have flee with him to Denmark.'

So, with the help of Asgar and me, the womenfolk climbed over the boat, to the playful calls of the fishermen, and onto the wooden fish-landing hythe. Once ashore, guided by Asgar, we walked the muddy path.

True to his word, the St. Benet, Abbot Aelfwold's ship, was moored less than one hundred paces away. Small but beautifully kept, it was polished, roped and rigged, and even now the butsecarls were aloft doing whatever it is that seamen do.

Something happened then. I often think of the Fates these days, all the twists and turns that have led us to where we are. The Fates are subtle; sometimes their gifts are not what they seem. Take the men of Sumorsaete and the monks who joined us for the besieging of Castle Montagud. They seemed a boon, but in the end led us to do things that proved the death of many.

Now there was a cheering in the distance and loud shouting arose and crept nearer, and from the north a motley crowd of men came towards us. Earl Morcar of Northumbria led them; with him were Aethelwine, Bishop of Durham, and Siward Barn, a noble thegn of the land, holder of more than one hundred carucates. They had come to join us and with them many hundreds of men. It was all the encouragement we needed to draw nearer to our doom, to choose to stay and wait before we fled.

Not all the news was good. Morcar had a long face, grieving because his brother Edwin, Earl of Mercia, with whom he had been hiding in the forests, had been slain by treachery. This was a great blow, for otherwise more men might have been brought to us from Mercia or at least the Scots or Welsh stirred up again to draw some of the king's army away.

As it happened Edwin had gone to the Scots' king, Malcolm Canmore, seeking aid to draw William away to the North. The idea was to waste his army man by man, in constant conflict. There were, after all, only a fixed number of Normans and many more Scots, Welsh and English, and the longer the fight and the more the dead, the harder it would be for William to find new trained soldiers to take their place. The tale that came back to Morcar, carried by a loyal hearthman, was that some men, brothers, sick of the never ending fighting and bad weather, had decided to leave and go home. Earl Edwin tried to prevent them by force and was killed. He never was a good leader of men or for that matter a warrior, so Morcar told us. He did not have the instinct for it, which is how Harald Hardrada had managed to fool him at Fulford Gate, for Edwin had let the Norwegians draw his men into a trap from which they could not escape the slaughter, except by drowning in the river.

When the sad greetings were over and the shoulder patting and the shaking of hands, we boarded the St. Benet with some of the fighting men and were rowed to the Lynn to join the forces of the others there. Our own boat was towed behind at the end of a rope. At the Lynn there were flat-bottom boats to carry the fighting men to Ely. As for the St. Benet, she went to and fro to Grimm's Haven for the rest of that night and then, guided by torches set in the mud, to the nearby isle where Hereward built his Burh and where more marsh boats awaited to carry the new arrivals.

Although Hereward remained war leader and commanded all raids and resistance, Morcar, as the greatest of the land now there, took command of the island fortress. This was a great mistake, for as we were to discover, like all the lords of this sad country of England, Morcar put more weight on his own position and wealth than he did on the country folk placed in his care. Like Asgar after Hastings – and Eadric as it was to prove before Stafford – he was open to the Bastard's lies if what they promised was to his own advantage.

We? We were forgotten in all that excitement and sat on the hythe of the Lynn, pressed together against the cold for much of that night. Our boat was tied up beside us and we thought at first to shelter in the bottom, but the sea had sprayed and soaked the bottom boards, which were now inches deep in water. I thought this very rough treatment of our queen and said so. But Edith smacked my hand and laughed.

'There is a time for everything and all must be as it should be for that time. Now they all prepare for war and their stomachs tighten for they do not know the outcome, whether they will survive, whether they will lose limbs. And so they bend all of their minds to make ready to do their best. Respect to past queens is only to be shown in idle times when all else is done. Think, young Edmund, if a Norman came out of a mist now with his sword bared, would you strike him with the heel of your stick or turn and kneel to me? Do not worry; all will come into order if all goes well.'

As it happened, we were not entirely forgotten. I know Asgar had spoken to Eadric when first we came and our steersman must have told Hereward of our arrival, and like Prince Bleddyn, our Hereward was a prince by nature, if not by dub or birth. When the shifting of Siward Barn's men was finished Eadric the steersman came to us and bent the knee to Edith.

'I sorrow that my tasks have kept me from my duty to you, my lady, but we make a fortress and time is short.'

Edith smiled and waved her hand to say it was no matter of importance to her, she understood that he was busy; she was content to wait. How she said all that in one wave of her hand I do not know, but that understanding passed to me and I know to the steersman also, for he in turn bowed and then looked up smiling.

'My lady, now Earl Morcar is here he will lead, but our commander of milites and pedites is Hereward, the greatest soldier in the land. He asks that you and your party be carried to safety at Ely.

'I thank Lord Hereward,' said Edith, 'but we are hoping for a ship to carry us into exile in Denmark.'

'There are none here at this time, my lady, but many are promised and when they leave, to carry you with them would honour them greatly, but if we beat William in battle you may wish to stay.'

For a moment Edith said nothing, looking over towards the setting moon, and then, 'If Commander Hereward has a fire we may warm beside that would be a great boon to us all.'

'I will have you taken there now, my lady. You can all go in your boat and then it will be there should you need it. I will bring forth men to row who know their way.'

'That is kind of you Lord Eadric, I shall remember it.'

Notwithstanding the water in the bottom of our boat, the five of us climbed in and settled ourselves on the benches, lifting our feet to keep them from the cold water. Within the time it took Eadric to walk to the St. Benet and back, there were six butsecarls standing on the hythe and awaiting our leave to come on board. I was much impressed, for butsecarls are not ordinary sailors but huscarls who can also sail boats and who understand the ways of the sea. They train as huscarls until they are the best warriors in the world for a straight contest behind a shield wall. Then they train in boats and how to plough the seagulls' fields. I knew we would be safe amongst these warriors though few in number.

Edith waved them on board. They jumped down with a thunder that rocked our boat violently. Their shields they put under their feet, their spears along the side benches. Gytha and Wilda still sat on the rowing cross benches looking in wonder at these armoured men with their great bushy moustaches. Those sailors, whose seats they had taken, grasped Gytha and Wilda by the arms, picked them up without effort and put them on the side benches, to much laughter from the womenfolk.

Once settled on the rowing benches, the butsecarls picked up the oars and at a word from their captain at the steering oar, our boat was fended off, the oars placed against the thole pins and we were pulling away from the hythe smoothly and with hardly a sound.

Edmund's voice ceased abruptly and there was silence for the time it took the village folk to understand that Bowdyn had ceased speaking. They sat watching him wondering whether he would carry on with his story and if so why he had stopped.

After the Cold Cot had fallen entirely silent, beyond the restless creaking of the benches and shuffling of feet, the flow of the story entirely broken and all eyes on Bowdyn, he waited, but not for long, for old Alf raised his hand, like a child seeking attention.

'Yere,' he said, 'You'm a galloping on Mister Bowdyn zir. There is so much I don know Oim getting lost. You've told's about Hastings but where is Fulford Gate and what 'appened there?'

'Ah Alf, Lord bless you, for when I forget myself and gallop on, you are there to remind me that there are things our folk do not know and that sometimes I need to stop the story and set the scene.

'You remember when the warriors set out for the North before Hastings?'

'Ar oi do,' said Alf. There were murmurs of agreement from the listeners.

'They went to fight a battle with an army of invaders from Norway.'

'Where be Norway to?' said Alf.

'East across the sea,' said Bowdyn.

'Oh ar, roight,' said Alf.

'When they got there they thought the warriors of Edwin and Morcar would join them, but they could not for most were dead. The earls had brought the Norwegians to battle at Fulford Gate near York and had been soundly defeated by Harold Hardrada. He was the greatest warrior of his day, but not so great that when our King Harold met him at Stamford Bridge there was not a great slaughter of the sons of Norway and their defeat in turn. It was after then that our army, tired and battleworn, returned in haste to its own defeat at Hastings.'

'Ar, oi'm with ee now. Thank ee kindly Maaster Bowdyn.'

Bowdyn smiled. 'We come to a point in Edmund's story where you may wonder why much is not said. Two strong stories have come together here. One is the tale of Edith Swanneschals, and this story is hers. The other is the tale of Hereward the Outlaw – outlaw maybe, but strong enough to challenge a king.

'While we learn much of Edith in the tale I now tell, of Hereward we learn little, for like the battle at Hastings, many people have told his tale and it is not for me to retell it. I will tell you something of Hereward as a man, but not the whole story of the defence of the Isle of Ely.

'The son of a king's thegn, rich in land having many thousands of acres, Hereward was wild in his youth and was banished to Flanders by his own father. There he learned the art of warfare. Whilst he was serving in Flanders, William, Duke of Normandy invaded our poor country. Hereward returned home to find his brother murdered and his land stolen. Well trained for war, he revenged himself on the Norman murderers of his brother and then took to the lakes and fens of East Anglia where, much like Swein Icgson in the fells and dales of Yorkshire, he lived the life of an outlaw, committed to resisting the Norman invaders.

'About him he gathered some mighty men: Earl Morcar of Northumbria; Abbot Aelfwold of Holme; Bishop Aethelwine of Durham; Maerlswein, Sheriff of Lincolnshire; Ordgar, Sheriff of Cambridgeshire; Siward Barn, a king's thegn, and Thorkill Cild, also a king's thegn. Amongst them were Eadric the steersman and many others of lesser rank.

'William's fear of Hereward's growing strength eventually drove the king to spare no efforts in seeking to crush him and his fortress of Ely. Abbot Brand of Petersburh, Hereward's uncle and a true Englishman, had stood firm, but sadly he died and it was the trouble caused by Abbot Turold, his replacement, which proved a threat too much for King William and drew him to Ely with all the might he could muster.

'Our story touches on this. Some things I cannot avoid telling because they link to our tale of Edith and Gytha, but it is not my purpose to speak of the battles of Ely; perhaps that is a tale for another season.'

He paused long enough for the benches to start to scrape and clatter and then looking around, spoke.

'Now I think it is time we went to our rest. I bid you good night until next time, when we shall see whether Edith succeeds in her wish to go into exile. We shall also meet William Malet once more, for his destiny and that of Edith is entwined and has been from the beginning of her story here and will be until we come to an end.'

They village sat silently, taking in what he said and then there was the usual hubbub of thanks to my father and mother and to Bowdyn and a further clash and clatter as the benches were restacked at the end of the Cot.

With called goodnights interrupting the rumbling of talk dying away in the distance, the workers of our farm and the villagers went noisily to their beds.

Chapter 27

Edmund's Tale: Hereward

The word was passed around and it was the following Sunday, after church service that we gathered together in the Story House. Bowdyn greeted all, reminded them that we awaited Edmund continuing with his tale of Hereward in the marshes and then he sank back into the shadows and the familiar voice of Edmund spoke out.

By the time we had rowed perhaps two miles through the fen, word of our coming must have been carried before us, for as we arrived at the hythe there was a figure standing alone, awaiting us.

As the butsecarls moored the boat and I helped Edith ashore so the figure went on one knee before her and I got my first sight of Hereward.

You must understand that in my young life all of my protectors during childhood had been big men, warriors. This had made me trust Earl Waltheof without second thoughts. His betrayal had come as a blow to everything I believed in. Now I knew not how I would feel if our protector was another giant hero, but when he rose to his feet, I could see that Hereward was no giant. Of middle height, thick set but without any sign of fat, he was a man who looked solid as a tree planted deep in the soil. I felt that if I pushed his chest with all my strength it would be my feet not his that would slide.

There was nothing striking about his face, no villainous scars arising from his outlaw life. The most striking feature was his warrior's bushy lip hair. His forehead was high and his jaw strong with a prow of a chin leading him wherever he moved; it was a strong face and yet a kindly one. A face a man could trust. There was no sign of the mind that could plan the cruellest of shifts, for Hereward was the master of using the land itself to fashion weapons to kill Normans. Looking at his honest face, his frank blue eyes, I could not have foreseen the screaming Norman milites all sinking through crusts of ground into the pits he had dug and filled with burning peat. Nor horses and riders sinking without trace through the false ways he had laid over quicksand.

He stood; head slightly bowed, drew his sword and placed it on the ground to one side, then shrugged his axe off his back placing it on the opposite side. Again he knelt, and with his hands pressed together as if in prayer, pushed them towards Edith. She enclosed them in her hands in the ancient ritual of Handgang.

'My Queen, I beg you, please accept me as your man.'

Edith bowed, just slightly. 'I do accept you into my service as my man.'

Whatever misgivings I might have had, I suddenly felt very safe. Hereward was now the commended man of Edith. It was his duty to obey her, help her and if necessary die for her. Anything less and all right-minded men – and there were many – would shun him. I smiled inside, for if William caught us what would such shunning matter? We would all be dead anyway once he had twisted the whereabouts of Harold's grave and the Wessex ring out of Edith. As always the thought made me feel sick. Watching the Handgang I wondered if I too might be 'commended', but rather than make a fool of myself in front of Hereward I thought I might ask my lady when we were alone.

It was much later and much had happened before my chance arose. By then the smoke of burning was always in our eyes and nostrils and we knew that soon we would need to run if we could find a way through William's army and William's ships. When I did ask her, she answered thus.

'Why would you want to and why would I want you to? You are not my servant or my sworn man, Edmund. You do not need to be, for we are friends and I know I can trust you to the utmost to do everything you can to help and support me. I truly believe that you would die in defence of me and Gytha.'

I fell to my knees. 'It is true my lady. I have always known I would die for you from when you first came to our hall. I love you my lady.'

'I know you do Edmund and I value that above all things, but it must be our secret, you must never say it out loud where others could hear. It could make things tiresome and might even be dangerous for you. Better it stays our secret. As my man, do I have your oath of silence?'

'You have my lady, I will never say it again, except in my head, one hundred times each day.'

'Sweet Edmund,' she said. Smiling she laid her hand on my head. 'I fear we will part soon for if a ship comes to carry me away you will then be able to go home.'

'I do not think I have a home any longer, my lady. I fear for my mother and that I will find our land held by a Norman.'

'Perhaps that is so,' she said, 'but even if true your people will need you. If, God forbid, your mother and father are both dead and your brother is broken, then all who are left will need you to speak up for them. It is your duty.'

'Asgar told me long ago my duty was with you. It is too late for me to try to save what is left in Lutgaresburh. Unless you drive me away my lady, for better or for worse I will come oversea with you.'

'Then kneel and hold out your hands.'

I knelt before her and put my hands together as in prayer and thrust them towards her. She folded them in hers and completed the ritual of Handgang.

'I offer myself to you to be your man.'

'I accept you as my man and will always treat you as a commended man should be.'

And it was done. I would go wherever my lady went for as long as she needed me.

Chapter 28

Edmund's Tale: The Defence of Ely; Trapped

There was a time of peace. At first perhaps the Bastard did not care. And then perhaps he did not think it worth his trouble to subdue us.

Then the Danes came and still he troubled us not. It was, I think, the knowledge that the Northern earls and bishops were with us that made him finally see danger. And then, as we found out when we reached Ely, our time of peace was at an end. Abbot Brand, Hereward's uncle and strong support, had died in Holymonth in the year of Our Lord, one thousand and sixty-nine. Hereward and the monks had thought it would not matter, that there would be another abbot and he would support us, for abbots were Englishmen and hated the foreigners and their working to remake the English church in the way of that across our channel. But they were wrong. For the new abbot was a Norman, Turold by name: a rough man, who had to leave his abbey at Malmesburh when he and all his monks had a violent disagreement. I heard from somewhere that William said, 'If he wants to fight send him to Peterburh where he will find someone to match himself against.' And so William had thought it good to send this fiery monk to Peterburh, whence in time he came with a train of one hundred and sixty horseback milites.

The monks of Peterburh knew of him from when his harshness had brought his own monks to mutiny. They also knew him to be a man who had taken the treasures of his abbey and sent them to France, and they feared what he would do to the rich hoard of Peterburh. Hereward said he would sooner the Danes had it than the Normans, and so the plot was hatched.

In June of the year of Our Lord, one thousand and seventy, four years but two months since we lost our liberty and just before Abbot Turold came to Peterburh Abbey, it was understood that Hereward, with the help of the Danes, would sack the abbey, stripping it of all its gold and silver so that there would be nothing for Turold to loot and send off to Fecamp in France.

At that time, with no abbot to take control, the monks became confused, some understanding the truth of the matter and some thinking they were under attack by outlaws. Thus Hereward's men had to fight their way in and much of the abbey was burned, only the church was spared. All the gold was carried for safety to the ships of the Danes, which is like storing egg-laying hens in a fox's lair.

It was this, the sacking and burning of the abbey that finally drew the king to us. Or perhaps the joining of the North once more with the Danes made him fear for his crown. Anyway, he came and with ships and soldiers.

At first it seemed that we could not be stormed. The Norman horsemen, the greatest weapon in William's army could not fall upon us. Many were lost in the swamps, meres and fens, trying. And then there was a lull and another peaceful time.

Then the duke – or king, as he would have it – tried something that seemed to show he thought us simple. It gave us many a laugh around the cook fires of the camp. If he thought it would frighten us it won the opposite, for it made us think that perhaps he was not so strong after all, at least between the ears. I dare say his Norman monks thought it up, but then they are bedevilled.

What happened was this: we woke one morning to the noise of shouting and hammering. Across the fen to Stuntney, the nearest dry land to us, the Normans were erecting a tower. It was just beyond bowshot. I know, for many tried.

When the tower was completed we saw a bedraggled woman climbing the ladder, slowly, with many halts, to the top. Some knew her as the Witch of Soham. Those who knew her feared her not, other than that she might drink the alehouse dry, for she was more known for her fearsome drinking than her fearsome spells. Anyway, Elga the Witch of Soham gets to the top and stands on the platform. Grasping the rail and shaking her fist at us she starts to shout what sounded like a load of drivel. We guessed that they had poured a pot of wine into her to get her up there. The Normans are great drinkers of wine and care not for ale the way we do.

Anyway, after she had screamed this drivel at us for a while she slumped to the platform and, as far as we could see, went to sleep.

Sat around our fire laughing I don't know who came up with the idea first, for it was cruel, but it showed the Bastard what we thought of him. We gathered kindling in a goatskin. Brazenly one brave fellow swam across behind a branched tree holding a glowing brand. He ran to the tower, spread his kindling, still dry from its voyage in the goatskin, blew on the brand and made a fire around one of the legs then ran and swam back. What guards the Normans had posted, if any, must have been sleeping for the whole tower was burning brightly before anyone noticed it and raised an outcry.

This woke old Elga who started to scream for someone to do something. The higher the flames reached the more she screamed until just before they reached her and she started to burn she jumped, to the roaring laughter of the cruel bastards around our fire, who had no respect for witches and wanted the Normans to know we had no respect for them either. It was a high tower, but the ground was soft peat. From the noise she made when she hit the ground she survived her jump.

There were other cruel tricks we played on our attackers. Much of the solid-appearing ground was peat. It is strange soil for if dry it burns if you set a brand to it. Not with bright flames like wood but with a slow smouldering that spreads until the fire is broad and deep. Now it is possible, if you are careful, to dig a narrow pit and set light to the peat underground and then fill in the pit. This causes a deep fire, but with a crust of grass and sedge on top such that it looks like normal ground. We would set these and then mock the Norman milites, tempting them to chase us. When they did they were swallowed up in a fiery grave. We caught many in that way before they became wise and refused to chase us. This pleased our bowmen mightily, for whilst many of our enemy stood watching and refusing to come-on, we speared them with arrows. And so we got them to the point that as soon as they saw us beckoning them on they withdrew.

The next ruse was to use stones and planks to cross quicksand and mud and lay false pathways, the stones laid carefully to look like the top of a causeway. But, of course, any who attempted to cross it, whether on foot or on horseback, would go straight through and be swallowed up by the swamp. In these ways we had the Normans frightened to move, even more in those places where we were not than where we were. Of course they took to always having bowmen with them and so we always must carry our shields. In place of our light round ones we made up long ones that we could ground and shelter behind. We also sent for and used the Welsh longbow, which, for those with the strength to pull it, had greater range than the Norman war bow. And so, although our numbers were less we defended the island of Ely and had hopes that in winter the Normans would leave. In this again we did not count on the Bastard's raw lust to win, at whatever cost in life and treasure.

He had known war his whole life, all of which he had spent fighting. He could see clearly that our land was rich, our water ample, he could besiege us forever and we would grow fat and laugh at him. He saw that as things were he could never come at us by land and he could not come by sea for he had no ships of a sort that could sail the fens. So he did what he did for the taking of England, he built the ships he needed and as there was no road to approach us with his mounted soldiers, he resolved to build one. I cannot look into his mind, nor would I wish to, any more than drink from the privy, but I saw what he did and in what order and thus knew the thoughts that had led to it.

The first that happened was that one day about late summer, in the year of Our Lord, one thousand and seventy-one, our fishermen brought back the tale that the rivers were jammed with boats filled with armed men, our escape to the sea cut off.

The next thing was that the king built a hythe at Stuntney. Here lines of fishermen landed timber and stones and sundry things and as we watched he had this rubbish tipped at the edge of the land and so, bit by bit, began a causeway towards us.

During the night Hereward had us sneak over, kill the Norman guards and any fishermen delayed there and tip the piles of painfully gathered rubble all along the edge where it was useless and could not be got back.

The next day the overseer and his troops arrived on the island and saw what we had done. After that, during that day and the next there was no work and we thought we had won. But the following day many pedites came; hundreds. With them came wagons loaded with timber. As we watched they started to dig and raise a mound and before our eyes within seven days a wooden motte-and-bailey castle was raised up.

That stopped any more storming to wreck the causeway. It mattered not as it happened, for the causeway they built was too narrow and they abandoned it.

Next there came boats carrying timbers and sheep bladders. We built a Burh on the shore where they might land so that they would have to take it to come ashore. William then put together his siege machines, pelted our earthwork with rocks and destroyed it. We retreated and watched while they built a bridge of timber floating on the swollen bladders. We formed our shield wall to fight to the last as they came across and landed. We need not have troubled ourselves, for they crossed in a rush, the end section sank and threw them into the water to drown. The threshing about caused the middle section also to collapse with great loss of life. And so ended the first try to invade our little island; pity it is that William's coming ashore at Pevensey had not met with such ill fate.

Many would have given up at that time or found their men would not obey, but a madness drove the Bastard and all his men were sore afraid of him. They knew that if they offended him he would be revenged, and so they tried again. They took what they had learned in their first attempts and went to another place. It was a place that was nearer to Ely, got at through a winding causeway, one that only a monk would know. Another betrayal.

Again they brought together logs and hurdles and sheep bladders, but now we saw that some of these they filled with sand not air for the shallow water.

The worst betrayal was that at this time the Danes went away. They floated their ships at dawn and rowed away to sea. On board they still had all the hoard of Peterburh Abbey. The king's ships let them pass. William the Norman had bought them off with English treasure.

Now we started to feel some little fear that the king might get onto the island and that our stronghold might fall. But before our small band around Edith could decide what we might do for the best, a strange thing happened. The night that the bailey wall was put up around the mound and the building of the Norman's castle was finished, there was some shouting and clashing of arms by the shore of the river and then the shouting came closer and we saw that some of our guards had caught someone. The spy, for that we thought him, was brought into the tent of Hereward and then word was sent for Edith and Asgar. As they answered the call so I trailed along after them, appearing to guard Gytha, for I wished to know all things that involved Edith.

When we arrived at Hereward's shelter there were guards outside but only one other than Hereward inside. Had I been holding the crown of England itself I would have dropped it, together with my jaw, for the man standing with Hereward was none other than William Malet.

On seeing Edith he dropped to one knee. 'My Queen, I told you that I would find you. I am here to pass oversea with you. I cast off my oaths to William and would swear those oaths of fealty and vassalage to you, my lady. If he comes here before we are gone he can take my life for I shall die in your protection.'

Then he held his hands prayerfully towards her and she, smiling down on him, took them in her own and he became her commended man. I smiled secretly; if warriors kept coming to her she would have her own hearthband in no time. William Malet? He was, I suppose, a good man, and loved her as I did. It was then I realised my cause was hopeless. Until the time I came to accept it as the way of the world, out of envy I came to dislike Lord Malet, although he had never done anything beyond that one thing to harm me. Even that he did without knowing he did it, for the truth was that she was a queen and he a lord, while I was just a ceorl.

The final betrayal happened as the king's road came closer to our shore and we massed to repel his army. We were greatly outnumbered and so had little chance of success. We were denied the chance, for at this time Earl Morcar put out in a boat and went to seek out William. Who knows what talk they had or what lies the Bastard told? When Morcar came back he said that he had surrendered the island and that all the common men were safe and William would let them all go home. As most of our soldiers were common men, as soon as they heard that, at a stroke we had no army.

Once more Edith and Asgar were summoned to Hereward's shelter and once more I gathered together Gytha and Wilda and followed them.

Edith stood before Hereward, who bent the knee before her. 'My Queen, all is lost here. I will not wait for William. It is nearly dark. The Normans will not move in darkness for they fear the fens. I can move as easily in the dark as daylight for I know them better than I know my own face. I beg you, come with me. There are many here who seek to flee from Ely. I fear very much for the men of quality who yield to the king. I foresee they will be roughly hewn for their timidity.'

'And do you go into exile Sir Hereward?'

'No my lady, I go with others of like mind to the forests. For our amusement is the destroying of Normans and life would not be the same without it.'

'Thank you my lord, I accept your offer of escape as long as my brave company can come with me.'

'Of course,' said Hereward. 'There are boats coming together at another place; I lead, they follow. If you go to the boat you came in I will send butsecarls to row it and guide it for you. We will meet up at the Lynn where I will find a Danish ship to carry you.'

'You are a noble man and a friend indeed,' said Edith.

'I am your man in all things my lady, how could I do less?'

As seemed to be the way with any trip I did by boat it was dark, after nightfall. My sole duty was to be quiet. In the dark unable to see and with hardly anything to hear except the oars, sack-muffled in the thole pins, the only noise was that of my thoughts within my head. In there was tumult.

I was Edmund the cripple. I had hardly ever left my dwelling place. Because of my leg I was passed over for warrior training and even for games with the other boys of the town. Whence came my skill with the quarterstaff you might ask? And my only answer is thus: from constant practice and strong shoulders.

And yet, here was I, going to join a ship full of Danes to take me oversea as guardian to a queen, slipping through a marsh with those I guarded sought by a king. Who would have believed it? Had you told me before the world turned upside down after the battle at the Lake of Blood, certainly not I.

AD 1072-73 Roskilde and
the Varangian Way

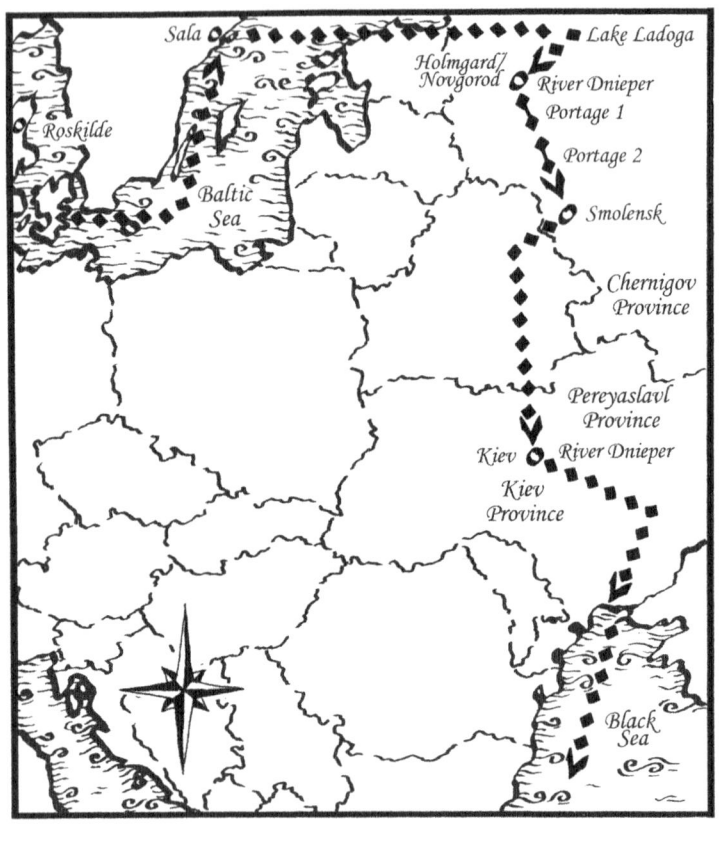

The Varangian Way to Byzantium

Chapter 29

AD 1071

Edmund's Tale: The Seagulls' Way to Roskilde

True to his word, Hereward found my lady and her daughter a Danish ship to carry them oversea, along with we her escort came Abbot Aelfwold and others fleeing into exile. This was not King Sweyn's ship, nor even that of his brother Osbjorn; they had gone on ahead with the treasure ships.

Once we slipped away from the Lynn we could see the land on both sides and then it passed behind us and we were in the open sea with England dropping away. Our ship sailed alone on an empty sea and was commanded by a shipman. I asked him how we would know our way. He showed me how at night we took a star that was always in the north and put it on our port side, and in the morning we put the rising sun on our starboard side. As long as we did that, he said, and as long as the wind blew from the west, we would find the land ahead in six days. When we saw the land we would turn to starboard and put the morning sun on our beam and from there it would be easy, for there was a line of islands to take us all the way to Roskilde Fiord. Easy, he said, as long as the sea was kind.

Indeed the sea was kind to us for the time of year, it being the end of the sailing season. It truly was the seagull way, for they followed us most of our journey, calling and complaining, but little food got they from us. As we went I remembered his words and saw what he meant. Just as he said it would be so it turned out. The first island they said was called Lasso, which we brought fine on our starboard bow. Once we passed it by we saw another island ahead, this they said was Anholt, which we left close to port. Ahead was yet another island; Hesselo. This one our shipman gave good clearance to port, for there were rocks nearby, he said. Once we were well clear we came to the last two islands and steered to keep the two in line. We were now heading towards the land again, but as we neared it so a great chasm opened up between the high ground on both sides and shortly we brought out the oars and dropped the sail and were rowing into Roskilde Fiord.

High ground stood on either side and there were many twists and turns, which our shipman followed, until ahead of us, built on the flat lands between the hills, we saw the royal capital of Roskilde. The king's hall or palace and the wooden cathedral stood out amongst the low wooden houses of the town.

As we slid alongside the hythe and made fast Asgar spoke.

'My lady, I beg you to stay on board a while. The king does not know we are coming and we must not take him by surprise. First I must go and speak with him to let him know a queen of England craves sanctuary and hospitality in his land.'

He turned to William and me. 'You must stay by our lady and prepare to defend her with your lives.'

We nodded. I do not think either of us felt it was needful for the thegn to instruct us in this. I know that I, and I was sure William also, would have done so without the telling. But as the ship drew alongside, as the oars were brought in and ropes sent ashore, we could see that people were waiting on the hythe.

The shipman touched Asgar on the shoulder, 'See, the king's Godman awaits us. Adam is his name, from Bremen. He will guide you to the palace.'

And so it proved, for once the gangplank went down so the Godman came onto the deck and spoke to the shipman, who pointed to where we stood watching, then he came across to us.

'My Lord Asgar I am Adam; the king has sent me. Horses are on the land for you and the queen. The others in your party will need to walk I fear, but it is not far.'

It seemed we were expected after all and I wondered how that could be.

Edith and Asgar mounted. My lady pulled Gytha up behind her and Asgar, out of courtesy, did the same for Wilda. William Malet, Aelfwold and I walked behind Adam along a road paved with small stones that followed a straight line from the port to the palace, which towered above the town at the end of the road. Some of the townsfolk out of curiosity lined the road to look at us others leaned chattering from windows.

I was all amazed at this for I still could not understand how the king and the folk knew we were coming. It was simple really, for it was law that the king must not be taken by surprise at anything, whether an attack or a visiting guest. I learned later that as we had entered the fiord so a swimmer was put over with the news. He told the harbour watch and they sent a horseman off at a gallop to alert the palace and the town.

The road ended at great open gates of wood. These were carved in tangled detail with heads at each centre post and each hinge post. As he entered, so Adam cast his gaze downward and crossed himself. I guessed the carved heads were those of the heathen gods of Denmark. Inside the gates was a courtyard where the womenfolk and Asgar dismounted.

'Please follow me,' said Adam, leading us through a doorway. Guards on each side looked very keenly at us, but seeing no harm in us and encouraged by the presence of Adam, they let us pass without hindrance. Inside was a passageway leading into the great hall of the palace. To either side of us as we entered the hall were doorways to private rooms. This pattern was followed on the side facing us and also off a gallery running around the upper part of the hall. At the end was a raised area on which were placed double thrones. It was clear that this great room was both a feast hall and a throne room.

We followed Adam as he turned to the other end of the hall opposite the thrones and climbed the stairs to the gallery.

'These are rooms of honour,' he said. 'Only the greatest of the king's guests are harboured here.' He waved his hand at the doors facing across the stairs and down the length of the hall to the thrones. 'The centre rooms are for the queen and her daughter and her lady in waiting. That to the left is for the Norman.' I frowned then realised he meant William Malet. 'The rooms to the right are for the Englishmen, Lord Asgar, his servant and Abbot Aelfwold.'

My lady thanked him warmly and asked that he should pass our gratitude to the king. He bowed and left us to settle into our rooms.

Edith had barely time to finish unpacking what little she and Gytha had when I heard a knocking at their door. I looked out of my own door as was my duty as her protector. It was the king's Godman again, the monk, Adam.

'My lady, the king begs that you attend on him.'

Chapter 30

AD 1072

Edmund's Tale: King Sweyn

When Edith emerged from her room I fell into the place of guard behind her. Startled, Edith looked back at me then smiled and continued down the stairs.

King Sweyn sat upon his throne before the fire staring moodily into the flames. He and his flanking huscarls looked keenly at me but seeing I bore nothing but my staff, and that Queen Edith walked confidently ahead of me, they said nothing of my presence.

The king got to his feet and offered his hand to Edith, drawing her to a chair beside his own. When she was seated he returned to gazing moodily into the fire before speaking.

'My lady, you are a queen,' he said, 'thus you know that nothing is as it seems. A king can only rule those who obey him and until someone plunges a dagger in his back...' He paused for a moment as if seeking the right words.

'You are welcome here madam, and I will do my best to guard you. That you should come to harm under my roof would be a great shame to me and to Denmark. And yet I cannot guide everything. I rule a kingdom of savage and greedy men. I sent my brother to fight against William in England. When he should have struck with the Northerners and perhaps have won a kingdom, what does he do? He comes home with his pouches full of Norman gold. That is the power I have. I have banished him, but the deed is done, a kingdom lost.

'What I am saying madam, is that I cannot be sure I can keep you safe whatever oath I swear. William wants you and will no doubt offer much gold for you. If you stay here, perhaps one day I will look for you and find you gone and a chieftain also, who will go smiling into exile – another betrayer with his bags full of Norman gold.'

I watched Edith's face as King Sweyn spoke, her beautiful eyes clouded with anxiety. 'What can I do?' she asked the king.

'I will think on it,' he said, 'and until I think of what is best, I will guard you well, I have some nobles here on whom I can rely.'

'Thank you my king, I place all my trust in you,' she said.

The king bowed in respect to my lady then turned away and waved to his servant who trotted to the door beyond which we could see a line of supplicants. Edith's audience was over and she and I returned to our rooms.

For six months we lived well in the court of King Sweyn. We joined in the Yule time feasting and merrymaking, although I often saw my lady looking away into the past with sad eyes.

I bathed in the warmth of her friendship, although I knew she saw me, as she once said, as a favourite nepos or nephew when I would have had it otherwise. Be that as it may, I often sat with her as she mused on the course of her life. I know she grieved still for murdered Harold. Often I would sit silent whilst she wept. I longed to take her in my arms and comfort her but did not dare for she was a queen and I but a farm boy. I think it was that which let her grieve before me. Had I been of a quality that could move to give comfort she would not, I believe, have let the clouds gather and the rain to fall.

Once she brought forth the ring of Wessex, the arm band with the white Saxon dragon on one side and the red dragon of Wessex on the other, chasing each other nose to tail around it. She looked at it for a long while; for long enough that I began to shift, for my backside was paining me on the hard wooden stool on which I perched.

'Such a small thing to cause so much misery,' she said.

I did not know what she meant for surely it was the crown and William's lust for it that had brought all the misery down on our poor land.

'It was not just the crown you know,' she said, as if seeing inside my head and correcting me. 'Any fool can fashion a crown. Certainly fools have worn the crown of England.'

She turned the ring in her hands, following the race of dragons around its band. 'It is Wessex that is the heart of England, from Wessex that the Gewissae made the broken land one, and a rich one at that. Did you know that the people of Wincaester were still called the Gewissae?'

I nodded, how could I not know, my folk accounted themselves part of the Gewissae and the tales had still been told around the hearth, until the Normans came that is. This made me think of my home, my lost mother and father and I felt unmanly tears start to well up behind my eyes. I sniffed and looked quickly at my lady to see if she had noticed. The tears were rolling down her cheeks. She wiped them with her hands.

'Enough. Enough tears have been shed. I shall put the ring away and look on it no more, not even to rejoice that the

Bastard has it not. No more tears, Edmund. If we would live then the years to come must be planned for,' she said.

She wrapped the ring in its plain cloth wrap and dropped it carelessly, like some spat-out plum stone, into a sackcloth bag and laid it in her clothes chest.

Not long after that the wheel of our fate turned again and our lives, or at least those of Edith, Gytha, Wilda and I, took a new and unlooked for direction.

The others in our band had already taken to our new life in exile. Asgar, with all that he knew of the running of a great and wealthy country, had a life of ease as counsellor to King Sweyn. Abbot Aelfwold was in earthbound heaven as a tutor to Prince Knut who, if he lived and took the throne, would one day be King Knut IV. William Malet was torn between his love for Edith and his love for land. I sometimes thought of it as a war between his English half from a loving mother and his greedy grasping Norman half. This was just my thinking, for he never said aught to me of his father. Anyway, the king offered him a demesne in the south. In fairness it was a generous offer but the king needed all the proven loyal war leaders he could get and to have a Norman bound to him pleased him. It was a hall with one hundred carucates of good land, so said William after he had travelled to see it. I think the bird of the land being in his hand as compared to Edith who might never nestle there was the turning point for his acceptance of the king's offer.

Thus were we broken up according to that we wished for. I clung hopelessly to Edith, now the last of her protectors, although King Sweyn gave her four trustworthy huscarls from his own household. William became a landholder and sworn man; Asgar a courtier and sworn man; Aelfwold a missionary for Our Lord Jesus. Wilda feared to leave us and was content to be Edith's maid. Our exile seemed almost complete. I could not know that Edith, Gytha, Wilda and I had but started ours and had many miles yet to go.

Siward Barn, who had travelled into exile on the same ship as us, did not seek a place from King Sweyn; neither did he seek our company. He knew where he was going and what he would do there. He planned to join the Varangian guard in the service of the Emperor of Byzantium, as had many of our best fighters already.

In the court of King Sweyn there were those faces we grew to know and those that arrived, performed their tasks and left. Many of these were ambassadors from Sweyn's distant ventures, some of trade, some of conquest. We were not a part of this being only guests in his palace and court, so it was with some surprise that Edith, Gytha and I were summoned to attend the throne. We had been accustomed to not descending the stairs until the day's end, when all the business of rule had ended and the evening of hospitality began. Then we came down to eat at the king's board. For as a visiting queen, so his courtesy ruled that Edith should always sit at his left hand and he at her right. Of course, this was a clever rule, for it left his right hand for the seating of important visitors and envoys.

Chapter 31

AD 1072

Edmund's Tale: Ambassador from Kyjev

One day was much like another, such that on that one particular evening when we arrived before the throne we were not to know that something important was about to take place; something that would change our lives forever.

As usual, King Sweyn sat on the throne guarded at the foot of the dais by two huscarls. What was not usual was that he wore on his head the glittering diadem of the ruler. Standing between the huscarls, but off to one side so that he faced us without turning his back to the king, was a man who to me looked more like a bear than any man I had seen.

His hair and beard were long but bushy and on his head he wore a bushy fur hat. Only his eyes peering out through all this hair told me this was a man and not some wild thing from the forest. His looks were made more feral by the clothes he wore, which were entirely of animal skins, bear I think, with fur side outermost. It was winter, of course, and such clothing was sensible outside in this snow-bound land, but the hearth in the throne room was burning high and the warmth must have made this fur-clad bear of a man unbearably hot and uncomfortable.

He looked at the king who nodded towards us. The bear

then turned and went on one knee before Edith. He glanced up at her and speaking with a thick accent said, 'My lady, I am your servant.'

What I thought strange was that after the first glance at Edith his gaze never left Gytha, who sat with Wilda on a bench at the side of the hall, out of earshot. If you asked me I would say the bear-man examined her as if he were buying a horse, except he didn't pry her mouth open to look at her teeth.

Getting to his feet he leaned close to Edith and I saw her nose wrinkle. His gaze darting towards Gytha he spoke in a low voice, 'Excuse please, Majesty, that your daughter? The Princess Gytha?'

Edith nodded, one eyebrow raised.

'Excuse please, she is virgin and has never known man or borne children?'

Surprisingly, at least to me, Edith laughed but then spoke almost in a whisper, although she smiled as she did so, the absurdity of the event clearly pleasing her. 'Sir, I know you not. I will not answer such questions about a princess of my country. These are not proper for you to ask.'

'Excuse please, I am sorry, the king gave his word I might talk to you. I am Oleg the Ambassador of Vsevolod, Grand Prince of Pereyaslavl.'

Edith waited, saying nothing and seemingly not awed by his words.

The bear-man was clearly taken aback. He paused, waiting, and when Edith still did not answer he bowed and said, 'The king has given his word. Grand Prince Vsevolod is a great man. He may even take the throne of Kyjev Rus one day.'

'You say so? That must be good for him, but what is it to me?'

'Please let me tell you my meaning. I begin this all wrong,

320

my Danish not so good, my English worse. Please, your Majesty, I bow before you, I kiss your feet.'

Edith shook her head, waving her hand from side to side to show that he must not.

He fell to his knees before her. 'Please, I start again, yes?'

'Yes.'

'Thank you, thank you,' he grasped the hem of her robe and started to kiss it. She pulled it from his grasp and backed away beyond arm's length, but I could see a smile twitch again at the corners of her mouth.

'Start again,' she said.

On his throne, King Sweyn watched all this, his eyes sparkling and a hand over his mouth to hide his smile.

'Thank you, thank you; I am Ambassador of Grand Prince Vsevolod of Pereyaslavl.'

Edith waited silently.

'The Grand Prince has a favourite son, his eldest, Vladimir.'

Still waiting, Edith said nothing.

'Vladimir is of the same age as your daughter Gytha I believe, for he also was born in the Christian year one thousand and fifty-three.'

How he came by this knowledge I knew not. I looked hard at Wilda across the hall but she would not meet my eyes, her gaze sliding away from mine. 'Ahah,' thought I.

Edith held up her hand to the ambassador to stop him saying anything more. She turned to her daughter and raising her voice said, 'Princess Gytha, pray return to our room and take Wilda with you. This is royal business; we will speak later.'

Gytha looked startled but hurried to obey. In silence the two women climbed the stairs and on entering their room closed the door behind them.

'You were saying, Ambassador?' said Edith.

Haltingly, the bear-man continued. 'Prince Vladimir must marry soon, but this not easy. Polotvsian princess may quiet the Polotvsians, but anger the rulers of other lands, they wish their blood on the throne of Kyjev Rus. The marriage must bring peace, you understand?' His face red and perspiring had an expression that pleaded for understanding. 'The marriage must be to a noble lady of a far land who will birth noble children. The mother of Prince Vladimir was Anastasia, a princess of Byzantium. She was such a one. Now, she is dead and Byzantium has no more princess. We hear a queen and her daughter come to Roskilde. We hear they seek a safe land. Grand Prince Vsevolod send me to see if princess is fitting.'

'And what, Ambassador Oleg, would you say makes a princess good enough for the Grand Prince of... where did you say?'

'Pereyaslavl, but your Majesty, there is every reason to think he might one day rule Kyjev Rus.'

'Ah yes, the throne of Kyjev Rus, and where is that?'

The bear-man saw that Edith was playing with him and lapsed into silence.

'Speak Ambassador Oleg, what will tell you that Princess Gytha is good enough for Prince Valodya, son of Vsevolod of Pereyaslavl?'

It seemed to me later, when I knew more and understood what she had done, that Edith had used the familiar name of the prince to let Oleg know she knew more than he perhaps thought. So are things played out amongst the powerful.

'I speak only as I have been told to speak by my master, the father of the prince, your Majesty.'

'Speak on.'

'He asks, "Is the princess pleasing to the eye?" I shall say that she is.

'He asks, "Is the princess a virgin?"'

'Yes,' answered Edith.

'I shall say that she is. He asks, "Has the princess ever borne children?"'

Edith's eyebrow lifted, 'the answer to that is contained in the last. Unless she be Our Lady Mary come again, the answer is obviously no!'

Ignoring her tone, Oleg continued with his master's questions. 'He asks, "has she dower enough?"'

'The answer to that is that she has no dower at all and if your master seeks marriage with my daughter he must start his hunt with a gift of gold.'

'My master trusts my judgement and empowers me to say that the Princess Gytha is good enough for his son. He wishes to ask you that he might marry her to Vladimir and make her a princess of Kyjev Rus.'

'Tell your master this. Such a marriage is possible if I say so. The princess is obedient and will abide by what I, the queen, her mother, decide. We must meet with this Vladimir at his father's expense, and if all comes to nought then we must be returned here, also at the Grand Prince's expense. It must satisfy the Princess Gytha that Vladimir's looks match her wishes for a husband; that he is kindly to those he loves and who love him; that he is fierce and severe to his enemies and will protect her against all evil; that he has gold enough that she may not want for food or clothes.'

'In all of those things there is nothing that will hinder this wedding, your Majesty. Prince Vladimir is tall, well built, in good health and reckoned to be of pleasing looks. He shows promise to be a good war leader, far better than his father, and even now sees to the defence not only of his principality of Pereyaslavl but also that of Kyjev Rus. Pereyaslavl is a wealthy land lying across the main route for traders between the North and Asia, It lies close to the Varangian Way and yields much in taxes. The princess may dress in amber if she wishes and eat salted white fish of Caspia.'

My lady appeared to consider this.

At length she gave her reply. 'Very well, Ambassador Oleg, we are in agreement. All that remains to be decided are the means by which we travel to Kyjev and Pereyaslavl for we, my daughter, our servants and I, cannot – will not – walk halfway round the world only to walk back. Even to ride on horseback will be slow progress.

The bear-man smiled at this. 'Your Majesty, you will travel in the greatest of comfort, you can if you wish keep to your couch day and night. We go to Kyjev along the Varangian Way.'

Then he told of the 'Way' but as we were to find out, he did not tell all.

I knew not what Gytha would make of all this, but could see that to Edith it was a windfall from the Fates. She had told me of the dangers to us should William offer gold for our return to him. The marriage of Gytha to a good man would put her daughter out of harm's way. It would also form a safe harbour for us. If that good man were also a great man, a ruler, then Gytha would have what she had lost with the death of her father.

'We,' my lady said to me later, 'will also be beyond the reach of the Bastard and much as he might rage and storm he will not find the body of the king, nor will he recover the ring of Wessex.'

It was small revenge, a pinprick compared to the dagger she wished to plunge into him to cut out his evil heart, but nevertheless something from which she could take a small fulfilment. So, when Ambassador Oleg had retired and we had returned to Edith's room, she approached Gytha with a joyful face as if the greatest good had come to pass.

'Gytha,' she said, 'the most wonderful thing has happened.' She rushed on, 'you are to be married to a great prince. He is tall, handsome and rules a great land and will sometime rule a greater. He is rich and kind and will love you and make all your dreams come true.'

The princess stood open-mouthed, expressions of dismay, fear and then sullenness crossing her face. She rushed at me and threw her arms about me, to my great amazement.

'Are you going to let them do this to me?' she cried. 'Please, please, save me, anything, run away with me. I don't want to marry anyone else.'

Both Edith and I looked at her and now it was we who were open-mouthed. I knew that Gytha gave me regard above my deserving; that she saw me as her protector, but I had not known it to have gone so far. Since then I have thought about it. I was protected from her by my love for her mother. What if I had not been? Would I have spurred her on, breached my duty as the commended man to Edith, run away with her, lain with her; ruined her life? Fate had it that I loved another and that love protected us all.

Edmund's sudden silence surprised all us listeners in the Cot. It had seemed that his voice, which we were so used to hearing now, would go on forever. Slowly we came to understand that the telling of the story had ceased and we came back from the palace in Roskilde to the Cot in Somerset. It was the gleeman's voice that drew us in, that took us away from our daily lot and into lands and places and stories, which somehow seemed more real than the day-to-day happenings of our lives.

We looked to Bowdyn and waited for him to carry on or tell us to go. He saw we still sat willing him to tell us more, and smiled.

'Well, my friends, we have come to the end of this story for today. Queen Edith seems to have escaped the clutches of William, at least for a time. Gytha's life is changing for she may be married to a great noble, far from the land where her father was killed and where his murderer sought her. She at least, if all comes to pass, will have found safety. So Edith and Gytha are to leave the doubtful security of King Sweyn's court and travel the Varangian Way, Edith as the mother of the bride to be. With her go Wilda as her maid and Edmund as her defender and servant. Siward Barn is the last of the gang of warriors who also travels on. He goes to Byzantium to join the Varangian guard; Edith's little band will leave him when they arrive at Kyjev.

'Who, you might ask are the Varangians? They are no single race of men; their name means "the oath sworn". That is because they are often bound to the Emperor to serve on his personal guard. Some who travel the Way are merchants and go to trade and are oath sworn to deal honestly. Some Varangians come from Denmark, some from Norway others from Sweden, some, since the battle, from England.

'The Way itself is by ship, down many rivers leading to the Black Sea. Here most take the right bank and follow it around to Byzantium. Some, merchants, take the left bank to the Sea of Azov where they enter the Don River and thence with many portages to the Volga and down to the Caspian Sea, meeting the silk route in Baku or Samarkand.

'You look at me with puzzlement and I know these names mean nothing to you. But you do know of the lands of the Northmen and you have heard of the lands of the fabled East and its riches of silks and spices. In between these two is the land of the Rus. Kyjev, to which Edith, Gytha, Wilda and Edmund go, is in the middle of that land.

'I think, my friends, this brings us to the end of the story in Roskilde. Next time we meet, Edmund will continue the story. He will also get the chance he seeks to risk his life for the safety of his unattainable beloved. There will be more peril for Edith where there should be none, but she lives in dangerous times and travels lands where the rule of law is loose. Perhaps William, in spite, thinks that if he cannot have her returned alive he will be satisfied with her death. For dead she can tell no one where Harold's remains lie. He might hope that his assassins may even steal the ring and bring it to him. Perhaps he sends his spies to Sigtuna to offer gold for her death and the ring. Who knows? That is one story that fits something that otherwise is a mystery. We cannot know, for those concerned took their stories over the blood red roads to Valhalla.'

Bowdyn paused, but when nobody asked a question, each of us trying to understand all the strange things he was telling us, he continued. 'So, having resolved to go to Kyjev and at least consider the marriage of Gytha to Vladimir, Edith must first find a ship to carry them. King Sweyn agreed to provide one for the first short leg of the journey. But to board it they must cross the land from Roskilde to the merchants' haven. From there King Sweyn's ship will carry them thence to the

Sala River and then they must find another to take them to Kyjev.

'So I bid you good night my friends. At our next meeting you will hear what happened.'

Chapter 32

AD 1072

Edmund's Tale: The Sala River

The sea lay calm with scarcely a ripple as our butsecarls rowed King Sweyn's ship along the coast of the Swedish lands. The oars raised more of a swell than the light airs over the sea. The weather was bitter cold and we huddled in the furs the shipman had loaned us. Light flurries of snow, tiny ice stones, swirled through the air and lay crisp on the deck. Breath froze on beards and lip hair and we drew scarves across our faces. They did not much improve our comfort for they stiffened as our breath soaked through and turned to ice. I for one wished I had never left the palace hall. I could well understand why Ambassador Oleg chose to look like a bear. Sometimes patches of the sea were covered with thin ice and crackled as we broke our way through it.

By the second day there was a gap in the mountains. The shipman stood talking with Siward Barn, who then crossed to where Edith leant on the rail gazing into the water.

'That is the Sala River,' said Siward. 'We will row up the river and then anchor where it enters Lake Malaran. Our time is brief for our shipman says that within a week the river will freeze and we must leave or be caught fast. If any ship comes it will be the last of the year. No more will come until the spring.

'Any ship leaving Sigtuna to sail the Varangian Way must pass by here. We must put out towards him in a small boat or he may think us pirates and wish to fight. We will bargain then to be given passage for it is very far. To walk would be to risk death many times over but to get passage, first we pay and then we must agree to put our shoulders to the portages, for there are many, which is to say that in places we must all help take the ship and its cargo overland. Does my Lord Abbot understand that?'

The Abbot of Holme, wanting to put as many miles as he could between himself and King William, and thinking to bring the English Church to those many Englishmen now employed in the Varangian Guard, had also set out to travel with Siward Barn to Byzantium. But it now seemed that his time as tutor to Prince Knut had shown him another, godlier way.

'I do,' said Aelfwold, 'I have taken thought on it and for that reason among others I shall not be coming with you. In Byzantium they are barbarians. They follow a Greek church; they are strangers to Holy Mother Church. I can do nothing there, except provide a target for their stones. Here I may do good deeds, for in Prince Knut, who one day will be King Knut, the fourth of that name, there is much that might be saintly. I would sooner offer him my faith and knowledge of Church and Holy Scriptures than carry a ship or its goods halfway across the world to be stoned to death by heretics.'

Our party was now much shrunken; only Edith, Gytha, Wilda, Siward, Oleg and I now remained. Whilst we sailed with Sweyn's butsecarls I feared nothing. But when we joined a ship on the Varangian Way there would be three womenfolk and only Siward a warrior, for although I had killed for Edith, I did not carry a warrior's weapons. The ambassador I knew nothing of, whether he would fight in a time of danger or not. I would fight, but only had skill with my staff. I found the safety of my lady a problem and worried at it like a dog with a bone.

Two weeks we lay at anchor with the ice forming around us or drifting by in flat rounds with raised edges like pan-melted cheese, waiting for a trading ship to put out from Sigtuna. When one did it was not the best ship we had ever seen. It was smaller than our own ship and somehow had an unkempt look. We excused that because we had no choice. It was this or wait in Roskilde, alert for the Bastard's hirelings until the spring.

Siward and Oleg helped the womenfolk climb down into the rowing boat tied at the stern. I followed, cursing my useless leg. One of our shipman's butsecarls then rowed us towards the newcomer and hailed it. The ship backed water and drew to a stop. The captain called down to us, and by shouting he and the butsecarl conversed in Danish over the cold, shivering air.

'Who calls?'

'Where bound?'

'The Varangian Way to Byzantium.'

'I have six passengers for you.'

'Can they pay?'

'Payment in Kyjev from the Monomach.'

'I have heard that merry tune before. And shall I go to war with Rus if the Prince does not pay? Payment must be made in full on boarding, and for all costs, including food. Are they strong and well? Passengers who cannot carry at the portages are no use to me.'

'They are one warrior, one servant, a Rus and three strong women.'

'I heard there is a queen going south. Is one of these a queen?'

The butsecarl gave a misleading answer, 'Do you see a queen here?'

'No matter, a queen should not carry at portages. No queen; everyone carries.'

He then told us what our passage would cost us. It sounded a vast amount to me. Oleg laughed and called up, 'Do you want to take the whole hoard of Kyjev? Rob us and take half.'

The Varangian captain shrugged. You can walk for nothing if saving the wealth of Kyjev is your aim. If you wish to ride the price is as I say. Now decide for I must be on my way.

While we sat and shivered wrapped in our cloaks, shorn of our borrowed furs, Oleg climbed on board and counted out the gold, slamming each coin down into the Varangian captain's hand, for the price was high. Without Oleg even Edith's purse would not have stretched so far. But without Oleg and Gytha's wedding we would have had no choice but to stay in Roskilde and watch for William's men coming in the night to murder or make off with my lady.

When Oleg had paid we were allowed to board also, climbing the boarding net with some difficulty. Once over the rail we waved goodbye to our butsecarl and across the water through the falling snow to the shipman of Sweyn's ship.

'You will sleep in the passenger house, it isn't much but this ship carries cargo first, passengers second,' said our captain. There are two others; soldiers going to Byzantium.'

'Englishmen?' asked Siward, coming alive.

'No, Flemings they say.'

'They say?'

'I have trod and sailed the Varangian Way most of my life and for Flemings they speak good French and only French.

They must think me simple. I know you are English and I know you have much to hate the Normans for, but there must be no fighting in the passenger house or you will be walking to Kyjev. Am I clear?'

We all agreed he was entirely clear.

Chapter 33

AD 1072
Edmund's Tale: Holmgard

There was a hatch and a ladder from the main deck to the passenger house deck. The hatchway let the only daylight in, although an oil light swung from the beams when the hatch was closed in bad weather and gave enough light to lie in bed or eat by. When the weather was bad there was no food to be had from the ship, but Oleg had known that and made sure we all carried a bag of cold food.

The so-called passenger house was in fact just a hold; an empty space in the middle. All along the wooden outside and cross walls of the ship were beds of a sort: ten in all, four on each side of the ship's shell and one on each forward and after cross wall. They were narrow beds with wooden slats and we lay on them wrapped shivering in our cloaks, which did little to keep us warm in this winter season. Only Oleg appeared comfortable.

Siward went to speak with the Varangian captain. I don't know what he had to say to him, but he came back laden with stinking, flea bedevilled, but warm furs. The best of these went to my lady, and then to Gytha, and then Wilda. We men took what was left. The stink was greater, but they were no less warm so I did not care. We could neither change clothes nor wash and for our needs there was a thunder box at the stern. This was just a screened framework of wood with a large hole in the base and the open water beneath. We did not use this needlessly for it was uncommonly cold. We were lucky; the weather was good. In bad weather I daresay there was danger of one's bottom being immersed in surging icy water.

Our two fellow passengers were well stored for they had brought their own furs, softer and better smelling than ours. Mindful of the captain's words we treated these strangers civilly but distantly. They seemed upright, which just goes to uphold what I have learned in these times. It is unwise to judge someone by looks or even sounds. Watch, wait, judge by deed, and keep your seax sheath oiled. Somehow, having made a good judgement of our fellow passengers we forgot that.

They had little to say but they watched us keenly. Mostly it was Edith they watched and this set an alarm drumming in my head. But they made no move towards her and the ship moved on. We crossed an icy but calm sea and entered a river. Here also there was some ice, but nothing to stop our rowers. By the time we had passed through a great lake and entered another river we had become used to the other passengers and thought nothing of them. Our mistake.

Our ship lay alongside the town of Holmgard to take stores. We passengers were wanted to fetch and carry, as we had agreed we could. We left the womenfolk in the hold for the weather was very cold, and told the Varangian captain that we men would work twice as hard to make up for their absence. I did not notice that the two so-called Flemings were missing for long moments and it was not until I heard a scream from the ship that it came to me as baleful.

I ran, but with my leg I was not as fast as Siward, who pushed past me. We slid down the stairway and landed heavily on the hold deck ready to fight.

Edith was crouched, bloody bodkin dagger in hand. Gytha, crying, the tears running down her cheeks, stood behind her with Wilda, their backs pressed against the boards of the forward bed space. On the deck in a pool of blood was one of the Flemings, the other faced her at bay, his sword raised ready to strike.

Hearing us behind him on the ladder he turned and thrust the blade at me. I thought my death was at hand, but the point of the sword missed its target as I turned and sliding against my skin caught in my clothes. Before he could strike again, Siward, who had drawn his sword as we ran, cracked him over the head with it and he fell to the ground.

Edith straightened up and smiled. She smiled! Bending, she wiped her dagger on the tabard of the blood-soaked corpse. 'So foolish,' she said. 'They came at us with drawn swords, they could have killed all three of us if swift enough.'

'What happened?' I said.

'They keep their brains swinging between their legs, Edmund. This one,' she stirred him with her foot, taking care to keep it out of the pooled blood, 'told me they were going to kill us and then walk ashore. He said they had William's money to spend and that a finger, a lock of hair and the ring I carry would bring them plenty more. Instead of killing me he wasted time boasting. And then he said that before they killed me they were going to have some glee. He had never had his old man up the kunte of a queen or a princess. Now was his chance while you, Siward and Oleg were carrying stores for the ship, which gave him plenty of time. He came up to me and as he reached for me so I drew my bodkin and thrust it

337

quickly in his heart, you know, under the ribs and up, and he fell where you see him now. That fetched the other up short and Gytha screamed. It is a talent of hers.' Edith fell silent and slipped the bodkin back into its sheath in the back of her mantle. White-faced, Wilda said nothing, but reached forward to place a comforting arm around Gytha's shoulders.

I went to fetch the Varangian captain and begged him come. He clattered down the ladder and glanced around. I was fearful that he would put us off the ship. When he sold a passage it was not expected by any passenger that they would be killed whilst on board, such happenings would be very bad for business, I thought, and he had already warned us about fighting. However, I need not have feared. When Edith had told him her story he looked down at the remaining Fleming, who was now attempting to stand.

'Go now, before I kill you. Go as you are, if you freeze to death then good.' The captain turned to the seamen who had followed him into the hold. 'Take this wretch and throw him off the ship. Do not let him back on board.' Then he kicked at the dead body, 'And when we sail tonight take this dross and throw it in the water.'

As the seamen did as he bade them, the captain went up to the Flemings' beds and began to sort through their baggage. After a while he turned to Edith. 'They tried to force themselves upon you; you have killed one of them justly. All that was theirs is yours,' and he dropped a heavy purse on the eating board in the middle of the hold. He then picked up the furs belonging to the Flemings and put those beside it.

'These also are yours my lady, as are these,' he took the dead Fleming's weapons, his sword and dagger and handed them to Edith. 'Please find a use for these, he no longer needs them.'

Which is how I got my first sword, for Edith gave it to me, and a very fine sword it was. The dagger she gave to Gytha, saying that it was past time she could defend herself.

And so at last I felt we could take our ease, for we had passed beyond the vengeful reach of William the Bastard, Duke of Normandy, now king by conquest of our ravaged and grieving land of England.

With some of the extra money that we had from the dead Fleming we were able to pay the captain to have a heater in the hold. This was an oil lamp contained in a swinging metal pail. A plate of metal was placed over the top and after a while this glowed red-hot and took some of the chill off the hold.

Chapter 34

AD 1072 - 1073
Edmund's Tale: The Varangian Way

From the Sala, where we had joined our ship, the Sjaelland, we rowed on many rivers as we travelled down the Varangian Way: the Neva to Lake Ladoga, then the Vikhov and so to the Lovat, Kunya and the Seryoza. It was here we found out what had not been told to us at Roskilde, for from Seryoza to the Toropa was a portage. That is to say, the ship had to be taken overland. Clearly, Ambassador Oleg, so eager to get Edith to agree to the marriage of her daughter to his prince, had not only concealed the truth about this journey, he had told a barefaced lie.

Passengers and seamen alike worked to discharge all the cargo and we carried it on our backs all the way to the banks of the Toropa. Then the ship was dragged on rollers stacked ready at the end of a dragway. The womenfolk, strong as they were, could not carry a normal load and so Siward, Oleg and I carried more. It was work that would break your back and tear your groin if you were careless. At one point Siward's foot slipped.

'Shit and fall back in it!' he exclaimed. 'I have hurt my apples. I will never breed again.' He had fallen to his knees, for though a mighty man the weight had carried him down.

He struggled to get up but the cargo was too heavy.

'Young Edmund, I cannot rise. Please take some of the load off my back.'

'I cannot, for I can lift no more, my leg will not take it.'

I looked all around, but none of the seamen had waited and were some way ahead, as was Oleg. In truth they may not have seen Siward slip. The loads were so heavy that the mind went numb; the eyes were cast down looking all the time at the ground for secure footing. This was important, for sometimes the groin would twist so much after a stumble that the man could die. We were told that this often happened and ordered to be careful. If a man was injured and could not carry, he was left to make his own way and if he died, he died. The worst of it was that his load had to be shared amongst the rest so the orders were for everyone's good.

I was wondering what to do when my brave Edith came once more to our rescue. 'I can lift more,' she said, 'be still.' She unstrapped the top packages of Siward's load and with some unwomanly grunts lowered them to the ground without her legs giving way under the extra weight.

After unloading two she put her arm under Siward's. 'Now,' she said and lifted as he pushed, until he, still moaning about his apples, was back on his feet again. 'Will you live?' she said.

'Barely, but I shall never breed for I have ruined my bits.'

Edith's lips twitched, 'some men would think that a good thing; glee without cost. Now turn and face the path.'

She reloaded his back with the two packages and lashed them firmly and somehow she did all this while still carrying a load that would kill an ass. I admired the willpower of our women; they never complained, even the smaller loads they carried were hard on them.

We moved about six miles each day and the cargo portage took us twenty days, the ship on its rollers somewhat less.

And so the year moved on. At the start of the portage it was bitterly cold and although the work warmed us somewhat, the ice on the ground added to the danger. By the time we had finished that portage, the snow and ice had turned to rain and puddles.

Once the ship was afloat in the Toropa we passengers could rest, but after a short spell the crew were expected to take their place on the oars. At first this was downstream and an easy row to the Western Dvina, but then they were working hard pulling upstream to the Kasplya. From there was a portage to the Katyn and so it started again. At the end of this portage was a city, Smolensk. Here we unloaded all our cargo, checked and marked any leaks the dragging overland had caused to the ship's timbers and bought black tar, which the seamen melted and used to plug the damaged woodwork of the shell.

While this was going on Edith came to me. 'Edmund, please ask if there are any inns in this town. We have money, we will be here for some days and Gytha and I would like to wash our clothes and ourselves in something cleaner than muddy river water; eat food that is not everlasting stew, be warm and lie in a warm, clean bed in which we might sleep and sleep and sleep. Ask the captain if you and Siward might come with us for our safety in a strange town. I have the Flemings' gold, I will pay.'

I asked. The captain was glad to see the back of us for we were eating his stores, getting in the way and adding nothing of work to the tasks he had to finish.

And so, gleefully, we went to the town. Finding an inn was hard because Oleg had gone off somewhere and no one spoke our language. Eventually we were pointed towards a Varangian who did. He had settled in this town as a sworn guard in the gate watch. He showed us to the town's only inn and there we soaked in hot water, sat around a fire, ate roast meat and good strong bread and eggs and cheese and all the things we had forgotten the taste of. And then we took ourselves to our rooms. The womenfolk to theirs, Siward and I to ours and then we slept and slept – for as long as the fleas would let us.

Seven days we stayed there, repairing ourselves while our ship was being similarly repaired in the port, and then we had the call to re-join and our rest was over.

After the Katyn and Smolensk, we joined the Slavuta and the worst of our journey was almost over, except that the Slavuta had rapids. We were lucky, our captain knew them well; had he not then we would have been portaging around them also. We had faith in our captain who had lived through many other passages down the Varangian Way, but the rapids on the Slavuta worked wonders at keeping our personal motions loose. Taking all the times together, I must have spent at least twenty white-faced paternosters in the thunderbox rigged hanging from the rail on the ship's quarter.

Edith seemed unaffected; she stood in the bow her face flushed with excitement as if she enjoyed the rocks racing towards us. I did not. I was ashamed for the number of times I had to say, 'Please excuse me my lady,' and break off our conversation to run along the centre of the deck to the stern. But Edith was a queen and diplomacy had been her life for years. She made no sign of noticing anything unusual and every time I reappeared she restarted our conversation as if I had never left.

'Oh look at that,' she would say, 'do you see between waves how the base of that rock is so green, how the white of the foam shines against it?' And I would stand wide-eyed whilst the rock to which she pointed loomed overhead and rushed by our side. Sometimes we would slide along a huge flat rock jutting from the foam. There would be a squealing, grating noise and the whole ship would start to turn. The seamen on the same side as the rock would sit with their oars upright whilst those on the other side backed water to keep us straight.

Edith would laugh. 'What a noise, Gytha would be better here with us, she cannot be sleeping with all this banging and crashing going on, silly girl.' She turned to me and took me by the arm. 'Gytha is not like her father or her brothers. Harold feared nothing and they fear nothing also. They are tough briar stock, thorny and hard to kill. Gytha is a primrose patch; she needs shelter; that is why she clings to you for you have always stood between danger and us. That is why, if her prince is strong and good, she needs this marriage. Do you see?'

'I see clearly my lady, but there is nothing for my part between Gytha and me, I love another, as well you know.'

She was silent for a while staring at the mad white foaming of the river. Then she patted my arm, 'You are a good boy Edmund, thank you for being my oathsworn.'

Gytha of course, like me, was frightened and had no reason to pretend to be brave. She had remained in the passenger house where she could not see the rapids. Wilda kept her company and diverted her with light chatter, but Gytha could not ignore the noise. I too thought she must be more frightened by it when she could not see what caused it. There were rocks that could break our hull and drop us all in the white foaming water, but our captain knew of these and steered the ship around them. There were shallows where the bottom of our ship ground its keel, where we could be swung broadside on and being swept onto our sides lost to the raging waters. On drawing near to these spots the captain had all those not rowing run to stand aft. In that way the after end was at its deepest and grated on the bottom, whilst the racing waters swept the bow to face downstream and thus save us from broaching to. Slovenly the upkeep of the Sjaelland might be, but I was thankful for the knowledge and the skill of that Varangian captain.

Eventually there was a stretch of calmer water where, off to the right-hand side, we passed another river joining the Dnieper. The captain seeing me on the hatch to the passenger hold, a place we had taken to sitting now the weather was warmer, waved me over.

He pointed, 'that is the Pripet River. Please tell your lady we will be at Kyjev, all being well, in two days.'

Edith was thankful, Wilda relieved and Gytha fearful. I understood that. We adults had only to look forward to a life of ease after the dangers and hardships of the journey. Gytha had the fear of marriage to a man she did not know. He might be ugly and earn her revulsion, foolish and earn her contempt, cruel and earn her fear. As she had said, she did not want to marry anyone; she wanted to stay near me. This was shaming for me, for I did not want to hurt her feelings nor disclose those I had for her mother, but I knew that if she married this prince then our plight would be over and all would be well. I felt like a betrayer.

Regardless of the guilt that bore down on me, the water calmed and within the two days forecast by the captain we were sliding down behind the offshore sandbar and rowing alongside the staithes of Kyjev.

Here we said goodbye to Siward and wished him good fortune in the service of the Eastern Roman Emperor. It made me sad that a good and brave warrior such as Siward Barn was forced to leave his own country and pledge his life to a foreign ruler, but I should have felt greater sadness for us, for Edith, for how were we any different? We too had been forced by our fear of a cruel and spiteful foe to flee our home and seek a haven in a strange land.

AD 1073 Kyjev and
the Polovtsi

Chapter 35

Edmund's Tale: Kyjev

Oleg, now on his home ground, told us to wait and climbed ashore disappearing from sight towards the town. While we waited we looked over the ship's rail at the place that might be our home for God knows how long. Certainly for as long as William lived.

As our gaze settled on the city of Kyjev we were struck silent with awe. It was the magnificence of the place that made us dumb. It was a town of stone buildings, tall walls and domes: domed gates, cathedral domes next to monastery domes. Some were covered with gold and flashed fire in the spring sunshine. Where we had expected a wood-built rural town we saw the capital of a great and rich empire. One of which, perhaps one day, Gytha would be queen.

The gangplank had no sooner clattered down than Oleg returned. A man, who by his rich dress could only be a wealthy merchant or some member of the ruling household, accompanied him.

Coming aboard, Oleg took him by the hand and presented him to Edith. 'This is Count Vassily, Master of the Grand Prince's Horses, he has come to greet you and invite you and your people to a feast, and to give you the chance to rest before you start again towards your wayfaring's end.'

'Start again?' said Edith. 'I thought at Kyjev our wandering was over?'

Oleg made a comical sad face, 'I am sorry my lady, but there is one more river passage to reach Pereyaslavl where Prince Vladimir awaits his bride. The glad tiding is that there will be no portages, here the Dnieper is wide and calm and so you may rest all the way.'

'I am not sure I should trust your word on that, Oleg' Edith said, but she smiled and he bowed deeply then held out his hand ushering the prince's envoy forward.

Count Vassily faced her and dropped to his knees. 'Your Highness, the Grand Prince Sviatoslav of Kyjev welcomes you and your daughter and begs that you attend him so that you might talk of the marriage of the Princess Gytha to his nephew, Prince Vladimir, who sends his humble regrets that he is not here to meet you himself, but he and his father are leading an army at this time and have grim business in hand.' This message he delivered in clear Danish, clear at least to Edith and Gytha, understandable to me.

'An army?' said Edith, indicating that he should get up off his knees.

'You have come to us at a difficult time, Highness. It is why Prince Vladimir cannot be here to meet his lovely bride.' He bowed to Gytha and her face lost its sulky look and became brighter.

'After you have met with his uncle the Grand Prince here in Kyjev, I will take you to Pereyaslavl on the Trubizh and Alta rivers. By land on horseback would normally be quicker but now certainly not safer.'

'And why is that?' asked Edith.

Count Vassily turned his mouth down; his shoulders did not move but if ever a face shrugged, his did then.

'Three years ago at the Battle of the Alta River the Povlotsians defeated the sons of Yaroslav the Wise. They tore down the frontier barriers, filled in the hollows. Now they ride their horses over the earthwork snakes, and gallop unhindered through our lands unless we catch them and bring them to battle. Where they go the land is emptied, they are like some great plague. If you set out overland, your Highness, you are more likely to end your travels in a Polovtsian tent than in the Palace at Pereyaslavl. When they tired of you then you would be sold at the slave marts. My prince would be very angry with me were that to happen. But no matter,' he said, gesturing with his hand and posing and posturing in a comical manner, 'for I would have died in defending you.' Then he smiled and Edith and Gytha smiled with him.

'I am sure we will be safe in your brave hands,' said Edith and I felt a lump in my heart for I knew that my reign as the hero protector of my womenfolk was over. I had feared William Malet, his nobility, his easy way with my lady, with him in our company I felt merely a servant. When I found he loved land more than my lady that freed me of fear. But now Vassily was one of a court full of gallants. Once more I felt humble, a mere servant. My fear would not leave me so easily this time.

Feeling saddened by this thought I looked around me and found Wilda standing by my side looking about her as if lost. Perhaps because I suddenly felt as lost as she looked, I reached to my side and took her hand in mine. She grasped it eagerly like a wandering child found by a parent. As Count Vassily explained the war against the Povlotsian nomads to Edith, we stood hand in hand like two orphaned children. Had we been alone I would have hugged her and hoped she would hug me back.

While we stood thus, gazing about whilst Vassily talked,

there was a bump and a lurch and the boat that was to take us to Pereyaslavl came alongside. We crossed the deck to look over at it. It was long, sleek and cleanly painted. The seamen, or river men, whatever they were called, were all dressed alike in war gear and I understood this to be a fleet craft belonging to the Grand Prince Sviatoslav. On the deck between the forward and after rowing benches was a deckhouse, which it seemed must be for the comfort of passengers, for it had both a door and a window and looked to be far superior to the passenger house on the Sjaelland. I was to learn later that it also served as a shelter from arrows.

Edith had found a more pressing worry. She now spoke with authority, sounding more like a queen than ever I had heard her.

'Count Vassily, neither Princess Gytha nor I have any clothes than the ones you see us in. We set out for a simple journey to an abbey, and now we are here, halfway across the world. We cannot meet the Grand Prince looking like the poorest of servants. I have gold; you must first take us somewhere where we can buy clothes that are more fitting.'

'Fear not, Your Highness. When we arrive at the palace you shall go first to meet the ladies in waiting to the Grand Princess Oda. She is from the Rhinelands; her uncles are a pope and an emperor. She will be able to guide you in the ways of the Grand Prince's court. Her ladies will help you to everything you might wish: hot perfumed baths, fresh clothes, drink and sweetmeats to relax you. The attentions of the finest most expert ladies maids, so that when you meet the Grand Prince it will be as if you stepped from your palace into his.'

'Count Vassily, if all that comes about and is but half of what you promise, you are an angel indeed,' said Edith with a smile.

'Then with your permission, your Highness, let us go to

the palace, for you must rest. It is not far, closer than the city. It is in the Grand Prince's village of Berestiv, in the Perchesk district, where we are now.' He bowed and gestured with his hand to the gangplank, which now was tied securely to the hythe. I went ahead to test the safety of the way to the land. Satisfied, I offered my hand to my lady, and then in turn to Gytha and Wilda.

Waiting on the hythe was a golden box with paintings of great beauty on the outside panels. It was taller than it was wide with doors on both sides, and inside were two facing seats covered in red velvet. From half way up the box there were two shafts, but no horses and no wheels. As Gytha and Edith clambered inside they looked back with regret at Wilda and me. But I had no regrets. Queens and princesses rode, servants walked, I understood that. Eight soldiers, two on each shaft end, lifted the box and set off swiftly, following Vassily and Oleg, who rode ahead on horseback. Linking hands, Wilda and I followed at a lively stride.

Vassily spoke truly for I doubt we went four hundred paces before we were flanked by guards and entering gates leading through the palace walls into a courtyard. This palace was a strange building, unlike any I had seen in our country or for that matter in that of King Sweyn. For a start the greatest building was in stone two stories high, but the palace, whilst of great extent, was otherwise made up of many smaller buildings around courtyards each joined together by galleries. Beyond the walls surrounding us I could see higher walls and a great gate with golden domes. This I learned later was the Golden Gate of Kyjev.

Through the smaller gate we had entered was the first of the courtyards and to the left a porch. The bearers put down the golden chair and Edith and Gytha stepped out in front of the porch. They had not stood for ten breaths looking around them, when a vision in silks and jewels burst from the doorway bowing so low he scraped the ground with his fingernails. He spoke in Danish to Edith, in a high piping voice.

'Your Majesty, your Highness, my Queen, I am Aleixos. I am yours to command. Please to follow me I will show you and her Highness the Princess Gytha to what will be your dwelling place until you continue with your journey.'

Chapter 36

AD 1073

Edmund's Tale: Of Enemies and Friends

This Aleixos was as strange to me as the palace itself. He was a eunuch, a servant of the dead Anastasia from Byzantium, where there are many such. Or so I was told. He it is that dealt on her behalf with the Varangians who came to trade. Now he would serve my lady, to fetch and carry and instruct.

This place was very different from anything we had known and we found it difficult to understand. Aleixos, who in a cloud of fragrant perfume continued to bow and scrape to my lady and Gytha whenever they spoke to him or he to them, helped us to unravel the weavings of Kyjev Rus.

When we were settled in our 'dwelling places', Edith's spacious, ours small, but all clean – though draughty and cold – furnished with padded benches, wooden board, bed with furs and chests to hang or lay our clothes, we sat with Aleixos and Edith questioned him. I say sat, but the eunuch had trouble with the idea of sitting in my lady's presence; he seemed most unworried when we let him kneel on the floor.

'Now,' said Edith, 'we must know who is who and what is happening all around about. Can you tell us?'

Screwing up his face, Aleixos made a lip-smacking noise and shook his head. 'I will try, but it is as twisted and dangerous as the River Dnieper.' He was quiet, thinking a moment and then he started his tale.

'There was a great ruler of Kyjev Rus, Yaroslav the Wise. He had three sons who may reign in Kyjev: Iziaslav, Sviatoslav and Vsevolod. There was also Vseslav of Polotsk, who was not a son of Yaroslav but who also, for a short time, reigned in Kyjev. Grand Prince Yaroslav's favourite son was the youngest, Vsevolod, the father of Prince Vladimir, your husband-to-be, Princess Gytha. Vsevolod is, as you know, Prince of Pereyaslavl.

'Perhaps the best place to start is with the Steppes, for all that is bad starts out there. Kyjev, its cities and its farmland, is surrounded by savage foes. These are the Polovtsi. They are nomads; they wander on horseback and steal or destroy whatever they can. There is no chance for peace, for Kyjev would farm where the Polvtsi would herd and roam free.

'Five years ago in Pereyaslavl, on the Alta River, Grand Prince Iziaslav of Kyjev was defeated by the Polovtsi in a great battle. When he returned to Kyjev, the Veche – the gathering of the people – asked him for arms and horses that they might make good his failure. But he would not give them what they asked so they unseated him. At that time, held in the dungeons of Kyjev was the sworn enemy of the three sons of Yaroslav the Wise. His name was Vsevslav of Polotsk. When the mob sacked the palace they freed Vsevslav and he took the throne of Kyjev. He ruled for only seven months, fleeing to Polotsk when Grand Prince Iziaslav finally took back his throne.

'Now, this very year, Iziaslav has again been unseated, this time by his brothers, Sviatoslav and Vsevolod. The Grand Prince Sviatoslav has the hearts of the people, for with a smaller army he defeated the Polovtsi at Snov. And so he now rules Kyjev, while the Grand Prince Vsevolod rules Pereyaslavl. Should Sviatoslav die then Vsevolod will inherit the throne of Kyjev and after him his son, Vladimir.'

We were still sitting with our heads spinning from the strange names of ambitious princes and their dance around the throne of Kyjev, when there came a knock on the door.

Aleixos sprang to answer it and bowed to our caller. Tall, of regal bearing, bejeweled, I took this to be the Grand Princess Oda. Wilda also bowed, but Edith and Gytha stood waiting for Aleixos, who spun around, bowed again and said to Edith, 'Your Highness, may I present Countess Lebid; she will serve you in all those things proper to a queen and a princess. Later, Grand Princess Oda will meet with you when you are rested and ready.'

The countess, a lady in waiting to Queen Oda, as I found out, smiled and bowed to Edith. 'Please, my lady, would it please you to come with me? All things to delight are awaiting you.'

Edith smiled, arose, wriggled her fingers in farewell to Wilda, Aleixos and myself, seized Gytha by the arm and followed Countess Lebid from the room.

When my lady returned I gasped in wonder. Her travelling clothes were gone and in their place she wore wafting material of a fine silkiness I had not seen before and in a hue of blue that could only have been plucked from a rainbow. About her forehead was a jeweled diadem and about her slender neck a necklace heavy with precious stones. Around her wrists coiled golden serpents, and yet none of this was uncouth; she looked nothing if not queenly.

Edith spun around for us, lifting the gown on the air as she did. She raised her hands to her face and then drew them downwards, calling us to see the difference. Gone from her face were the marks of travel; gone the wear from months of grief. Still there no doubt, but hidden by the art of the beautifier. Her cheeks were the delicate colour of a rose; her eyes seemed somehow larger and sparkling, her lips darker and fuller. Framing all this colour, the ice whiteness of her hair, bouncing now and waved, the brown tips – the last remnant of Frida's dye - cut off; the snood put away.

Gytha had the sweetness of youth and had been given the same attention, but did not have her mother's beauty. I feared if Prince Vladimir saw them both together he might choose the mother instead of the daughter. But then, that is my simplicity; I thinking marriage something you do when your heart beats so that nothing less will calm it. Marriage amongst princes is to do with the throne and the begetting of boy children. For that the youngest wife must be chosen, for the best chances lie with the span of years.

Wilda and I, as servants, stayed in our travelling clothes, although there was a basin of water in our rooms so that we might wash the grime of travel from our bodies. However, we now found that Aleixos had the ordering of us. He wrinkled his nose as he gazed at us, looking us up and down, measuring us with his eyes. Then he directed us to the kitchens where we might find pails of hot water.

'Get hot water, wash away the dirt. On your beds I will have clothes laid out for you. These you must wear at all times.'

We did as we were bid. When we returned from the kitchen I found outer clothes on my bed: a jacket and trews striped in the blue and yellow colours of the royal house of Kyjev. I donned them, admiring Aleixos's judgement, for they fitted me perfectly. All else was not perfect though, for amongst the seams and folds were the eggs and the mothers of fleas. I cleaned them out as best I could, but was to learn that fleas infested the palace. All the servants had red bite marks around their wrists.

I met Wilda in the passageway. She looked very elegant in the royal colours. In her case a dress of yellow and a blue brocaded sleeveless jacket nipped in to the waist and flaring over the hips. It was the first time I had seen her shining clean and in clothes that were not soiled and travel worn. Her hair, long since grown back, was dark and lustrous and I saw that the prettiness, of which I had seen the remains when first we met, had now returned entirely.

Aleixos told Wilda to await my lady's wishes within her room during all the daylight hours unless ordered otherwise. He told me to wait outside my lady's door day or night until she dismissed me. I was her servant in my heart in all things so I did not protest, but I had little to do and almost wished us back on the road to Kyjev.

Chapter 37

AD 1073

Edmund's Tale: Separate Ways

Everything changed for me after some days. During this time Prince Vladimir arrived fresh from the Steppes to meet his bride to be. I caught but a glimpse of him but it appeared that Oleg had spoken truly. He was tall, upright every bit the warrior. He was older than me of course, but young enough to be my uncle. The two met and became acquainted under the care of Princess Oda.

It seems that whilst Gytha was presented to Prince Vladimir, Edith spent much of her day in the company of Count Vassily and continued her learning about the passions of the princes of Kyjev and their restless struggles, on the one hand to possess the throne for themselves and on the other, to bring about peace and safety. My lady told me that their talks, as did all in that land in the end, came round to the Polovtsi. Amongst the many things they talked about, Edith learned how, after the lost battle of Alta when the plains were laid bare to them, the Polovtsi had ridden wild across the land. Count Vassily mourned the loss of the defences, for nothing now stopped the Polovtsi from raiding wherever they willed. It took time to muster men and it was hard to bring them to battle, for by the time the army arrived they had gone. He told

Edith how the Polovtsi roamed only on horseback. They carried no weight for they warred in their daily furs and took with them only their bows and arrows. Each Polovtsi warrior rode with a string of horses, which never strayed but always followed the leader. This leader changed with time, for the warrior leapt from one to the other so that each horse took turns to bear the weight of a rider. Also, each horse ran with a nosebag of food, so the Polovtsi never stopped moving. A war party could ride further in one night than warriors from Kyjev could ride in six days. A Polvtsi war party stopped for nothing and left nothing behind. They collected wealth and slaves, stripping the land bare.

To rebuild the defences now the Polovtsi were so strong was impossible, even after their defeat by Prince Sviatoslav. At every try, the Polovtsi fell upon the workmen and slaughtered them or swarmed up to the new palings and pulled them down whilst the workmen cowered in their camps. If the army protected the workmen then the Polovtsi struck elsewhere. They played a game that gladdened their hearts and broke those of the city men.

It was just a chance remark by Edith that brought about the change to my life. She had told Count Vassily how quickly the motte-and-bailey castles of the Normans were built. He had asked to know more so she described how the one at Hastings had been brought in pieces and put together in seven days. Even working with raw timber one could be thrown up in a month, she had said. Vassily asked her many questions, she told me later, and she had explained how guarding the builders was easier, for the land would be laid bare of guardians for only a short time whilst the first castle was thrown up. After that the soldiers and horse soldiers inside could sally out to protect the fence builders. A chain of such castles could protect the rebuilding of Yaroslav's whole wall. Best of all, the mounted nomads would be helpless to overthrow them, for whilst the soldiers inside the castles would always be protected, they could be ready to sally out at any time.

Count Vassily had asked Edith how much she knew about the actual building of such castles. Nothing, she had told him, but Edmund knows much for he has worked on building one and was at its storming when the men of Sumersaete were defeated.

And that is how I found myself being taken by Count Vassily to meet the Grand Prince Sviatoslav.

Veliky Kniaz is what they called him in Kyjev, which seemed to mean either 'Grand Prince' or 'King' and as there was no one above him I thought of him as King Sviatoslav. All the princes in these parts, for all their outlandish Slavic names, seem to be the children or grandchildren or great-grandchildren of Varangians. The Varangians still pass through for trade and sometimes to fight as mercenaries, and so the ruling houses have never lost their Danish tongue, although they talk to each other in some Slavic tongue that is drivel to me.

Thus we were able to talk together. There were some differences, but then so there are for a Wessex man travelling through Mercia and especially York in the old days, and I could understand what King Sviatoslav said to me. When I first came into his presence I knew him only by his seat on the throne, for he wore no crown or other trappings of kingship. He scratched his scrubby short beard and pointed at my leg, laughing.

'We ask you for your wisdom and here you are lame, it is a good omen.'

Not being able to connect lameness and wisdom in my head I failed to understand and turned to Count Vassily, who was smiling.

'The king is making merry with you, Edmund. You see, Yaroslav the Wise died but twenty years ago, he was one of our greatest rulers. The Varangian sagas name him as Yaroslav the Lame. So you see the king's meaning?'

'I fear you have been misled, Highness,' I said, 'for I have no wisdom that might be of use to your kingdom.'

'Ah, but you have, for the lady Edith has told it to Count Vassily and he has told it to me.' He spoke slowly and clearly, 'I have heard that you know how to build a castle of wood in four weeks. A castle that will keep out foes whose main weapon is to be very light and quick on horseback.'

'I could not build one myself Highness, for I am no carpenter or craftsman of any sort, but I know how it is done for I was at the building of one but four years ago and took great care to watch that we built it right. I could advise a proper builder how to shape such a castle.'

'And would you go with such a builder and be his right hand whilst the Polovtsi gallop all around and fire their darts at you?'

'I would, Highness, but I would be loath to leave Lady Edith, the mother of the bride of Prince Vladimir, unless I could be sure that she was well protected from the spies and murderers of William the Bastard, King of England.'

'You may be sure of that, young man, even a great army could not bring harm to these two ladies whilst my roof shelters them. Go with Vassily and he will take you to Mychajlo my builder of wooden churches. You will show him how a church builder who works in wood can also be a castle maker.

'And hearken to me, there are dangers. You may die from disease for the Steppes are harsh places to be. The Polovtsi may kill you or take you and sell you into slavery. But if you survive I will reward you beyond your dreams.'

He paused and then, 'Here is what you must do. First you must travel with Queen Edith and Princess Gytha to Pereyaslavl for the wedding. Queen Edith has asked most firmly that you do. Once that is over you must go with Vassily to meet with Mychajlo on the Alta River, for it is there you must start to rebuild King Yaroslav's snake earthworks.'

With that he turned to one side to talk to a noble of some sort or another, who stood by his right side. As he did so the king waved his hand at me and when Vassily tugged at my arm I understood that I had been dismissed.

I followed Vassily from the throne room. He didn't speak but walked quickly from the palace through courtyards and along pillared passageways until we came to a room where even from the outside, I could smell the sweet resinous scent of wood. I knew well the smell of resin for I was one of those who had used it to make watertight the tanks of Montagud castle.

Count Vassily knocked sharply on the door. It was thrown open and framed in it stood the church builder, perhaps the least churchly person I could have thought of. In many ways he was almost the brother of my bear-man Oleg. He wore no hat, but his dark hair sat his head like some great bush and balanced the great, black, bushy beard that joined it. His eyes as black as the beard would have been frightening in the fierceness of the scowl he rested on us, were it not for the network of laughter wrinkles that surrounded them.

'What!' he shouted. 'Don't you know I'm busy?' He shouted this in Danish so I knew him for a Varangian although his colouring belied that.

Then he stopped, 'Oh, it's you Vassily. What can I do for you?'

Vassily told him our purpose. How the king wished him to speak to me and listen while I told him how the Norman

367

invaders of my country could build castles in a matter of days. 'The king is of a mind that a chain of such, thrown up quickly and simply, might help with the rebuilding of Yaroslav's wall,' said Vassily.

'Hmmm, come in, come in. What's your name? Edmund? Well mine is Mychajlo. I build churches, but if the king wants me to build fortresses then I shall build fortresses, or stables or dog kennels or anything else he wants. I am his servant in all things.'

I began to feel that Mychajlo, whom I would always think of as Michael, was not pleased with the king's orders. And I would have been right, so I found out. As the king had said, castle building in the lands roamed by the Polovtsi was likely to be dangerous. It was not the wont of a church builder to be at risk. Perhaps, I thought, Mychajlo had chosen church building as his work to avoid putting himself in the way of Polovtsian arrows.

'Thank you Count Vassily, please come in Edmund, we will talk, you will tell me everything you know about castles then I will take you back to where you sleep.'

I thought that a strange way of putting it, but as soon as Vassily had walked away I thought no more about it, for Mychajlo pulled me in through the door and slammed it shut. Inside beside a small whitened stack of slates stood a young man, clutching a stick of charcoal, clearly a scribe of some sort.

'Sit, sit,' said Mychajlo, and while I did so he poured water into a beaker and held it out to me then turned and poured another. Facing me he raised his beaker, 'Good Health,' he said.

To be polite I raised the beaker and swallowed. As soon as this 'water' hit my throat I gasped and coughed, for it was like liquid fire in my mouth and all the way down. 'What is that?' I croaked. 'Have you poisoned me?'

'Poisoned you? No. It is good for you, like beer or wine but much stronger. It is iced rye wine. Made on the coldest nights of the year when breath hangs in icicles from your beard. Good no? Have some more. We will sit and drink until the room spins and you will paint a picture with your words of how the castle you worked on took shape, from the beginning to the end.'

And so I did, taking cautious sips from my beaker as a warm glow began to fill my belly. As I spoke so Mychajlo spoke to his scribe, who drew pictures with charcoal on white painted slates. He showed them to me and I said yes or no and if no, where he was wrong. By the time the room started spinning and I felt sick, forced to ask the whereabouts of the privy to puke, Mychajlo had a motte-and-bailey castle in his head and in drawings. When I returned I felt woeful and bade him goodnight. As promised, he took me to my bed and I must have fallen face down with my clothes on, for so I was in the morning.

I woke to knocking like thunder on my door and a head that felt as if it had been split in the top with an axe, which someone with a mallet was hammering home in hope of splitting me like a log, from top to bottom.

'Oh... Oh... all right! I'm coming. Stop, for Jesu's sake stop!'

It was Vassily, his arms piled high with furs and boots and a belt hanging down. 'We don't want to lose you right away,' he said, smiling, 'so the king has ordered me to find you proper clothes for the Steppes. Not now, but you will need them when summer passes and the winter approaches.'

'Could you not have waited?' I asked, holding my head together with both hands.

'Wait, wait? No, this is the king's business. Your carriage, our supplies, our workmen and our escort wait in the courtyard with Mychajlo. They go by land; you must join Queen Edith, Prince Vladimir and Princess Gytha on the prince's ship. They are going right now. You do not know your luck for, curse it to hell, I must go with the wagons, overland.'

I groaned at the cruelty of even such an order when all I wanted to do was to lie in bed and sleep forever, or at least until my head knitted back together. When I gathered up the furs and stepped outside the door I gasped at the sight that met my eyes. It seemed that the king either was a magician or owned one, for the caravan that awaited Vassily was huge. It stretched from the porch across the courtyard and all the way along to the palace gates and beyond. There was a golden wain, all covered in, like a small hut on wheels and drawn by two horses with a man on a bench at the front to drive them. I thought this must be for Mychajlo, his drawing assistant and Vassily. There were ten other wains, larger and open, each holding at least twenty men, workmen I guessed. Lined up along the road was what looked like another two hundred men, but these were mounted soldiers wearing armour. As I watched, the golden hut moved away and I saw that Vassily was not to ride within for he mounted a horse and trotted over to me. As he passed me he leaned from the saddle.

'Don't just stand there, if the ship sails without you the king will be unhappy and take your head. Although from the look of you, you might be glad of that! Go to the hythe.' With a grin, he trotted away to the front of the column of soldiers. Vassily was going to lead this force into the lands now owned by the Polovtsi. As he moved off, my womenfolk came out to wave him goodbye. Edith and Gytha knew where the ship was and I, shamefaced at the fog I was in, followed them back, my arms full of furs.

Having boarded the sleek ship we had seen when we arrived, we set out for Pereyaslavl by river. Prince Vladimir had come to Kyjev not only to greet his bride but also to lead Edith and Gytha's escort, taking time out from his war with the Polovtsi.

'I am glad you are here now, Edmund,' said Edith, 'but do not worry about us when you are gone building castles; we are quite safe. We shall look forward to your return in glory.' She smiled and my heart felt it might break.

'Oh Edmund, I also am glad you are with us,' said Gytha, 'but I have met and am pleased with my future husband, he is handsome and brave and will be a great ruler one day, so he tells me. He will take care of us while you are gone. Imagine, when you come back I may be a mother!' She blushed and looked down at her feet, but Edith laughed. It was a tinkling, joyful sound and I could see that she too was content to have Prince Vladimir as the father of her grandsons.

Wilda threw a bundle of furs she was carrying through the window of the deckhouse. 'My Lady Edith has released me to serve you, Edmund. I am to come with you when you leave for the Steppes. Someone has to see the cooking does not poison you, or filthy wet clothes make you sick. She says that as you are about the king's business you must have a servant until you return, and that's me.'

We had become friends on our journey and I felt warmth in my heart at her speech. Reaching for her hand I helped her through the door into the deckhouse then did the same for Edith and Gytha, both of whom were smiling. 'Thank you, my lady, it will be so much better to have a friend with me, thank you.'

At that moment there was much shouting at the front and the banging of feet on deck. With a jerk the ship swung away from the hythe and out into the stream and with a clatter of oars started to move off downriver.

Edith and Gytha walked to the window. 'Farewell for a while,' they called to Kyjev, 'be safe until we come back.' Gytha turned to me smiling, 'Of course that will only be when Vsevolod or Vladimir is Veliky Kniaz and I a grand princess or a queen.

Our escort of mounted soldiers rode along the bank whilst our oarsmen rowed us downriver. As our ship followed the river round a bend so Vassily's long caravan was lost from view.

The River Dnieper was wide at this point and quiet. Vladimir told us we rowed towards a river called the Trubizh; Pereyaslavl lay between it and the Alta River.

When we entered the Trubizh we found that some Polovtsi were camped on the bank. As we rowed past they shot arrows at us. Straight away Vladimir hurried over to the deckhouse, which I now saw was more for protection than comfort. It seemed the Polovtsi had been giving this some thought, for next they sent fire arrows at us, which started to catch light to the roof. The rowers had to ship their oars, take pails and put out the fires.

Vladimir ran a red flag to the masthead to signal our escort to close up to help. There was much whooping and hooting from the bowmen on the bank. They mounted their horses and were gone before our escort reached us. There looked to be many Polovtsi, but although fifty horses galloped away I counted only ten bowmen. I think perhaps they were amusing themselves frightening us rather than mounting a serious attack. That, I think, was Vladimir's view too, for he was laughing as he gave his orders to the fire-fighters and still laughing when we pulled into the bank and he called across to his chief of horsemen to keep closer to us. They shouted back cheerfully and all in all, as I said to the women, I didn't think we should take it too seriously, as long as we came inside the deckhouse when the arrows started to fly.

During our wayfaring down the Dnieper and up the Trubizh, when the banks looked peaceful we spent time in the bow just watching the land glide by and listening to the calm dipping of the oars. Often we talked of the future. I told Gytha I had heard the wedding would be ruled by the rituals of Byzantium not Rome and asked if she would mind that. It was not until then that I learned how bitter she was about the death of her father.

'No, I would like that,' she said. 'The Pope in Rome plotted with the Bastard to murder my father and ravish our country. I damn him and his Church to Hell. I damn Normandy and France to Hell, if I could live to see the day that Englishmen run wild across their land and destroy it I would be happy to live in misery until then.

'I will be Queen of Kyjev Rus and I will fight for the Church of the East against Rome with all the strength of my body and mind. To have that chance I would marry the devil himself. I am lucky that Vladimir is a good man, a strong warrior and with my help will be a great man and the father of kings.'

I sat thinking, weighing with myself whether I would be betraying Eadric if I told her of my find in the stable of Clun, which now seemed so long ago, and the secret he had told to me. To talk to someone of power, as Gytha was soon to be; one who so hated the pillaging churchmen of Normandy, was too great a chance to let go.

And so I told her about the Wild Hunt and she made me promise to help with their task of frightening and killing the greedy; to talk to the huntsmen and make them believe in blood for blood; make them want to ruin French land as the Normans and their French lickspittles had ruined ours, to have their starved bodies lie dead in the fields and streets as ours did.

I swore to obey her if I saw any chance, and she in turn swore to help in any way she could, she would, she said, befriend Princess Odda and through her would drop poisonous words into the ear of her uncle the Emperor, she would plot to deprive the Pope of the land of England and tear away the other lands to the north. She would do this by spreading the influence of the Eastern Church, or would support any heresy that would spite Rome.

Her resolve startled me. Gytha was at that time only twenty years old, even now I still saw her as a child. I had never thought to find such hatred in her. Her childhood love for her father was greater than I would ever have believed.

When we arrived at Pereyaslavl, a town smaller than Kyjev but with mighty walls as befitted its position on the border of Kyjev Rus lands facing the Polovtsi, we were taken straight away under escort to the palace. Twelve servants clad in Pereyslavl colours of red and gold carried Edith, Gytha and Vladimir in the now familiar golden chair. They were to meet Grand Prince Vsevolod, Vladimir Monomakh's father. Wilda and I, as servants, were given a corner of the kitchen in which to wait and saw nothing of this meeting, though we did see the wedding – Edith had insisted we should, she told me – and caught our first sight of the Grand Prince, a great, brooding, long-bearded hulk of a man. Perhaps his failures against the Polvtsi had made him sour.

Princess Gytha and Prince Vladimir were married in a domed cathedral. Though smaller than many churches, it was a cathedral because the Eastern Metropolitan had his seat in Pereyaslavl. He it was who would conduct the rituals of the wedding the day after we arrived and had rested in the prince's palace.

Her ladies in waiting laid out Gytha's clothes and dressed her, Wilda told me her surprise at the simplicity, even plainness of the wedding clothes, but when we went inside the cathedral I understood why the princess was dressed so plainly. I gasped at the golden, jeweled and frescoed decoration inside. The magnificence of the surroundings would have made any adornment on the bride tawdry and uncouth.

I remember some things about the wedding, which seemed foreign to me, and yet I found it very moving, Wilda also, for she cried. Strangely, the first part was a ritual of betrothal. Then there were two rings, one each. First the bride's ring was worn and then the groom's, then they were changed over so that each wore the other's ring. On their heads they wore floral crowns of myrtle, joined one to the other with white silk. There were dances around the altar and much reading from the bible. All in all it left no doubt that little Gytha and Prince Vladimir were well and truly wed. While I stood there listening to the deep-voiced singing and watching Gytha, who looked so beautiful and every bit a princess, I was seeing something very different. Drawn from my mind's hoard I saw her, a young girl, shrieking and floundering in the waters of

375

the Gwy. I felt her warmth through the sleeve of my coat and remembered the way she had so trustingly looked to me as her protector with no thought for my crippled leg and humble state. Now she was gone far beyond me and as I wished her the best of life I felt my eyes well up.

When the wedding was over and Gytha away with her new husband, Wilda and I said goodbye to Edith and sought out Vassily. He showed us back to the ship where he had posted guards and where we would sleep. He told us we would be leaving at daybreak and by the end of that day would be at our destination. There we would meet with Mychajlo and he and I would plan the work on the first of the motte-and-bailey castles.

Chapter 38

AD 1073

Edmund's Tale: Polovtsi on the Steppes

The border fence we were going to restore lay six days to the south of Kyjev – six days for us, that is; for the Polovtsi barely one. That is the reason for the snake embankments. They slowed the Polovtsi and enabled beacon fires to be lit, warning Kyjev to man the walls and bring out the army from Belgorod. There are three rivers flowing through the plain. Kyjev lies on the Dnieper then to the east is the Desna and to the south the Sula. Our task was to restore the barrier between these three rivers and when that was done, to bring more timber to line the tops of the detinets – the defences – of Kyjev, Chernihiv and Pereyaslavl, to protect against the arrows of the Polovtsi and thus protect the cities of the plain. This circle lay at a distance of twelve days' travel from Kyjev. To defend the barrier when we rebuilt it would take twelve castles at equal distance along it. As each castle was built so a garrison would be sent from Belgorod.

Our escort of two hundred would build the first castle, be joined by a fresh hundred from Belgorod and go on to build the second castle leaving the garrison of one hundred behind in the first – motte-and-bailey castles can hold only a small number of soldiers, perhaps one hundred, hardly more for they are not large – and so each castle, when our protection was least was built by two hundred with a garrison of one hundred being left behind in each completed castle. As we built more castles so more soldiers would come from Belgorod. With them would also come the provisions they would need in the early days; after that they must live off the land.

And so we set to building and I forgot the most important lessons I had learned from the storming of Montagud. I forgot that when we were looking up we should have been looking down. Oh, we had a watch posted all right. We could see our foes coming and take shelter, but once bottled up how were we to get relief?

This problem was soon brought home to me. We were finishing the second castle and had placed our one hundred soldiers in the first. We had the motte mound piled up and had built the bailey wall inside the ditch, but had not yet started on the tower atop the motte. For reasons only they know, the Polovtsi chose that moment to storm us.

The thing about the Polovtsi is that they don't come sneaking. They gallop up on five times the number of horses, as many as a thousand to two hundred warriors. Unless the weather is very wet the dust cloud can be seen for miles. And even if it is wet, the drumming of their hooves gives plenty of time to take shelter inside the bailey and mount the fighting step. A castle is likely to have more fighters than the attackers, but that is not always so and today we were outnumbered by at least two to one.

We saw the dust cloud coming and took cover within the bailey walls. We even kept working on the motte, except for the bowmen who manned the walls. The garrison commander told me that after we killed or wounded some of our foes from our arrows, the rest would gallop away and leave us in peace.

This always happened, always, so he told me, thus I was not overly concerned. This time, however, they did not.

The Polovtsi had soon discovered what I had seen with the Welsh: whilst light horsemen may have an advantage over those who are heavily armoured, they have none when attacking a secure and manned castle. But if there are enough of them to encircle the bailey, they can trap the castle defenders who then must rely on relief coming. If it does not, then the besieged start to run out of stores and water. They must attack or die a slow death. Our Polovtsi outnumbered us. Our attack would fail. If we were lucky they would kill us quickly, if they took us alive then they would sell us in the slave marts of Cherson. This is what would have happened to us, had the fates not smiled on us, for this time the Polovtsi camped around us. They even set up their round houses of skin and felt. We could have been easy in our minds about this but for the fact that we had not got to the point of unloading our stores or filling the tanks we had dug ready. In our rush to shelter in our castle we had left our wagons of stores in their pen outside the bailey wall where the Polovtsi were even now enjoying them.

We leaders, for as the adviser I found myself being counted as one of their number, met to decide how we might get relief to drive the enemy away. Unusually this time there were too many Polovtsi for us to fight, for we had only our hundred soldier workers, the new recruits from Belgorod had not yet joined us. We could light a fire high on the motte, the first castle where our other one hundred soldiers were living would see this, but we had left it too late to bring up large numbers. We must have fires that Belgorod could see, fires lit along a chain of towers would bring the reserve army hurrying with perhaps a chance of bringing our foes to battle.

This thinking did not solve our present problem. The only blessing we had was that our besiegers did not know how little food and water we had. This castle was at a distance from the river so that gave the Polovtsi a problem as well because they needed to water their great herd of horses, whilst we only needed to water ourselves. I thought to play out a lie to the horsemen surrounding us so they would not think us short of food and water.

It was dangerous, for bowmen encircled us; even to show myself was a risk. It was not a cold day so at least that was good. I took up one of our few full skins of water then stripped naked and climbed up to the fighting step. There I displayed myself to the watching Polovtsi. I expected their darts to come flying towards me and was ready to drop out of sight, but as I had hoped, my antics aroused their curiosity and although some raised their bows, none released an arrow. I made a great show of sniffing my underarms and pulling a face at the smell then I scratched my crotch, sniffed at my hands and grimacing, held my nose. Finally I raised the goatskin over my head and started to trickle the water over myself, rubbing under my arms and other places. I took some time over this. When the bag of our precious water was empty, I stepped down from the step. I could only guess that so bemused were they by my apparent lack of concern that they had not skewered me with arrows. Perhaps they thought me a madman – but one who clearly had water to waste. Once out of their sight my legs gave way and I sat to let my madly beating heart slow down.

Later that day I had the watchman on the fighting step eat a leg of meat, sheep I believe. When he was halfway through he patted his stomach and tossed the meat down to a watching archer, who grabbed it and wolfed it down.

I think these simple ploys must have convinced the Polovtsi

that they were wasting their time, for the next morning as the sun rose we saw that the little skin and felt houses had all been packed away and the camp was gone. Our foes no longer encircled us. We sent a troop to get food and water from the other castle and stuffed ourselves to get rid of the feeling of hunger and then, apart from the watch, we slept. I had learned lessons, stores must be protected at all times and we must arrange a way of signalling for relief.

The next day I visited Michael in his work tent, where he went to make his drawings and to drink the iced rye wine he had a liking for. I told him what I thought. He agreed and drew a tower with a fire on a platform at the top. The danger was, of course, that the fire would spread to the whole tower, he shrugged, 'no matter, it could always be rebuilt.'

As they were my idea I undertook to build them. We kept to the forests, choosing the tallest, straightest trees to be the centre point of our beacons. I say we kept to the forests; there was a reason for this. The Polovtsi loved the open Steppe. Galloping over that was a joy to them. Threading their way through trees and under branches they felt to be unnatural and so they avoided the forest when they could. We worked as silently as tree felling would allow. The tallest tree we used as the stable corner, and then we cut two more as long as we could find and leaned them against the father tree to form a three-legged pillar, lashing them together with thick rope. This was how Michael wanted it, three together. Then we built a ladder to the top and at the very top we made a platform. On this we stacked kindling and lightwood all soaked in cooking fat. Over this we built a sloping roof to keep off the worst of the rain and snow. Of course the roof would burn but no matter. And thus we built our beacons.

When we had a line stretching far enough that we could see Pereyaslavl from the last one, then we sent a messenger to the city to tell them what to watch for. Whenever they saw flames they should turn out the reserve from Belgorod and send them to us. Either they would be in time to relieve a castle or they would find a large army of Polovtsi broken through the defenses. It would perhaps be too late for us, but they could at least bring our foe to battle and avenge our deaths.

We would not see Kyjev for another three years. First there was timber to find and fell and then the winter when nothing could happen and we would huddle round our fires, then in the season the building would begin again. When one castle was complete we would move on and start all over. We tried sending men on ahead to find and cut timber so it would be ready for us at each site, but the Polovtsi burned it and killed any tree feller they caught. Our men refused to go, even the soldiers protested. We kept all our men together after that.

The work went well, we manned the castles and our soldier builders taught our foes that they could not besiege us and win.

I understood how that felt for had I not been in their place? There was something else also, working under Hugh's lash had made the building of the castle on St. Michaels Hill a hateful and painful task but strangely working on these castles nearly overwhelmed me with sadness for my lost home. Without Wilda whose reason for sorrow was so much greater than mine, to whom I could give and from whom I could receive comfort, misery would have cast me down.

Most of our soldiers came from Belgorod for the pay and were a mixed lot. There were some Varangians, many Poles, some from the seacoast to the far north; there were many East

Slavs and strangely, some Polovtsi. It was from these I found out that not all Polovtsi were the same; some were at war with each other. Our Polovtsi were Pechenegs, this had been their land once until our foes, the Cumans, had driven them off it.

When fewer than a hundred or so Polovtsi crossed the earthworks then the castlemen attacked them. If a whole army of Polovtsi passed by, the castlemen stayed secure behind their walls until the horde had passed by. Then they lit the beacons to warn the towns and bring out the army. Finally the castlemen mustered together to block the return of the horde. The Polovtsi, weighted down with slaves and booty and followed by the army from Kyjev pressing at their heels soon found that they were caught between two forces and either they fought and took many losses or had to abandon their booty and run. Either way the horde took little gain from crossing the boundary and raids began to dwindle in number. The barrier and the castles proved successful and were popular with the Veche; to my surprise my standing as a valued advisor grew.

When we were working hard at building I hardly saw Wilda. If we returned to camp, which often we did not, then there she was, a welcoming smile on her lips and hot stew bubbling over the fire.

Coin I got from Vassily as much as I wanted, I gave this to Wilda and she saw that I was always fed and had a change of clean clothes. How she managed this I never did find out, but I think she knew who in camp was short of coin and who had spare things that I might need, for I found that when she took my clothes to wash and mend, there were others to change into that I had never seen before.

Because we were moving along the barrier and building we never stayed in one place for long, so it was a waste of time, men and materials to build wooden huts only to abandon them to be burned by the Polovtsi in hit and run raids. Count Vassily, who was old in the ways of the Steppes, used our Pecheneg troops to build us round houses of skin and felt, which could be taken down and moved to each work site. Wilda lived in mine when I was away and kept it clean. In awareness of my importance, third in line from Vassily and Michael, we set our little house inside the bailey of each castle as we moved on to build the next. I was happy that my friend was safe within the castle walls and not at risk from the Polovtsi.

Was there anything more than friendship between us? Of course, what else? We were man and woman together, each to soothe the loneliness of the other. This is God's purpose. As we passed the winter days and nights huddled around the fire in our little round house of skins, we talked. We talked of the old happy days in Lutgaresburh before the Normans came to wreck and pillage our land. Eventually Wilda was able to talk of her lost family without tears. There had been many at the start, but in that first winter we spent together she came to accept what had happened. When she had talked it away I too began to speak out the beast of my fear for my family and I also came to accept that my feelings for Edith were madness. As time went on Wilda and I came to see that we were two lonely people far from home with only each other to cling to. And cling we did, seeking greater relief from our loneliness.

I married Wilda by handfast without a witness, just the two of us together under the snow-covered roof of our house of skin and felt. I took her hands in mine, bound my right hand to her right hand with a strip torn from my tunic, gave her my sole gold coin, which Vassily had passed me in a purse full of silver, and gave her my vows to love and protect. Then she gave her vows to me and as man and wife we banished our loneliness.

Afterwards, thinking about it, I was sure this is what Edith had foreseen when she had released Wilda into my service.

Of course the Polovtsi attacked while we were building, but they soon learned that such attacks were at great cost in lives. I saw then the wisdom of sending us with soldiers to do the labouring work, many of the men in the wagons had been craftsmen, carpenters or builders, skilled in laying out foundations or making sure that walls were straight along and straight up and that the corners met. But the labouring was done by the two hundred soldiers that always came with us as escort, for each time we completed another castle, we were sent a further one hundred men to replace those we left behind.

When the Polovtsi had attacked us during the building of the first castle, the watch had seen them coming from miles away. Before they neared us, our soldiers were behind shields and ready for them, bows, spears and slingshot instead of tools in their hands. I remember one time, when what was left of the Polovtsi had galloped away, that out of curiosity I went to look at a dead horseman. He lay on the ground where a well-cast spear had brought him down. I had thought them some kind of demon with horns, but he was just like us, more like a Dane really. His hair, beard and warrior's lip hair were corn yellow. The eyes I closed with my fingers were cornflower blue. I remembered then what Aleixos had said. The Polovtsi wanted the Steppe for herding while Kyjev wanted it for farming and so the war went on between them. Sadness swept over me as I looked at the dead herdsman. These two ways of life each fought for the land on which to live it. That was the cause of so much death and destruction. Only when one had swept the other from the steppe would peace come to this land.

I should tell you of my next meeting with the Polovtsi. It makes me look foolish but I am over that now and some find it mirthful. It was towards the end of the building of the first castle. After it I learned to be more careful, for what happened was very dangerous to me. We met, in the open, without a castle to retreat to or soldiers to protect me.

Our builders had dug the water tanks and coated them with clay from the riverbank. I, wanting to be useful, wandered into the forest to look for trees with resin to line the tanks. Not that I could collect enough, but I wanted to show it to the workers so they would know what to look for.

Why I went alone I don't know to this day. I knew better than to wander off. None ever moved away from the camp unless in a crowd. Michael did not need me to help or advise at that time and so I was kicking my heels in our little house. Wilda had been unwell and now recovered had chosen that day to put our lives, our home and our clothes in order. I was keen to leave our dwelling and get out from under her feet, which is when I thought of the resin. Thinking all quiet and having no real reason, so I thought, to summon soldiers to escort me, I decided to take a quick look to see what I could find. And so like a fool I wandered off alone. I suppose it was that which saved my life, though at some cost to my pride.

I was beyond the forest edge, past the birch trees that are so common in the forests of this land, and had found a stand of pines. It was gloomy under the trees and the thick carpeting of brown pine needles muffled the sound of my footsteps and cast a shroud of silence below the branches. It was this that led to what followed.

I leaned my staff against a tree where resin was leaking and drying and was levering this off with my fingers, cursing that I had not even picked up my seax let alone my sword. It is strange how fate works. We think we sometimes have bad and sometimes good luck. And yet, if we think hard it is often the good things we do that turn bad and sometimes the stupid things we do which make that luck good. How can we plan for that? For in the end we must believe it is fate and the Fates decide for us the actions that will lead to the end they have chosen. For in wandering off without weapons, probably the most witless act I could have done, it nevertheless also saved my life.

I had just levered off a strip of resin and put it in my sack when I heard a noise, a low whistle. I looked up and my heart lurched in my chest. There facing me was a warrior, a copy of the one whose eyes I had closed. He had the same yellow hair, the same blue eyes. At first I thought him a ghost, but he had a cone-shaped helmet on his head, wore a padded sheepskin jerkin and carried a bow. As I gaped, others drifted out from the trees until they were standing in a circle around me. Now I knew he was not a ghost. I also knew I was a dead man and would be a ghost myself soon. I hoped someone would look after my Wilda, so much sadness in her life.

What could I do but die with pride and make the cost of my killing as high as I could? I seized my staff and made my snake strike towards the Polovts facing me. Faster than I would have thought possible he bent from the knees, swaying his body so that my strike flashed past him, missing by a thumb's breath. Sheep skulls didn't do that nor had the men I had killed. Worse, his hand reached up, a blur, and he grasped my shaft so that I could not draw it back. I have strong shoulders and I tried but I might as well have been trying to draw Arthur's sword from its rock.

My Polovts looked at my staff, bent his head to press his ear to it and rapped on the wood, listening. Then he spoke to the Polovtsi around us.

'Drevesina!' He pointed to my staff and said the word again. Even though I didn't understand what he said, from the look on his face I caught his meaning: 'It's a stick, he tried to hit me with a stick!'

The other Polovtsi burst out laughing. I thought perhaps I should laugh too and so I did, although I felt more like running to the privy to puke or empty myself than laughing. But laugh I did. The laughter tailed away and they stood looking at me. I could see they had noticed my leg. And then one who seemed to be the leader waved his hand in a backhanded sort of way. I hoped he was saying, 'A cripple with only a stick is not worth killing,' and it must have been something like that, for he seized me by the back of the neck and gave a lively kick to my arse that sprawled me in the mud. I waited face down for the arrow to enter my back. After the space of one hundred breaths – not long, for my breath was coming very fast – I looked up to meet my fate full face.

They were gone; melted away as quickly and quietly as they had come. I could not be sure, but I thought I heard laughter in the far distance.

When I arrived back at my little half-apple shaped home and told the tale to Wilda, strangely she could not see the funny side. Not only did she not laugh, she threw herself into my arms and cried until I stroked her hair and soothed her with kisses.

I had not been far out in my thinking. We had set out to mend and strengthen the earthworks in the year of Our Lord, one thousand and seventy-three, and three years later we came back to Pereyaslavl. Much had happened in that time. King Sviatoslav of Kyjev, who had sent me off to build castles, had died and Iziaslav had returned to rule for the third time. Of course, as was always the way in Kyjev, it was not as straightforward as that. In fact, when Sviatoslav died his brother Vsevolod had inherited the throne. Perhaps because of his Varangian roots Vsevolod had decided to trade it and had sold the throne of Kyjev to Iziaslav for the principate of Chernogov. And so that is how Iziaslav became King of Kyjev for the third time. Perhaps Vsevolod was just tired of fighting with his brother for the throne, or perhaps he looked ahead to the time when his son Vladimir would be Kniaz of Kyjev and Prince of Chernogov and Pereyaslavl.

Being off on the Steppes for three years I had, of course, missed how well the marriage of Princess Gytha and Prince Vladimir Monomakh had gone. By Edith's account it seemed that at least now, at the end of three years of marriage, it was one blessed by God. Gytha was very happy with her Valodya as she called him, and he with her. Already there was an heir to the throne and one in waiting.

Edith seemed quiet when I returned. She was glad to see me, glad that I was safe. I was bursting to tell her of my stay between the rivers and she seemed as stirred as I by my story of my meeting with the Polovtsi in the forest and pleased at my marriage to Wilda. But when it came time for her to tell me what was happening in her life she was quiet. She told me the news of Sviatislav and Vsevolod, which I already knew from Count Vassily, but nothing of herself other than her joy at Gytha's marriage. I waited patiently, sure there was more and then, like a river bursting its banks, her unhappiness overflowed and she told me of it.

'There is nothing for me here Edmund. Gytha is happy in her marriage. Vladimir is a good man, kind and strong. Gytha is busy, I hardly see her; she is bound up with her husband and his deeds. And such is the way of things here in this land that I have little time with my baby grandson.

As mother of the queen in waiting I am too high for some and having no power, too low for others. Apart from my ladies, whose language I do not understand, I have no one to confide in, no one to talk to. I have now said more to you than I have spoken this last six month.

'Oh Edmund, I am still young, I cannot spend the remaining years of my life like this, I am so lonely I live in my memory and that starts up the sadness again.'

She was silent for a while, I think struggling not to weep, and then, 'Oh Edmund, I am going mad!'

'My lady, it saddens me to hear you so cast down. What is to be done?'

'I do not know, I go around and around in my head. I think I must leave here. I think I will go back to Denmark – at least they are my own folk – and spend time there until Gytha's children grow, then perhaps there will be need for the wisdom of a grandmother. There may be some task for me in that.'

For some reason, although with my marriage to Wilda I had put aside my unreachable dreams of my lady, my heart sank. Perhaps she did not know what she meant or was merely concealing it, but I knew. She was thinking now of William Malet. Of that I was sure. But then, if she was so unhappy here and her heart led her there, who was I to judge? I was still her man in all things.

'My lady, if that is your desire then Wilda and I will accompany you, although when you are settled and have no need of us perhaps we may come back. We like it here. As servants of the Kniaz we stand higher here than we ever have, either in Denmark or in England. We long for home, but the sadness is too great, we can never go there. In Denmark with you, or in Kyjev with your daughter and grandchildren, is where we will end our lives if the Fates will it so.'

My lady held me with her gaze, reading my face. When she saw that I meant what I said the tears trickled down from her eyes. 'Oh Edmund, you are the best of my friends, how can I ever thank you?'

Something happened then that was so amazing that even now I find it hard to believe. I don't know if it was, as claimed, the outcome of my service to the Kniaz in building his motte-and-bailey castles and repairing the snake earthworks, or whether my lady, as queen mother in waiting, asked it as a windfall for me. It's just that I remember my last words to her in that first talk after I came back from the Steppe, saying how high we stood in Kiev, more so than anywhere else.

All I know is that a member of the royal guard came and summoned me to the presence of the Grand Prince Vsevolod. After Gytha's wedding, he and I had met to talk about the earthworks, for he was Prince of Pereyaslavl and they ran through his land. Now he was king in waiting of Kyjev Rus, for when Iziaslav died Vsevolod would once again inherit the role of Velikiy Kniaz of Kyjev, but for the time being he remained Grand Prince of Chernigov and Grand Prince of Pereyaslavl.

He beckoned me to come closer as I came before him. His chin rested on his left hand, his right hand clutched a vellum roll.

I knelt. 'My Kniaz.'

'Stand up, stand up, Edmund, Tell me about your battle with the Polovtsi.'

I told him about my capture, my fear, my forced laughter

and my miraculous escape and he laughed until the tears ran down his face. 'We must give our soldiers a stick each,' he said. 'Perhaps it will save their lives.'

He quietened, became serious. 'After the good service you have done in the repair of our defenses and after your successful battle with the Polovtsi in which they retreated before you, I must reward you, as indeed King Sviatoslav promised. Henceforward you will be one of the counts of Belgorod, as is Vassily, under the command of the duke. This will give you land within the line of the Stuhna River. I have had the papers drawn up.' He pushed a scroll towards me, 'Greetings Count Edmund of Stuhna. Should you ever leave our service then the land will come back to me for its fair value in gold.'

I stared at him and had to pinch myself to be sure I was not dreaming.

'Well,' he smiled at me. 'What say you, Count Edmund?'

'I am speechless, my king. Thank you, I am your servant in all things, although I have promised the Lady Edith that my wife and I will go with her and serve her on the way to Denmark.'

'Then so you shall. Mark well, the title will stay with you all your life, but if you wish I shall equal the land in gold, which you also may carry with you if you dare the thieves upon the way.'

'My king, I will take the gold, for if I am robbed then I am robbed and you shall hear nothing of it, but if I perish still holding the land it will go uncared for, which may be hard on some. Perhaps if I return with the gold intact I can buy the land again?'

He turned his head in doubt, 'Perhaps.'

Taking back the scroll he threw it in a box with other papers. 'Before you leave, my chancellor will meet you and give you a pouch in which will be a fair price in gold for your land. I am pleased Lady Edith has so trustworthy a protector. You shall have as a guard six valiant knights of Kursk.'

I could not believe what had happened. I sped as if on winged feet back to our dwelling to tell Wilda.

'Wilda, Wilda, your husband is a landed count and you are now a lady!'

She in her turn listened in amazement to my tale as I spun it out. And then her joy ran away and changed to a stern look.

'Does that mean we must stay here and work the land?'

'No, no, my love, for we may leave and if we do Vsevolod will give us the value of the land in gold. We can go anywhere we wish. When the Bastard is dead we can even go back to Lutgaresburh!'

We sat and stared into the west, to where our homeland lay and thought about that. 'We could maybe buy land from the Bastard's son and have a barony and a hall of our own,' I said.

In silence, each with our own thoughts, we sat thinking this through and then Wilda turned to me. 'I do not think I could bear the sorrow in Lutgaresburh.'

'And I do not know what has happened to my mother, I must think some more.'

So we chose to wait, not choosing until the time to make up our minds came upon us, but going to Denmark with Edith was a promise and that at least we must do.

AD 1076 Return to Roskilde

Chapter 39

AD 1076

Edmund's Tale: The Return to Roskilde

We waited until the six mailed knights of Kursk, Prince Igor's grey wolves, came knocking at our door to escort us to the Sala. The king's Varangians were already in Kyjev. In two days they would set off up the Varangian Way about the king's business. It being summer our guardians would rest under covers on deck and would help with the portage. I was mightily relieved to learn that Edith, Wilda and I would be free of that task.

We were told to say our farewells and get ready to board our ship. The goodbyes to Gytha were not as hard as I had thought they would be. Edith made hers first and then we. With the usual inward-looking of the young, Gytha, now deeply involved with her husband, who was forecast to be the next king of Kyjev, had other things on her mind and meetings to go to. Wilda and I said our goodbyes and wished her luck and that the fates would be with her. She in turn wished us a safe journey then giving me a long look Gytha came close and whispered, 'May your hunt prosper.' She made no mention of our new standing or good fortune, so I knew her mind was not with us but somewhere else. This was good for we had thought there might be tears and there were none, only a goodbye to loyal servants from a great lady, wife and mother of a future king.

And so we joined our ship, a much better ship, greater and cleaner than the Sjaeland. As it was the king's ship it was called the Kyjev, what else?

Carpenters had been busy and Edith had a small cabin for just herself. So did Wilda and I. And so we went to Sala. We travelled this time in comfort and safety with nothing to do but sit and talk. During the portages we ambled along free of burdens and able to take in our surroundings, those that we had not seen because we could barely raise our gaze to see, when we had come. It was then Edith got around to saying that when we were at Roskilde she might, just might, had she the time, call upon William Malet. I, who had known this in my heart from the first, was not surprised. Nor was Wilda for she and I had talked of this and we knew what we must do.

'We will come with you my lady, and stay until you bid us leave.'

'Thank you Wilda, thank you Edmund, I have heard nothing and so do not know what might await me. Perhaps William is married, perhaps dead. To travel back to Roskilde on my own in either case would be hard.'

I exchanged glances with Wilda, wondering if Edith knew she had let slip her hopes of Malet, for otherwise why would it be hard to find him married?

As it happened everything turned out well. As the Kyjev was a king's ship I told the captain of the gold I carried and my worries for it. He laughed.

'I can give you paper for that and in Roskilde you can turn your paper back into gold.'

I had never heard of such a thing and frowned at him, thinking he joked. But Edith had heard of it. Not all merchants, even Varangians, were to be trusted, she said, but as this was a king's ship and a king's servant then his word would be good. And so, bowing to her greater knowledge and with many a qualm I parted with my gold and took the captain's paper. Edith read it and told me that it was simply a promise that a merchant of Roskilde would give my gold back into my hand.

At Sala we were lucky and found a king's ship sailing for Roskilde, which offered us passage.

When we arrived at the Danish court it was to learn the sad news that King Sweyn Estrithson was dead. We were announced as Edith, Queen of England and Grand Princess-Mother of Pereyaslavl, the Count Edmund of Stuhna and his wife the Lady Wilda.

Sweyn's son, Harald, now King Harald III, greeted us. After his welcome, he bade us meet him for the evening meal when, as he said, we must tell him all, for it seemed much had come about whilst we were in the court of Kyjev.

We had a happy meal in which we each related our good fortune. Harald in turn told us he did not plan to make any more attempts to win the throne of England. With his brother Knut, now the student of Abbot Aelfwold, they and their father had sailed to be at the storming of York. They had both seen it all come to nothing and he did not want to spend men's lives needlessly again; it did not seem worth the loss. All he hoped was that the Bastard would die soon and in a most painful way.

He was awed that Gytha was now the wife of Vladimir Monomakh and so related to the houses of Kyjev and Byzantium. He had me tell him over and over as much as I knew of the Polovtsi. He, like Vsevolod, laughed at my adventure in the forest.

'It is better,' he said, 'to be lucky than to be rich, for if the Fates are with you, everything will follow along, as it has. For there you were in the forest with but a stick to your name and now you are a Count of Kyjev with gold in your belt and land if you want it. Perhaps they will write the saga of Edmund. I will send my skald to talk to you before you leave; he is always looking for a good tale.

'William Malet? Yes, his hall is south of Roskilde, perhaps half a day's ride. The land is quiet; if you want to visit I will give you a horse-drawn wain and huscarls to drive and guard it. With Edmund's stick you should be safe. There are no Polovtsi here.' He winked at Wilda and laughed again. The new King Harald seemed a merry soul. Unlike his father neither he nor his saintly brother wanted to go to war.

True to his word, the following day a servant called us early and by the time we had dressed, a beautifully carved and painted wain with four horses, a driver and two mounted huscarls waited by the platform for us to enter. There were horses for our six grey wolves of Kursk. The three of us settled onto the padded seats and the driver set off at a rattling pace until we reached the country roads outside the town. There the ridges in the mud road slowed us down to a bone-rattling crawl, though a safer pace. Nevertheless, as the king had forecast, within the half-day, we arrived at a hall set in farmed land, some to wheat, some to cattle and some to forest, where I judged there was good ground for pigs to roam. It seemed a rich land dotted with the cottages of tenants. Everywhere were the signs of careful husbandry and from that it seemed that William Malet had found the good land and the peace for which he sought.

One of our huscarls dismounted and went to the door to announce us. William was at home and came out to see who called. When he caught sight of Edith he became very still and then rushed forward and bowed the knee.

'My Queen!'

'Lord William, we are returned from our travels, Gytha is to be a queen; we thought to see how the Fates are treating you. As you see, Edmund is still with me, and Wilda, who is now his wife.'

William's eyebrows rose as he took in the richness of our clothes, but he said simply, 'Come, come into my hall, we will take refreshment. You must stay as long as you can and tell me everything that has happened since last we met.'

We followed him into a hall; warmly coloured like most, with a good fire in the hearth, again like most. We sat around the board attended by servants who set off at a run to bring drink and food before us.

'Now tell,' he said.

Edith laughed, 'You first, William.'

The laughter went out of his eyes, his mouth turned down and frown lines came to his forehead.

'I have earned my carucate from the king with the blood of my farmers,' he said. 'At least, that was true. Things are better now, for Harald has no interest in war. Before Sweyn died there was much fighting with Norway for little gain. I am bound by my word, but I am sick of the sight and stink of dead men.'

'Will the king take back his land and release you?' this from Edith.

'Better, King Harald has promised to release me, but he thinks I have earned my land. Only if the Crown is attacked will he call on me and my land holders and then must we ride to war.'

His smile returned, 'And now you.'

As we spoke so the frown came back to his forehead as he struggled to understand the great changes four years had wrought.

Then he smiled. 'Hail Count Edmund, hail milady Wilda, all hail Queen Edith, mother of little Gytha, Queen of Kyjev.'

'Not so little now,' Edith laughed, 'she has borne her husband an heir and has another on the way. But the princes of Kyjev dance a merry dance about the throne. For now she is but Princess Gytha of Pereyaslavl, though the omens are good, Prince Vladimir Monomakh is a strong young man with blood binding him to Byzantium.'

Two days we stayed enjoying William's hospitality and good company. We talked much of the state of England and our escape, these now being the old times of our lives and fit for tales of past events. There was one piece of news I thought good. Earl Waltheof, after having betrayed us to the Bastard, had been taken back into his service. But Waltheof could not rest quiet and had joined with the magnates of England in another plot against the king. The earls' revolt had failed, Waltheof was taken and the Bastard had his headsman sever the betrayer's neck. I rejoiced at this, but of the death of King William there was no news. It was then that Edith told us she had made a vow that she would never go home while he lived. She would stay in Denmark and die, the place of her beloved Harold's burial locked forever in her head. All she would say was that it was somewhere he had loved; close by the sea. His arm ring she would keep hidden where none would ever see it again.

At the end of those two days, fearing that we and our six husky knights of Kursk might be eating all William's winter stocks, we bade our goodbyes, had our wain made ready and set about our return to Roskilde.

As Wilda and I walked ahead towards the wain we saw that Edith had hung back. She and William were turned towards each other and held hands. They stood thus, each searching the face of the other. I could see that they were speaking. Then William looked across to where I stood with Wilda. He gazed fixedly at me and bowed his head, just a hint, and I understood his meaning. My wife was before me, for she was tugging at my arm.

I bowed to William and he bowed in return, then Edith waved to us and mouthed, 'Thank you'. Then she placed her finger across her lips, the sign for silence; we placed our fingers likewise, our promise that we would guard her fate and whereabouts from the world.

Holding tight to Wilda's hand I turned away and we continued to the wain. When I glanced back it was to see my lady and William Malet walking hand in hand towards his hall. And then I knew that my queen had no further need of me, her servant, and in my heart I was glad for her.

I never saw, or even heard from or of her ever again.

And so my story of the fate of King Harold's handfast wife and their youngest daughter ends here. I hope that Edith put aside her sorrow and for the rest of her life found some measure of happiness with her noble Norman friend.

Gytha, of course, did become queen of a great kingdom and through her Harold's blood will travel down the ages. I heard from a passing Varangian that she had five children by Vladimir, all of whom became princes and will each perhaps one day be kings of Kyjev, the eldest one, Msitislav, is king and is already called 'the Great'.

My story ends with Wilda and myself. We had thought to wait for the Bastard to die and then to go back to England to our home in Lutgaresburh. We thought long and hard about our return, but in the end we could not face our home with so much tragedy around about it.

I loved Wilda my handfast wife and would go where she wished, but I felt bound by my duty to search for my mother. Torn between two desires at odds with each other we crossed the country from Roskilde and I sat staring west over the sea for many a day. I knew Wilda could not go back with me the grief was too strong. I knew that if my mother did not survive there was nothing I could do. There were many who cared for her to hem her about if she did survive. My brother, my sister and her household would all cluster around her. She would have no need of me. And so, as Asgar had said I should, I finally grasped that life is full of hard decisions and I made mine to stay by my wife's side in this foreign land, which was now our own.

As for the Wild Hunt I heard nothing more about it, as should be expected of an enterprise wrapped in secrecy. I did hear the Varangian sagas called Gytha's eldest son Msitislav the Great, Harald, after Gytha's father, our slain king Harald II. I also heard that the Eastern Church held our dead king to be the last Eastern Church king of England and the enemy of the Roman Church. It seemed to me that Gytha at least remembered 'The Hunt' and was doing what she could to fight those it opposed.

Thus, amongst many from our sad country, we stayed in exile in Denmark. We wandered the west coast where at least we could see over the sea towards our old homeland. We found a Hide by the coast running down to the Eider River. It was a blessed spot. The good land was three miles from the sea, but from it there was a marsh brimming with fat eels. The marsh was two miles in width, after that the pools grew brackish, but the edge of the sea was shallow and for the most part the surf was easy for the launching of fishing boats. Off the sea's edge was a small island within swimming distance.

We spoke to the tenants on the land. We asked them what they could tell us of the place, they told us it had been farmed for as long as any could remember and had been the king's demesne since before the recall of any. The skalds had called it Hold of the Ancients but they had forgotten those songs now and none knew the story only the name.

As the land was the demesne of King Harald I asked him if we might hold it from him. I said we were prepared to pay and showed him the Varangian paper. He was kind and said for that amount he would sell it to us as book land and have his scribe draw up the deeds. And so I, Edmund the cripple, now a count of Kyjev and my Wilda, Lutgaresburh Inn pot girl, but a countess as my wife, bought our barony. There were landholders and cottagers who worked the land and when it became mine so did they and their food rent kept us in comfort.

Sometimes in wonder at our unexpected nobility, we rode our horses over our land, just to see it, to touch it, to walk over it, to stand on it. There was a vantage point that looked out over our entire holding. If we looked south we could see the whole carucate with the marsh, the beach and the sea on its right hand side. If we looked north when the sun was right we could see the sparkle of water through the trees that lined the banks of the Eider, to the left was the opening where the river joined the sea.

There was a mystery about this place, for one day, walking

about it; in a gap between two rocks that stuck up from the red soil I saw a glint of white. I drew my seax and scraped at it and around about.

'Wilda, come look.'

She came to my side and looked towards my working.

'What is it?'

'It's a body, or the bones of one, but no head. What a strange place.'

'Perhaps someone was killed by bandits and hidden between the rocks.'

'Perhaps just a fight between rivals.'

'What secrets does it hide I wonder?'

We stood musing for a little while and then I scooped earth back between the rocks until the bones were once more covered. We mounted our steeds and walked them quietly and gently back to our hall, quietly, for we were lost in thought, and gently, for to our great joy, Wilda was with child.

Edmund's voice came to a stop and there was silence in the Cot. Then Bowdyn spread his hands apart and we knew that this story was finished.

'So you see,' said Bowdyn, 'many times in life things come in full circle. If you don't understand my meaning think back to the first story of Creoda and Gewis at its very beginning and perhaps that will tell you where it is that Edmund and Wilda came to make their home. And if they are fruitful then some of the folk of the Gewissae will one day have come home in freedom to the East Holding from whence their forebears left. Those in Lutgaresburh will still have far to go to recover their freedom, but perhaps it is not so far off now as

I speak.' He paused waiting for silence in the Cott and no doubt weighing his next words.

'Let me give you some news to take home tonight to nurse you in your sleep.

'Days ago Staatholder William of Orange landed in our country. King James has fled without a fight. We have a glorious and bloodless revolution and soon a new king and freedom in the land. This new king will grant to us, his people, a Bill of Rights to protect us in the future from all abuses such as this Scottish king has imposed on us. At last, my friends, we will be free under the law and the rule of those our landowners elect.'

There was silence, fright, for he was talking treason.

'Be this true?' eventually asked old Alf a quiet voice out of the silence.

'It is true,' said Bowdyn, 'I would not make such a poor jest.'

Then there were thin cheers from a few, quicker on the uptake than others. These grew and grew into a shout of joy that made the old Cold Cot shake.

And so for the first time ever, that I can recall, Bowdyn and my mother and father left to talk over the news in milord's hall and without the thanks of the village echoing behind them. I do not think the village even saw them go. This, they said, was good news they rejoiced in it, so different from poor Monmouth's earlier attempt, which had cost them so dear. And I alone among that joyous crowd knew of those who had worked in the shadows to bring about this revolution and change in our fortunes: the Huntsmen of the Wild Hunt, whose task would never end.

For those with more between their ears than peas pudding there was a lively talk with others who were 'not so daft, neither.' About freedom, come in not one, but two circles. For there was Edmund and Wilda living free on the land on which the old folk had died rather than live in servitude, and there was a new king coming to bring freedom back to the land where Monmouth and those who had been with him had died trying to keep that freedom safe.

Author's Note

As with the previous two volumes much is speculative and is therefore fiction. On the other hand, unlike the Dark Ages, where the records are patchy and partisan so that the two volumes set in the 5th Century had plenty of unchallenged scope for speculation, the period around William the Conqueror's invasion is far better documented and so the fiction must be woven, as far as possible, within the known or apparently known facts.

What do we know with reasonably certainty of the various protagonists, alive and dead, within this story?

King Harold II died at Hastings, but even the manner of his death is in doubt.

The arrow in the eye was a recognized symbol; it was of course God's punishment aimed at a perjurer and ex-communicate. On the other hand the description of his death at the hands of four mounted warriors including the Conqueror, whilst perhaps more likely, redounds with little credit on William's valour and holds considerable danger, in that his survival from the deed says much about God's attitude to the murder of God's anointed, removing a level of protection he would need to rely on when he took the throne. It seems that the poem of Guy, Bishop of Amiens is a double-edged sword. Nevertheless, bearing in mind the trouble that William went to in order to get the support of the Pope and to declare a religious crusade, it seems likely that the arrow in the eye was propaganda, so I have ignored it.

As for Harold's burial, whilst William wanted the cairn on the cliffs, there is a tale that monks recovered him and buried him in the grounds of his foundation at Waltham Abbey.

Edith it seems, disappears off the scene after Hastings, there is no firm information about where she went or what happened to her. The last glimpse we get, and that perhaps mythical, is her task with William Malet to identify Harold's remains so that Duke William could inter them without 'Last Rites' and with mockery in a cairn on the cliffs.

There is, however, a mystery. Earl Harold ruled Wessex, and his best-loved part of it was Bosham. It is from there that he set out on his ill-fated voyage to Normandy.

In the Saxon church at Bosham there is a Saxon coffin containing the bones of a tall man in his forties, missing his head, one leg completely and the lower part of the other leg. Injuries consistent with those described by Bishop Guy.

What is particularly interesting is the present day refusal to allow DNA analysis of these remains, especially when compared with the recent enthusiasm to use DNA analysis to identify the Plantagenet Richard III. Perhaps some groups might think such identification to be politically inconvenient, just as there are other groups likely to treat the grave of the martyr as a suitable site for pilgrimage. Certainly the excuse that such testing would desecrate the remains seems specious when they have already been disturbed and the stone coffin opened.

It is this burial that I hint at when touching on Edith's secret interment of Harold with funeral rites.

There is argument whether the Pope conspired with William to declare a crusade against England because Harold reportedly perjured himself on saints' bones, and because the

Church in England observed rules not approved by Rome. These intolerable differences included the holding of services in English rather than Latin.

Interestingly, the Orthodox Church has declared Harold II to be roughly the equivalent of the Catholic 'Venerable' i.e. a 'Passion Bearer' or even a 'Martyr' and is considering him for sainthood as the 'Last Orthodox King of England'. Take from that what you will about the differences of the English from the Roman Church at the time of Hastings. Could it be that the location of the remains of this 'Martyr' and a site for pilgrimage is sufficient reason to deny DNA testing even in this day and age?

There is some argument over whether the Pope was involved but the suggestion is strong that he excommunicated all those who fought for Harold and gave the Conqueror a Papal banner to show his support. Perhaps as some hold, Pope Alexander, and Hildebrand the arch plotter were innocent. William was expert in the use of fraud as a weapon. Perhaps the Pope's support, the crusade, the banner were all Norman propaganda. Certainly, the Pope seems to have been horrified at the 'Harrowing of the North' and even the massacre of Lutgaresburh led to the penitential construction and endowment of a priory under the shadow of St. Michael's Hill. The gatehouse to this priory is still in existence today.

Swein Icgson's promise to go overseas and take vengeance even if it took one hundred years, in fact took much less. William in waging war on Maine took many English with him in his army. As the Anglo-Saxon Chronicle states for 1073:

'This year led King William an army, English and French, oversea, and won the district of Maine; which the English very much injured by destroying the vineyards, burning the towns and spoiling the land'... (Not for the last time!)

The Halig Rood, hanging on a wall of Waltham Abbey, was hoped by Harold and the English to be a counter to the apparent malevolence of the Pope and the battle cry of the English forces at Hastings beside the traditional 'Ut, Ut,' ('Out, Out') was 'Halig Rood, Halig Rood, Holy Cross, Holy Cross.' Unfortunately, William's propaganda was stronger and may have prevented Harold's forces from being at full strength, as did differences of opinion on the disposition of the loot from York. But that is another story well told by others.

As for the Wild Hunt: I take the evidence for its existence from the Anglo-Saxon Chronicle entry in the Peterborough Chronicle for 1127 AD concerning the Abbot Henry of Poitou, of which it says:

… 'there he dwelt right so as a drone doth in a hive. For as the drone fretteth and draggeth fromward (sic) all that the bees drag, so did he. – All that he might take, within and without, of learned and lewd, so he sent oversea: and no good did there – no good left there. Think no man unworthily that we say not the truth; for it was fully known all over the land: that as soon he came thyther, which was on the Sunday...

...Immediately after, several persons saw and heard many huntsmen hunting. The hunters were swarthy, and huge, and ugly; and their hounds were all swarthy, and broad eyed, and ugly. And they rode on swarthy horses, and swarthy bucks. This was seen in the very deer-fold in the town of Peterborough, and in all the woods from that same town to Stamford. And the monks heard the horn blow that they blew in the night. Credible men, who watched them in the night, said that they thought there might well be about twenty or thirty horn-blowers.'...

Of course the idea that it became a secret society working against tyranny and injustice is fiction. How would I know?

It's secret!

James M. Hockey, Bristol, October 2014

List of Characters

Aldan Hamal existed and was an outlaw, was captured and imprisoned by Harold's brother, Tostig, and released after Tostig's death at Stamford Bridge, fighting against Harold.

Asgar existed. The landholder at the time of the finding of the Halig Rood on St. Michael's hill was Tovi the Proud, standard-bearer to King Knut the Great. Asgar was Tovi's grandson. Athelstan, Tovi's son and Asgar's father, was improvident and lost much of his inherited land, including Waltham.

Asgar, wounded and borne on a litter, is reputed to have met with William during his procession around London and conveyed his terms favourably to the city leaders, who surrendered London and the country to the Conqueror.

Abbot Aelfwold existed. He was Abbot of St. Benet's at Holme. He guarded the east coast at the time of Stamford Bridge and Hastings. William exiled him and he fled to refuge in Denmark.

Eadnoth the Marshal. Although a high official of Harold's administration it is said that he held back the western levies for fear of excommunication by the Pope thereby contributing to the defeat at Hastings. Certainly he entered William's service very early on and died fighting against Harold's sons in the west country. Significantly his son Harding inherited his land and went on to receive permission to build a castle in the west country.

Eadric the Steersman existed. Subordinate to Abbot Aelfwold he was in charge of the English ships defending the east coast. Exiled by William together with the Abbot he found refuge with King Sweyn in Denmark.

Eadric the Wild (or Silvaticus) existed, did burn Hereford and Shrewsbury and did unsuccessfully storm the castles there, in company with Welsh troops of Prince Bleddyn. He did make his peace with William, after withdrawing from the battle of Stafford and contributing to the defeat of the Welsh forces. He received his lands back and fought by William's side in his campaigns against the Scots.

Edith Swanessa (or Swanneschals) existed. Sometimes miscalled Edith Swan Neck, sometimes Edith the Fair, she was Harold's wife through a handfast ceremony, in the manner of the Danes. She had seven children by Harold. Their marriage was not recognised by the Pope and for purposes of state he also married Eadgyth of Mercia, the widow of the Welsh king Gruffydd, in a Christian ceremony. They had two children.

Edmund is a fictional descendant of the Gewissae.

Gytha of Wessex ends up in Kyjev, as happens in my story, married to the ruler of Kyjev Rus and giving birth to a line of famous children. This bloodline, I have read, connects to our present Royal Family through Edward III and so, if true, Harold's blood runs in them even now.

Harold's five other surviving children by Edith Swannneschals were not so successful. Of the four boys: **Magnus**, **Godwine** and **Edmun**d Haroldson raised armies in Ireland but no enthusiasm in England; they lacked their father's charisma and never provided serious opposition to the Conqueror. Magnus may have been seriously wounded in the battle in which Eadnoth the Marshal was killed. It is possible he ended his life as an Anchorite in St. John's, Lewes. **Ulf**, a long time hostage in Normandy until released by Robert of Normandy drops out of sight and may have lived out his life as a knight in service to a Norman magnate.

One daughter, **Gunnhild**, entered a nunnery and then escaped to freedom, first by abduction and then by choice and led a notorious life marrying sequentially two Breton brothers, both of whom were named Alan, one 'The Red' and the other 'The Black'. Each of these marriages appears to have been a love match for she resolutely refused to return to the convent.

Hereward of Ely existed, the last effective resistance fighter against the Normans.

Prince Bleddyn existed, held by all to be a gentlemanly and temperate ruler. He joined with Eadric the Wild in his campaigns against Hereford Castle and the Normans.

Siward Barn existed. A thegn and landholder he went into exile and travelled to Byzantium to join the Varangian Guard.

Swein Icgson existed and was a bandit, an early Robin Hood stealing from the wealthy religious foundations. He was active in the Freelands mostly in the vicinity of York. He was the sworn foe of the French Abbot of Selby.

Sweyn Estrithson existed and was King of Denmark. He sent expeditions to assist the English in the retaking of England from the Normans.

Ulf the thegn's chosen is, of course, fictional although the mutilation of those not killed in the massacre of the shire is historical. Although the Bishop of Coutances wielded a mace from horseback during Hastings and killed many I have not found a statement anywhere that he participated in the maiming of those involved in the storming of Montacute Castle. I have seen it suggested that it was those in his employ who were guilty. I have invented Hugh the Vavassour to be his whipping boy for these mutilations.

Wilda the pot girl is a fictional descendant of the Gewissae but the story she told of the massacre of the shire is not. It is said that the folk of the area around about that part of Somerset were darker of hair and complexion due to the slaughter of everyone the Normans thought looked Saxon; that is, Nordic-looking with fair hair and blue eyes. Whether that is still true today I can't say.

William Malet, the gallant Anglo-Norman of this novel existed, was with William at Hastings; was Harold's friend; was charged with Harold's interment in the cairn; did reputedly send for Edith to help with the finding of the body; was the Sheriff of Yorkshire, captured in York castle and was one of the few, with his family, to escape with his life. He took part in the campaign to take Ely, entered the Fens and disappeared. I have built a web of fiction around these facts. It is fiction. I do not purport – and can produce no evidence – that it is true. It is a fabrication crafted to fit the facts, as we know them.

Wirt the warrior elder brother of Edmund is fictional

Kings and Princes of Kiev.

For the purposes of this story we are only interested in the Kingdom of Kiev and the principalities of Chernigov and Pereyaslavl (see map).

Before this story begins Yaroslav the Wise (or in the Varangian sagas, Yaroslav the Lame) ruled as High Prince of Kiev and was to all intents and purposes, king.

Yaroslav existed and had three sons in contention for the throne of Kiev. These sons were:

Vsevolod (his favourite) and father of **Vladimir Monomakh**, ruled Kiev 1078- 1093 also Prince of Pereyaslavl. **Iziaslav**, ruled Kiev 1054-1068, 1076-1078 (enthroned three times) also Prince of Chernigov.

Sviatoslav ruled Kiev 1073-1076

When **Sviatoslav** died in 1076 **Vsevolod** inherited the throne but ceded it to **Iziaslav** in exchange for the Principality of Chernigov.

When Iziatoslav died in 1078 Vsevolod again inherited the throne of Kiev but was now also Prince of Chernigov and of Pereyaslavl, all the important territories of Kiev Rus except Novgorod in the north. These he passed on to Vladimir the husband of Gytha of Wessex. He ruled Kievan Rus as Vladimir II (the name Monomakh comes from Anastasia of Byzantium, being her Imperial family name).

Glossary

I have chosen where appropriate to use Old English spellings for places still in existence today. As this may cause some mystification please find translations below.

I have use **Burh** for places built around Alfredian fortresses. The Modern English would be **Bury** or **Burgh** or **Borough** but without the implication in modern times of being a fort.

I have done the same where the modern spelling would be Castle or Chester. Hence: **Caester** is modern Chester.

I have used the measure **carucate** in quantifying land. This is equivalent to about 120 acres.

Chernogov or **Chernihiv**, **Pereyaslavl** are still the chief towns of their Oblast or district, although I have romanised their names from the Cyrillic.

The **Dnieper River** is still the **Dnieper River**.

Grimsby (Grimm's Village) still bears that name and is still a fishing port.

Holmgard was the Varangian name for **Novgorod** the Great

Ilcaester is modern Ilchester

Kyjev is the East Slav spelling of **Kiev**, which still thrives as the chief city of modern Ukraine.

Kniaz means king but where there is a higher authority it means Prince. Alternatively **Veliky** means high or chief so **Veliky Kniaz** means king.

Lutgaresburh would be Lutgaresbury. In the modern village of Montacute, old Lutgaresburh, there is an open area known as the borough, I have made the assumption, perhaps wrongly, that that is the place where the old fort would have been.

The village in all probability takes its name from the defunct and disassembled castle Montagud (**Montacute**). The village sprawls around St. Michaels Hill, which seems a more likely title as Robert of Mortaine sailed under this banner. The Montagud of the castle was reputedly in honour of the first castellan, Drew de Montague at the request of his friend the Conqueror.

Peterborough and Ely still exist with their names intact.

Polovtsi refers to the nomadic mounted tribesmen of the Steppes at constant warfare with the town dwellers and farmers of Byzantium and **Kyjev**. Polovtsi was a generic name for these nomads but tribally they went by alliance groups such as: **Kipchaks**, **Pechenegs**, **Cumans**.

Roskilde is no longer the Royal City of Denmark but still exists with that name.

The **Sala River** is renamed the Fyris River and rises in modern Sweden; the Varangian Way is no longer the trade route between northern Europe and the Black Sea..

Scaepterburh is modern Shaftesbury.

References

This is not a scholarly work and so I will not be attributing claims I have made to specific works of reference. But, I have erected this volume, this story, for what it is worth, on scaffolding made from information I have mined from the works of many scholarly writers. Without doubt some facts I have misunderstood, other facts I have distorted to make them fit my story. Most of the story is fiction made up from the unknown, grafted onto facts. By so doing I have created the possible/plausible answers to a number of questions: What happened to Harold's remains? What happened to Edith? What happened to William Malet? How did Gytha become queen of Kyjev Rus? If you are a historian with published works about the history of this period I have probably mined them. Don't be alarmed, all the mistakes, distortions and inaccuracies are mine and mine alone. I shall not name you and therefore you will not be associated with my cavalier approach to known, confirmed historical research. It is just fiction after all.

CPSIA information can be obtained at www.ICGtesting.com
Printed in the USA
LVOW05s0621161014

408932LV00007B/16/P